TOP-SECRET RENDEZVOUS

Linda Hudson-Smith

BET Publications, LLC
http://www.bet.com
http://www.arabesquebooks.com

ARABESQUE BOOKS are published by

BET Publications, LLC
c/o BET BOOKS
One BET Plaza
1900 W Place NE
Washington, DC 20018-1211

All Kensington Titles, Imprints, and Distributed Lines are available at special quantity discounts for bulk purchases for sales promotions, premiums, fund-raising, and educational or institutional use. Special book excerpts or customized printings can also be created to fit specific needs. For details, write or phone the office of the Kensington special sales manager: Kensington Publishing Corp., 850 Third Avenue, New York, NY 10022, attn: Special Sales Department, Phone: 1-800-221-2647.

First Printing: June 2003
10 9 8 7 6 5 4 3 2 1

Printed in the United States of America

This novel is dedicated to all of the nation's women and men who so proudly and honorably serve their country as members of the United States Armed Forces. We love and appreciate you for what you do 24/7, 365 days a year. As the proud wife of a dedicated Air Force retiree, and a supportive member of the military family, I salute your commitment to excellence.

We thank you for your dedication.

We thank you for your vigilance.

We thank you for your love of country and its citizens.

In loving memory of all fearless veterans who proudly served the United States of America, in times of peace and war.

A special tribute to the loving memory of my personal heroes:

Jack Hudson—World War I, USA

Oscar Hudson—World War II, Korean War, Vietnam, USA

Richard Henry Ward III—United States Army/Pentagon, USA

Ross Grinage—World War II–Casualty of Port Chicago, USN

Charles Lawson—World War II–Tuskegee Airman, USA

R.J. Brinson—Vietnam War, USN

Edward J. Smith—World War II, USA

George Holman—Vietnam, Desert Storm, USAF

George Glenn—Vietnam War, USMC

A.L. Blackmon—Korean War–Purple Heart Recipient, USA

ACKNOWLEDGMENTS

To: Rudolph A.L. Smith, Senior Meteorologist, United States Air Force, Retired—I want to send out a very special thanks to you, my dear husband, for assisting me with weather and military terminology and the other difficult technical details of this story. I appreciate you sharing your expertise in both weather phenomena and military service. Your love and patience is always duly noted. You're one of the very best men that the world has to offer. I salute your honor, dedication, and continued commitment to excellence as a dedicated retired member of the United States Air Force.

To: Lt. Colonel Willie Blackmon, United States Air Force, Ellington Air Force Base, Texas—A heartfelt thanks for helping me to interpret and develop an understanding of Air Force directives and instructions as they pertain to fraternization. I salute your honor, dedication, and continued commitment to excellence as an active member of the United States Air Force.

One

"Hi, beautiful, what are you drinking this afternoon?" Smiling at the rare beauty daintily perched on a high, cane-back barstool at the Hotel Meridian's poolside bar, Zurich Kingdom lowered his hulking frame down onto the stool next to hers. "I'd love to buy you a refill when you're ready for one."

Hailey Hamilton took her good old time in sizing up the newcomer. Her amber eyes shamelessly roved his physical attributes with a definite spark of interest. As her gaze came to rest on his sun-bronzed face, she decided that she loved the warmhearted smile still pasted on his sweet, juicy-looking lips. As his smile broadened, she got a good glimpse of toothpaste-white teeth, all of which appeared free of cosmetic dentistry. His twinkling sienna-brown eyes appeared sincere, but she didn't know if she should be flattered or annoyed at the reference to his opinion of her looks. It had slipped off his tongue a little too easily for her liking.

"Would you like me to supply my measurements for you?" he asked.

"That won't be necessary, since I've got twenty-twenty vision. But you can tell me your name if you like." She playfully purred from deep within her throat. "I bet it's a strong one."

"Zurich Kingdom." He grinned. "How's that for strength?"

"It's packed with power and it personifies your physical

make-up—tall, strong, Marine-like build—yet you seem so tender and sincere. There are a lot of manly powers packed into your six-foot-plus physique. I would be surprised if your ancestry didn't include royalty. I can imagine you running an entire *kingdom* single-handedly or commanding an entire army of men and women. Zurich brings to mind the majestic ambiance of the Swiss Alps. That thought definitely conjures powerful imagery. I can see you raising the flag of victory after your strength and fortitude has allowed you to scale your way to the very top. However, your approach needs a little polishing." Smiling smugly, Hailey was pleased to share her own brand of bull.

"Please don't stop, lady, now that you have me falling in love with myself. No, I'm only kidding, but enough about me for now. What's your name?"

"Beautiful! But I thought you already knew that since you said it when you first sat down." Her amber eyes flickered with devilment.

He nodded, smiling broadly. "Okay, okay, you got me there. Sorry for being a little overly flirtatious and forward, but I certainly wasn't lying. You *are* a very beautiful woman." He quickly arose from the stool and walked away. He only took a few steps before he turned around and came back to claim his seat. "Hi, I'm Zurich Kingdom. Mind if I join you for a drink?"

She tossed him a dazzling smile. "Hailey—with an 'i'—Hamilton won't mind if you do."

"Now that name certainly speaks to mystifying allure. I like it way more than *Beautiful*. How is it that your name is spelled like that? Isn't it different from the normal spelling?"

"I think some people spell it the same as I do."

"I don't know why, but I'm fascinated with the spelling. Is there a story behind it?"

"The story on the origin of my name is a long one."

"Am I already running out of time in your engaging company?"

"We've got a little time yet, Zurich."

"Good!"

Zurich summoned the cocktail waitress. Upon her arrival, he found out what Hailey was drinking and asked that the waitress keep both of their glasses refilled. It surprised him to learn that Hailey was only drinking lemonade, the same sort of refreshment that he enjoyed. A glass of wine or two was the only alcoholic beverage he ever indulged in, and even that was infrequently.

"Ready to tell me your name-related story, Hailey with an 'i'?"

"I guess I can tell you the story without going into all the boring details, which my parents, Martin and Marie, love to do. They lived in the small town of Palatka, several miles from the hospital in Gainesville, Florida. A horrible hailstorm had hit the morning my mother went into labor. As the conditions worsened, my father pulled off the road to help me into the world. I was born in the backseat of his car. From what I'm told, I was also conceived there. That's a longer story; another weather-related one. To finish up, my father decided to name me Hail. When it was typed into the official records, two additional letters were accidentally inserted. But I think someone felt sorry for me and decided to show some mercy, thus, Hailey."

"After hearing the story, I'm even more intrigued than before."

"Daddy wanted to change it when he first saw it, but Mom loved it. She wasn't too keen on Hail from the beginning, but there are times when she and Dad shorten it to just that."

"A beautiful story befitting a beautiful lady. In what twentieth-century year did that miracle of miracles occur?"

"In 1975. So, what's your story? What are you doing here on South Padre Island?"

"Vacationing. But I never thought I'd find literal paradise in my favorite Texas coastal city. Silky auburn hair, sparkling amber eyes, an indescribable figure packaged in a hot tangerine-orange bikini, soft-looking burnished-brown skin; all highlighted by a winning smile and a bubbling personality add up to my definition of a living, breathing paradise. Earlier I was in Dallas to honor my old football coach, Clyde Foster, during a special weekend event at my alma mater, Buckley Academy. I always make the Meridian Hotel Resort my playpen when I'm here in my great birthplace of Texas. That is, after a couple of days at my mom's modest ranch."

His loquacious description of her didn't earn him so much as a blush. Referring to her as *paradise* had awarded him the same number of points as his earlier reference to her as *beautiful*—zilch. "I've heard a lot about your alma mater. Buckley Academy is the most prestigious prep school in the country."

"So I've been told. I attended Buckley from 1981 to 1985. I also played football for the Buckley Eagles. It was sort of a reunion for all the students, especially the football team, though we were really there to honor our coach. Three of my friends, Neal Allen, Haughton Storm, and Nelson Wainwright were on the team with me. We're still the very best of friends. All of us live in different parts of the country, and travel extensively, but we always manage to stay in touch. It was good to see them again."

"I'm glad your reunion was a success. Mind if I refer to something you said earlier?" After his replying shrug she asked, "You used the word *playpen* in reference to the resort. Now that's an interesting choice of words. Do you consider yourself a playboy, a player, or just a mischievous baby boy needing a safety net in the form of a playpen for security?"

"None of the above. But that was kind of cute if it wasn't meant as an insult."

"No offense intended, Zurich."

"No umbrage taken. To answer your question, I'm no player. I came here to relax and thoroughly enjoy myself. I want to have lots of fun without any emotional entanglements. Whatever I get into in the next couple of weeks will definitely end when I leave here. I have the kind of job that keeps me moving. I'm single and I want to keep it that way, that is, until my professional obligation is stable. I wish I knew how not to come off so direct, but I don't."

"A man after my own heart. It seems like we have a lot in common; I'm here for the very same reasons you are. I like all the cards to be placed right out there on the table where I can see them. I'm leery of people who keep less-than-desirable traits hidden and then spring them on you after you've given them your complete trust and loyalty, usually based on their false representation of self. I like to refer to that kind of person as the poker-playing hustler. I don't play cardshark-like games with others' emotions and I don't allow anyone to play me, period. What profession are you in, Zurich Kingdom?"

Zurich's eyes narrowed. "That's highly sensitive information, classified as top secret."

Zurich was surprised and pleased by her mature attitude. But in no way did he think she was the kind of woman who was going to take pleasure in having a physical tryst with someone for a couple of weeks only to have it end abruptly. In his thirty-five years he'd run into every type of woman imaginable. After numerous failures to read the signals right, he had finally learned how to easily differentiate between the women who were in the game strictly for pleasure, the ones in it for money and prestige, and the ones who weren't interested in either. The kind of woman who loved without reservation, without expecting anything in return, was a rare find indeed. That's the same sort of love Zurich wanted to offer to his wife when his career finally allowed him the freedom to marry.

It was his opinion that Hailey belonged to the latter group. He'd be willing to bet the ranch on his hunch. He might be eight years her senior but she seemed to have as much savvy as he had in how the game of life was played.

"Wow, we really do have a lot in common. I have the same type of job as you do. Maybe we're both members of the FBI, the CIA, the Secret Service, or some other covert organization. This vacation is suddenly starting to look up. I never thought I'd meet a very interesting man here at the resort, let alone one as fine as you. What's so amazing to me is that you like to play by the very same rules as I do: no hang-ups, hassles, or heartbreak."

He didn't know whether she was kidding. Her expression gave nothing away, and there hadn't been a hint of sarcasm in her gentle tone. Zurich didn't know what to make of her, but he couldn't recall a single female whom he'd ever been more impressed with or totally intrigued by. Hailey Hamilton had already scored an exorbitant number of points with him, effortlessly. Zurich was truly hoping that they could spend more time together.

As he studied her alluring profile, he cursed his profession under his breath. That was something he couldn't ever remembering doing, since he was extremely proud of his chosen field. In fact, it was all he knew, the only job he'd ever had. There were countless married folk in his line of work, but he wasn't the type of man who could divide his loyalties. Plain and simple, Zurich was married to his job and he loved it as much as he could ever love a woman.

"Hailey, are you saying that you and I can hang out and have a good time without having any hang-ups or hassles when the vacation is over?"

"That all depends on your definition of hanging out."

"Dinner, a movie or two, dancing, and enjoying the sunsets. And, if I'm really lucky, perhaps we can even share in a few sunrises."

"Sounds like you're making a bid for exclusive dibs on my time. Are you?"

"As much of it as you're willing to share with me."

"That seems like a great way to spend the next two weeks. However, if at any point I decide that I'm not having such a grand time, I'm back on my own. Okay?"

"As long as it cuts both ways."

"Absolutely. I believe wholeheartedly in equal opportunity and treatment. As for the sunrises, don't count on Lady Luck. The odds aren't in your favor."

He grinned. "Don't be so sure about that. I don't have any aces up my sleeve, but I think you'll be genuinely pleased with me as a date. I'm a man who knows how to treat a lovely lady. By the way, sunrises can be enjoyed from a variety of locales. So if you're thinking I'll be trying to get you up to my room, you're probably right, but not for any X-rated activity. I only make love to a woman when there's mutual consent. Lovemaking can't possibly be the beautiful, intimate experience it was intended to be if both parties aren't willing participants."

"My instincts tell me that I'll be completely safe with you. If they somehow fail me, be forewarned. My feet are registered as lethal weapons." She winked at him as she got up.

He laughed heartily. "I thought we had more time. Where are you off to all of a sudden?"

"Up to my room to get a few winks of beauty rest before our first dinner date. I'll meet you in the main restaurant at seven. You can have the hotel operator put a call through to my room should you need to cancel. I'm registered under my intriguing name. No aliases or secret code names were used this time around. I save those babies for when I'm on a special undercover assignment." *If only he knew the truth, he'd probably run.* She laughed inwardly.

"Lady, I do like your style. You're utterly fascinating! The only call you'll be getting from me is the one I'll make if you fail to show up at the appointed time and place."

"In that case, see you at seven sharp, Zurich. It's been such a pleasure."

"You can say that again." He stood and then leaned down and kissed her cheek. "So long for now, Hailey Hamilton. This is one evening I'm more than looking forward to."

"The feeling is mutual, Zurich Kingdom."

Totally intrigued, Zurich stood stock still as he watched Hailey disappear into the hotel. The woman had certainly left him with a lot to think about. He didn't know if meeting her was luck or a curse, since their relationship wouldn't last beyond the next two weeks. A blessing was a more accurate description of his first-time meeting with one Hailey Hamilton. It had felt like the angels were smiling down on him the entire time they were together. Grinning, Zurich prayed that the angels would continue to smile on him for the duration of his vacation.

Hailey awakened to a loud knock on the door. Wondering who could possibly be on the other side, she looked at the clock. She'd been asleep a lot longer than she'd intended. The steaming-hot shower had relaxed her completely. As three short raps sounded on the door, she thought of Zurich. No, she mused, he wouldn't come to her room, not without calling first.

Quickly jumping out of the king-size bed, Hailey slipped on a loose-fitting cover-up, dashed across the room, and asked who was there. Upon learning that it was a hotel service employee, she became a little leery. She hadn't ordered anything from room service. Further inquiry let her know that the gentleman had a package to deliver.

Curious as to who'd sent her a package and why, Hailey flipped the locks and opened the door. Her eyes grew bright with surprise when the deliveryman handed her a large, white wicker basket wrapped beautifully in lavender cellophane and tied with a huge purple bow and curly streamers. Since the basket was done in her favorite color, she suspected her parents. It had to be from them. They were the only people who knew where she was. Smiling, she thanked the young man and closed the door.

The sensuous smell of Tresor perfume wafted across her nose. Body lotion, shower gel, and a host of other fine toiletry items in that same heady scent filled the basket. The lavender heart-shaped candle touched her deeply. Looking at the accompanying card, she saw that the gift wasn't from her parents. Zurich was the one who'd sent it to her. That made her smile.

As she thought about his statement, *I'm a man who knows how to treat a lovely lady*, she laughed. He certainly hadn't been lying about that. This was such a nice way to start a first date, as well as the gift being such a lovely gesture. After all the cards had been laid out on the table in front of them, she'd felt relieved. His plans fit perfectly into hers—no hassles, hang-ups, or heartbreaks. Once the vacation time was up, she and Zurich would go their separate ways. Her next mission was far away from home; she had to be fit for duty, both mentally and physically.

Hailey didn't know if Zurich was serious about his job, but she certainly was about hers. She was so close to her ultimate goal, so near to fulfilling her lifelong dream. If all went as she hoped, a promotion was imminent. Six more weeks of intense technical training would be no problem for her. She never once regretted all the blood, sweat, and tears that's she'd already poured into her job. Hailey was extremely proud of her career.

Hailey decided she wanted to look extra special for Zurich. What to wear out to dinner wasn't a problem for her. Everything she'd brought along with her was versatile. Hailey had chosen articles of clothing fashioned in fabrics of linen, silk, spandex, or pure cotton in soft but bright colors, solids, subtle prints, and basic blacks. She could go casual, classy, or dressy by simply adding or subtracting an accentuating piece or two. A couple pairs of denim jeans, linen blazers, lightweight shells, and sleeveless tops completed her fashionable wardrobe.

Since the basket was cellophane-wrapped in her favorite shade, she decided to wear her lavender silk dress with the bandeau top, which was classy and sexy with or without the matching jacket. If Zurich had chosen the color scheme for the basket, then he just might appreciate her wearing the same hue to show her appreciation of his choice.

Hailey plugged in her portable steamer after filling it with tap water. While waiting for the small appliance to heat up, she sat down on the side of the bed and put on fresh silk undergarments. She then seated herself in front of the mirrored dressing table and applied a fresh layer of foundation to her face. Earlier, before her nap, she had given herself an herbal facial.

After steaming her silk dress, she slipped into it. Her jewelry, a pair of diamond dewdrop earrings and matching pendant, came next. The two-carat diamond tennis bracelet she had a hard time fastening was a gift from her parents when she'd recently earned her college degree. Cute lavender-and-white medium-heeled sandals were her choice in footgear. While dabbing the Tresor on her pulse points, Hailey made a mental note to leave for the date early in order to purchase a thank-you card for Zurich from the hotel gift shop. She suddenly realized that she hadn't given the delivery guy a tip. Hailey recalled what he looked like, so she could easily remedy her mistake the next time she saw him around the hotel.

There were numerous first-rate hotels on South Padre Island, but the Meridian was Hailey's choice because it was smaller and more intimate than the larger resorts; it was also easier to recognize the staff and get to know them. There would be no touring or other outside activities on this trip since she planned to stay inside the self-contained entertainment complex and get caught up on her rest and relaxation, just another of her reasons for choosing the Meridian. Her next work assignment would take her far away from the comforts of home—and her next opportunity to take a vacation wouldn't come anytime soon.

A last minute glance into the mirror left Hailey satisfied with her stunning appearance. Smiling smugly at her image, she reopened the bottle of Tresor and dabbed a bit of the engaging scent onto the base of her throat, just in case Zurich desired to shower one of her more sensitive pulse points with his affection. He seemed like the romantic type, and she couldn't wait to find out if she was right. She needed a little romance in her life; romance without the worry of commitment was the best kind. But she definitely had her boundaries preset.

The thank-you card she chose for Zurich was lightly humorous, but with a sincere message of gratitude. She had purposely looked for a card in the same lavender color he'd chosen to have her gift wrapped in. Hailey felt really lucky when she'd found the cute one done in lavender and white. Two boxes of chocolate-covered raisins, one of her favorite treats, and a roll of wintergreen Lifesavers completed her gift-shop purchases. Hailey had less than two minutes to make it to the restaurant, but it was just a few steps away and around the corner from where she was. She wouldn't have to run, but she'd have to step lively.

Zurich's sensuous smile caused her pulse to quicken. All this man wore was a crisp white shirt, dark pants, and a designer blazer that defined his broad shoulders, yet he looked the part of a highly successful businessman. Zurich also seemed extremely relaxed.

His hand came up to her face and tenderly stroked her cheek. It was an innocent enough gesture, and certainly brief, but it made Hailey sizzle. The pleasurable experience lit up her eyes like sparklers.

"You look radiant, Hailey. And I just love a woman

who's punctual. Did you bring a good appetite along with you?"

She smiled sweetly. "A ravenous one." She handed him the special card. "This is for you, Zurich. I hope you like it as much as I loved the gift you had delivered. Thank you so much."

Zurich was taken by the way Hailey showed her appreciation for the gift. He raised an eyebrow. "My thanks to you, as well. Mind if I open it once we're seated?"

"Not at all, Zurich."

He took her hand. "Let's go inside and get our table. I reserved one by the window. We should have a great view of the Gulf. It won't matter once it gets dark, but we still have an hour or so of daylight left."

Zurich gave his name to the willowy, blond hostess, and she instantly directed them to the cozy, elegantly set window table. The restaurant was practically empty, but Zurich knew it would quickly fill up with patrons. With that in mind, he hadn't objected when Hailey had chosen a time for their date that was about thirty minutes earlier than the most popular dining rush hour. Le Meridian was one of his favorite places to dine when he visited the island.

Hailey gave Zurich a dazzling smile as she sat down. "Did you arrange for this little surprise?" She picked up the placard with her name on it. "Miss Hailey Hamilton," she read aloud, "AKA Beautiful."

He seated himself directly across from her. "I'll only 'fess up if you're impressed."

"Intrigued is more precise. It's also a very sweet gesture. As I looked around at the other tables, I didn't see any other placards, so that's why I asked. When did you request this little extra nicety?"

"Right after our first date was set up. Glad you're not offended by it."

"Quite the contrary. Why would you think I'd be insulted?"

He grinned. "Earlier, you weren't too thrilled at being referred to as beautiful, so I thought I'd like to show you that I wasn't using the term flippantly. As I said earlier, you *are* beautiful, Hailey, and I am being sincere."

"Thank you, Zurich." Hailey looked up at the waiter as he appeared at the table. "Looks like it's time to order dinner." Hailey positively loved Zurich's unique way of expressing himself, as well as his seemingly romantic nature. She could hardly wait to see what else he had up his expensively tailored coat sleeve. He seemed as sweet as he was handsome.

"What do you have a taste for in the way of appetizers, Hailey?"

She picked up the menu. "Maybe I should first take a quick peek at what they have to offer. It'll only take me a minute or two. This is my first time eating here."

"Take your time, Miss Hamilton. I have no desire to rush us through our evening." Zurich looked up at the waiter. "We'd like a couple of more minutes to look over the menu, please. In the meantime, I'd like to request a carafe of chilled sparkling cider."

The waiter nodded at Zurich and then quickly moved away from the table.

As his eyes zeroed in on his lovely companion, Zurich's breath caught. Bathed in the soft glow of the candlelight, Hailey's near-flawless complexion had an angelic appearance. Her full, ripe lips were the next of her delicate features that caught his eye. Zurich imagined that a lot of women would love to have a sensuous mouth like hers. He could almost taste its sweetness.

Hailey made eye contact with Zurich. The softness exposed in the depths of his eyes made her heart tingle. "I'd like a shrimp cocktail for my appetizer, Zurich. What about you?"

"I love their stuffed mushrooms and fried mozzarella

cheese. I even order the same from room service every time I stay here. This is my favorite restaurant in the hotel."

"How often do you come here?"

"Every time I visit my mom; at least twice a year. I love visiting this island. It's so quiet and peaceful here." He removed a couple of colorful brochures from the inside pocket of his jacket. "I picked these up from the hotel lobby so we can decide on a few fun things to do. I used to venture outside of the complex for my entertainment pleasures, but on my last few visits I've just stayed around here. I'm sure there have been a lot of changes on the island since then, and I'd love to re-explore this paradise with you." He handed the brochures to her.

She laid the pamphlets next to her place setting when the waiter reappeared with Zurich's beverage order. The young man removed the carafe of cider from the tray. After pouring the liquid into the crystal goblets, he set them in front of the couple.

"Are you ready to order, sir?" the waiter asked, dining check and pen in hand.

"Appetizers first." Zurich wasted no time filling in the waiter on their pre-dinner choices. Zurich then decided they should go ahead and order their entrees at the same time.

Once the waiter took the meal orders, he hurried from the table.

Hailey picked up one of the brochures and glanced it over. "I had actually made up my mind not to leave the hotel complex. I planned on catching up on my reading and relaxation. A lazy, daily stint of lying out by the pool was also on my slate of things to do. I want to get my tan on, too," she joked, laughing.

He smiled at her. "Your coloring is already perfect. But I'd love to rub the suntan oil on your body for you. Interested in my hands-on services?"

"Maybe, maybe not. However, I do have a hard time reaching my back. I just might let you handle that area for me, but only if you can control your hands and keep them from roving into the 'no trespassing' zones." Her smile was a tad smug, but the laughter within was joyful.

The waiter's arrival kept Zurich from responding verbally, but the responsive thoughts in his mind had him laughing inwardly. Controlling his hands was the easy part. It was his inability to exercise restraint over the lower part of his anatomy that had him worried. Just the thought of massaging oil into Hailey's sexy body already had him physically aroused.

Hailey hadn't expected the pink, plump shrimp to be so large. After squeezing lemon on her appetizer and then dipping one into the cocktail sauce, she bit into the seafood delicacy. Her taste buds instantly went wild. The red sauce had a tangy, gingery flavor to it, different from anything she'd ever tasted. She could barely refrain from moaning with pleasure, but her amber eyes had the tendency to give away even her simplest thoughts.

Zurich was mesmerized by the expression of utter satisfaction he saw in Hailey's eyes. "You look like you're having a divine culinary experience over there. Is it really that good?"

"Hmm, you'll have to see for yourself." Taking another shrimp from the glass rim, she dipped it in the sauce. With a slight arm stretch across the table, she held up the shellfish to Zurich's mouth. Hailey's heart rhythms accelerated when his tongue made slight contact with her fingers. Wondering if the look on his face matched the one he'd seen on hers, she laughed. "What do you think, Zurich?"

"I think I need to place another order. From the heavenly look I saw on your face, I get the feeling you may not want to share another one of those delectable shrimp with me."

Repeating the same steps as before, she offered Zurich another one of her appetizers. The totally unselfish gesture caused him to eye her with mild curiosity. This time, he allowed his tongue to linger a little longer on her fingers. His attempt to effect a tender moment between them didn't go unnoticed, nor was it unappreciated by Hailey; her smile told him at least that much. The sensuous connection had been made, and each of them was feeling it.

"Thank you. That was very generous. There are people who don't like to share."

"I guess you could say that, but since you're the one paying the bill, I can afford to be generous." Although she was joking with him, she kept a straight face.

"Oh, it's like that, huh? How is it that I'm paying when you're the one who asked me out to dinner? Or was I mistaken in my assumption, Hailey?"

"I know I don't have amnesia, but you're remembering something that I'm not."

"I distinctly recall someone saying they were going to their room to rest before our first dinner date. Does *I'll meet you in the main restaurant at seven* ring a bell?"

Hailey couldn't have lied even if she wanted to. There was no denying what he'd remembered. Her own words rung in her ears with such familiarity. "Well, in that case, it looks like this dinner is my treat. But I don't mind if you order another appetizer. What's a few dollars when you're having a wonderful time?"

His eyes fell softly on her face. "It's nice to know you're enjoying yourself, Hailey. And I wouldn't think of having you pay the check. I realized you were joking when you made the statement about me paying. The laughter in your eyes allowed me to ignore the poker-bluffing look on your face."

"Oh, so you think you can read me that easily, Mr. Kingdom?"

"No, but I'd like to learn how." His expression turned pensive. "I know you and I have already set the ground rules, but what happens if one of us falls in love?"

She raised an eyebrow. "One of us? Why can't it be a mutual thing?"

He shrugged. "It can be. It happens all the time. I didn't

come here looking to fall in love, but I didn't know I was going to find you here, either. We said a lot of things earlier about what we are and aren't looking for during our vacation time and what we're going to and not going to do. I'm now wondering if perhaps we made a mistake by doing that. What's your take on it?"

"We made those comments because we both knew that we weren't in a position to look back when it's time to go our separate ways. I think we're the type of people who have to keep it real. I know that every comment I made earlier about my life was an honest one. What about you, Zurich?"

Zurich gave Hailey's comments a minute of thought. "It has often been said that I'm too honest. But in my opinion, honesty is the only way to fly. The story will always be the same when you're telling the truth. Lying is the most confusing to the one doing it. You're right about keeping it real. It's easier that way. To answer your question, I was honest with you."

Zurich definitely knew how to keep it real. But what he didn't know was if it was going to be so easy to leave Hailey Hamilton behind without looking back. Their imminent separation might indeed be a hard one to pull off, especially without bringing about some sort of a change in him. For the better or the worse? He just didn't know. But this woman was truly different.

"*I wish I knew how not to be so direct, but I don't*. Do you remember who said that?"

He cracked up. "Sounds just like me. Well, here comes the waiter. We'll have to get deeper into this conversation after we eat. Okay with you?"

She nodded. "Fine, but what about ordering another appetizer?"

"It was good, but I really had enough. The main course is here now, so I'll be just fine. Thanks, Hailey."

Zurich quickly picked up the envelope he'd received from Hailey. He then opened it and read it. The simple words of thanks put a smile on his face. "This was really nice of you. I appreciate the way you show your appreciation. You're very thoughtful."

"I'm glad you like the card. It was the least I could do to show how much your gift meant to me." She stretched her arm across the table and put her wrist under his nose. "How do you like the perfume on me?"

His heart raced as he traced her wrist with feathery kisses. "It smells divine on you. It looks like I picked out the perfect scent for you. You two were definitely made for each other."

Seated across from one another in one of the popular lounges inside the hotel, where a live band played top-forty tunes, Hailey and Zurich had yet to experience an awkward moment as they enjoyed getting further acquainted. It was a little difficult to communicate above the loud music, but they somehow managed to converse despite the noise level.

His lips grazed her ear as he spoke into it. "Do you want another ginger ale, Hailey?"

"That would be nice. While we're waiting for the waitress, I'm going to slip into the ladies' room." She stood and reached for her purse.

Smiling, he got to his feet until she walked away.

After coming out of the stall, Hailey washed her hands. She then stood in front of the mirror as she freshened her lipstick and dusted her nose with corn silk. A slight smile appeared on her full lips as she thought of the good-looking man waiting back at the table for her. Zurich came off as a very genuine person, and she had to admit that she already liked him a lot.

Too bad they only had two weeks to click with each other. She could really get into Zurich, but when duty called she had to be ready and all set to go. Even if they did make a love connection, they'd still have to go their separate ways. Each of them had laid down the ground rules from the start: two weeks of fun in the sun and then it would be all over for them. The fact that Zurich thought they might've made a mistake in laying down the rules surprised her. Sighing with dismay, Hailey picked up her purse and left the ladies' lounge.

Two

Zurich stood as Hailey approached the table, but then he noticed that she had stopped all of a sudden. Another person had stepped into his view, making him lose visual contact with his date. Once the obstacle was cleared from his sight, he saw her talking to an extremely tall man. Her back was now to Zurich, which made him think she'd possibly turned around to respond to the guy with whom she appeared to be chatting.

What Zurich saw happen next blew his mind to smithereens. He was nearly in shock. Hailey had practically flipped the guy she'd been talking to upside-down, and he was now sprawled out all over the floor. From where Zurich stood, the guy appeared to be unconscious, out cold. Just as Hailey stepped over the prone figure, loud clapping broke out all over the lounge. Zurich was both stunned and amazed.

Zurich went forward to meet her. Cupping his hand under her elbow, he walked her back to the table. Once they were reseated, for several seconds all he could do was stare at her. Laughing hard, he shook his head. "I'm almost afraid to ask what that was all about. But I gotta know. What did that guy do or say for you to physically abuse him like that?"

Hailey put her hands together and squeezed them. "He obviously doesn't understand that n-o spells no. He asked me to dance, and when I told him I was here with someone, he decided to put his hands on me; one of the things

I hate for any stranger to do. I told him to please take his not-so-clean paws off of me, but he ignored the urgency in my request. Alcohol had built up his false courage; Hailey Hamilton was left with no choice but to tear it down."

Zurich whistled. "I can see that you're one bad girl! He sure paid a serious price for not listening. I'm over here in pain for him myself. You really physically abused that brother."

She pointed to the guy, who was being helped up from the floor by security. "That man there, my friend, is the abuser, not me. I can tell by the way he confronted me that he's used to pushing and knocking women around. He just happened to pick the wrong sister to mess with this time. You shouldn't feel anything but contempt for him. He's not worth your agony."

"I agree with you. I would've come to your rescue, but my vision was blocked. You were coming toward the table and then you stopped. By the time I got you in my sight again, you were busy knocking that guy flat on his behind. I hope you don't think I'd just sit by and let someone manhandle you like that. Where'd you learn to take someone out with such ease? Should I be scared of you, prizefighter Hamilton?"

Hailey laughed heartily. "I think he was the one that got handled—woman-handled. As you witnessed, I didn't need rescuing." She placed her hand on top of his and smiled into his eyes. "I don't want you to be scared of me, but I do have boundaries. I don't like to be touched by strangers or to be maliciously ridiculed. Other than that, I'm tamer than tame."

"You answered all my questions but one. Where'd you learn your techniques?"

"It goes hand in hand with my job. I'm highly trained in self-defense. For all you know, I could be a member of the Secret Service. We seem to have that job secrecy thing in common."

"I'm beginning to think you really are a member of

some covert organization. There aren't too many men who could handle themselves any better than you did."

"Well, according to you, your gig is just as undercover as mine. I bet you could kick some serious butt, too, especially if someone challenged you the way I was just now."

"I was serious about the kind of job I have, but I thought you were just putting me on about yours until now. Whatever your profession is, it seems that you have to be physically and mentally prepared for it, and you are that. Girl, you had everyone in the lounge cheering you on. He must've made a nuisance of himself with a few other women before you, since the crowd seemed to think he got exactly what he deserved."

Tears came to Hailey eyes, but she blinked them away before Zurich could see them. Hailey deeply grieved her best friend, Kelly Gardner, who'd been horribly abused for several years, both mentally and physically, by her jealous husband, Will Brockman. Less than six months had passed since Hailey had attended Kelly's funeral. Will had finally murdered Kelly. While in one of his jealous rages, with his bare hands, he'd strangled the life right out of the body of one of the kindest, most loving women that Hailey had ever known. Hailey and Kelly had grown up together and had loved each other like sisters. Hailey's career had separated them, but in distance only. Their spirits had stayed connected no matter where Hailey's job took her.

"I bet he'll think twice before he grabs hold of another woman. Zurich, do you feel up to taking a walk around the complex? The cigarette smoke in here is killing me. Texas has yet to adopt 'no smoking' policies for public places. A smoking section is not enough to combat the deadly hazard. The acrid smell travels." She needed more than fresh air; her head needed clearing.

"Hailey, can I ask you one question before we leave?"

"Of course you can."

He looked into her eyes. "I've already called you out of your name, though it wasn't anything vulgar. I've also dared to touch you, though it was innocent. I'm a stranger, too, so what kept you from taking me down to the hard deck?"

Her eyes twinkled with laughter as she successfully warded off her desire to cry. "That's easy to answer, though I think you just answered your own questions. Being called beautiful isn't such a bad thing, and you touching me the way you did wasn't the least bit repulsive or inappropriate. Strangers are people that I've never laid eyes on before, period. I'm simply dead set against abuse in any form. But I'm on a date with you. Now, if you were to do me the same way that jerk just did, you'd get the same kind of treatment he got. No exceptions to that rule."

"I somehow believe you." Zurich found himself wondering about her matter-of-fact statement. He didn't get the impression that she'd ever been abused, but it seemed that she had strong feelings about the issue. The tears she'd tried to hide from him hadn't just come right out of the blue; some sort of emotion-stirring memory had caused them. He stood. "Let's take that walk now. Is it inappropriate for me to hold your hand, Hailey?"

Without comment, she stood and then slid her hand into his. Zurich was surprised by the warmth and softness of her palm. With the type of physical training she obviously indulged in, he had expected her hands to be a tad rough or even somewhat calloused. He was also astonished by the spine-tingling sensations he'd felt the minute their hands had entwined.

The night air was muggy, thick with humidity, but the beauty of the grounds and the soft lighting that brought them into plain view made up for the sticky weather. Hailey's sense of smell was heightened by the heady scents of a variety of colorful flowers and luscious plant life. The sparkling pool water looked cool and inviting, but that was only a mirage. After the insufferable heat of the day, its temperature was nearly as warm as bath water. The blazing sun had made the Jacuzzi even hotter than what was considered normal. Hailey had even asked for the heat in the spa to be lowered. Hailey and Zurich had used both pools earlier in the day, but not at the same time. It was after their use of each that they'd met at the poolside bar.

The silence between them was amicable. It was as if each sensed the other's desire to be at one with the tranquility surrounding them. Hailey was far too aware that she wouldn't have this kind of peace again anytime soon. With her next assignment, even if it were in a place she positively loved, she'd have her share of serious duties to be concerned with.

Zurich loved the great outdoors, whether he was in the desert, the mountains, or on the beach. Walking had been a part of his daily regimen for as far back as he could remember. Zurich was a hiker, hunter, and avid fisherman. He considered himself more of a wild game tracker than a true hunter, because he'd never think of killing an animal for sport. He loved to track the animal and capture it in the scope of his hunting rifle, but never once had he pulled the trigger. The thrill for him was in the hunt, not the kill. He also loved to capture game on film.

Hailey and Zurich had practically walked around the entire complex, both outside and indoors, before they finally seated themselves on one of the plush sofas adjacent to the piano bar. The couple had planned to listen to the melodic music from the ebonies and ivories without actually going inside the lounge; it would be much easier for them to converse that way.

Zurich briefly touched Hailey's hand. "Before I get too comfortable seated here next to you, would you like something to drink, Hailey?"

Hailey patted his knee. "I'll pass on it since you already look so comfy. And if you're anything like me, you must be tired after all the walking we did. You need to relax. I can just wait until I get back to the room for that drink."

"Hailey, I can't imagine that any man has ever dared to make you wait for anything you wanted." He got to his feet. "I'm not a follower by any stretch of the imagination, but I have no intention of being the exception either, not in this case. What do you have a taste for?"

You. He did look icy-cool and delicious enough for her to drink right up. She thought that, alone, his moist-looking lips would probably be enough to satisfy her thirst. "I'll take a tall glass of cranberry juice with a big splash of orange juice and an even bigger splash of 7-UP, over crushed ice, garnished with a fresh slice of both lemon and lime. Let me warn you, the bartender's going to look at you strangely. But they'll mix the drink right up for you. I promise."

His eyes danced with wild abandon. "And I promise to get you exactly what you want, by hook or crook, Miss Hailey. Please don't duck out on me while I'm gone."

That warm, sexy Texas drawl of his heated her up all over. Too bad they were only ships passing in the night. This was one dreamboat she wouldn't mind colliding head-on with.

Her smile was warm and sweet. "Wouldn't think of it, Commander Kingdom. I'll be seated right here when you return."

He turned back and looked at her curiously. "Why did you call me that?"

The tone of his voice made her think she'd somehow offended him. The look in his eyes wasn't too friendly either. "I guess I was looking at you and thinking of how I'd described you earlier, like a man who could run a kingdom single-handedly or command an entire army. Remember me saying that? I meant it no differently than you did by calling me beautiful."

He looked rather relieved at her explanation. "So it seems that I need to take your comment as a compliment and not as an insult. Sorry if I misread your intent." He smiled, but his embarrassment was apparent. Her calling him "commander" had set off his internal alarms for many reasons.

Puzzled by his strange remarks, Hailey watched Zurich until he disappeared into the piano bar. Deciding not to make too much out of his oddities, she took off her shoes and curled her feet up under her. The tinkling sound of the piano keys was relaxing and she laid her head back against the sofa to await Zurich's return. Thinking of the time they'd already spent together made her smile. He was a nice, gentle man, and she was rather taken with him.

Minutes later, upon opening her eyes, Hailey heard a seductive female voice call out Zurich's name as he made his way back to the seating area. As Zurich turned to look behind him, Hailey saw a woman advancing toward him rapidly, as if she were afraid he might take off before she could get to him. Hailey blinked hard, as though she couldn't believe what she was witnessing. The young woman had thrust her body against Zurich's while her hands entwined all up in his hair. Hailey was as shocked as Zurich had been earlier when he'd watched her encounter with the man who had bitten off more than he could chew.

Slightly amused by Zurich's reaction to the bold woman who'd thrown herself in his face, Hailey smiled as she watched him try to extricate himself from the human noose hanging on to his neck. Almost in the same instant that Zurich gave Hailey a pleading-for-help glance, she got out of her seat. Not bothering to put her shoes back on, she walked toward him and his brazen companion.

Hailey removed the drinks from Zurich's hands. "Darling, there you are," she cooed. "I was getting worried about you."

The woman spun away from Zurich as if she'd been caught doing something she knew was wrong. While backing away from Zurich, the woman took time to size up Hailey. "I'm sorry," she stammered, "I thought he was someone else. A simple case of misidentification."

Liar, Hailey accused her inwardly. She had clearly heard the woman call him by his first name.

"Really! There's not another man on this planet who looks like my handsome husband. There's only one of his kind in this world. Aren't I the lucky one?" Hailey asked, smiling up at Zurich as if he were her very own personal hero. Her next move stunned even her; the fiery kiss she put on him had his loins screaming for mercy.

Hailey and Zurich howled as the woman took off down the hall as fast as she'd come. They watched after her until she disappeared around the corner.

Mindful of the drinks she held, Zurich pulled Hailey to him and gave her a warm hug. "Thanks. You covered my butt quite nicely. I was definitely in the grip of a of she-tiger."

Hailey's smile was smug. "You're welcome, but I'd like to hear what that was all about. She called out your name before she wrapped you up like her own personal Christmas present."

Zurich shook with laughter. "That was a good one, Hail. She did have me bound. Come on, let's sit back down and talk. This has been one incredible evening. First off, some guy gets up in your face—and you end up decking him. And now this aggressive woman comes along and practically climbs all over me. Lady, this has been some first date, but I don't think I'd wish for an encore, at least not featuring any of the bizarre incidents we've just encountered."

"Okay, dispense with the small talk and the stall tactics," Hailey teased as she reclaimed her seat on the sofa and set the drinks on the table. "How did that woman know your name?"

Sitting down beside her, he shifted until he'd made himself comfortable. "I ran into her the first day I was here, outside the gift shop. It was only for a couple of minutes. She asked my name and then she told me hers. I told her how long I'd be a guest at the hotel, but only after she asked. That was it, end of story, Hailey. I hadn't seen her again up until now."

"I would've never guessed that by her bold behavior. It still doesn't make sense as to why she threw herself at you that way. I thought you two were well acquainted, possibly even in the Biblical sense. That possibility definitely crossed my mind."

"She's certainly a fine-looking woman; the right bait, but the wrong hook. But nothing about that brief first meeting with her indicated any personal interest in me on her part. You just never know what goes through a person's mind. I'm sure you never thought that that guy was going to start pulling on you when you responded negatively to his request, but it happened. The lady was all up on me, but it surprised me as much as it did you."

"It's a crazy world. People today are more forward than at any other time. There are ladies who no longer wait for the men to make their acquaintance, and it seems that some men actually expect, even prefer, the women to approach them first."

Zurich had a good idea that he might get into trouble with Hailey, but he was too curious not to voice his inquiry. "Do you consider the way you kissed me as being forward?"

She had no control over the color she felt rising up in her face. "That was nothing more than a rescue attempt on my part. You looked uncomfortable with her all over you like that. I thought your eyes were sounding the emergency assistance siren when I looked your way. You shouldn't read anything into that kiss. It was nothing and it meant even less."

Hailey wished she could find a ten-foot deep hole and jump in it. The kiss might not have moved him, but it had shaken her very foundation. Her mouth on his made her feel like her blood had caught on fire. Just reliving it had her flesh burning up as she gulped down the cool drink.

"Didn't you think the 'husband' line was enough to do the trick?"

She shrugged with nonchalance. "Now that's what I would call being a bit forward. But I saw it as a solution to the problem. And it worked. Sorry if it didn't meet with your approval. I'm sure you can find her later and tell her I was lying. Whatever suits you is fine with me."

Her arrogant statement tickled him, but he hid his amusement. "I have a question about your earlier remarks. Which way do you prefer, Hailey, to lead the chase or be chased?"

She took a moment to think about his question. "I like to be chased. I still favor the man making the first move. But I'm not against introducing myself to someone that's interesting to me. As for my personal preferences, wanting to meet a member of the opposite sex is not always about romantic notions. I'm most intrigued with a man's mind and his value system. If I could have my idea of a perfect man, he'd be spiritual, humble, intelligent, confident, sensitive, honest, and possess a great sense of humor. He'd also have to be a genuinely caring individual."

While sipping his drink, his eyes carried a glint of deep intrigue as he studied her closely. "I noticed that the spiritual characteristic was first on your list. Why's that?"

"A person's spirituality is important to me because I'm spirit driven. I believe that women and men develop stronger relationships when they possess kindred spirits. To otherwise get involved is to fight against your own spiritual fiber. It's a battle that simply can't be won."

"Let me get this straight. Are you saying that opposites can't have a good relationship?"

"In a way, but let me explain what I mean. Two people can be opposite in many ways and still develop a strong bond. For instance, he can be a neat freak and she can be a slob, or the other away around, and they may get along just fine. He can like sci-fi movies and she's into nothing but romantic sagas, but that doesn't necessarily mean they're not compatible. In these instances, they can come to a happy medium just by accepting each other for who they are. But when the spirits are opposite, that can be a little harder to overcome. If one believes in God, and the other believes he is god, we have a definite case of opposing spirits."

"Hmm, never heard it put that way." Zurich was impressed with her analysis. "So when people say a couple is unevenly yoked, they're not necessarily speaking in terms of them not being from the same religious denomination, but rather in their having unmatched spirits."

She shrugged. "I don't know about anyone else, but that's what I understand it to mean. If I believe in God and you're a devil worshiper, our spirits are unevenly yoked. If you love your brother as you love yourself, and I hate practically everyone on the planet, we can't possibly claim kindred spirits. On the other hand, if you're one denomination and I'm another, and we both believed in one God, our spirits can still be of one accord. There are a lot of obstacles a couple can overcome in a relationship, but overcoming a vast difference in spiritual makeup isn't one of them. In my opinion, being spiritual and being religious are not one and the same. Does that make sense to you?"

"Perfect sense. What religious denomination are you, Hailey?"

"None. It's not about that for me. I merely strive daily to have a personal relationship with God, Zurich. I'm just human, with lots of human frailties. I struggle with the forces of good and evil and how to differentiate between good and bad choices just like everyone else."

I have a job that has trained me to kill or be killed, one that demands I take up arms when warranted. But you'll never know that about me. In two weeks you and I are on separate planes back to the lives we led before we met. Why do I suddenly feel that our day of separation will be a sad one, Zurich Kingdom? I truly believe I would enjoy a deeper relationship with you.

"Hey, I think we've let this conversation get way too serious. Do you still have the brochures I gave you earlier?" Zurich asked.

Hailey dug around in her purse until she came up with the entertainment pamphlets. "Let me see what we have here, Zurich." She took a brief look at all the brochures. "Well, we have several nice choices. Dolphin watching sounds intriguing, a water park is not really my cup of tea, but I'm willing to try most things once. Horseback riding on the beach stirs my taste for adventure, and a sunset cruise sounds romantic. Going over into Mexico on a shopping spree doesn't appeal to me at all. It's not something I'd want to risk."

Zurich frowned. "How's that a risk?"

She shook her head. "Just the horror stories I've heard about people, mainly women, going into Mexico never to return. So what if we do everything but that? I'm up for it."

He laughed at how easily she determined things. "I can live with your choices. Let's start with having breakfast together in the morning. We can finalize our plans while we eat. Are we on, Hailey?"

"Only if it's bright and early. I'm a morning person, Zurich. I like to sing along with the birds as the sun rises. But I'll let you sleep in for a couple of hours. Is eight too early for you?"

"You've got to be kidding! My days have always started before five A.M. since I was eighteen years old. If it's the sunrise you're interested in, I'm a man who can appreciate that. What about meeting out by the pool just before old Sol rises? We can watch the rising sun from the outdoor patio."

"We have a date." She looked at her watch. "I guess we'd better call it a night. It's late, but I always have to read and meditate an hour or so before I go to sleep. What do you do to get yourself calmed down enough to check out of consciousness for a few hours?"

His smile was tender. "Girl, I'm gone at the same time

my head kisses the pillow. I don't need to do a thing but climb in. Beds are for sleeping in. That's all I do in mine."

She raised an eyebrow. "Really? *All* you ever do in bed is sleep?"

"That's a loaded question. The devilish expression on your face says you know it, too." He winked at her, mischief twinkling in his eyes. "I'm going to leave that one up to your imagination. I'm not about to walk into that loaded minefield." *Just being around you is explosive enough.* "Ready for me to see you to your room, Hailey?"

"Yeah, but let me pull my foot out of my mouth first. Then I can put my shoes back on."

Noticing her bare feet for the first time, he smiled at how uninhibited she was. "You sure know how to make yourself comfortable, don't you? I like that about you. You seem content with everything, including your surroundings. That's kind of rare these days. It usually takes a long time for most people to grow relaxed with one another and a new atmosphere, but it's been real easy for us. At least, it's been that way for me."

"I feel the same as you. I'm also extremely comfortable with me, Zurich. That one trait can make a big difference in how we see and deal with others, as well as what's around us."

"How'd you get so comfortable with yourself? That's another rarity."

"I guess it has a lot to do with the way I was brought up. I was taught never to define myself by the opinions of others. My parents are very positive people who wouldn't think of using destructive criticism and harsh berating as a form of punishment. I grew up in a very safe and loving environment, always encouraged, never discouraged in anything I attempted to accomplish. I can't remember going to bed without hugs and kisses or waking up the next morning to the same sweet affection. If I couldn't find a comfort zone anywhere else, I always knew I'd find it at home. You seem pretty comfortable with yourself, not to mention confident."

Zurich stopped to allow Hailey to precede him into the elevator car. After pressing the button for her floor, he leaned back against the railing. "My story is nothing like yours. Affection didn't come in abundance in our modest home. My mother was warm and caring, but our father, Macon, was an evil tyrant. He ruled his entire family with an iron fist; we considered ourselves lucky when we didn't find our mouths and noses at the end of it. My mother wasn't so fortunate. I don't think she had a single body part that escaped contact with his angry, destructive hands."

Hailey looked distressed as she and Zurich stepped out of the elevator. "Is she still with your Dad? Or did your parents eventually divorce?"

"Our father died several years ago, but we all left home as soon as we turned eighteen. Each of us was born a year apart. I'm the middle child. Had my two brothers and I stayed around our hometown, we might've ended up in prison for first-degree murder. My mother finally left our abusive dad right after my youngest brother flew the nest. However, she ended up taking care of him in his last days. She actually brought that evil man back to her home, where she took care of his sickly body for nearly a year. They never divorced. My mom is now enjoying her senior years on the small Texas ranch that my brothers, Zane and Zaire, and I purchased for her. She lives in Brownsville, just down the road from here."

Hailey felt as if another chunk of her heart had been broken off. "Your story is more common than you might realize, Zurich. Happy homes nowadays are the exception rather than the rule. Your mom is very fortunate to be alive. My best friend didn't survive her abusive husband. He strangled her to death nearly six months ago."

He wasn't stunned by her remarks, but he certainly felt deeply saddened by them. Her comments had also answered the earlier question in his mind when it looked as if she had tears in her eyes. He was right on both accounts. She hadn't been abused herself—and she did have firsthand knowledge of an abusive relationship, one that deeply affected her.

"So that's what the tears were about a short time ago. I saw you wipe them away, even though you didn't seem to know that I was aware of it. I'm deeply sorry for your loss, Hailey."

"Thank you, Zurich."

In seeing her grief, his heart went out to her. "Was your girlfriend on your mind when you took that guy out in the club? Your reaction was rather swift."

"Not really, but I did think of her immediately afterward. I would've reacted to him in the same manner no matter what. He was completely out of line, just the same way Kelly's man was. Kelly didn't deserve to be treated the way she was, but her husband had her permission to do whatever he wanted with her."

"Her permission? What do you mean by that?"

"When she didn't press charges against him the very moment the abuse started, she let Will know that it was okay for him to beat her black-and-blue—without consequences. Each time he did it, she'd threaten to leave him. Then he'd convince her that he'd never touch her again. But he did, with each beating worse than the previous one."

Zurich took a hold of her hand for comfort. His inner feelings were in turmoil. The things Hailey mentioned had him thinking hard about something he hadn't yet come to grips with. He often wondered if profound fear of becoming an abuser just like his father was the real reason he didn't allow himself to get too involved with women. Had he been using the instability of his career as a way to keep himself from getting caught up emotionally?

Zurich had always had a short fuse, which he believed

was born out of his father's brutal treatment of his family. Although he'd never raised his hand to a single person, there were times when he'd feel angry enough to cause serious bodily harm to the one who'd aggravated him.

At one time, there had been things about his career choice that he couldn't deal with, those things involving acts of aggression and violence. He'd eventually learned to make peace with all that his career-field expected of him. Leaving home had been uppermost in his mind when he'd chosen his destiny. Staying around his abusive father wasn't an option for him, especially since he wanted to stay out of real trouble. His career choice actually saved his life.

At the door of Hailey's hotel room, Zurich reached up and gently lazed his forefinger down the side of her smooth face. "Are you going to be okay by yourself after all the things you've gone through this evening?"

She briefly touched his hand. "I'll be just fine. I don't allow myself to dwell on unpleasantness. It serves no purpose. What is done is done. I'm already over it."

"What about enjoyable experiences? Do you ever take time out to dwell on those?"

Hailey laughed inwardly. "Are you by chance asking me if I'm going to spend some time thinking about you and the pleasurable parts of our evening?"

He grinned with knowing. "I guess you could say that I'm a little curious about it."

"I can't imagine not thinking about you and the evening. Both have been very pleasant."

"Thanks." He leaned down and kissed her cheek. "See you at sunrise, Hailey Hamilton."

Her arms went around his waist as he brought her head against his chest for a warm hug. "Thanks for such a nice first date, Zurich Kingdom. I can't remember having an evening that was any nicer than this one." Her light, airy kiss to his lips left him trembling.

Hailey quickly moved away from Zurich and was inside her hotel room before he could respond to her gentle affection. He stared at the closed door, wishing it would open up for an instant, just so he could have another glimpse of the beautiful spirit inside.

Three

Still unable to fall off to sleep, Hailey had been tossing and thrashing about on the king-size bed for the past couple of hours. In the beginning of her restless night it was only the thoughts of the evening's numerous unsettling events that had kept her wide awake. Then the sweet memories of Zurich had entered her mind and had removed any possible chance for sleep. The different expressions that had crossed his handsome face, the tender feel of his hands, the warmth of his heart reaching out to her, were all she could think about.

This man had her feeling things she'd sworn never to allow herself to feel, warm and wonderful feelings. Kelly's abusive situation had made Hailey terribly fearful of getting involved in any kind of serious relationship. Hailey had had her share of close male friendships, but she'd never given her heart away to anyone.

At times, her fear of romantic love was so much bigger than she was. Hearing Zurich talk about his mother's abusive marriage was just another confirmation that love did nothing but cause pain and suffering. While her parents' marriage was the exact opposite of what she feared the most, she had convinced herself that their relationship was the exception, not the norm.

Kelly's horrific suffering at Will's hands began when both girls were only fourteen years old; Will was two years their senior, handsome and popular. Love had blossomed for Kelly and Will during the yearly summer vacation at a youth camp. Will's abuse of Kelly first began once school reconvened that September, the week after Labor Day. Any guy that looked at Kelly sent Will into a jealous rage. Never did he confront the guy; Kelly was the weaker target.

The main reason Kelly hadn't told her parents about the abuse was the fear that her dad would end up in jail for going after Will with a vengeance. Her love for Will, and the fact that she thought she could change him were the other excuses Kelly had always made. Thirteen years of abuse proved that Kelly hadn't been able to change Will Brockman one iota. Her violent death at his hands was the strongest proof of all. And it had also become Hailey's burden of guilt because of the secret she'd been forced to carry within.

Although Hailey knew she'd never let anyone abuse her that way, just the thought of some man attempting to treat her like that was enough to make her vow to keep her heart to herself. While she didn't believe she was in any imminent danger of losing her heart to Zurich, she was aware that the odds of her not falling in love with him definitely weren't in her favor.

Hailey drew in a shaky breath. The beauty of the rising sun had her mesmerized; the beauty of the strong black man enjoying the sunrise with her held her spellbound. Straddling the same lounge Hailey occupied, only seated behind her, Zurich had his hands on her shoulders; they were tender and comforting as they gently massaged her muscles. His chin pressing into the top of her head and his warm body pulsating against her back aroused her physical desires.

He kept his eyes to the east. "I almost stood you up," he whispered.

"Why?" She didn't make any attempt to turn around to face him. His chest against her back felt too good to disrupt the contact by moving about. His chin still rested atop her head.

"Fears."

"Of what?"

"For one, how you make me aware of things. I already feel as if I'm an important person in your life. My eyes have never followed a woman's every single movement, yet I can't keep them off of you. You're confident, but I also sense quite a bit of vulnerability in your make-up."

He moved his head around until his cheek lay against hers. "I haven't been able to identify the areas in which your defenses aren't as tough as you seem to portray. I feel a strong desire to protect you, even though I've witnessed firsthand your ability to take care of yourself. All of these things add up to what I'm beginning to believe is my worst fear: one day falling hopelessly in love with someone, only to turn around and abuse them like Dad did Mom."

Her insides trembled with the compassion she felt for him. His fears were exactly the same as hers, only she was the one who feared the abuse. But did she dare tell him that? Was he the one she could bare her soul to? Their relationship wasn't going any further than the end of the vacation, but she already felt a special kinship with him. Could she and Zurich build a solid friendship, especially when it was so obvious to her that their attraction was both emotional and physical? Hailey thought it was better to have him as friend than to lose contact with him altogether. But she wanted so much more with Zurich Kingdom, desired it badly.

As he rubbed his cheek against hers, her body eagerly responded to his sweet caresses. His hands continued to massage her shoulders, but his face so close to hers was what she enjoyed most. His skin was baby soft and she loved the feel of it next to hers.

He squeezed her shoulders. "Aren't you going to comment on my fears, Hailey?"

"No, because I understand them. I fear abuse, too. I

guess my girlfriend's situation keeps me afraid. I don't want to end up like her."

He brought her shoulders back toward his chest. "What makes you think that would happen to you, that you'd end up being hurt that way?"

"The same things that have you fearful. You think if your dad abused your mom that you might do the same to someone else. Right?"

"That's exactly what I believe. I just don't know how someone gets like that. Do you? Knocking the hell out of someone isn't something that I'd think would come easily for me."

"A learned behavior, more than likely. Perhaps he was battered by one of his parents."

"Maybe so. But I've never heard mention of it. Dad was a nasty, mean one, sober or drunk. He didn't care which one of us he lashed out at, but Mom suffered more."

"Violence runs in cycles. And men aren't the only ones who become abusive. Women dish out cruel treatment as well; you just don't hear about it as often as you do about men. I just happen not to believe that anyone is born into the world with the deadly temperament of a venomous snake. Something horrible has probably happened to these people who take their frustrations out on others in a physical manner. That kind of behavior doesn't come out of the blue. It doesn't just happen without a reason. Still, it's difficult to deal with."

"Hey," he said softy, "I have an idea. Why don't we lighten up this conversation a bit? I think it's weighing us both down. Let's do pleasantries, okay?"

"I like your idea, Zurich."

"Did you sleep well, Hailey?"

"Barely slept at all. But if I told you why I couldn't rest, we'll end up negative again. What about you? Did you go out as soon as your head hit the pillow?"

He laughed. "I wish. Sleep made a liar out of me last

night when it didn't show up immediately. I couldn't get there for thinking of you. How's that for honesty?"

"Uplifting. I thought about you, too, Zurich. It was the only good part of my sleepless night."

"I like the sound of that." He drew her head back even closer to his chest and then wrapped his arms around her waist. "A lot of my time lying awake was spent wondering what it would feel and taste like to kiss you. Is that too much information?"

"Not enough."

"Really! Did you find yourself wondering about intimate stuff happening for us as you lay awake?"

Hailey's heart sighed with longing. "No, just envisioning them."

He laughed huskily. "Do you think we'll get a chance to satisfy one or two of our intimate curiosities?"

"I sure hope so, Zurich."

"It's nice to know we're on the same page, Hail."

"Only for the next two weeks." Only family members called her by a shortened version of her name, but she liked the sound of it coming from him. There were people who didn't care to have their names chopped up or mispronounced, but it never bothered her. As long as she wasn't called anything vulgar and disrespectful, she was tolerant when someone didn't get her name exactly right. After all, the world was full of never-to-be-perfect humans.

"Don't remind me of how short our time is. The strangest thing is that I'm already dreading for when the time will end. This has never happened to me. I've always been prepared to move on, 'cause that's what I have to do. This time is different. That I can't do anything about it is the only thing that's the same. When my job cracks the whip, I have to make the trip."

"Same scenario here. Commitment and dedication to one's job does suck at times, Zurich. But I love what I do. More so, I love the reasons why I do it."

Zurich was growing more and more curious about her profession. The fact that she wasn't willing to reveal any more to him than he himself was willing to tell about his job made him want to know that much more about Hailey Hamilton and her seemingly undercover life. Due to September eleventh, he couldn't divulge information about his own employment; he had to give her the same respect and not pry into her private affairs. That two people with mysterious jobs would meet on a beautiful island in paradise was one odd occurrence. *Or was it fate?*

Seated in a less formal hotel restaurant than Le Meridian, Hailey ate heartily of her soft-scrambled eggs, sausage, toast, and jelly. She couldn't believe how ravenous she was. It wasn't like her to eat this heavily during the first meal of the day. It was during lunch that she normally ate the most food. For the latter part of the day she preferred lighter dining, nothing akin to the feast they'd eaten the previous evening. Hailey was thoroughly amused by Zurich's manly appetite. His plate was piled high with pancakes, eggs over easy, a thick cut of breakfast steak, and homemade biscuits. The hash browns and sliced tomatoes had been served on the side, but he'd already devoured most of them. The boy could put it away, but it didn't seem to affect his finely tuned physique. He might eat like a horse, but Zurich was in great physical condition.

He smiled lazily at her. "The look on your face tells me exactly what you're thinking."

"And what am I thinking, Mr. Kingdom?"

"That I should be grossly overweight and terribly unhealthy to boot, from all the fattening foods I like to eat. How close am I to your thoughts?"

"I am amused by the amount of food you order and then devour, but I'm impressed with the way you keep your body so well conditioned. There's not an ounce of fat anywhere on your anatomy. You're leaner than lean and your muscle tone is extraordinary. You eat each of your meals as though they might be your last, but it's obvious that you also adhere to an extensive exercise program. You *are* a cut above being physically fit, Zurich."

"Thank you, ma'am. I appreciate the compliments. Am I at liberty to tell you what I think of your body?"

Smiling broadly, Hailey raised an eyebrow. "I think you let me know that when we first met. *An indescribable figure packaged in a hot bikini* is the first comment that comes to my mind. Then you said something about my *physical attributes adding up to your definition of a living, breathing paradise*. How's my memory?"

"Sharp as a tack. Well, I *was* being honest when I said those things. You're also a fine physical specimen. From the looks of things, I'm not the only one who works out regularly."

"It's a good thing that we're both health-conscious," Hailey remarked. "Exercising isn't the easiest task to perform, but it is one of the most important when trying to keep yourself healthy. Both my profession and lifestyle dictate that I maintain top-notch mental and physical conditioning. This girl is no couch potato. Swimming, jogging, bowling, and playing tennis are my favorite pastimes. I also indulge in a little kickboxing. Can't leave out reading."

"Yeah, I recall that your feet are registered as lethal weapons. That's something I'm not about to forget. I'm sure the homeboy that ran up on you won't have a problem remembering the way he was taken down, either. Girl, I still can't get over what you did to 'J. Smooth'."

Hailey laughed at Zurich's joking name for the guy she'd injured. "I've *been* over it. Are you ready to get on with the beginning of our adventurous day? Time is not going to stand still and wait for us to get our groove on." *It would be nice to have it stand perfectly still for us.*

Laughing hard, he looked her attire over. "You sure got

the right kind of clothes on: loose fitting and casual. I'm glad to see that you're also wearing proper footgear. I've actually seen a few sisters try to go sightseeing with heels on. Looking cute should be the last thing on someone's mind when touring any city. Comfort is what's happening when you've got a lot of territory to cover, especially on foot. The sisters that want to be cutesy probably end up carrying their shoes, wishing they'd dressed for comfort instead of slaving to fashion."

"I traded cute for comfort a long time ago. Most of us women don't do that until we hit middle age, but I learned not to wear uncomfortable shoes after getting a serious blister on my big toe. Now that's what I call unfashionable. That painful foot malady put a cramp in my style for days. I could barely walk because my toe was so sore and tender."

"I can only imagine. I've never worn shoes that were too tight, too small, or any shoes with stacked heels. Other than the footwear I work in, I'm into wearing the softest in leather."

Zurich got to his feet and then helped Hailey to hers. Time suddenly did seem to stand still as they came face to face. His eyes embraced hers, a fiery warmth burning in their depths. The desire for her in his heated gaze was undeniable. He looked as if he wanted to kiss her, but it seemed as though he was uncertain of what her reaction might be. His hand, closed into a fist, reached up and touched her face. As his knuckles brushed downward against her cheek, the longing to melt her body into his attacked her with sweet vengeance.

Their waiter seemed to appear out of nowhere, breaking the enchanting spell.

"I can settle the check for you, sir."

Without taking his eyes off of Hailey, Zurich handed the waiter the check and his American Express card.

"I'll be right back with your receipt, sir." After getting no immediate response from Zurich, the waiter hurried off.

Zurich took Hailey's hand. "Where were we?"

"I don't know. It seemed to me as if we'd somehow gotten lost. Where do you think we were, Zurich?"

"We were so into each other it only seemed that we were lost. I know exactly where we were—in a sweet trance. I hope we can stay there for a while. It was a nice place to be with you."

"Very nice, serene. I enjoyed being there with you, too."

So sure was she that he was going to kiss her, her eyes immediately closed in eager anticipation of his lips tenderly introducing themselves to hers. When his mouth only made gentle contact with her cheek, she felt disappointed and relieved at the same time. Disappointed because she'd expected to be kissed, relieved because, had he kissed her, she couldn't have hidden her deep desire for more than just the taste of his mouth; her body had already begun to crave his.

Being an independent woman didn't stop Hailey from allowing Zurich to be the perfect gentleman as he helped her aboard the large floating vessel scheduled to take them out into the Gulf of Mexico. Zurich's touch had a way of making Hailey's spirit dance. He seemed no less affected by hers. His eyes smiled every time they captured the slightest glimpse of her. Zurich loved the graceful way Hailey moved. She was a classy woman, and her sweet, soft-spoken voice was music to his ears. Her laughter enchanted him and her beautiful smile had a way of brightening the atmosphere. Zurich had been in the company of many awesome women, but Hailey's genuineness seemed to radiate from deep within.

Her eyes were bright with excitement as she leaned over the railing to watch the crew working diligently to untie the boat from the dock and get it on its way. There were several children playing about her, which caused her to smile. She loved kids of all ages, but she had a way about her that especially appealed to teenagers. They found her easy to talk with and the teens loved the fact that she was non-judgmental. Hailey worked with teenagers through volunteering at community centers whenever an opportunity arose.

"Have you ever been seasick, Hailey?"

"Not that I can remember, but I don't find myself on boats very often. I've been on a couple of cruises, but they were several years apart. What about you—and all that food you ate?"

"Being at sea won't bother me. I'm a fisherman and I also have a strong stomach."

"Fisherman, huh? I haven't done that in a long time. My dad used to take me fishing with him. I remember it being fun." The loud whirring noise coming from the boat's motor caused Hailey to look around with a start. She laughed at her own ready-for-battle reaction since the noise was very similar to that of a gun being fired. She was trained to be on guard.

"Hey, we can remedy that. We can go out on a deep-sea fishing boat tour early tomorrow morning. I think you'd have a lot of fun, especially if you're lucky enough to land a big one."

Hailey frowned. "Is it okay if we leave a day or two in between boat tours? I'd love to go fishing, but back-to-back boating trips could leave a girl a little green." She smiled sweetly. "What about the day after tomorrow?"

"You got it. I'll make a reservation for us as soon as we get back to shore. We can rent all the fishing equipment right onboard the boat. Where do you want to eat tonight?"

She laughed. "We just ate, Zurich. I can't even think about eating right now. I'm still full. But I'm sure we'll come up with something that'll interest both of us."

He snapped his fingers. "I know the right spot, a casual diner with great seafood and lots of down-home cooking." He was familiar with all the cooks; one he knew personally.

It was when Hailey failed to respond to his enthusiastic announcement that he noticed the look of utter amazement on her face. Her eyes were actually glistening with tears, but he couldn't see what had her so misty-eyed. He couldn't believe how affected he was by her every mood.

As she clapped her hands and jumped up and down, Hailey squealed with excitement. "Oh, look at the dolphins, Zurich. They're magnificent!"

Zurich still didn't see anything, but he heard several of the others also shouting with joy.

Hailey pointed down at the water. "Right there, Zurich. The dolphins are swimming right alongside the boat. My gosh, I can't believe my eyes. These two are so close to the vessel."

Zurich finally spotted the two dolphins as they resurfaced. His breath caught as they dived below as quickly as they'd come up. He waited with bated breath for them to show up again. This was the first time he'd taken this particular tour—and he was so glad that he had, especially being able to experience something this magnificent with Hailey. It appeared that the sea had come to life right before their eyes.

He positioned himself behind Hailey as his hands gently spanned her waist. It was only seconds later that several more dolphins appeared near the boat. Zurich's eyes caught sight of a pair of the big fish that appeared stuck together. Every time one surfaced, the other one did also. It looked as if one was right on top of the other.

"Look at those two," he told Hailey, pointing at the two sea creatures. "They seem fused together. Or I'm seeing double."

Hailey tossed her head back against his chest and smiled up at him. "They are. I think they're mating. They're probably making little baby dolphins."

The wondrous expression that crossed Zurich's face broadened Hailey's smile. He appeared totally in awe of what natural beauty his eyes had beheld. She also thought that the dolphins were one of the most beautiful creatures that the sea and nature had to offer. She'd never seen anything like it until now. All the sea life she'd ever laid eyes on had all been living in captivity. Hailey couldn't help wondering what it would be like to swim alongside them. She was sure the experience would be nothing short of awesome.

Hailey looked around at all the others who shared her and Zurich's enthusiasm over such unbelievable sightings. She closely studied the faces of the men, women, and children. Their joyous expressions nearly brought her to tears. It wasn't that long ago that she'd seen sadness and deep pain etched on the faces of her fellow Americans. Hailey would never forget the haunted, grievous looks she'd seen in the eyes of those she worked side by side with, day in and day out. The suffering was indescribable.

The events of September eleventh had left behind such devastation. But to see Americans laughing again and enjoying themselves thoroughly was very rewarding. It also made her job that much easier. Practically every day of her life was spent doing what she was trained to do so that each of them could have the freedom to enjoy breathtaking moments just like this one. Unfortunately, there were many citizens who didn't understand or even know about the profound sacrifices constantly being made by dedicated people just like herself.

Zurich turned her around to face him. "Are you okay? You've gotten mighty quiet for someone who was so bubbly only minutes ago."

"Just observing how America is valiantly bouncing back from the tragedies in New York, D.C., and Pennsylvania. But the horrific memories of how terrorism nearly destroyed the hearts of Americans while turning this country inside-out will never be forgotten." Hailey shuddered. "That's what brought on the sudden melancholy mood. I'm sorry for that."

He kissed her forehead. "Don't ever apologize for what

you and every other person in America are constantly feeling. It's still hard for me to talk about it in depth."

"Did you know anyone who was personally affected by the tragedies of the day hell rained down on us, Zurich?"

"Many. I knew several people who didn't survive that day. Some worked at the World Trade Center, but the majority of the ones I knew worked in the Pentagon. What about you?"

"I also knew quite a few people who worked both places. It's a small world, isn't it?"

"Smaller than we think, Hailey. There are times when I can feel it closing in on us."

"Can I hug you?" she asked right out of the blue.

No sooner than he opened his arms wide to her did she find the safe harbor he had offered to her. Her heart thumped wildly inside her chest as he squeezed her ever so gently. As he lifted her head with his two fingers under her chin, she felt as if she might faint. He was so near and he smelled so good despite the fishy scent gliding on the sea air. Her heart began to hammer away as he slowly bent his head and then grazed her lips with his own. Hailey waited for the kiss to deepen, but when it didn't, she still felt grateful for what little intimacy he'd shared with her.

He held her slightly away from him. "Are you feeling better?"

She looked up at him. "Yeah, I am. I just needed a little comforting. Thanks for giving me that. How about you? Doing okay?"

"Better than okay. This has been a great day so far. We've shared a lot of things. I like that we can be so honest and open with each other. It's not always easy to share some of your innermost secrets with someone you just met. That usually comes a lot later, once trust has been established. I think we've learned a lot about each other despite our short time together, though there are things that we will never get the opportunity to learn. Kind of sad, huh?"

Hailey had no comment. She wished that they didn't keep reminding each other of how short their time was. Maybe he was trying to keep her from building up her hopes only to have them dashed away. He really didn't have to worry about that. She knew better than anyone that a long-term relationship was impossible for them. It was sad but true. Zurich had no idea of the world she lived and worked in, even if he did have some sort of covert job. Her job was a highly technical one, and it was an extremely important one.

"Do you think maybe we could stop dwelling on how much time we have left on the island? I promise not to turn sappy and weepy-eyed on you and confess my undying love. I don't expect any more from you than what we share from one moment to the next. I'm not a schoolgirl with a crush on my first boyfriend, just a young woman with dreams and aspirations and a job that requires my undivided attention for right now. I have no intentions of breaking our rules. I have as much at stake as you do." *And probably way more to lose: my heart.*

"Are you through?"

She shrugged. "I didn't mean for that to come off sounding like a lecture. I'm through."

"Good. I promise not to mention the subject again. It's taboo with me. Okay, Hailey?"

Hailey wasn't going to waste one more second waiting for him to kiss her. She had kissed him before, during the episode with the strange lady. And that sweet kiss had left her wanting more of the same. Her eyes were magnetically drawn to his lips when she looked at him.

Since she'd made her position perfectly clear to him, she didn't see a problem with them sharing a little intimacy. Unless she was wrong, he wanted to kiss her every bit as much as she wanted him to. They were on a boat out in the middle of the Gulf, the perfect atmosphere for a touch of romance. Hailey would not go to bed another night without at least one delicious memory to take with her; her mind was made up.

Hailey cupped Zurich's face between her hands and her lips pressed tenderly into his. Her mouth moved up to his face and then returned to his lips. The next kiss she gave him was full on the mouth, but she had reservations about using her tongue to find his. As he deepened the kiss, she let her doubts fly free. His tongue had already found hers.

Zurich came up for air, but only for a moment. In the next second, his mouth reclaimed hers feverishly. He had to assume that she knew what she'd gotten started since she'd made the first move, but he had to wonder: Did she know how to corral the passion before it got too far out of control? He sure as hell didn't.

Hailey clasped her hands behind his head as the tip of her tongue tickled the base of his throat. She felt the thickness of his manhood when he pressed his body even closer to hers. Excitement welled in her breast and her nipples grew taut with the desire for his heated touch.

The moment Hailey thought about where they were, out in broad daylight, on board a boat with numerous other tourists, many of them children, she pulled slightly back. "I think we should put this on hold for now. I only have eyes for you at the moment, but I'm sure there are many eyes on us. For a moment there, I forgot where we were. Can you believe it?"

He laughed at how the natural color in her cheeks had deepened. "It was too easy to forget, Hailey. I'm glad you put the skids on us 'cause I wouldn't have given a minute's thought to all the probing eyes. Can we pick up later where we left off?"

"If I should forget, though I doubt that's possible, will you promise to remind me?"

"That's one promise you can count on." He kissed her lightly on the mouth. "Until later."

* * *

Bill Withers' "Lean On Me" floated from the patron-packed diner's old-style jukebox. The place had a heartwarming homeyness, saturated in the delicious scents coming out of the kitchen. Hailey liked the sentimental feeling she got being seated in a worn red leather booth with Zurich right next to her. Having grown up in a small town where diners like this one were the in-place to hang out for the locals, Hailey felt downright comfortable and very much at home.

Hailey thought she'd zoomed back in time when several patrons took to the fairly decent-size dance floor; it was only the middle of the afternoon. Well, she thought, the oldies music was hard for the body and feet to resist. Her own feet had been moving every since she and Zurich had sat down. The constant bobbing of his head was a good indication of the effect the soulful music was having on him. The songs belonged to a couple of generations ago, but classics were like old soldiers—they never died. Unlike the soldiers, the top oldies rarely faded away.

Countless times, her parents had taken her down to the town's local diner, where they dined, danced and listened to music. The thought of her dad dancing her all over the place filled her with warmth. But it was the occasions she'd danced with both of her parents that were the most precious. When her daddy had held his two best girls, as he often referred to them, in his arms, Hailey had always felt like she was dancing on a cloud in heaven. Hailey and Marie had to share Martin's forehead when they slow danced. She could almost feel their foreheads touching one another. Those were indeed special occasions in the life of Hailey Hamilton.

"This is a nice, cozy place, Zurich. It's also very lively. I love it already."

"I'm glad I thought about it when I did. I come here on every single visit. And I was pretty sure you'd like the place as much as I do. It never ages and nothing ever seems to change. That same old jukebox has been in here for as long as I've been coming. Unless they're replacing it with exact replicas, I believe it's the same one. Are you ready to order?"

"If you don't mind, I'd like to just sit here and watch the dancers. But you should go ahead and order if you're ready. I know how much you love to eat. I can play catch-up."

"No problem. I can wait on you. It's not that serious. Instead of just watching the dancing, do you want to take a spin or two around the floor? I promise not to show you up."

Hailey grinned. "Think you're that good at it, huh? Boy, I bet I can dance rings around your sorry butt. I have rhythm like you wouldn't believe."

"Well, I guess we're going to find out." He slid out of the booth and held out his hand to her. Hoping he hadn't talked himself into a big-time embarrassment, he escorted Hailey onto the dance floor. His laughter rang out as the soft melody of a slow song began to play. As Teddy Pendergrass's sultry voice swept into the room like a silky, magical web, capturing the souls of everyone present, those who were seated crowded onto the dance floor.

He pulled Hailey into his arms. "I know I can out slow dance you, especially since I get to lead. Close your eyes. You're in for a real nice treat."

"Or sore feet."

"What's that supposed to mean?"

"Step on my toes—and you just might find out," she teased him.

His eyes were soft and seductive as he looked down at her. "Baby, I'm way too smooth for that." Placing the palms of his hands firmly against her back, he drew her in close to him. "Relax, Hailey. Let Teddy P work his miracles on us. Your toes are safe with me."

She giggled at his last comment. "I think all of me is

safe with you. But if I get any looser, I just might fall asleep. I don't think that would be too cool."

She laid her head against his chest. Involuntarily, her eyes closed. "Hmm, this feels so good." Her arms entwined around his neck as she allowed him to lead her in the most electrifying slow dance she'd ever shared in.

Several songs later Hailey and Zurich made their way back to the table, feeling even closer to one another than before the dancing started. He made her feel warm and safe and she made him feel just downright happy and content.

Zurich hadn't smiled this much in a long time; Hailey had broadened the horizons on even his smile. She had taught him how to reflect outwardly his inward joy. Although he was quite satisfied and extremely happy with his life just the way it was, Hailey made him realize that he may have allowed himself to miss out on some of the other important elements that life had to offer; for one, the absence of a good woman.

It wasn't that he hadn't dated other women or hadn't ever been involved romantically; his mindset was totally different now. He viewed romance and emotional love as two entirely different matters. His family and his job, which he considered his second family, were the only things in this life that he was emotionally connected to without reservations; nobody should dare to mess with either. Inasmuch as his dad had been an abuser, Zurich was a fierce protector of both home fronts. He was not only committed to both entities, he would fight to his death to honor and to preserve each.

The little time he'd spent with Hailey had him thinking about the added enjoyment life could hold for him now, as opposed to waiting to find it after his career was over. Hailey had him wondering about all sorts of life's wondrous possibilities—the kinds of heartfelt things he hadn't ever given much thought to.

Zurich brushed the back of Hailey's hand with his fingertips. "Did you work up an appetite while you were working me over on the dance floor?"

Hailey smiled beautifully. "I hope you brought along a lot of money. After looking over this menu, I want to sample practically everything on it. But you only have yourself to blame for that since you've been telling me how mind-blowing the entire menu is."

He grinned. "You're what's blowing my mind." Slightly rising up from the seat, he removed his black leather wallet from the back pocket of his pants. Smiling at Hailey, he checked the contents of his billfold. Looking directly at her, he frowned. "Nothing but lint in here, girl. How much cash do you have? I might need to borrow a few bucks to fill your order."

Hailey rolled her eyes at him in a playful manner. "They take credit cards. I saw all the symbols on the door when we first came in. You invited me here to eat, Zurich."

He laughed. "But I didn't make you pay when you invited me out to dinner."

"That's your fault, not mine. I offered."

"So, it's like that, huh?"

"How come you guys always use that tired phrase 'it's like that, huh,' when you don't have a sure-fire, or at least a reasonable, comeback?"

He got to his feet. "Hold your sassy tongue, woman. I'll be right back."

Hailey couldn't help wondering where he was off to. When it looked as if he'd gone behind the swinging doors, which she thought might be the kitchen, her curiosity increased. *What was he up to now?* She had no idea, but Hailey admitted to loving the delicious intrigue.

A few minutes later Zurich slid back into his seat, smiling smugly at Hailey. "I'm back now. Do you remember the nature of the conversation we were having before I left?"

"It's not as important as me finding out the nature of your disappearance. Where'd you go, Zurich?"

"Let's just say I had a little private business to take care of. Cool?"

Hailey looked embarrassed, thinking he must've gone to the men's room. Talk about a subject that was taboo! That was one intimacy that she had never understood. Both her parents constantly ventured in and out of the bathroom when the other mate was in there. It was one area in a person's life that she thought should be totally sacred. She couldn't imagine using the bathroom while someone else was in there, spouse or not.

Less than a quarter of an hour later Hailey was amazed at all the small dishes being placed on the table, along with a couple of larger ones. Looking over at Zurich, she hunched her shoulders. "What's up with all this?"

"Did you not ask to sample the entire menu?"

Her look was one of disbelief. "No you didn't!" Her laughter was uncontainable as she realized he was telling the truth. "Oh, my goodness, you *did* go there!"

All the smaller dishes on the table held a variety of mouthwatering samples of practically the entire menu. Thank God they weren't in a four-star restaurant, she thought in amusement. She was beginning to believe that she'd have to be careful what she requested from Zurich. His comment about not being able to imagine any man denying her anything she wanted came to mind. She'd never required anyone to cater to her every whim, but Zurich's desire to please her sure made her feel extra-special.

Reaching across the table, she took his hand in hers and kissed the back of it. "This is too special, and you're way too much for me to try and define. Thank you. My heart weeps with joy."

His heart became full at the affection swirling in her eyes. "You're welcome, Hailey. Go ahead and dig in. I want to sit here and watch you take pleasure in devouring the feast that I had specially prepared for my black queen.

My mom, though retired, prepares a variety of the menu dishes for the diner. Watching you enjoy your meal is my dessert."

Hailey looked shocked. "Your mom works here?"

Zurich basked in the warm glow of bewilderment in her eyes. "No, but she used to. She prepares the food items in her own kitchen. The driver of the diner's catering truck picks up everything from the ranch and delivers it here. Hailey, I would've had Mom join us had I thought of eating at the diner sooner than I did. I know she'd fall in love with you instantly."

Hailey realized he'd rendered her speechless when she couldn't come up with a fitting response. Just him mentioning his Mom and her in the very same breath had her overwhelmed.

Four

Hailey was very tired by the time she and Zurich returned to the hotel. Both had decided to take quick naps and showers before seeing what else the island had to offer in the way of nightlife. Her plans to stay inside the complex and relax and read had been all but forgotten. Being with Zurich was much more exciting than the vacation she'd initially had in mind. Never in her wildest dreams had she expected to meet anyone so interesting and so down-to-earth as Zurich Kingdom. But she had—and she couldn't be happier about it.

A soft knock came on the door in Hailey's room, immediately followed by a much stronger one. Not expecting a soul, she looked at the clock. She had several hours left before she was to meet back up with Zurich, and she hadn't ordered anything from room service, so neither of those things were any help to her in determining who stood on the other side of the door. The only sure-fire way to find out what she needed to know was to answer the knock.

Realizing she had nothing whatsoever on under her robe had Hailey scrambling for something acceptable to put on before making another move. The persistent knocking caused her to abandon the idea of dressing as she moved quickly toward the door. After putting the security chain in place, Hailey cracked the door. She felt instant relief at seeing a woman standing there. "How can I help you?" Hailey asked through the small opening.

The statuesque brunette smiled at Hailey as she pointed at the name tag pinned to her white lab-style coat. "My name is Rhoda Butler, Miss Hamilton. I'm here to deliver a very unique present for you. I am an employee of the hotel, a masseuse. A friend of yours, Mr. Zurich Kingdom, has requested that you receive a full-body massage from the spa staff, at his expense. I can render the services in your hotel suite or you can come down to the health spa. The choice is yours, of course. I can get all the equipment needed should you decide to have it done now. "

Hailey looked down at her attire, laughing, as she thought about her state of undress being totally appropriate for receiving a massage. Hailey removed the safety chain and allowed the hotel employee to enter her suite. "Come on in, Ms. Butler. I'd like to do it here."

The masseuse wheeled inside a metal cart laden with lotions, oils, and a host of other products and tools used in her profession. After finding an appropriate spot for the cart, she removed a two-way radio from the pocket of her white coat. Hailey listened in on Rhoda's conversation as she requested that a portable massage table be delivered promptly to Hailey's room.

"This must be a nice surprise for you," Rhoda remarked.

"Mr. Kingdom is such a thoughtful person. I can certainly use the massage, but it may render me incapable of keeping our date for later on. I guess I'll have to worry about that when the time comes. What do you need me to do?"

"You can just make yourself comfortable until the table arrives. I'm going to turn on the Jacuzzi tub in your bathroom. You'll want to relax in there for a short time after the massage."

"Oh, I can see that I'm going to be good for nothing when this treat is over. I'm sure he didn't think that his wonderful surprise might interfere with our plans."

"He might end up kicking himself. But it seems that his

heart was in the right place," Rhoda said as she left the room.

When another knock came on the door, Hailey didn't hesitate to open it, since she knew the table was to be delivered. Instead of an employee with the equipment, another hotel employee stood before her holding a large tubular-shaped vase of long-stemmed yellow roses.

"These are for you, ma'am. Where would you like me to place them?"

Speechless, Hailey pointed to the credenza. There was no end in sight to Zurich's generosity and thoughtfulness. He was the kind of man she had hoped to meet one day. Unfortunately for them, their chance meeting of a lifetime had occurred on the wrong day, within the wrong month and the wrong year.

Hailey felt a little self-conscious lying on a table nude, with only a thin white sheet covering her body. Hailey attempted to block out everything else once the massage had begun in order to receive maximum benefits. Rhoda was good at what she did, darn good. Her hands, fingers, and palms were working wonders on Hailey's anatomy. According to Rhoda, the soothing music playing on the portable CD and the candlelight had also been arranged by Zurich.

Zurich Kingdom was some man, Hailey mused. The brother *did* know how to treat a lady. No one had ever scheduled her an appointment with a masseuse as a gift. That in itself was unique. With her eyes closed, Hailey thought of the sweet kisses they'd shared at her prompting. It didn't matter to her that she'd initiated their first deep kiss. Earlier, she had admitted to him that she liked to be chased, but it felt rather good to do the chasing. In her opinion, Zurich didn't seem to mind getting caught.

The memories of them dancing at the diner only slipped into Hailey's mind for a hot second. She fell asleep in the next instant. The relaxing massage had knocked her out.

Zurich was puzzled and unsettled that Hailey wasn't answering the phone. He had only called her room three times within the last ten minutes. When she wasn't down in the lobby at the designated meeting time, he'd come back up to his room to phone her. His next call was to the front desk, but he hung up before anyone could answer. He had decided to go down to the desk and ask that security check on Hailey to make sure she was safe.

Zurich's strides were purposeful as he made his way to the door. Just as his hand reached for the knob, the phone rang. He rushed across the room and picked up the receiver. A look of relief came over his face the instant he heard Hailey's voice.

"Hey, girl, I was worried about you when you didn't show up for our date. Are you okay? Has something happened to you?"

"I'm okay, but I have a little problem. I can't make our date. I called but you were already gone. Sorry I missed you. I had hoped you'd go right back to the room. Glad you did."

His brows knitted together with worry. "Me, too. Is there something I can do to help out with your problem?"

"Well, it's really not something I want to discuss over the phone. Think you can come up to my room?"

"Sure, Hailey. When?"

"Twenty minutes or so."

"I'll be there. Are you sure everything is okay with you? You sound strange."

"Yeah, I know. I am feeling a bit odd, Zurich. We'll talk when you get here."

After hanging up the phone, Zurich began pacing the room. He had to admit that he was seriously worried about Hailey. That was unusual, as Zurich wasn't a worrier. He was the kind of person who normally took everything in stride. The little time he'd spent with Hailey had somehow changed him. It wasn't so odd that he felt deep concern for someone other than his mother and brothers, because Zurich also genuinely cared a lot about the men and women that worked for and with him.

But the level of concern he had for Hailey was a different sort of feeling altogether. Not only was he concerned for her, but he had the desire to take on any problems that might arise for her—and wanted to be the only one to help her solve them. It wasn't easy for him to admit that his distress for her might be prompted by a deeper emotion. Naming the particular emotion he felt was even harder. That he might be falling in love with Hailey Hamilton wasn't something he could easily come to terms with. Being in love wasn't an option for him at this point in his life. He was no longer sure that the choice was his to make; his heart was in control.

It came as a shock to Zurich to find Hailey looking like a million bucks in a seductive, curve-hugging basic black pants set. Since he'd convinced himself that she might be feeling a little under the weather, Zurich had expected to see her looking somewhat pale and drawn. As he stepped further into the hotel suite, he took in the romantic ambience created by the soft yellow glow of candlelight and the mellow music. Then he saw the beautifully set table. But it was the lovely centerpiece that had him doing a double take; the overt display of the yellow roses he'd sent Hailey touched him deeply.

He took her into his arms and tenderly kissed her forehead. "Saying I've been had by you might be a bit of an understatement, Hailey. You've knocked my socks right off my feet." He gazed into her amber eyes with adoration. "Assuming you did all this for me, of course."

Hailey kissed his cheek. "It was absolutely done with

you in mind, only you. You've already arranged so many unique treasures for me—and I really wanted to show my appreciation for your thoughtfulness, even though I knew you didn't expect a thing from me in return. Come on in and make yourself comfortable. Room service will deliver dinner shortly, my treat this time around. Sorry I led you astray, but it was necessary if I was to pull off my surprise."

He didn't know how to get his heart rate to calm down, but it was a must if he didn't want to have an outright attack. No one, but no one, outside of his family members, had ever done anything this special for him. His experience of any special treatment was limited to the big fuss his mom made of his birthday on every one of his thirty-five years. No matter where he was in the world, Bernice Kingdom made sure that Zurich had an extraordinary birthday surprise on his special day. In fact, Bernice used any and all means available to her to make a big deal out of the birth dates of each of her three sons. In turn, he and his brothers went all-out for their mother on her birthday and Mother's Day. They did their best to make every day a special holiday for her.

"Dinner, too! You certainly duped me. I thought you might be ill and I might have to order you some chicken soup or something else light from room service. I'm flattered by everything you've done, Hailey. Thank you so much. I'm going to enjoy every second of this evening. It has certainly started out with a big bang."

"It's going to end with an even bigger one." Hailey turned to face the entry when she heard the knock. She then hurried over to the table and pulled out a chair for Zurich to be seated. "I'll join you in a minute." Hailey kissed him lightly on the lips before rushing away.

Looking astonished, Zurich watched the white-coated waiter roll in a portable cart laden with silver-domed covered dishes, a silver bucket with a bottle of sparkling wine nestled inside, and two crystal wineglasses. Although

Hailey had mentioned having dinner delivered, he really hadn't expected such fanfare. Candlelight, mellow music, an elegant dinner, and a man and a woman who were very much attracted to one another all added up to a very romantic evening. Zurich was quite pleased with the way things were going thus far.

Hailey joined Zurich at the table as soon as the waiter took leave. Her eyes were all aglow as she saw how handsome he looked. His appearance was never anything less than impeccable. Zurich wasn't a flashy dresser by any means, but all of his clothes fit him perfectly. He had both class and style. For a second or two she allowed herself to wonder what he'd look like totally nude. The tingling sensations caused by her torrid thoughts made her shiver. As engaging as her heated thoughts were, she dragged herself out of her sweet reverie.

Smiling at Zurich, Hailey carefully removed the domed tops from the covered dishes. The delicious smell of the filet mignon, baked potatoes, sauteed mushrooms, steamed petite vegetables, and hot rolls hit them full force. They both moaned with pleasure at the same time.

Hailey set the silver tops aside. "Well, what do you think, Mr. Kingdom?"

"That your dinner choices are excellent, Hailey. If it's okay, I'd like to say the blessing."

"By all means." She immediately bowed her head and closed her eyes.

Zurich's prayer of thanks was short and to the point. It was also very genuine.

Zurich poured small amounts of wine into the two crystal glasses and handed one to Hailey. "I know we don't imbibe much, so we should take it slow with the potent grape juice." He lifted his glass in a toast. "Here's to us and to a wonderful evening, Hailey."

Hailey clinked together her glass with his. "Hear, hear."

They both took smalls sips of the wine and set the glasses back down.

Zurich picked up his fork. "How was the massage?"

Hailey rolled her eyes expressively. "Heavenly! Thanks so much. I actually fell asleep on the sofa right after Rhoda was through with me. I don't even know when she left. That scared me when I woke up and found myself alone. I had to be really tired to be that careless. But if the masseuse had been a guy, I don't think that would've happened."

He laughed heartily. "Why's that? Afraid a male might've made a serious play on your beautiful body?"

"Something like that. Falling asleep with a strange man in the room wouldn't have been a wise thing to do. You can't be too careful nowadays."

"You're right about that."

For the next several minutes as they ate their dinner, silence ruled. Zurich ate as he always did, like a horse, and Hailey was just as amused as ever by his healthy appetite. Though silence permeated the space, Hailey and Zurich were very much aware of one another. Every time their eyes connected, their fluttering hearts seemed to skip a beat or two.

Once their meal was finished, Hailey wasn't sure if she should call room service and have them clear the table or just leave it for later. Not wanting to deal with it later, she quickly made the decision to arrange to have everything cleared away. Hailey thought there were way too many items for her to just set the dishes outside the door.

Side by side on the sofa, hands entwined, Hailey and Zurich sat quietly listening to the mellow music slow dancing gently on the air. Hailey didn't know how she was managing to stay awake, but she had a pretty good idea that being in Zurich's presence had a lot to do with it. He was an exciting man. Unbeknownst to him, he had the kind of presence that practically commanded the undivided attention of others. He was a great conversationalist, which also made him very interesting company.

Hailey couldn't imagine any woman having the nerve or the need to fall asleep on the one and only Zurich Kingdom. Despite her fatigue, Hailey didn't have the guts or the desire to drift off to never-never land while in the company of such an appealing man. As the marvelous voice of LeAnn Rimes seduced the silence, Hailey let out a deep sigh of satisfaction.

Zurich gave Hailey a strange look. "You like country-western music?"

"I love it. Doesn't everyone?"

Laughing, he slapped his knee with an open palm. "I don't think so! But I do. Just surprised that you enjoy it. What about attending the rodeo?"

"I've only been a few times. I had no idea that watching grown men roping cows and riding bulls and wild horses could be so much fun. I fear for the cowboy's safety during the entire show, but it doesn't put a damper on how excited I get. I was yelling and cheering just like everyone else. I don't think anyone guessed that it was my first rodeo. I was once lucky enough to be out in southern California when the black rodeo came to town. Now that was an awesome experience for me. Being from Texas, I guess you're a pretty big fan of the sport."

"I'm definitely a huge rodeo fan. I love to ride horses, but I'm no daredevil. You won't see me riding a bucking bronco or a ferocious bull, mechanical or otherwise."

Hailey reached for Zurich's hand when one of her favorite cuts by LeAnn Rimes came on: "How Do I Live." Hailey knew the words to the song by heart—and she couldn't begin to imagine how she'd live without the unforgettable Zurich Kingdom; she just knew she'd have to.

He brought her into his arms. "It seems that you like that song. It has a nice sound."

"I like both the song and the singer. LeAnn can sing her

butt off. Some country-western songs are so sad and bluesy, but I love most of them."

"What other country-western artists do you enjoy, Hailey?"

"Reba McEntire, Clint Black, Trisha Yearwood, Faith Evans, Wynonna Judd, Bonnie Rait, just to name a few. I also have a few golden oldies by Charley Pride and most of the songs recorded by Kenny Rogers. The last two artists are Dad's favorites. I'm also into Latin music."

"Wow! You really are into the country-western genre. I like a little Latin music myself. You must carry a lot of CDs with you when you're traveling around."

"Just the ones I love and can't do without hearing for long periods of time."

He looked right into her eyes. "We have so much in common, yet we can't do much about it. Where are you off to when you leave here?"

She rubbed her cheek over his. "That's top secret. You'd need a security clearance in order for me to share any sort of sensitive information with you." Leaning forward, she placed her forehead against his. "Us being here together like this is so nice, huh?"

He sighed out of frustration. "Maybe too nice." He pulled slightly away from her. "I don't know if I can continue to do this. I'm finding it terribly difficult to live by my own rules. I'm thirty-five, yet I'm feeling a lot of emotional stuff that I haven't ever felt. I don't know how to deal with most of it, Hailey. Am I the only one experiencing these unfamiliar emotions?"

Hailey ran the back of her hand down the side of his face. "No, you're not alone. I'm feeling them, too. But we agreed from the very beginning not to get emotionally involved. I guess it hasn't been as easy for us to do as we initially thought, at least, as far as I'm concerned. Do you have any suggestions, Zurich?"

"None that are pleasant, none that will resolve our situation. I don't want us to even try to stop what's happening between us. But if we don't do something about it, one way or the other, we may end up with deep regrets. I have to admit that I want you fiercely, Hailey, but I know that's not nearly enough justification for me to try and take this relationship to another level. Involving myself in a deeply emotional relationship with you and then just walking away is not an option for me. I respect you too much for that. I'm sure you feel the same."

"Are you suggesting a physical relationship in the absence of an emotional one?"

He scowled hard. "How in the hell did you come up with that conclusion? I never mentioned a thing about anything physical, but I *did* say how much I respect you."

Moving out of his arms, she winced at the sharpness in his tone. "You also talked about wanting me, or did I misinterpret your meaning?" She sat back down on the sofa.

"You sure in the hell did! Maybe I should clarify myself. I want your companionship, your friendship, and your personal attention. In short, I want you in my life far beyond the next two weeks, Hailey. That's the type of *wanting* I was referring to. I'm not going to deny a strong physical attraction to you, but that's not what I meant by the comment you've questioned."

Hailey pushed her hair back from her face as she blew out a stream of unsteady breath. Things between them had now gotten complicated, something she deeply regretted. What was she to do? Just cutting the ties between them wasn't going to be easy, but it suddenly seemed essential. Whether the tie breaking was necessary or not, she and Zurich would be staying at the same resort hotel for the duration of their vacation. That meant they'd probably run into each other from time to time. What were they to do then? Hailey didn't think she could stay in the same hotel with Zurich and not want to be near him: emotionally and physically. To exile him from her life while living in such close proximity to him was utterly impossible.

Canceling the rest of her vacation stay was the only solution she could come up with. She thought of checking into a hotel on the other side of the island, but that wouldn't work either. She could control herself in staying away from him and the places he might hang out, but she didn't think she'd be able to get him out of her head or evict him from his place in her heart.

"Our evening isn't turning out so good, is it, Zurich? That wasn't my intent."

The anguish in her eyes upset him. The last thing he'd wanted to do was to cause her pain. Like or not, he was already emotionally involved with Hailey, deeply involved.

He dropped down beside her and pulled her into his arms. "Ah, Hailey, I didn't mean for our date to turn out like this either. Is it possible for us to turn our good thing back around? I want to at least try. What about you?"

Her lips responded for him, hungrily, ardently. The kiss she engaged him in was long and passionate. As her hands entwined in his hair, he lost his fingers in her silky tresses. As his tongue gently plunged in and out of her mouth, she wished that she could control Father Time.

Hailey desperately wanted to turn back the hands of time, but that was also impossible. However, she planned to make the best of the remainder of the evening. Short of actually making love to him, she was up for whatever intimacy occurred between them.

As for future contact, Hailey planned to check out of the hotel first thing in the morning.

While the light foreplay had already nearly driven her insane, the hardness of his arousal pressed against her moist intimate treasures with feral urgency had her trembling with desire. Hailey's fever-pitch passion matched his own as she opened her legs wider to receive him. As he slowly entered her, his tender hands firmly in place beneath her shapely buttocks, he kissed her deeply, making her coo like a newborn babe. Hailey's insatiable hunger for him burned deep within her inner self. Her fingers dug into the flesh on his back; the fiery passion heightened as he rocked back in forth inside of her. Deeper and deeper, fervent stroke by stroke, he sank his manhood into her molten heat.

Hailey felt every hardened inch of Zurich's long, smooth, tender strokes as he made wild, sweet love to her. Each time he withdrew and reentered her moist core, her soft inner flesh felt as if was exploding from the heat of his passion. Drowning in ecstasy, Hailey manically moved her head from side to side as Zurich's delicious assault on her overheated body continued.

As the loud buzzing noise of the alarm pierced her ears, Hailey sat straight up in the bed. The sweat trickling down her body was real enough, but the images of Zurich making love to her had occurred only in her dreams. Moaning, she threw her head back against the pillow.

While things had become extremely heated between her and Zurich on the previous evening, wild passionate lovemaking had not been the eventual outcome, despite the strong desires. Zurich hadn't spent the night with Hailey, but in the midst of her dreams he had slept in her bed, had made nonstop love to her up until the early hours of the morning, and had kept her safe and secure in the warmth of his strength. Hailey wiped the sweat from her face as she thought about the numerous erotic dreams she'd had of her and Zurich engaged in sensuous lovemaking.

After climbing out of bed, feeling sad and blue, Hailey trudged into the bathroom and turned the shower on full force. She brushed her teeth before stepping into the downpour of hot, steamy water. Thoughts of what she had to do for both of their sakes made her ill.

Hailey hated to run out on Zurich, but she'd been left with no other choice.

* * *

With her bags packed and stationed near the front door,

purse in hand, Hailey looked around the room to make sure she hadn't left anything behind. As for airline reservations, she had to opt for standby since her ticket was nonrefundable. She'd also have to pay a few dollars more for a ticket upgrade just to be eligible for standby. While she hadn't planned to go back to Florida for more than a couple of days before departing for her next duty assignment, she loved spending time with her parents. Normally kids had a favorite parent, but Hailey was equally crazy about both of hers. Martin was her hero and Marie was her heroine.

Feeling terribly apprehensive about leaving without saying anything at all to Zurich, Hailey opened the front door to see if the bellman was somewhere in the vicinity of her room, and was shocked to find Zurich standing there, poised to knock. Her bags were in plain sight so she couldn't even tell him a lie if she wanted to. Feeling like a kid with her hand caught smack-dab in the cookie jar, she just stood there, shuffling her feet nervously.

His sienna eyes immediately zeroed in on her suitcases. Without comment, he pushed her back into the room and closed the door. Before she could even utter a protest, he picked up the "Do Not Disturb" sign and hung it on the outer doorknob.

Zurich turned back to face her. The thundercloud look on his face gave her a good indication of his mood. "Where are you going? Have you been called up to go out on one of your covert assignments?" He eyed her suspiciously when she didn't respond. "Well, I'm waiting to hear why your bags are all packed and you look ready to take flight."

The stern look on Zurich's face made her feel like a little girl who'd done something bad for which she was about to be scolded. Stalling for time, hoping to find the right words, Hailey walked over to the sofa and sat down. Realizing that she had to be open and honest with Zurich, she patted the sofa cushion beside her. Appeasing him wasn't going to be easy, she knew.

She saw the slight hesitation in his step before he finally decided to join her.

Hailey took his hand and looked into his eyes. "I'm checking out of the hotel and I hadn't planned to say good-bye to you. I thought it was the best thing to do considering . . ."

"Considering what?" he interjected.

"That our emotions are taking a severe beating. Neither of us is able to live up to the rules and boundaries we've set for ourselves. We both believed they were realistic ones, but we didn't count on getting emotionally involved this way, not to mention so soon. I don't know about you, but this has been a horrendously trying year for me, Zurich. Coming here to the serenity of this island was supposed to be all about recreation and relaxation before I have to get back into the daily grind of duties, obligations, and physical and mental challenges. I didn't plan on this outcome. I didn't plan on meeting a wonderful man like you, Zurich. Not at all."

His eyes softened a tad. "Why were you running out on me if I'm so wonderful? We're not kids, Hailey. As adults, we should've been able to discuss this and bring our issues out in the open. Do you think running away from our feelings is going to solve this for us? I can tell you this. It won't do it for me."

"We have been discussing it, Zurich. That's how I knew you were going through the same changes I was. And we both know there are no other alternatives for us. We have other serious commitments that aren't going away simply because we've carelessly allowed our emotions and our fantasies to carry us far away from our stark realities. I didn't want to leave without explaining myself to you, but I just couldn't face the pain of saying good-bye. Nor did I want you to see me cry. I guess that makes me a big old coward, huh?"

A knock on the door, despite the sign, kept Zurich from responding. He looked at her with a soft expression as his hand caressed her cheek. "We need to talk, Hailey. Can I have the privilege of telling the bellman you're considering staying on for at least one more night?"

Tears welled in her eyes. "Yeah, Zurich, why don't you go ahead and do that." *I can manage to get through this for one more night. But what am I going to do tomorrow when I'm faced with the same decision that's staring me down right now?*

Hailey couldn't control her emotional trembling as she waited for Zurich to return. She'd have to call the front desk and explain the change in her plans. She decided not to give an exact date for check-out; the length of her stay was now unpredictable. Her airline ticket wouldn't be affected since she hadn't actually cancelled it. Signing up for standby travel could only be done at the airport and her ticket wouldn't have to be surrendered unless the airline had a seat for her. To give herself something to do, Hailey quickly picked up the phone and put a call in to the desk.

Zurich didn't look so tense as he returned to his seat next to Hailey. "Thanks for giving us an opportunity to try and sort this all out. Are you sure you're okay with your decision to stay on at least until tomorrow? I know you didn't have much time to think it through."

She nodded. "I'm fine with it. This is the right thing for us to do. Zurich, I'm going to come right out with it. I'm falling in love with you despite the stupid rules we made. My head simply can't make the decisions for my heart. My head may know better, but my heart knows what's best." She pointed at her chest. "This little heart of mine has a mind of its own. It knows exactly what it feels, how deeply it loves, and no one can change its mind." She shrugged. "There it is, Zurich. Deal with it however you see fit."

His way of dealing with it was to kiss her hard on the mouth. She hadn't pulled any punches, and neither was he. The kiss grew in intensity and he wanted it to go on and on. He feared letting her go, lest she should regret her decision to stay.

With much reluctance, he finally released Hailey from his loving embrace. "I don't know what to say or do about us, Hailey. But I do know that I feel exactly the same way about you as you say you feel for me. Is it love that I feel? I don't know. But if it's not love, it's sure has me going around in circles. Feeling as I do about you is a new emotional experience for me. It feels darn good and I don't want to let go of those wonderful sensations. I have a lot of personal issues, Hailey. We've already discussed my fear of becoming an abuser like my father."

Hailey caressed his cheek. "Our fears parallel in that regard, Zurich. My heartbreak over my girlfriend's terribly abusive experiences with her husband has taken a serious toll on me, leaving me fearful of the same thing happening in my life. Many of our issues seem to run along the same vein. We both have jobs that we can't discuss, or refuse to, and we live the sort of lives that make it nearly impossible to get involved in a serious relationship with anyone. If I get the promotion I'm hoping for, it'll be like starting my career all over again. Other drastic changes will occur in my life should the promotion come through. It just seems to me that we may be right for each other but that we've merely met at the wrong time. Do you agree?"

He pulled her back to him. "Wholeheartedly. We could probably manage this if my career wasn't constantly moving me all around the world. I'm rarely in one place for very long. But I have to admit that I love what I do with a passion. I can't imagine doing anything else. I have seventeen years invested in this job, and I'm shooting for thirty. There are times that I have to leave town with only a moment's notice. In my opinion, that's no life for a wife and children. If you were my wife, I wouldn't want to leave your side for a short period of time, let alone for weeks and months in one clip. I already know the type of husband I want to be should I ever marry. Being an absent spouse and father is not for me. Do you see what I'm saying?"

"All too well, Zurich. The demands of your job sound exactly like mine. Like you, I love what I do. Because of Kelly's situation, I've never allowed myself to dream of marrying and having children. Just as yours has, my career has made a globetrotter out of me. I admit to getting tired of traveling at times, but then the next vital mission comes up or something intense and all-fire important occurs. It's those sorts of things that get my adrenaline pumping hard again and makes me proud of the role I've been called on to play. I can tell you this much, I have an important job, one to which I'm totally dedicated and committed."

Zurich wasn't sure exactly what Hailey did for a living, but their jobs certainly seemed to have a lot in common. He wouldn't be surprised if their careers were similar in nature, perhaps even involving covert government work, but he in no way thought Hailey could withstand the rigors and dangers found in many aspects of his career field. Hailey was tough, but she was also soft. He wasn't a male chauvinist, but what he was thinking certainly bordered on such. When he took a minute to recall how she handled the nuisance of that guy in the club, "J. Smooth," he thought he might need to do a serious reassessment of one Hailey Hamilton.

Perhaps Miss Hamilton was much tougher than he was giving her credit for. He honestly didn't know where to go from here with their relationship. But he had already decided that he wanted to make a serious attempt to find a way for them to work out something they could both live with. Long-distance relationships rarely worked, or so he'd heard. But when two people were willing to make sacrifices, perhaps the outcome could actually be a positive one.

At this point in time, all he knew was that he had to give this relationship his best shot, long-distance or otherwise. The absence of the lovely Hailey Hamilton in his life was an option he no longer wanted to consider.

Holding her in his arms, Zurich looked down at Hailey as he kissed her forehead. "Can I make a couple of suggestions, Hailey?"

"Please do, Zurich."

"For one, I don't want you to cut your vacation short. You obviously came here to relax and have a good time. I think you can still do that, with or without me. However, I'd prefer it if we can manage to do it together, as originally planned. Another suggestion is that we don't hold back on our feelings for each other and that we stop trying to analyze to death our complicated situation. If it's any comfort to you, I definitely don't want our relationship to end when our vacation time is up. I'm certain of that much. I know we'd have to do the long-distance bit, but I want to give it a try. Will you at least think about my suggestions? We don't have to decide on our fate right this minute, Hailey. If I have my way, we'll have plenty of time left for that."

Hailey held her emotions in. Knowing he wanted the same things she did filled her heart to overflowing. "I'm not going to undermine your suggestions by asking if you're sure. I can see that you are. I think your suggestions are excellent ones." She looked at her watch. "Time is getting away from us. Think we can get on with the plans we'd already made for today?"

His smile was bright with anticipation. "That's an excellent idea. We're supposed to head down to the beach and soak up a few rays. Then we'll take our time relaxing in the Jacuzzi." He closed his eyes. "My lucky stars are already shining; it's not even dark outside. I can already see you in that tangerine bikini, Hailey. Wow! What a sexy image."

She laughed at how his eyes had rolled in the back of his head. As for sexy images, she'd had quite a few of him in the buff while sleeping last night.

While thinking of their previously planned itinerary, he put a finger up to his temple. "Early tomorrow morning is deep-sea fishing aboard the charter boat. The water park comes the day after that. But first things first." Zurich kissed Hailey gently on the mouth. "I need to feed my baby. Where do you want to eat before we head to the beach?"

Hailey moaned. "Food is the last thing on my mind. It seems that all we've done is eat. However, I could use a salad or something else light."

"Since I'm already here with you, we can order from room service."

She gave him a suspicious look. "Not on your life. If we stay in this suite any longer, we'll probably get seriously sidetracked in satisfying other hungers. Let me change out of my travel clothes and then we can go downstairs to eat."

"I'll meet you in the lobby. I need to go to my room and grab my swim gear. I came here this morning to have a serious talk with you. That's why I don't have all the things I need for our outing. I didn't know you'd planned to leave, but I'm glad I got here in time to ask you to change your mind. I'll see you in half an hour."

She wrapped her arms around his neck. "I'll be waiting in the lobby for you, Zurich. Also, I'm glad you caught me before I made the biggest mistake of my life." Her mouth sought out his to show him her deepest gratitude. "Thank you, Zurich. I'm looking forward to when we can one day have our very first top-secret rendezvous!"

He pressed his finger onto the tip of her nose. "I like the sound of that."

Zurich had definitely rescued her—and she felt that

she'd somehow rescued him, too. Now who was going to save the both of them? Hailey prayed hard that their relationship wouldn't ever need rescuing. She wasn't sure if a long-distance relationship would work, either. But, just like Zurich, Hailey had decided to give his suggestion all she had.

Five

The sun, although hot, was not yet unbearable, but Hailey had taken a quick dip in the Gulf just to douse her body before soaking up the rays. She was now seated on a huge beach towel ready for some serious reading and tanning. After removing from her straw satchel a container of suntan lotion and two books, *Prodigal Husband* and *Awakening Mercy,* two inspirational novels by the wonderful novelists Jacquelin Thomas and Angela Benson, Hailey laid the books alongside her. She first needed to lather her skin with the lotion so as not to overcook her body. She had sensitive skin, the kind that burned quickly without protection.

Zurich plopped down beside her and took the lotion from her hand before she could even get the top off the plastic bottle. "You told me you might let me do this for you. Get comfortable so I can take real good care of you."

"So I did, but with restrictions in certain areas." Laughing, Hailey stretched her full length out on the towel and closed her eyes. "Make sure you behave yourself, Zurich."

"Oh, I'm going to do that—and still enjoy the heck out of myself. You're going to enjoy it, too, Miss Hamilton. Those statements come with a money-back guarantee."

"I like a man who's that sure of himself, rather than too sure," Hailey cooed.

Her poignant observation made him smile. Although he had no doubts that he was a self-assured man, versus one who was overtly cocky, her comment still made him feel great.

Zurich squeezed a fair amount of the sunscreen into his hands and commenced to massage it into her tender flesh. Looking much closer at her body than he had on the day they first met, he noticed that the rest of her skin was as soft and smooth as her face.

Hailey had surprised him by not wearing the tangerine number he'd complimented her on that first day. When she'd peeled off her white shorts, he found himself a little disappointed. But then he saw that her arresting jade-green one-piece swimsuit looked just as tantalizing next to her burnished brown skin as the other, brighter color once she had discarded her white pullover. Low-cut in the front and nearly nonexistent in the back, the body-hugging swimwear was very provocative.

As his hands neared the exposed flesh on the sides of and below her buttocks, he immediately handcuffed temptation. He'd just have to imagine his hands there, since he didn't want to experience a hardening arousal on a crowded beach. The brief-style cut of his black swim trunks wouldn't help any in hiding his more-than-adequate sexual endowment. Besides, that particular area of tempting flesh was probably one of Hailey's "no trespassing" zones.

Hailey moaned inwardly as Zurich's hands roved over her flesh like a silken glove. It was hard for her to keep from cooing like a lovesick dove. He probably didn't need any amount of encouragement from her. She could only imagine that he was also struggling to keep himself morally correct. She couldn't fathom any man rubbing a woman's body in the stimulating manner he was massaging hers and not feeling any physical excitement from the sensuous contact.

He squeezed her shoulders. "Please turn over on your back, Hailey, so I can finish up."

Hailey slowly rolled over. Flat on her back now, she

looked up and gave him her brightest smile. "Am I going to get the opportunity to do you?"

Shaking with laughter, he eyed her with a seductive gaze. "Maybe you should explain your definition of 'do' before I answer that one."

Hailey felt like burying her embarrassment deep into the sand, but she made no outward showing of how mortified she really was. "Perhaps you should tell me what you think it means. Better yet, in what context did you take my question?"

He outlined her full lips with his index finger. "I know exactly how you meant it, but I couldn't pass on that one. It was too tempting to just leave alone. However, the thought of you *doing* me is rather intriguing. I'd be honored to have you *do* me. I'm almost done here. Then you can have your way with me." His taunting smile was just as alluring as his suggestive comments.

Hailey wished she could stop blushing like a teenager who'd just heard her first erotic innuendo from the opposite sex. Zurich's verbal foreplay had her body feeling things it hadn't felt in a long while, sexual awakening. She couldn't help wondering what it would really be like to *do* him, lending the word a totally different meaning than her original intent.

"Do you want the tanning lotion on your face, too?"

Hailey tucked away her delectable thoughts as she reached into her satchel and came up with a tiny plastic container. She handed it to Zurich. "I use this. It's a special skin conditioner manufactured exclusively for the face."

Zurich read the label on the jar before opening it. He then put a dab on his finger and inhaled the light coconut scent. Leaning forward, he lowered his head and placed a feathery kiss on her cheek. He then dabbed the spot of cream on the same area, repeating the same enticing procedure until her face was completely dotted with the conditioner. Using only the soft pads of his thumbs, Zurich gently massaged the moisture-rich lotion into her lovely face.

Zurich looked into her eyes as his lips softly grazed hers. "Ready for you to *do* me, anyway you choose to *do* it? I love a woman who has a flamboyant imagination and an uninhibited spirit when it comes to doling out the type of pleasures only the hands can give."

Hailey felt immediate heat invading her cheeks, not to mention the other intimate areas on her body. She fought hard her desire to taste his lips with her tongue and then kiss him breathless. He had a luscious mouth, and his full lips looked as if they hungered for her attention. The battle with her cravings came to an abrupt halt when he suddenly moved. Sweating from within, she licked her lips as she watched him reach over and turn on the portable CD player.

The yummy tones of Maxwell's engaging voice gently rent the air.

Zurich stretched out, turned over on his stomach and handed her the lotion. "I'm all yours, Hailey. I need you to know that this brother loves a slow, gentle hand."

Hailey hadn't spoken a word in the last several minutes simply because he'd kept her speechless and in breathless anticipation. Although she knew Zurich's comments were mostly joking, they still made her body sizzle and her mind effervesce with thoughts of him in her bed, his maleness deeply nestled inside her molten heat. She sucked in a trembling breath as her inner muscles contracted from their need to be stroked and caressed from within.

In her desire to fulfill his requests, Hailey straddled his lower back and began to apply the tanning oil he'd brought along, starting with his broad shoulders. The oil was slicker and went on much smoother than the lotion. Hailey wasn't a masseuse, but she had strong hands. She had the strength to give him a good working over, but he'd made clear his preference for gentle hands.

After working the oil into his shoulders, she used only the tips of her nails to draw circles onto his flesh, hoping he'd feel the same pleasurable tingling sensations she'd felt. His soft moans told her she'd accomplished her mission.

As Hailey tended to his lower back, she inched herself backward just enough to where her buttocks settled atop his powerful thighs. She ignored the temptation to lower his trunks slightly in order to reach the small of his back. With that portion of his anatomy being so close to his perfectly rounded buttocks, she didn't want to risk losing control of herself. Massaging his sexy derriere might invite the sort of consequences she wasn't ready to deal with.

Using the heels of her hands, she kneaded his back clockwise and then counterclockwise. His moaning increased in volume. For the next ten minutes or so Hailey used a combination of her strength and the smooth touch of gentle hands to totally relax Zurich.

Sure that Zurich had fallen asleep, she relaxed her knees, leaned her body forward and rested her head on his back. Smiling with smug satisfaction, Hailey closed her eyes, thrilled that her gentle handiwork had lulled him to sleep. Zurich had gotten just what he'd asked for, a slow, gentle hand, a flamboyant imagination, and an uninhibited spirit.

Knocked completely off balance when Zurich suddenly raised his body, Hailey found herself flat on her back in the sand. In one quick motion, he straddled her, careful not to settle his full weight upon her. With her arms pinned over her head, he nipped wildly at her succulent lower lip. As quickly as he'd moved into that position, he rolled over, turned on his side and laid his arm across her stomach to keep her stationary.

Looking at her with a soft expression, he caressed the

side of her face. "You'd better be careful whose back you fall asleep on. I could've mistaken you for the enemy."

"I wasn't asleep, just indulging in a bit of meditation. Since I've been on vacation, I've gotten away from my normal morning and evening routines, so I took a couple of minutes for spiritual restoration. In the midst of such serenity, I felt that it was the perfect place for me to get in touch with God and my inner spirit. When you fell off to sleep, I just closed my eyes and rested my head against your back. By the way, your back makes a nice pillow."

"Glad to have been of service." His grin was devilish. "I wasn't asleep, either."

Hailey sucked her teeth. "Yeah, right! Not only were you asleep, you started snoring after a short while. If there were any trees around here, they'd all be cut down by now. You had your buzz saw hard at work."

He laughed heartily. Then his expression suddenly turned somber. "You know something, Hailey, people don't talk anymore, not like we used to do. We no longer take the time to get a true sense for the people that we come across in our daily lives. Nor do we try to really get to know them. I want to know you, to learn as many things about you as I can. I know that discussing our jobs isn't something either of us is comfortable with, whatever our reasons, but it's important to me to learn other relevant things about you and your family."

She sat up and rested back on her elbows. "Anything in particular come to mind?"

"I think in learning who your parents are, I can get a better of understanding of who you are. Our parents, one or both, can have such an impact, positive or negative, on the kind of person we eventually become. You've talked a lot about your dad, but you haven't mentioned what profession your mother's in. And how does your relationship with her differ from the one you share with your dad, outside of you both being females? What's your mom's greatest passion in life?"

"Besides my dad?" Hailey laughed. "We enjoy a wonderful relationship. Marie Hamilton was, and still is, a homemaker, a calling that's somewhat frowned upon today, yet is the most important job in the world to some women. Mom is one of those females who thrives on and celebrates in her job as wife and mother. She made her own money, but she did it from home."

"A home-based business?"

"Not in the same sense as the term is used today. She made silk flower arrangements, and unique gift baskets like the one you had sent to me, as well as many other creative works of art. Ceramics is also one of her biggest passions. The idea of nurseries and baby-sitters didn't set well with my mother. She thought it was her responsibility to be there with me every single day, just as her mother had done. Making money at home is just another way of asserting one's independence."

"That she didn't want to work outside of the home after you were school age comes as a big shock to me. My dad denied Mom the opportunity to work away from home. She wanted to, yet yours chose not to. The only work Mom was allowed to do was to take care of us and him."

"When I started kindergarten, and was gone from home a half a day, my mother did whatever she needed to do outside of the home in those few hours. Her outside freedoms increased as my hours at school grew longer. I use the word freedom, but she never thought of being away from me as liberating. Mom's liberation was in proudly taking excellent care of her husband and only child. The word freedom has been used a lot in the last twenty-one months. Although African-Americans have been aware of the high cost of freedom for countless years, the events of September eleventh have served as a reminder to all of us who may have forgotten. Homemaking is not the ideal job for every woman, but it's what Mom wanted to do. I have found that in doing those things we truly have a passion for, we can find a much greater joy and sense of peace than in doing something we absolutely detest. That in itself is freedom."

"I know that's right. Life is so short. If we didn't realize it before, we've been left with no choice now but to come to grips with that reality. People are now taking a serious look at their own mortality. In less than three months we will once again relive one of the greatest tragedies in the history of America, on the second anniversary of September eleventh." Zurich closed his eyes for several seconds as if he'd suddenly been compelled to send up a silent word of prayer.

Hailey prayed within her heart as she waited for Zurich to resume the conversation.

Zurich opened his eyes and reconnected with Hailey's. "In an attempt to lighten things up, though this might sound like a silly question, did you have any pets, Hailey? I know these are things a lot of young brothers wouldn't ask a woman, but I'm from the old school of thought."

Hailey thought of their heart-to-heart session as very intimate. Intimacy and passion were achievable through simple conversation, indeed rare but so beautiful. "Your genuine interest in me is refreshing. It speaks to your values." Hailey took a moment to reflect, smiling when she thought of the family's present miniature collie, their third in her lifetime.

He kissed his forefinger and touched it to her cheek. "Flash of a tender memory, huh?"

"A quick reflection of the past. I've had three dogs. I had an image of Sirocco running alongside me in the woods behind our home. He's the latest of our three miniature collies, all of which shared the same name. When one passed on, we'd waste no time in getting another. Sirocco was a name we all loved."

"Sirocco is a type of wind common to the North African coast. You guys seem to have a real passion for things relative to weather. Your name seems to be just one of them."

"My father does. So much so that he told us that when

he passes he wants to be cremated and have his ashes scattered to the four winds. But it just so happens that he's a retired meteorologist. He's been in the field for over forty years. It sounds like you know more than a thing or two about weather yourself."

Zurich couldn't believe his ears. *Was this an omen of some sort?* He had to wonder.

"Not meaning to come off arrogant, but I'm knowledgeable in many areas. I also have to admit to a deep interest in atmospheric science. I do a little dabbling in weather myself." He instantly felt a tad guilty over the misleading statement he'd just made. "It's said that the apple doesn't fall far from the tree. Is your interest in weather as passionate as your dad's, Hailey?"

"It was all I heard about coming up! He kept us informed on whatever was going on with the weather. He loved to give the names of the clouds as he pointed them out to me. I guess I don't have to mention that I was the best physical-science student all through school. His constant predictions used to get on my mother's nerves after a while, but she'd never let him know it. She supports him in all his passions, even if she doesn't necessarily share in them."

Zurich stroked his chin thoughtfully. "Sounds like a match made in heaven. With parents that love each other like that, exception to the rule or not, I don't understand why you don't think you can have that same kind of relationship. I made the reference to the apple and the tree, but I pray constantly that my brothers and I turn out to be among the exceptions to that universal phrase. So far, so good. With that in mind, I guess I can understand your concerns."

Hailey gently stroked his arm. "Thanks for that. As for your situation, I don't think you have a thing to worry about. You seem like a real good brother to me. You've been so considerate, and nothing but a respectful gentleman. I can't imagine you hurting a fly."

He frowned slightly. "Speaking of considerate, I have something I want to discuss with you. I now realize I should've talked to you before I made the arrangements. I asked my mother to meet us for dinner this evening. I can cancel out, but I don't want to unless you object."

Hailey was astounded that he wanted her to meet his mother, even though he'd earlier mentioned something about wishing he'd had her meet them at the diner while they were there before. It was a nice gesture that he wanted them to get together; she wasn't going to read any more into it than that. Getting acquainted with his mother wasn't tantamount to a marriage proposal, despite what a lot of people had a tendency to believe.

The general consensus among the old womenfolk, her grandmothers included, was if a man took you home to meet his momma, he must have marriage on his mind. Marriage was the last thing she or Zurich had on their brains.

Embarking on a long-distance relationship was already enough for them to contend with. Zurich had no idea of the vast distance that would soon separate them. Whether to tell him right away that she'd be moving to Europe, or wait until after she saw how their relationship developed was her biggest concern. A continent-to-continent commute didn't seem the least bit realistic. The thought was, in fact, downright daunting.

"Well, are you going to tell me what you think about dinner, Hailey?" Zurich laid his head in her lap and looked up at her.

Dragging herself away from her thoughts, she looked down at him. "I can't think of a single reason for me to object. I'd love to meet your mom. I hope you didn't have to coerce her into meeting me. She's okay with it, isn't she?"

He grinned broadly. "Bernice Kingdom is just fine with it. She has three unmarried sons, old ones," he joked. "That should tell you something. She wanted to bring along her three sisters, my aunts, Dorothy, Josephine, and Ethel, but I talked her out of that since it was a first meeting. Mom is excited about the dinner, Hailey. No, I didn't have to coerce her the least bit."

Hailey blew out a steady stream of air. "I'm relieved at that. With so much family living close by, why do you choose to stay at a hotel when you come home?"

"After a few days with my mom and aunts, my brothers, my cousins, and I need a quiet space to get away to. They're always competing with each other to see who gives the best pampering. Each one loves to cook our favorites, and they usually end up nearly stuffing us to death with food. In wanting to show off their fine children, they're gung-ho about us visiting all their friends while we're in town."

"That's only natural when you're proud of your family."

"But them sisters can wear the Kingdom brothers and cousins down. The Meridian is far enough away, yet close enough for me to drop in on them when the mood hits me. I guess I forgot to mention that they all live together on Mom's ranch. It's a wonderful living arrangement, since they're all widows. They're also close in age: fifty-nine, sixty-one, and sixty-two. With no mortgage or rent to worry about, they can easily manage to share in the household expenses."

Hailey's eyes lit up from the joy she felt inside at hearing a more tender side of Zurich's family story. "Sounds like a beautiful family thing to me. That four women can live under one roof and get along is mighty astounding. They do get along, don't they? Do any of your brothers or cousins live nearby?"

"For the most part. They have their little tiffs, but it's never anything serious. They might squabble over who wants to watch what on television. If they can't agree, but they normally do, each of them has a television in their room. Now their biggest spats come when they're playing what should be friendly card games. But even those ones are in jest."

"Do they have any favorite card games?"

He grinned. "Believe it or not, poker! They're a trip. Those four sisters love each other dearly. If you decide to start some mess with one, you'd better worry about where the other three are. They do have each other's backs. Just like my brothers, cousins, and me. The children are scattered all over the country; no one lives nearby. But they have plenty of family visitors throughout the year. No one neglects them. My brothers come home as often as I do. We shoot for a family reunion every other year. We're due for one next August, the second weekend."

Zurich picked up his pants and removed his watch from the front pocket. "How come time doesn't fly like this when you're having what seems like the worst day of your life? Do you want to take another dip in the Gulf before we head back up to the pool area?"

Hailey ran her hands through her hair. "My hair is practically dry now. I'm going to pass on getting back into the water. If you don't mind, I'd also like to skip the soak in the Jacuzzi. With our special dinner date in mind, I want to have enough time to wash and style my hair. Where are we going to eat, anyway? Somewhere in the hotel?"

He scowled. "Would you believe back to the local diner?"

"You don't seem too pleased about it. If that's the case, why go there?"

He twisted his mouth to the side. "Mom's choice. I made the mistake of asking her where she'd like to eat."

"Ah, so! I got it. But don't look at it as a mistake. We just got through talking about how people are happier when they get to do what they want. She must like going there."

"You'd think she'd want something different since she cooks a lot of the food that's served there. But she and my aunts love to hang out at the diner and listen to old-old-school music. I think they got their eyes on a couple of widowers that frequent the place. They think they're fooling someone."

Hailey cracked up. "There's nothing wrong with that. These sisters seem like people I'd love to hang out with. Sounds like they know exactly how to get a party started."

Zurich groaned. "Whatever you do, Hailey, please don't encourage Mom in that area. It's hard enough for me to keep my eye on her when I'm home or close by. But I don't even try to imagine what she gets into when I'm not around. If I did, I'd probably go crazy."

Hailey covered his hand with hers. "Let her have some fun. Maybe she's just trying to make up for lost time. From what you've told me, she hasn't had an easy time of it. She's not too old to one day have a wonderful new beginning with someone who may truly value her."

"That's what I'm afraid of. I'd rather see her alone and lonely than have her end up with the kind of horribly abusive man she was married to all those years. He may've been my father, but I had no respect for him, nor did I ever dare show him any disrespect. Mom taught us to be better than that. Oddly enough, but fortunately for me, I stopped despising him long ago. He died without apologizing to her or my brothers and me. During the entire year she took care of his sickly behind, he never once told her he was sorry, or even bothered to thank her for taking him in. Despite loud objections from all the family, Mom did what she thought was the right thing to do. Her Christian spirit was the only reason she gave for her decision."

"I have to tell you this, Zurich. That's reason enough; I can't think of a better one. But it's all over now. She's alive and well, by the grace of God. She deserves whatever joy comes her way. You don't ever want to put your mother in a position to choose what you think is best for her over what makes her happy. That's what she had to do for years. Agree?"

"I see your point, Hailey. Thanks for the great advice."

Zurich began to gather the things that didn't have to be packed away. Hailey put her books back in the satchel without reading a single page. Conversation had taken precedence over everything else. She wouldn't think of trading in their little intimate getting-to-know-you-better session, which had actually turned out to be very informative. They both had learned a lot.

Once Hailey got to her feet, she helped Zurich fold the towels and put them away. Hand in hand, feeling good about each other, they made their way back toward the hotel entrance.

Hailey couldn't wait another minute to slip into a few moments of quietude. She pulled the drapes completely shut. After opening the midsize leather case she carried with her everywhere, she took out a polished teakwood square resembling a checkerboard and set it on the coffee table. In the center of the board, she placed four unscented tea-light candles nestled in tiny ceramic holders, followed by an incense holder. Hailey struck a match and lit each one.

The final steps in preparation were to insert into her CD player a disc featuring soothing music to mediate by, and then reading a couple of passages from an inspirational journal. Hailey lowered herself to the floor, crossed her legs Indian style, read from the book, and then closed her eyes. After a few words of silent prayer, Hailey felt prepared to attain peace during the blessed journey into spiritual healing.

For the next twenty minutes Hailey released the stresses of the day and a number of troubling concerns as she compelled herself toward completely relaxing her body and freeing her mind and spirit in order to transcend to a higher plateau. Hailey believed that meditation improved her very sense of being by allowing her to achieve total tranquility. She always followed her ritual by singing a gospel or inspirational song. Hailey knew she wasn't Grammy material, but she did have a decent voice.

* * *

Zurich had immediately noticed how beautiful and shiny Hailey's freshly washed and styled hair looked when they'd first met up in the lobby. Although she was simply dressed in casual attire—dark denim jeans and a stiff-collared white cotton shirt—to him she looked exquisite.

As he quietly sat back in his chair at a corner table inside the diner, he watched how she interacted with his mother, paying extremely close attention to both the languages she spoke, verbal and body. He loved the way Hailey periodically touched Bernice's hand as she talked.

Hailey's beautiful smile intrigued Zurich as she listened to Bernice chat about her sisters and how much they wanted to meet her. Earlier, when Bernice had stopped to talk to a diner employee before making it to the table, Hailey had told Zurich that she was surprised to find that she had pictured Bernice Kingdom all wrong. From the information he'd given her, she hadn't expected Bernice to be so stylish in looks and so youthful in body and physical health. With lovely, short, mixed-gray hair, pecan-brown eyes, and an attractive face, Hailey thought the five-foot-six Bernice had it going on. She was nothing like the grandmotherly type that Hailey had conjured up in her mind.

Although his mother rarely met any strangers, Zurich was never really concerned if she'd take to Hailey; she had, instantaneously. His mother loved all people, period, the good spirits and the bad ones. Bernice believed that good could be found in everyone and in any and every situation.

"Just take time to look for the silver lining," she'd always tell her boys. "It's there."

In some of his own life experiences Zurich had found her belief to be true enough.

Zurich's eyes narrowed as a tall black man approached their table. As the elderly man drew closer, Zurich recognized him as Morgan Cobb, one of his dad's old drinking buddies. When Morgan leaned over and kissed Bernice on the cheek, Zurich's hackles raised instantly. He eyed the man with cold suspicion as Morgan introduced himself to Hailey.

"Morgan, you remember my son Zurich, don't you?" Bernice smiled up at Morgan in a knowing way.

The starry look in Bernice's eyes made Zurich uncomfortable, putting him on high alert.

Morgan faced Zurich and extended his hand. "Of course I do. I remember all your boys. How are you, son? Long time no see."

Zurich hesitated briefly before finally shaking Morgan's hand. "Nice to see you again, sir. Yes, it has been a long time." *Not long enough if you're courting my mother.*

Morgan nodded at Zurich as he pulled out a chair and sat down next to Bernice.

Zurich didn't know what to think as he looked for any sort of reaction from his mother. The older man hadn't been invited to seat himself at their table, but that hadn't stopped him from intruding upon what was supposed to have been a private party. Bernice had yet to outwardly react, which kept Zurich guessing as to what was going on between her and Cobb.

"Zurich, I hope you don't mind that I invited Morgan to join us for dinner. We thought this would be a perfect time to tell you that we share a special friendship. We've grown very close over the past few months, and we also have been talking of a possible future together. We'd love to have your blessing on whatever we decide, as well as the blessings of Zaire and Zane. Morgan and I are good for each other."

"Mom, if you don't mind could we talk about the serious stuff a little later? I'll be coming by the house numerous times before I leave town. I brought Hailey out to meet you so we could have a good time. Let's just have fun this evening. Is that okay with you?"

Zurich couldn't hide his dismay, but he had successfully controlled his tongue. The fact that Morgan had hung out with his dad was enough for him to believe that his mother didn't need him in her life. Not only had they been friends, they'd worked together, had gotten drunk together. Zurich was of the opinion that birds of a feather flocked together. The only man who could possibly stomach Macon Kingdom was someone who was just like him.

Zurich's discomfort was not lost on Hailey. She felt his unrest. He looked shell-shocked because his mother had definitely dropped a bomb on him. Hailey recalled Zurich's earlier words. *I'd rather see my mother alone and lonely.* She had to wonder if Zurich saw Bernice's new beau as the same type of man his father had been. If that was the case, she could understand why he didn't look at all pleased by his mother's announcement. Hailey's attention was drawn to Zurich as he got to his feet.

Zurich extended his hand to Bernice. "Mom, let's show these folks how cutting a rug is supposed to be done."

Touched by how gently Zurich had spoken to Bernice, how he seemed to handle her with tender care, Hailey's eyes followed them out to the dance floor. She hoped Mr. Cobb didn't ask her to dance since she wanted to enjoy watching the best-looking couple on the dance floor do their thing. Many pairs of eyes were already glued to mother and son.

A few seconds later, when Mr. Cobb got up and excused himself, Hailey sighed with relief. She nodded and smiled as the older gentlemen took leave. Then, in an instant, her amber eyes traveled back to Zurich and Bernice.

Hailey was only by herself for a couple of seconds before three lovely women seated themselves around her table. She didn't need to ask who they were; Bernice's sisters all had a striking resemblance.

"Hello, Hailey! We're Zurich's aunts. I'm Ethel, and this is Josephine and Dorothy," the smiling aunt said with enthusiasm, pointing at the other two women. "We were at the bowling alley down the street. We decided to just wander in here to eat a light snack and listen to our favorite kind of music before going home."

Hailey had to laugh at that one, but she was gracious enough to do it inwardly. These three ladies were every bit as stunning and lively as Zurich's mother. Hailey would bet her last dollar that they'd come to the diner to get a sneak peek at Zurich's date.

"Hi. It's so nice to meet you. But how did you know who I was?" Hailey extended her hand until she'd shaken each one. The tender warmth she received in return from each firm but soft handshake was energizing.

Dorothy smiled endearingly. "We got here just in time to see Zurich and Bernice leave the table and head to the dance floor. We weren't going to come over, but you looked so lonely after Morgan left the table. Are you enjoying yourself, sweetheart?"

"Yes, ma'am. I really like this place. This is the second time Zurich has brought me here." The hopeful looks the sisters exchanged didn't get by Hailey. The magical look of maybe-this-is-the-one was undeniably in their eyes.

Josephine, seated next to Hailey, patted her hand. "That means you're special. I've never known Zurich to date anyone while he's here on vacation. This diner is a special spot for him. He hung out here as a teenager, as so many of the town's kids did. So, tell us, how did you meet our handsome nephew?"

"You already know the answer to that question, Aunt Jo. I already told my mother, so I know she told all of you. Couldn't stay away, could you?"

With his eyes playfully scolding his aunts, Zurich pulled out his mother's chair for her to be reseated. He had to pull up another chair from a nearby table, as his was occupied by one of the sisters. He saw that there also was no seat for Mr. Cobb, which he thought was a good thing. Maybe the older man wouldn't come back if he saw the small family gathering as an intimate one. Family Cobb wasn't, nor would he ever be, not if Zurich had any say in it.

"So, beautiful ladies, what brings you-all into the diner tonight, other than your uncontrollable desire to get a preview glance of one Miss Hailey Hamilton? And to be all up in our business." Zurich couldn't keep himself from laughing; these four sisters were a handful.

The three aunts looked slightly embarrassed at being publicly chided by their nephew.

Bernice laughed. "Son, I know you're not trying to tell us that you didn't expect your nosy aunts to show up here before the end of the evening. You already know that we sisters never leave our curiosity unsatisfied. That's why I asked to bring them along in the first place. I was merely trying to save you the embarrassment of having them show up here just like they did." Everyone laughed at Bernice's remarks.

Bernice leaned over and pecked her son on the cheek. She then turned to Hailey. "Please don't pay us any mind. This is how it is whenever we get together. We're just one big happy family. Sorry if my dear sisters injected themselves into our evening uninvited, but all of them are good girls—and they mean well. They were merely dying to meet you, just as I have been since the moment Zurich extended the invite to dinner. Hope you're not offended."

Though Hailey looked shocked to discover how eager everyone had been to meet her, she was touched by Bernice's other sincere remarks. "Of course I'm not offended! I think it's wonderful for Zurich to have such a caring family. I'm sure you ladies just wanted to make sure he's not getting himself into real trouble. I can tell you that he's not. He's safe with me. I've been taking real good care of him. I recognize a precious gem when I see one. And you can rest assured that I will treat him accordingly."

Hailey looked over at Zurich and winked her eye. The flirtatious gesture, her genuineness, and the humorous delivery of her comments had the other four women beaming all over; Hailey had instantly won each of their approval, hands down.

Zurich definitely approved of the way Hailey had handled

his aunts—and she'd done it with such aplomb, as well as with kid gloves. Her kind, gracious ways and her gentle spirit were among of her most endearing qualities; he loved these characteristics in a woman.

Dorothy stood, the eldest of the sisters; Ethel being the youngest. "Now that we've had the opportunity to meet you, Hailey, we're going to let you-all get on with your evening. We don't want to intrude any longer. Thanks for letting us join you."

The other two sisters, Ethel and Josephine, instantly got to their feet.

"Please don't leave now," Hailey practically begged, "we're having so much fun. It can only get better since the ice has already been broken. Not that I've felt a moment of chilliness from any of you. You're all so warm. Zurich, please invite your aunts to stay."

Happy to oblige without any prompting from Zurich, Ethel was the first to sit back down. "In that case, I'd love to stay. Can't speak for the rest of them, though."

"Aunties, please make Hailey and me very happy by staying on with us. I agree with Miss Hamilton. We *are* having a great time being here together, as we always do. Let's keep this lively party going, ladies. A statement I made to Hailey a while back keeps me from denying her anything she wants—that is, those things that are within reason."

With everyone laughing, the others reclaimed their seats as well. Josephine traded seats with her nephew so that he could sit beside his date. Before the seating exchange was complete, Zurich's laughter died on his lips. He'd spotted Morgan Cobb making his way back to the table. Morgan's presence was unwelcome as far as Zurich was concerned. Zurich quickly changed hats from the loving son and nephew to fierce family protector.

Hailey actually felt Zurich tense up when Morgan pulled up a chair and squeezed it in between Bernice and Dorothy's chairs. The sisters seemed genuinely delighted to have him at the table, and readily made room for him, but Hailey clearly could see that Zurich wasn't at all thrilled about his return. She touched his hand in hopes of bringing a touch of calm to the restlessness plaguing him. She didn't know what he held against the older man, but it was obvious to her that Zurich didn't like him. Hailey wondered if it was the statement that Bernice had made about them considering a future. Or was it something from the past?

In the next instant, Morgan stood and held his hand out to Bernice. She smiled up at him as she accepted his proffered hand. The sisters whispered a few comments to each other between giggles as the couple headed for the dance floor. Another gentlemen seemed to appear out of thin air to ask Josephine to dance. The smile on Zurich's face suggested to Hailey that he didn't object to his aunt being escorted to the dancing arena. Ethel and Dorothy didn't wait around for anyone to approach them. Having decided to dance with each other, they were out of their seats in a jiffy. While his aunts made a hasty departure, Zurich couldn't contain his laughter for another second. Looking over at Hailey, he took her hand and gently squeezed it with affection.

Hailey's eyes danced with glee. "They are too precious, and with so much energy."

He nodded. "I would have to agree. Want to join them out there?"

Her smile was beaming. "Don't mind if we do. I'm having so much fun. Thanks for making this happen. This is an evening I surely won't want to forget."

"Well, this is not exactly how I planned it, but I had a good idea that it might turn out this way. My ladies are practically inseparable, and I feel guilty for not inviting everyone in the beginning. I was concerned about overwhelming you by having you meet them all at once."

Smiling, Hailey settled herself into Zurich's arms. "It certainly has been an overwhelming experience, but a very delightful one. Mom would love each and every one of them. They are kindred spirits. Dad would enjoy them, too."

Zurich felt relieved that Hailey was so comfortable with the other women in his life. It actually made him very happy. The evening was turning out to be as pleasant as he'd hoped for.

If Mr. Cobb hadn't shown up, Zurich knew that it would've been a perfect evening.

Six

Seated on the inside deck of the charter boat, Hailey watched Zurich through the window as he placed some sort of large bait on the fishing pole provided as part of the early-morning deep-sea fishing tour. It was cool this far offshore, from the winds and all, but that had been expected. Hailey and Zurich had dressed warmly, both wore dark jeans and heavy sweatshirts. Each had brought along a jacket and had worn sturdy footgear.

Hailey didn't know much about deep-sea fishing because her father had only taken her out to fish in local Florida waters and other southeastern streams, and in lakes where fish were hand-stocked by man. However, Zurich was well informed on the subject and he didn't mind sharing his vast knowledge with her. He had even given her a small booklet that detailed anything and everything a person might want to know about deep-sea fishing: seasonal fishing; names and types of fish found in Gulf waters; fish sizes, weights, and lengths; and a list of restrictions on catch limits and other relevant matters. Although she had looked the booklet over, she hadn't read it in depth. Hailey knew that experience was the best teacher.

Hailey got up and walked over to where the coffee bar was located. After pouring herself a cup of hot brew and fixing it to her liking, she went to the outside deck where Zurich was. She arrived just in time to see him drop his line into the deep waters.

He smiled at her. "Hey, glad you came back out. Were you able to warm up a bit?"

"Pretty much. I thought I'd bring a cup of coffee out with me this time to help keep my insides warm. Would you like a cup?"

He shook his head in the negative. "I'll get it later. Have you taken a tour around the inside of the boat?"

"Yeah, pretty interesting. I've also talked with a few of the women. From the conversations, I can tell they love the sport as much as their men do. I guess I'm the only one on board who isn't really into it." Hailey sat down on one of the deck chairs.

"That's okay. No one expects you to be all into it your first time out. But after you try it a few times, I think you'll begin to really enjoy it. Mom and my aunts love to do this. The sisters also like to go on hunting trips, but them old girls don't go in for killing animals. They enjoy going up to our cabin in Cameron County just to play cards, cook, and talk trash."

Hailey frowned. "Do you go in for the kill, Zurich?"

"I'm a tracker. Love the hunt but not the kill. Just getting them in my scope is enough excitement for me. Getting the game on film is even more exciting. Now, my brothers, they'll shoot, but only if they're going to be home long enough to have it prepared for eating. Besides, there are a lot of serious restrictions on hunting and fishing. The Kingdom men heed them all."

Hailey looked relieved. "I'm glad I was right about you. I didn't think you'd get any sort of thrill out of killing innocent animals. Your mom and aunts are unbelievably active women. That's how it should be. When I get to be their age, no grass will be growing under my feet either."

"They're also incredibly stubborn women. My mother is the worst of the four in that department. There are times when she can't be reasoned with at all. I called her last night, but she wasn't trying to hear a thing I had to say. We had a major disagreement over the phone."

Hailey looked alarmed. "About me?"

Mindful of keeping an eye on his reel, Zurich dropped down onto the deck chair next to Hailey. He removed her coffee cup from her hand and drank a swig. He made a horrible face as he handed it back. "Girl, you must put coffee in your sugar! It's so darn sweet."

"Sorry, but I offered to get you your own cup. That's how I like it. What can I say?"

"To each his own. I take mine black, but I'll get it in a minute. Where were we?"

"You'd mentioned having a disagreement with your mom. I asked was it about me."

"I guess I really understated the nature of our heated discussion. Mom and I had an all-out battle over the announcement she made to us at dinner. I can't believe she'd get involved with a man like Morgan Cobb. He's not worthy of her!"

"What makes you say that, Zurich?" Hailey was concerned by the anger in his tone.

"He hung out with my father, that's why!"

"And?"

"And what?"

"Is that the only thing you hold against him?"

"Isn't that enough? Knowing what kind of a man my father was, how can you even ask me that question?"

"Are you saying Mr. Cobb is a drunk and that he abuses women and children?"

"He drinks, but I don't know anything about him being abusive."

"A lot of people drink, but that doesn't make them bad. So on what else are you basing your opinions of Mr. Cobb?"

"The fact that he hung out with my father tells me exactly who he is. How else could he stand being around Macon Kingdom if he wasn't just like him?"

"Zurich, that's an unfair assumption unless you have concrete evidence to back it up. Have you ever seen him drunk? You've admitted that you don't know if he's abusive. Does merely hanging out with someone make you just like that person? I don't think so."

"Damn right it does! Guilt by association! And, yes, I've seen him drunk. Not stumbling, falling-down, nasty drunk, but I've noticed him being intoxicated. What kind of man knows that another man is abusing his wife and children, and does or says nothing about it? You tell me, Hailey. What other kind of a man should I assume Cobb to be?"

"Is that a statement of fact, or another assumption, Zurich? Or are you being just plain judgmental? I don't think your father was out there in the streets bragging about beating his wife and kids. Men who are abusive normally do it behind closed doors. They often present themselves as kind, loving, and upstanding, especially when in the company of friends and peers. Did your mother tell her family that he was beating her?"

"She didn't have to. My brothers and I saw it happening. When we didn't see him hit her, we saw the evidence in her bloody and broken noses, black eyes, facial scratches, and black-and-purple body bruises. I can't remember when my mother's body wasn't showing some sort of evidence of his brutal hands."

"What about her sisters?"

He sharply raised an eyebrow. "You met them. What do you think?"

Hailey gave a hearty harrumph. "I think not! I also remember you saying when someone messes with one of them, they'd better know where the other three are. That alone tells me they probably didn't know."

"They didn't. My aunts all lived in different states. They didn't move in with my mom until after they all were widowed, only a couple of years ago. Mom had left him by then. My mom would've never told her siblings what was happening to her, nor would she have wanted us boys to tell it while she was still with him. However, she did tell them after she left my dad. That's why everyone objected vehemently to her taking him back into her home when he became so ill some years later."

"You made my point for me, Zurich. Trust me, your dad didn't want anyone to know about the abuse either. That's one of the things that makes abusers cowards. I find it hard to believe that Mr. Cobb, or any man for that matter, would know what harm your dad was doling out to his family and not try to do something about it. I admit to only spending a few hours with the man, but Mr. Cobb seemed very attentive to and extremely tender with your mom. Also, they sell liquor at the diner, but I didn't see him touch a drop of alcohol."

"Oh, Hailey, come on! You weren't born yesterday. He's not going to be on anything but his best behavior in front of her family, especially her sons. You just mentioned closet abusers. My aunts would scratch his eyeballs out and then feed them to him—and he knows that. What I'm worried about is what he's going to do to her once he gets her under his magical spell. More than that, if she agrees to marry him, what's going to happen once the doors are closed tight?"

Hailey shook her head in dismay. "I don't think you're giving your mother the credit she deserves. She's been there and done that. I, for one, don't think she's going to let any pattern of abuse happen all over again. And who said anything about marriage?"

"You didn't hear Mom say they were considering a future?"

"I heard every word she said. But she didn't say a future in what. They could just be thinking of taking their relationship to another level. Even so, *considering* a future is totally different from them having *decided* on one. I think you're jumping the gun here."

He blew out a ragged breath. "I don't know what you're really saying, Hailey. Are you telling me to stay out of my own mom's personal business?"

"Exactly! She's a grown woman. You don't want to run

the risk of alienating your mom, Zurich. Your dad kept her isolated enough. If you do that, you're the last person she'll come to if she does end up needing someone, because she may think that all she's going to hear from you is 'I told you so.' She's free now to make her own choices, and I refuse to believe that she's going to make anything but wise ones. If you want to continue being privy to everything that goes on in your mom's life, you'd better try to believe in *her* and not in what you think might possibly happen. Anything can happen, but until it does, you're simply speculating."

The visible tug on his fishing line kept Zurich from responding, but he hoped that Hailey didn't think she'd gotten in the last word. Once he landed what appeared to be a big fish, Hailey was going to finish hearing him out whether she wanted to or not.

Up until this very moment, seated at the dressing table in her room, Hailey hadn't given any more thought to the near fiasco of the previous day. Neither she nor Zurich had spoken again that night of his mom's relationship with Mr. Cobb. Zurich had stayed with her until well after midnight, and had only left then because of the early hour they'd gotten up in order to catch the charter.

Other than his arms around her, and a few kisses and warm hugs as they'd watched a couple of movies, no deeper intimacy had occurred between them. Conversation had also been limited. She gave a minute's thought to how easily they'd reclaimed their comfort zones with each other, yet seemed to have become a tad cautious in both speech and action. Hailey had been careful not to initiate any physical contact with Zurich. If they kissed or hugged, she'd made up her mind to let him make the first move. She'd already been too aggressive in getting involved in his personal family affairs, not to mention in stating her matter-of-fact opinions.

Knowing time was running out on her, she hurried to finish dressing to be on time for their next date. Zurich would be in the lobby in less than thirty minutes.

The horseback ride on the beach was going very well. Hailey hadn't ridden a horse in a while, but she was comfortable with the gentle one that Zurich had chosen for her. The sandy-colored mare, Cream 'n Sugar, wasn't nearly as big as Renegade, the dark stallion Zurich was riding, but her trot was just as lively.

Hailey appreciated that all the riders didn't have to stay in single file. No one was in a real hurry, and everyone appeared laid-back, which made the experience even nicer. The freedom to ride up and down the beach at will was the most appealing part of the adventure for Hailey. She and Zurich could remain side by side while sharing in delightful conversation.

Zurich looked over at Hailey and smiled. "This is some romantic backdrop we have right here. But it's even more beautiful on the beach at sunset. Maybe before we leave we can take another horseback ride around the time the sun is due to set. I know the magnificence of it all will blow your mind the same way it does mine."

Hailey winced inwardly as she wondered if he'd ever had a romantic liaison with another woman on the very same beach; it sounded as if he'd experienced a few sunsets on this particular shoreline. But she wouldn't think of asking him something that personal. The most sensible thing to do was to let go of her silly thoughts. Hailey knew she was hardly the first woman Zurich had ever had in his life, but she sure in heck hoped she might be the last. Hailey, for sure, knew that that last thought could get her in a heap of trouble.

First, second, or last? It really didn't matter. He was all hers for now. For the duration of their stay on the island she'd be the *first* at whatever new memories they made together.

"Have you ever shared a sunset on the beach with anyone special, Hailey?"

Surprised at his personal question, the exact same one she'd wanted to ask him but hadn't dared, she shook her head in the negative. "But I plan to." She blew him a kiss. "You are special to me, you know."

"The feeling's mutual." *You're more special to me than I'd ever thought was possible with anyone.* Zurich turned his attention toward the sky. Frowning slightly, he pointed out the dark clouds to Hailey. "It looks like rain."

"We're going to get a good downpour from the look of those thunder clouds." She pointed toward the northeast. "It's already raining over there. Maybe we should inform the stable master of what we expect to occur. The loud clapping of thunder could send the horses into a tizzy. That could prove dangerous to both the animals and the riders."

He laughed. "You sure know more than just a little bit about weather."

Hailey smiled smugly. "I should, with a meteorologist dad, remember? He still has a strong fascination with weather. He taught me a lot of what I know. I'm also very enthralled with meteorology." *Boy, was that an understatement.*

Zurich looked up at the sky again, closely studying the formation and dark coloring of the clouds. What he saw definitely pointed to unfavorable weather conditions. It didn't look good at all. "I think you're right about getting these horses back to the stable before the thunder and rain breaks loose. Lying on the beach and soaking up the rays won't be happening today, at least, no time soon." He winked at her. "But I'm sure we can think of something else to keep ourselves amused."

He grinned devilishly as his eyes roved her magnificent body.

"I'm sure we can," was Hailey's barely audible response.

Without so much as a peep to Hailey, Zurich took off down the beach. Hailey quickly turned the mare around and followed behind him, riding Cream 'n Sugar at a much slower pace than he was running Renegade. The scenery was breathtaking, and she wanted to savor it.

Inside his fifteenth-floor suite, Zurich poured two cups of hot brew and carried them over to the coffee table in front of the sofa where Hailey was seated. He sat down and placed one cup in front of her. Caught in the heavy downpour from parking lot to hotel, Hailey and Zurich had gotten soaked through and through. After getting out of their drenched clothes, they'd dressed themselves in thick, white terry-cloth robes. The one Hailey wore belonged to Zurich, and the other was a compliment of the hotel. Her clothes were drying on the towel bars in his bathroom.

Zurich picked up one of the hot wings he'd ordered from room service and held it up to Hailey's mouth. "Be careful now. Don't hurt yourself, girl. This is pretty hot stuff."

Hailey took a small bite of the chicken. "You call this hot? You've got to be kidding. I've eaten spicy foods with way more heat than this. You must have a punk stomach, Zurich."

Laughing, he raised an eyebrow. "I always carry a bottle of Tabasco sauce with me wherever I go. Do you want me to get it for you?"

"That would be nice. Thanks."

Eyeing her with a mixture of curiosity and admiration, more and more intrigued with her by the second, he went off to retrieve the condiment from the dining table. Zurich had called her bluff, but he could see that Hailey wasn't an easy one to call out. He was eager to see how Hailey would react after dousing the allegedly bland wings with one of the hottest pepper sauces around. He laughed while thinking that he should have a couple of glasses of water within easy reach, just in case.

True to his thoughts, he set down on the table the bottle

of hot sauce, a pitcher of ice water, and two glasses. "Thought the water might come in handy."

Hailey rolled her eyes. "I guess you think I can't handle it, huh? You just have no idea."

After taking the green top off the Tabasco, she doused it over a couple of wings. Hailey devoured the chicken in a matter of minutes. Although her mouth was burning like fire, she'd rather suffer in silence than let Zurich know it. Hailey was used to eating things super-hot, and loved most spicy foods, but she always had a glass of water handy to cool her tongue down between bites. With Zurich watching her so closely, she didn't know how long she could hold out; she just knew that she had to. She also knew she'd allowed her ego to get involved.

Zurich was impressed with her resolve. He knew she desperately needed at least a sip of water, but he could tell that she was a warrior. While he didn't associate Hailey with any type of military service, he still thought she'd be a tough nut to crack. The only thing she'd ever give up to the enemy under duress was her rank and serial number.

The lights in the room suddenly flickered off and on, and then dimmed. Zurich looked over at Hailey and shrugged his shoulders. "We didn't make it back to the hotel a minute too soon. There seems to be an even stronger storm brewing."

Hailey jumped up and ran over to the picture window to get a closer look. She saw the bright flashes of lightning and heard the loud sounds of rolling thunder, soon followed by more buckets of pouring rain. Hailey watched, in awe of Mother Nature as windswept waves crashed upon the coastline and rain beat hard against the hotel windows. She loved to look out at the rain, but her experiences with weather phenomena told her this wasn't just your run-of-the-mill shower. And it wasn't going to end that quickly.

Zurich went off to search the place for candles just in case the power failed completely; he also wanted to give Hailey a chance to cool off her mouth. Most large hotels had a back-up generator, but Gulf Coast storms had a way of wiping out everything in their wake. He had grown up living near the coast and had seen firsthand the damage that could occur when the weather took a drastic turn for the worse. The rains could simply blow over, but this had all the earmarkings of an intense electrical storm.

The moment Zurich left the room, Hailey dashed over to the table and downed one of the glasses of water. She then refilled it and raced back to the window.

A few minutes later Zurich walked up behind Hailey, pulled her back against his body, and rested his chin atop her head. His hands spanned her slender waist. After lacing his fingers together, he rested his palms on the flat of her abdomen. He was now dressed in denim jeans and a polo shirt.

He kissed the top of her head. "It's so beautiful to look at, Hailey, but this type of storm can turn deadly in no time at all. Are you going to be okay while I go down to the gift shop and purchase a few candles?"

"I'll be fine. And I know exactly what a storm like this can do. I shudder to think. These sustained winds must be blowing thirty miles per hour or better. Maybe we should turn on the weather channel and find out what's being said about this one. What do you think?"

He looked amazed. "I think your dad taught you a hell of a lot about his profession. If I didn't know better, I'd think you had a career in weather. But we both know that can't be. According to you, you have some sort of undercover job. At any rate, I need to get the candles. I see the possibility of a power failure. Sure you're going to be all right?"

"I'm okay, Zurich. You go ahead. I'm going to make a couple of phone calls on my cell."

When he didn't respond, Hailey tilted her head back and looked up at him. The look of horror on his face made her follow the direction of his stare. "Oh my God, the strong force of the wind is sweeping away that old couple!" she cried out.

Zurich was out the door before she had the chance to utter another word.

Hailey stayed rooted at the window, watching and praying as a couple of people immediately came to the rescue of the seniors. Only a few minutes had passed when she saw Zurich zip across the parking lot and join what looked like a concerned citizens rescue team. As she intently watched the emergency unfold below, she saw that things appeared to be growing worse. Totally forgetting that she wore nothing but a robe, Hailey ran out the door and raced toward the elevators. Recalling the danger of being in an elevator during a power outage, Hailey made a U-turn and rushed toward the stairwell.

Fifteen floors down, she thought, inhaling and exhaling deeply in order to pace herself.

Hailey was well trained in disaster preparedness, just as Zurich seemed to be. Her expertise in that area could only help. Still, she prayed that everything would be under control by the time she got there, that it hadn't gotten any worse.

Once outside, Hailey struggled valiantly against the gale-force winds. Though she was no match for the power of Mother Nature, she steadily moved forward, inch by inch like a soldier in battle taking a position on the front line. Her hair was limp, soaked through and through, as was the robe she wore, but she trudged on through the flooded parking lot. Although she could barely see her hand in front of her face, she diligently searched for Zurich and the others.

Zurich spotted Hailey as she spied the small gathering. A car suddenly came barreling out of nowhere just as Hailey ran toward him. He called out to her to stay back, but she didn't hear him. Nor did she see the speeding car.

Zurich nearly stopped breathing. Time appeared to

move in slow motion as he watched the car bearing down on the woman he'd come to love. The thought of losing her was even more frightening than the sudden discovery of his true feelings for her.

Right in the midst of serious danger, Zurich Kingdom realized he loved Hailey Hamilton.

Without wasting another moment, Zurich's feet rapidly burned a path straight to her. In the next instant, his body came down on top of hers as he pushed her to the ground. A second later would have been too late for him to save her.

What happened next nearly scared the life out of both Hailey and Zurich. They watched in absolute horror as the car hit a parked car, turned up on its side, and then slid all the way to the other end of the parking lot. Zurich pressed Hailey's face against his chest as the car spun around several times before crashing into a concrete beam.

Zurich made sure Hailey was okay before going off to join in yet another rescue mission.

Hailey was still trembling all over as Zurich helped her get dressed in dry clothing. He had already cleaned up and applied an antibiotic cream to the nasty scratches and bruises near her left temple. Hailey had nearly come out of her skin from the stinging sensations of the peroxide he'd carefully applied with a Q-tip. Her left arm was also badly bruised. Neither of them had thought the injuries, which had occurred when she'd made contact with the hard concrete, serious enough to seek out emergency medical treatment at a local hospital.

Hailey was gritty. All during her frightening ordeal in the parking lot she had held up admirably. It was when she'd learned who the driver of the car was that she had nearly come unglued. The intoxicated man behind the wheel was none other than Corbin Whitehall, Hailey's would-be suitor from the club. The driver of the car, and the man that Zurich referred to as "J. Smooth" were one and the same. Hailey couldn't believe her eyes when the paramedics had pulled him from the car. He hadn't received so much as a single scratch. For whatever reason, God had spared his life.

The storm was still raging on and the rain was now falling in sheets. Zurich had pulled the heavy drapes back all the way so they could watch Mother Nature continue to unleash her fury from within the safe confines of the hotel. Zurich had ordered dinner for them, but had requested that it not be delivered until the early evening, just a few hours away. He thought Hailey needed to relax for a short while to help speed up her recovery. She was still somewhat in shock from the terribly disturbing events in the parking lot.

Hailey squeezed Zurich's hand as he led her over to the sofa in her suite. The only lighting in all the rooms came from the numerous candles Zurich had lit. After making sure Hailey was comfortable, he put his arm around her shoulders and pulled her head against his chest. He gently massaged her right arm as he kissed her forehead.

Hailey looked up at him with fear in her eyes. "Do you really believe that he wasn't aiming his car at me? Or were you just trying to make me feel better?"

He shook his head. "Hailey, sweetheart, he was too drunk to know who you were even if he had seen you. Make no mistake about it; the guy was plastered. He was probably in the same alcohol-besotted condition, if not in worse shape, the night you flipped him on his sorry butt. I know you believe he was trying to kill you, but I don't think so. He simply lost control of the car because he was driving way too fast for the current weather conditions. Besides, no one should ever drive like a maniac in a parking lot, drunk or sober."

"But he looked right at me after he was removed from the car. And when the cops handcuffed him, he called me a bitch."

He smoothed her hair back from her face. "I'm sure that

all he could see was the figure of a woman, if that much. He would've yelled out expletives no matter who'd been standing there. I bet when they check his blood-alcohol levels he'll be way over the legal limit. You have to stop worrying. You'll go insane if you manage to convince yourself that he tried to kill you."

She rested her head back against his chest. "I guess you're right. But it's people like him that kill up half the nation. Drunk drivers rarely get hurt. It's the innocent that usually become the fatalities. It just doesn't seem fair. I'm glad the older couple didn't get seriously injured. They were so grateful to you and the others for helping them out."

"I know. They couldn't stop thanking us. I felt so sorry for Mrs. Drago when she saw how swollen her husband's right eye was. That tree branch could've easily put it out. She kept kissing him and petting him like a baby, crying all the while. She told me they'd been married for fifty-two years, Hailey. Can you imagine that?"

"I can. My parents have been married thirty-one. What's so amazing to me is that they're still crazy about each other. My mom and dad are all over each other every chance they get. They are so cute, and still very romantic. They do everything together; I do mean everything."

"They've been blessed. My father was quicker to hit my mother than he was to look at her. He was a drunk driver, too. We used to be scared silly in the car with him. My mother would pray out loud as he'd zigzag along the highway at seventy and eighty miles an hour in a fifty-five speed zone. Even when he'd shout at her and tell her to shut up, she'd keep on praying. Prayer was Mom's answer to everything. I often wondered why God didn't hear her."

Hailey looked up at him, her amber eyes awash in sympathy. "He did. She may not have been listening to his response."

He jerked his head back. "Say what?"

Hailey rested her palm on the side of Zurich's face.

"God hears everything, but we don't always listen for or hear his responses to our pleas. And if we do hear it, or even see it, we don't always recognize it as the answer to what we'd asked for. Or, on the other hand, we recognize it but choose to ignore it. Not hearing God was Kelly's biggest problem. She'd ask Him for a solution to the problem; then she'd go right on listening to what Will had to say, all the things she obviously wanted and needed to hear from him. 'I love you and need you.' That was only one of the choruses he sang over and over to her. 'If you leave me, I won't make it.' 'I'll kill myself if you walk out on me.' There were so many things he'd say to try and get her back in check. Any and all of them never failed to work. He killed Kelly's spirit first. In the end, he murdered her body. This may sound horrible, but there were numerous times I wished for Will to take himself out. I thought the world would be better off without him; Kelly would've been."

Zurich sighed hard. "I won't say it wasn't a horrible thing to wish for, but I can't tell you how many times I wished the very same thing about my father. I used to have dreams of attending his funeral. After his casket was lowered into the ground and everyone had left the cemetery, my brothers and I would dance all around the gravesite. A couple of minutes into the dance, he'd leap up out of the ground, screaming like a he-banshee and spitting out fire. Then he'd swing his thick leather belt at us, twirling it as if it were a lasso. That's when I'd wake up screaming and sweating something fierce." He looked at Hailey, his eyes glazed with moisture. "You're the only person I've ever told about those awful dreams. I wonder why that is?"

She snuggled in closer to him and wrapped her arms around his neck. "Trust. The same reason I've shared some of my innermost fears with you. I trust you." The kiss he gave her was so gentle it felt like a butterfly had landed on her lips for only a brief moment.

"I noticed you used the word 'some'. Do you have a lot of other secrets, Hailey?"

"Just one or two."

"Think you'll ever be able to share them with me?"

"I don't know. It all depends."

He looked puzzled. "On what?"

"How emotionally deep we get into this relationship. Like I said before, I don't sit around dreaming about getting married and having children. But there is one secret I promised myself that I'd only tell my husband. I probably made that pact with myself because I was so sure I'd never find anyone I'd trust enough to marry. It won't be an easy confidence to share."

He coughed nervously. "Do you have that much trust in me?"

She laughed against his chest. "Oh, no, buddy, I am not going there. That's a loaded question—and I'm not taking a walk through that minefield. We'd better move on away from such dangerous ground. Sound familiar?"

He laughed at the words that sounded very similar to his own. He recalled with crystal clarity Hailey asking him if sleeping was the only thing he did in his bed.

Flashing lighting suddenly lit up the entire room. The sound of rolling thunder followed soon after the unbelievable electrical light show. The fact that Haley didn't so much as flinch at the dangerous lightning or the loud noise of the thunder once again aroused Zurich's curiosity. A lot of the women he'd known would've reacted fearfully to both elements right off the bat. Not too much seemed to frighten her. He didn't think her fearlessness had a thing to do with being the daughter of a weatherman. Hailey was simply a woman of strong substance.

Zurich was of the opinion that there wasn't an ounce of false bravado in Hailey. She was as courageous as anyone he'd ever met, including the unbelievably courageous group of women in his family. The way she'd shown up in the parking lot had certainly impressed the heck out of him. Her sincere desire to help out strangers had brought her outside into a downpour of heavy rain dressed in nothing but a terry-cloth bathrobe. If that wasn't an act of bravery, then he didn't know the meaning of the word. Thinking solely of the safety of others had nearly cost her precious life.

"This is a magnificent display of weather phenomena, and we have ringside seats," Hailey enthused. "I normally like to sleep when it's like this outside. I know it may seem strange to you that I'd find peace amidst an electrical storm, but I do. I've been known to sleep through some rather bad ones. Much like the Texas coast, coastal and inland Florida is hardly a stranger to these kinds of unpredictable weather patterns. You're not the only one who grew up in a crazy climate. We have quite a few interesting and unusual things in common."

"So it seems." Zurich got up from the sofa. "Since you like to sleep when it's like this, I think you should go into the bedroom and lie down for a while. You've been through quite an ordeal. Dinner won't be here for a couple of hours. While you're resting, I'm going to stretch out here on the sofa if that's okay with you. Come on. Let me get you all tucked into bed."

Hailey stretched her full length out on the sofa and then rolled on her side. Looking at him in a most loving way, she patted the space she'd made for him. "I think it'd be nice for us to lie here on the sofa and take a short nap together. Don't you?"

He grinned broadly. "Real nice." He turned to walk away. "I'll get the extra blanket from the top of the bedroom closet. A couple of pillows won't hurt, either." Sorry for all that she'd been through, even though she'd braved it, he leaned over the sofa and gave her a light kiss. "I'll be right back, Hail. If you can't stay awake, don't worry about it."

"Oh, I'm not going to fall asleep. At least, not until you're lying right here beside me."

Smiling, Zurich winked at her as he moved out of her line of vision.

As Hailey fought the idea of sleep, she thought of how attentive Zurich had been to her. His gentleness while tending to her battle scars was only rivaled by that of her parents. His concern for his fellow man was obvious in that he'd risked his life to save the lives of Mr. and Mrs. Drago. She cringed as she thought back on her mention of sharing a certain secret with only her husband. His question about trust had caught her completely off guard. Yes, she mused, she trusted him enough to tell him her secret, but she wouldn't. Since their earlier conversation on that particular issue, she had decided it was a confidence she couldn't ever share with anyone. It was actually one that she couldn't bear repeating.

Hailey hadn't had her eyes closed for more than a couple of seconds when Zurich joined her on the couch. After placing one of the pillows behind her head and one where he'd lay his, he stretched out alongside her and then covered them with the blanket. The air conditioning had made the room pretty cold. Concerned that Hailey might catch a chill, especially with the good soaking she'd gotten earlier, he'd turned the unit down a notch while he'd been in the bedroom. The last thing she needed was to come down with a cold. She'd been through enough.

"Sleepy?"

She kissed him softly on the mouth. "A little."

He stroked her hair. "Close your eyes. You're safe with me."

She laid her head on his chest. "I feel that with you."

As he gently kissed each of her eyelids, his hand slid under the sweatshirt she wore. He knew she hadn't put on a bra when she'd changed into dry clothes, but the contact with her soft flesh still caused him to moan. Tenderly, he stroked her bare back with the pads of his fingers.

In a matter of minutes his tender caresses had her wanting him in the worst way. The throbbing ache of her physical need for him made her feel so weak. Hailey wasn't an overly aggressive woman; that's what kept her from telling him she wanted him to make wild, passionate love to her. She no longer cared whether or not they'd have a love affair once their vacation ended. All she was concerned with was what they had right here and now.

If sweet memories of him were the only thing she was going to take away from Texas with her, then so be it. They were hardly children at ages twenty-seven and thirty-five. The only thing she was worried about at this minute was if he had easy access to a condom.

As his warm hands came around and fondled her breast, she had already made a conscious decision not to resist what was happening between them. An unhesitant Hailey took his mouth with a fierce hunger; her kisses were moist and passionate. Zurich's tongue met with hers. The kiss deepened and quickly grew in intensity.

In one fluid motion, he rolled Hailey on top of him. His hands then slid down into the back waistband of her sweat pants and firmly gripped her buttocks. His hardened sex pressing into her thigh made her desire for him nearly explosive. But it was the wild, circular motions of his hands on her silk bikini–clad bottom that set her entire body on fire.

"Hailey," he whispered huskily, "do you want me as much as I need you? Please tell me you're feeling every emotion that I am."

She lifted her head and looked deeply into his eyes. "Yes, Zurich, I do want you. I'm feeling it all. Do you keep protection in your wallet for unexpected moments like this?"

Sighing deeply, he pressed his lips into her forehead. "I do, but I don't have anything with me. It's probably for the best." He pulled her head down on his chest. "Go to sleep, Hailey. Making love without a condom can't happen. We value ourselves far too much to even consider something so foolish as to make love without using protection. You wouldn't happen to have a condom around here, would you?" He joked to try and ease the sexual tension.

"Oh, how I wish! Thank you for understanding. I responded to you the way I did because you are a man who is true to himself, which usually means you can be true to others. You just proved that I'm right about you. I don't regret what almost happened, Zurich. Not one bit. I hope we don't have to wait too long for us to finish what we began. I'm also true to myself."

His heart leaped inside his chest as he thought of what she'd come to mean to him. "I love that about you. I also love how you get a serious flesh fire started. Something tells me I shouldn't have turned the air conditioning down. It's going to take more than a few minutes for me to cool off. Come here, Hailey. I just want to hold you in my arms while we take that long-overdue nap. I love how you and I fit so nicely together."

Before laying her head on his chest, she looked down at him. "About the condoms, Zurich. You should treat them like that American Express card of yours. Don't ever leave home without 'em." They both laughed heartily.

"I got you. And now I have one for you. Don't ever try to eat hot wings doused with Tabasco without having a glass of water handy. Oh, by the way, you forgot to replace the water you poured from the pitcher. I bet it felt good going down! Your mouth had to be on fire."

Knowing she'd been cold busted, all Hailey could do was laugh.

All through the delicious dinner of veal cutlets, wild rice, Brussels sprouts, and fresh garden salad, Zurich thought of what had almost happened between him and Hailey. Although she'd claimed to be ready for it, he had begun to have doubts. He was afraid they'd simply gotten caught up in the moment and in the romantic ambiance of candlelight and stormy weather. He wasn't even sure if he was prepared to take their relationship to that level of intimacy. There were still a lot of things for them to work out.

A long-distance relationship wouldn't be easy on either of them by any stretch of the imagination. Distance wasn't the only issue. The nature of their jobs obviously posed a problem, since neither of them had been willing to talk about what they did for a living. There were many reasons why he didn't feel comfortable getting into the duties of his profession, all of them legitimate; Hailey seemed to be faced with a similar dilemma, if not the same one.

September eleventh, 2001 had changed a lot of things, had systematically changed the way world situations were handled, not to mention the drastic changes that had occurred in the many lives that had been turned upside-down and inside out. It seemed that in today's climate everyone was guilty until proven innocent: the exact opposite of the way the law was originally intended. Zurich couldn't even begin to explain the drastic changes in himself and how he viewed his beloved country and the world at large. It all created great conflict within.

With much dignity and immeasurable valor, Zurich Kingdom had proudly served his country for the past seventeen years as a member of the United States Air Force. It was because of the countless numbers of brave men and women like Zurich that freedom continued to ring.

In the wake of the tragedies of nearly two years ago, though recovery had been achieved on many levels, the nation's healing was still incomplete. Issues of national security were yet to be fully resolved. The economy remained riddled with uncertainties, and the unemployment rate had taken a sharp rise. The United States was still in a deep state of shock. September eleventh and its tragic stories were still the major topic of discussion all over the world.

It was the day on which America the beautiful had received its harshest wake-up call.

* * *

Hailey watched Zurich closely as he wrestled with his feelings. The fact that he'd said very little since they'd sat down to dinner was only one of the indications that conflict brewed within him. The constant changes in his facial expressions were another good indicator. This was the first time conversation between them had been practically nonexistent. She hadn't tried to draw him into any type of discussion out of respect for his seemingly dark mood.

But Hailey had to finally admit that a bad case of nerves was beginning to take a serious hold on her. The nearly quarter-of-an-hour-long silence between them was terribly unnerving, to say the least, especially after the kind of deep intimacy they'd shared only a short time ago.

He looked over at her. "I'm sorry, Hailey."

Her heart skipped a beat as she drew in a shaky breath. "For what, Zurich?"

"For shutting you out. I realize I've been preoccupied over here. Forgive me?"

She nodded. "Not even an issue. I just wish I knew what it is that seems to have taken all of your attention. It's not like you to be so quiet for such a long period of time."

"It's nothing, Hailey."

She sharply cut her eyes at him. "Don't do that, Zurich."

"What?"

"Don't lie to me about what you're thinking and feeling. I view lies as disrespect, no matter how white or small they are. I deserve the truth. It's what almost happened between us, isn't it? You're deeply regretting it, aren't you?"

More to the point, Hailey feared that Zurich had lost respect for her because of her willingness to sleep with him. If that were the case, she'd never get over it. It suddenly dawned on her that she'd taken a serious risk, one that might've lost her the very things she desired most from Zurich—his love and respect.

His eyes closed for a brief moment. "It's not that I regret it. It has more to do with my belief that neither of us is ready for what nearly occurred. I don't regret any of what did happen, but I am relieved that it didn't go any further. Thanks for demanding complete honesty. I always prefer honesty, but I would've lied just to spare your feelings. I can see in your eyes that I've already hurt you. I can also see that lying about what I felt would've only added insult to injury."

Unable to speak without showing her emotional agony, Hailey got up and walked over to the window. Tears splashed from her eyes just as she reached her destination. Quickly, she wiped them away with her fingers. She'd already made a big fool of herself morally. She certainly didn't want to reveal to him that the pain he'd inflicted upon her was deep enough to make her cry. But she was sure he already knew how badly she was hurt. Her eyes were her worst enemy at times. They had a way of stripping her soul bare.

Hailey's spine stiffened when she felt him come up behind her. If he dared to touch her, she feared her emotions would give way to grief. Yet the yearning to have him take her in his arms and hold her until the pain eased was so overwhelming.

Thinking she might think him disrespectful of her if he allowed the front of his body to make contact with the back of hers, especially under the circumstances, he purposely left a fair amount of space between them as he placed his hands on her shoulders. "I know you're hurting. If I can somehow ease the pain for you, please tell me what I can do." He leaned in and kissed the back of her head without the rest of his body making contact with hers.

Unable to hold back her emotions, she allowed the tears to barrel down her cheeks. She lacked the courage to face him. "I could handle this so much better if you were to leave. It's hard for me to face you knowing you've lost respect for me. I'm sorry I gave you a false impression of me. I'm really no different from the woman you had come to respect. I was ready to give myself to you only because I'm in love with you. I admit to being filled with lust, but that had very little to do with my decision. Making love to you would've merely been my deepest expression of what I feel for you. I'm not a person who takes lovemaking lightly. I'm sorry if I disappointed you or possibly tainted your image of me."

"If what you've said is true, why can't you tell me to my face? Why does your back have to be turned to me when I hear one of the most wonderful things a woman can tell a man?"

"Because you've made me feel ashamed of myself, Zurich."

He spun her around to face him. His eyes pierced hers. "You have no reason to feel that way. If you do, it has nothing to do with me. I can't control your feelings one way or the other. I haven't said one thing to make you experience feelings of shame. I don't have that kind of power over you. You once told me that Kelly gave Will permission to treat her badly. You haven't given me permission to treat you other than with love and respect. I have not lost reverence for you, because you haven't given me any reason to. Besides that, you won't allow anyone to disrespect you. And for the record, I'm falling in love with you, too."

Her gasp was audible as he brought her to him and wrapped her up in his arms. "We have a few issues to deal with, Hailey, but disrespect isn't one of them. Am I getting through to you?"

She nodded. "Loud and clear." His sincere confession about his feeling of love for her had washed all her doubts away. He had no way of knowing how her insides danced with joy. Yet she knew they still had a rocky road ahead of them.

"Good. Now that we have that settled, do you really want me to leave? Before you answer that, I expect the same honesty from you that you demanded from me."

"No, Zurich."

He kissed her full on the lips. "In that case, let's make ourselves comfortable on the sofa and watch the DVD movies I brought from my room." He kissed her forehead. "Thanks for not kicking my butt out of here, Hailey. I would've been miserable the rest of the evening if we hadn't talked this through. I'm glad you changed your mind. Are we back on the same page?"

"I truly hope so, Zurich."

Seven

Hailey lay in her bed in the early morning hours thinking of all the things that had transpired in her life since she'd arrived on South Padre Island, Zurich being the very best one. It was hard for her to believe that there were only a few days left of her vacation. The time had flown by with the speed of lightning. She'd be returning to Florida for a couple of days before going on to her next assignment in Europe. She had yet to tell Zurich where she'd be living and she knew that time was running out on her. Although she didn't have an official address yet, he had a right to know she'd be living on the other side of the world. Especially since he still wanted them to try and work on a long-distance relationship.

Zurich hadn't revealed the nature of his job. Although he hadn't said exactly where he was working, he had mentioned that he'd be there quite a while longer. They had already exchanged the addresses of each of their parents' homes. No matter what, those two addresses were permanent for some time to come. They'd always be able to contact one another through their parents when no other way was possible.

Hailey couldn't remember having had a better vacation than this one. Meeting Zurich had been a godsend. It certainly wasn't something she'd ever expected to happen. Looking for a man had never been on the top of her list of priorities. But she hadn't had to look for this one. He'd waltzed into her life like it had been destined. How they'd manage to keep their destiny from changing was altogether another matter, but that wasn't something she could worry about.

All her life Hailey's parents had taught her to believe that she'd have whatever God meant for her to have in this world. So if God intended Zurich for her, Hailey had no choice but to believe they'd be together. If not, then she'd trust that He had something or someone even better in mind for her. However, she couldn't imagine any better man than Zurich was; the man was definitely for real.

For all the marvelous attributes Zurich possessed, Hailey had to admit that his growing anger over his mother's relationship with Mr. Cobb wasn't a favorable one. She thought he was being totally unreasonable about it; he though just the opposite. Hailey had been sure she'd convinced him not to interfere with Bernice's personal life. Before he'd left her the previous evening, she'd found out she'd been mistaken. Zurich had announced that he was having breakfast with his mom this morning; his intent was to tell her exactly how he felt about Morgan Cobb.

Zurich also intended to demand that his mom give up her friendship with this man whose character he questioned. When Hailey had tried to protest the unfairness of his intent, he'd told her that his word was final. He had had the last word simply because his tone brooked no argument. In fact, his tone had frightened her. It had also made her wonder what he would've done had she continued voicing her objections. He'd looked angry enough to hit something. Though she was sure he wouldn't have struck her, she didn't think it a coincidence that his abusive dad was the first person to come to her mind during those unpleasant moments.

Zurich took a sip from his coffee cup as he sat at his mother's kitchen table. "Mom, you object to what I'm saying, but what do you *really* know about Morgan Cobb?"

Bernice looked obstinate as she eyed her son with disappointment. "All that I need to know. What you need and want to know about him are what's really at question here."

Zurich grinned. "Would you mind expounding on your answer?"

Bernice shook her head. "Zurich Kingdom, I don't know what you want from me. But let me say this. I had one man who completely controlled me, and for far too long. As you youngsters would say, *been there, done that*. Right here and now I'm putting you on notice, your brothers on notice, and anyone else who thinks they have the right to tell me what to do, that I'm not having it. I'm an adult and I'm exercising my right to do my own thing, in my own way."

Zurich held up his hand to say something in protest.

"Put your hand down, son. This is not school, but I've been your teacher for thirty-five years. I wasn't a very good one and we've all suffered serious consequences for that. But I'm the one talking now. You'll just have to wait. When I got enough courage to walk out on your daddy, I vowed to never again disrespect myself in that way, or allow anyone else to. I stayed with Macon for a lot of reasons you'll never understand. But that's all over now, son." She held out her hands and kicked up her feet. "In case you haven't noticed, the shackles have all been removed, permanently. I'm free at last. Are you feeling me, son?"

Zurich remembered Hailey making some of the same remarks in reference to his mother's controlled past. *Been there, done that* was the same phrase she'd used. "Okay, I'm feeling you. I just want to know what it is that makes you think Mr. Cobb is someone you should be giving the time of day. He worked with Dad, hung out with him, and they were drinking buddies. He knew you were getting beaten black-and-blue, but he did nothing to try and protect you from his best bud. What kind of man is that, Mom? Don't you fear the same treatment from him after he gets you permanently settled into his lair?"

Bernice looked exasperated. "Although this is none of your business, Major Zurich Kingdom, I love you enough to share a few truths with you regarding Mr. Cobb, the man you are sadly mistaken about. Little do you know, but Morgan did help me, plenty. Your dad went to work every single day, made darn good money, but the truth is he drank up most of what he earned. Morgan gave me a good portion of his paycheck, every payday, so that I could buy food and clothes for my kids and myself. His generosities went far beyond what anyone can imagine."

Zurich's eyes were filled with the pain of his shame. Although it was hard from him to grasp all that his mother had said, the one thing he had seized hold of was that he'd been dead wrong about his mom's friend. The only thing that kept him from apologizing was his desire to hear Bernice out. Hailey had accused him of being judgmental; it looked as if she'd been right.

"In the beginning, I wouldn't take one red cent from him. When that happened, he'd go and buy the groceries himself and leave them at the back door. Then he'd call and tell me they were there. Even after I told him I couldn't accept them, he left them there, told me that I shouldn't dismiss God's blessings. He let me know from the start that there were no strings attached to his kindnesses, that he was just a man who believed in doing the right thing. Mr. Cobb, *Mr. Wrong* in your opinion, is the man who took care of us all those years. Had it not been for him we would've gone hungry many a night. The school clothes and shoes came from him, too. He even helped me get a fresh start when I decided it was time to leave. He's the one who gave me the contract to cook for the diner."

Zurich's eyebrows knitted together. "How could he grant you a contract for the diner?"

"He's the owner, son. Why didn't you know that? Because he's a very low-key person, a man who does a lot of good for many people but never brags about it. He owns businesses and property all over this town. How do you think we were able to afford Buckley Academy?"

Zurich nearly fell out of his seat on that one. "No way! I had a scholarship."

"You're right. And you were granted it on your own merit. However, Morgan contributes heavily to that particular scholarship fund. Still, there were other yearly fees that had to be paid, quite a few steep ones, such as the dormitory. He paid them all for us.

"Zurich, Morgan has never expected a thing from me in return for all that's he's done for us. And I've never given him a thing other than my undying gratitude and respect. He's never been married because he never found what he was looking for in a woman. The one woman he saw as the perfect mate was married to someone else. It was long after your daddy died that Morgan told me I was that perfect woman." She took a deep breath. "You can speak now. I'm through with this explanation—and I don't plan to ever expound on it again. So when your brothers start in with their loud protesting, you'll have to be the one to set them straight."

Zurich got to his feet and opened his arms wide to his mother. As she stood, he lifted her completely off the ground and hugged her tightly. "You *are* a perfect woman. I'm sorry I doubted you." He kissed her forehead before standing her on her feet. "I love you, Mom."

Bernice wiped the tears from her eyes. "And I love you, you big old boy. Am I right in thinking I have your blessing should I decide on some sort of future with Morgan?"

He grinned. "Not only do you have it, I plan to give you away should you decide to get married again. I stand corrected; my brothers and I will do the honors. Your happiness has always been our main interest. I can see that you are finally that, happy as can be. I'm proud of you, sweet lady." He looked at his watch. "I've got to run now, Mom. I don't want to be late for my date with Hailey."

Bernice eyed her son with curiosity as she walked

Zurich to the door. "She's the one, isn't she, son? Miss Hailey has done a number on you, hasn't she?"

He looked puzzled. "What makes you say that, Mom?"

"Boy, if you could see what I see every time you say her name or look at her, you wouldn't have to ask that question. I can't say that I've met more than two or three of your lady friends; that was way back when you were much younger. But I've never seen your eyes capture any girl the way they capture Miss Hailey. Girlfriend is working your heart but good!"

Zurich didn't look too happy about his mother's assessment. "Mom, I'm not sure what to do about Hailey. I'm scared of what I feel for her. Scared to death. Mom's she's some special woman. When I look at her, I see a million tomorrows for us. Then the fears take control."

"What has you so darn scared, Zurich?"

"What if I turn out to be just like Dad? What if I vow to love and cherish her, and then turn around and beat her to a bloody pulp? What if I knock her silly because I don't like the way she looked at me or the tone in which she spoke, or that she didn't cook my steak exactly the way I like it? I fear becoming like Dad more than anyone can imagine. Mom, I still have a lot of pent-up anger inside of me. What if I take that anger out on her one day?"

Bernice didn't wipe her tears away this time as she took hold of her son's hand. "You are not your dad, Zurich, plain and simple. Don't let happiness pass you by based solely on 'what ifs'. What if I'd stopped him cold the first time he hit me? What if I'd left him on the second time or the third? Those are the questions you might want to consider. Miss Hailey doesn't look like the type to let you get away with it the first time. An abused woman has to share in the blame. I don't know why I feel that way about Miss Hailey, but I do."

"Mom, I have to ask. I desperately need to know. What made you stay and allow him to inflict such inhumane treatment upon you? Please, Mom, help me understand."

"As smart as you are, I thought you would've figured that out by now. Where do you think I could've gone that he wouldn't have found me? When a man shows you exactly what's he's capable of, how do you make yourself think he's bluffing when he tells you he'll kill you if you dare to leave? Then, when he tells you he'll murder your babies if you even attempt to abandon him, what do you do when you're sure he won't hesitate to make good on his promise?

"Tell me, what choice would you make, son? Would you have left, knowing he'd make good on the threats? I was sure he'd come after me and kill me when I did leave, but my babies were safe by then. They were all grown up and out of harm's way. We can also thank Morgan that Macon didn't try to kill me. Morgan never told me this himself, but rumor has it that he paid some good old boys to put the fear of God in your daddy. I heard they'd threatened to kill him if he ever came near me again. That's supposedly when Macon picked up and left town. So there, son, you have it all right out there in front of you. I hope you have all your answers."

With tears in his eyes, Zurich brought his mother to him and wrapped her up in his arms. "I would've done just what you did, Mom. No more questions from me. I don't want you to have to relive another second of your life with Macon Kingdom. He's dead now. May he rest in peace, though I doubt he'll ever find a moment of serenity where he's going."

"As for Miss Hailey, Zurich, let your heart be your guide, not your daddy's evil ways. Love is what you make of it. Love isn't what Macon felt for me. It couldn't have been. But love and marriage can be a beautiful thing. If you and your brothers keep shying away from both, I'm never going to become anyone's grandma."

Zurich's scowl gave way to a huge smile. "Ah, so the truth has finally been told! You're more worried about not becoming a grandma than you are about us never being husbands." He kissed her cheek. "Just kidding, Mom. Thanks for the advice. I heard everything you said. And you're right about Hailey; the girl don't take no mess off of anyone. I'll tell you how I know that when I have more time. See you before I'm due to leave in a couple of days." Zurich looked down the long hallway. "By the way, where are my beautiful aunts?"

"They're not here. They said something about going to the WalMart super center. If they were in the house, they would've been right there at the table with us. I'm glad we had the opportunity to have this private mother and son chat. Be safe now. Give Miss Hailey my best and tell her that I hope to see her again. Love you, baby."

He hugged her tight. "Why do you keep referring to her as *Miss* Hailey?"

"Because that's how she strikes me. She seems to be the kind of person I wish I could've been at her age: brimming with confidence, sweet but with a tad of sassy spice, and highly respectable. She's what I call a sweet little miss."

Zurich smiled broadly at his mom's description. It mirrored his own of Hailey. "You might not see Miss Hailey before she leaves town, but you will see her again. That's a promise, Mom." He winked at Bernice as he took his leave. "I love you, Bernice Kingdom."

Hand in hand, Hailey and Zurich leisurely strolled the aisles of Just 4 U, a quaint little gift shop located right in the heart of South Padre Island. Hailey's eyes darted here, there, and everywhere as she looked around at all the interesting gift items that the place had to offer. Many of the trinkets for sale had been handmade.

Hailey wandered away from Zurich when the contents of an upright rack caught her eye. A sentimental looked settled in her eyes as she read the item she'd removed from the bracket.

"Look at this, Zurich." Hailey held up a beautiful glass bookmark.

Etched into the beveled glass, at the very top of the bookmark, the writing read: *You Are My Friend*. It then went on to poetically express what a true friend was.

"My very good friend, Alicia Richards, would love to have one of these. Isn't it beautiful? I'll be seeing her again fairly soon."

Zurich took it from her hand and read it. "This *is* beautiful, very elegant. I think your friend should like it a lot. Is she a lifelong friend?"

"No, I didn't meet her until way after I graduated from high school. We're always in touch. Alicia works for the same organization I do. I've known her for seven years now. We began our training at the same time. We actually became fast friends. We had a little mini-reunion, just overnight, up in San Antonio, before I came here. We stayed at the Sheraton on the River Walk, where we giggled and acted silly for the entire night. You two have your love for Texas in common. Alicia's a real Texas cowgirl."

"Sounds like you-all had a blast. If she's a Texas girl, I'm sure I'll like her. Think I'll get a chance to meet her?"

"I hope so. I just don't know when it'll happen, but I promise to work on it."

"That's good enough for me, Hailey, but I won't hold you to a promise that you really don't have any control over. We'll just wait and see what happens."

Hailey smiled at his thoughtfulness, eyeing him with a bit of curiosity. There was something a tad different about Zurich, but she didn't know what. He wasn't in a bad mood, just more of a somber one than normal. She wasn't sure if he'd gone to his mother's for breakfast; since he hadn't mentioned it, she wasn't about to ask him. God forbid that she should open up Pandora's box.

As Zurich turned the rack that shelved the lovely glass souvenirs, he saw that it also held a variety of other ones specially designed for wives, mothers, daughters, sons, and grandparents, and several spiritual ones, like the *Twenty-third Psalm* and *Footprints in the Sand*. The one entitled *Love* especially caught his attention. He quickly removed it from the rack and read it. Before Hailey could see which one he was reading, he put it back in haste and then gave the stand a full turn.

Although the gift shop held countless lovely treasures and an abundance of unique gifts, Hailey ended up buying several of the etched glass keepsakes for family members and several other special people in her life. No matter how many items Hailey looked at when out shopping, she always had a tendency to return to the very things that first caught her eye; this time was no exception. There were times when she'd decide to put her decision off and go back another day to make her purchases, only to find the items sold out, but she wasn't going to take that risk today. The selected gifts were not only perfect for "thinking of you" presents, they said exactly the same kinds of warm, wonderful things that she felt about the intended recipients.

For the next couple of hours Hailey and Zurich wandered aimlessly around the island's shopping district. Before returning to the hotel, they decided to have lunch at a Chinese buffet.

The modest-size restaurant was very clean and boasted the usual Oriental decor of petite colorful lanterns, red leather booths and chairs, and a variety of Chinese figurines and artifacts. Several large Oriental fans done in red, black, and gold graced the four walls. Every imaginable kind of Chinese food was served on the buffet.

Zurich handed Hailey the bottle of soy sauce for her egg rolls. "You were a big hit with my mom, you know." He watched closely for her reaction to his statement.

Her amber eyes lit up like golden flames of fire. "No, I didn't know. She told you that?"

He nodded. "Not in so many words. Just every other

word that came out of her mouth was *Miss Hailey* this and *Miss Hailey* that. She sounds a lot like me."

Hailey gulped hard. "She says it like that, too? Why?"

"Because that's how she sees you. She uses the title in front of your name with the utmost respect. It has nothing to do with mockery. You won her over. She told me to give you her best."

"Oh, wow, that was so sweet of her. I fell in love with all of your family. Everyone was warm and genuine." Hailey's heart fluttered wildly as she thought of the four loving women in Zurich's life. Each of them was a treasure to hold near and dear to one's heart.

"That's who they are." He looked right into Hailey's eyes as he gave a resigned sigh. "I learned some things today that made me feel terribly ashamed of myself. My mother and I had a no-holds-barred conversation this morning. It turns out that you were right about me being unfairly judgmental toward Morgan Cobb. It seems that he's in part responsible for the man I've become. According to my mother, he's not at all the kind of man I thought he was."

Hailey raised both eyebrows. "How's that?"

Zurich explained in painstaking detail the things he'd learned from his mother regarding Morgan Cobb and the integral role he had played in their lives. He told her the entire emotional story without giving way to the emotions he'd been holding back since leaving Bernice's home.

"I hope you're relieved by what you've learned, Zurich. Are you?"

He nodded. "Very much. It's all settled between Mom and me. She has my blessings. On some level I think she may've set me up. She has designated me as the one to tell my brothers the real deal if they start protesting her relationship. You think I've been had by her?"

Hailey's laughter was sparkling. "Simply coincidental. I think whoever was the first to protest landed the job.

You're it! And now it's up to you to tag the next person if you want to pass on the duties."

He laughed, too. "I see your point. To change gears, we don't have much time left here on the island, so what do you want to do tonight? I have something special planned for tomorrow, our last day in paradise. So you get to choose tonight's activities."

Smiling wickedly, she winked at him. "Did you ever locate the missing condom?"

Zurich grinned broadly. "Here you go with the drama! We've run into more active minefields since the day we first met. You'd think we'd be on safe ground by now. To answer your question, you'll have to wait and see. How about you? Are you hoping that I've found it?"

"In a word: Yes!"

Zurich felt in his loins the heat of Hailey's simply spoken word. "Moving on," he said in a joking manner, "What's your pleasure for the early part of the evening?"

"Coward," she mocked. "In another word: Karaoke!"

"You can sing?"

She grinned and winked. "In the words of Zurich Kingdom, you'll have to wait and see."

"I'll look forward to it." For a couple of seconds he eyed her intently. "Can we get serious for a minute?"

She felt nervous under his intense gaze. "Sure, but can we go back to having fun right afterward?"

He smiled. "You bet." Zurich cleared his throat. "Hailey, there are many things that you and I have yet to discuss. I don't know about you, but I'm dreading us parting ways, which will happen in less than forty-eight hours. That's when we'll have to kiss and say good-bye. It's going to be hard. Neither you nor I know what the future holds for us. It's obvious to both of us that we can't make a real commitment to having a long-term relationship."

Zurich leaned forward and covered her hand with his. "There are a host of things that we still need to learn about each other, but that'll all come in due time, as we become more and more comfortable talking about things. However, I'd like you to promise me, only if you can keep it, that we'll stay friends and keep in close contact by phone and mail. Hailey, I want us to stay connected. I need to have you as a part of my life in whatever capacity you can be there." He lifted her hand and kissed the back of it. "Can you do that for me, for us?"

"Oh, I can, Zurich, and I will. I want us to stay connected, too. I promise to write you and call. I don't want us to ever lose touch. We can be friends, even if we find it's too difficult or that there's too much distance for us to be anything else."

"I have plenty of vacation time each year, Hailey, and I have unusual flying privileges."

Hailey toyed with the idea of telling him exactly where her assignment was. After a few moments of deliberation, she decided to leave things as they were. The fear of him recanting what he needed and wanted from her kept her silent. At any rate, he'd find out soon enough. When he got that first letter from another continent, he'd get the message then, loud and clear. Hailey was aware that fear made people come to a lot of unfair conclusions and do things they wouldn't normally think of doing. She was no exception. Fear had a way of binding the heart and destroying the ability to reason even simple matters out with any degree of intelligence.

The man sitting across from her had stolen her heart when she never thought such a thing was possible. She had vowed to never give her heart away, but now it had been taken from her—and without the slightest bit of force. There were so many beautiful things between them, but would their very real fears and numerous acts of secrecy turn their relationship into an ugly, sordid mess? Their time spent apart would surely tell all.

"You look like you have something important to say, Hailey, but you don't know if you should say it or not. Do you want to share what's on your mind?"

"Just thinking of all the things we didn't get to do," she lied. "We didn't go to the water park, or the movies, and you didn't get to go over into Mexico. Our time at the pool and Jacuzzi was also cut short. But even with all that, we packed in quite a few events in the little time we had. We enjoyed the sunrises and sunsets, ate ourselves silly during our romantic dinners and casual lunches, had fun watching the dolphins, froze to death deep-sea fishing while I watched you lose what must've been the biggest fish in the sea. And we shared a magnificent horseback ride on the beach. I'd say we had a pretty fun-filled schedule, nothing like the boring stuff I had planned for my vacation."

Zurich laughed. "We didn't go to the movies, but we did watch a few. You didn't mention the stroll around the grounds or listening to the music at the club and outside. Then we had a few down-sides. J. Smooth came on too strong, I was nearly accosted by a beautiful woman claiming mistaken identity, and we had our differences of opinion over Morgan Cobb. We were literally rained on, and you were nearly run down by a car operated by your personal nemesis. I left home with my American Express card but without a condom, which left us out in the cold after the hottest moment of passion I've ever had. I'd say we've about run the gamut here. I don't know what we can do to top this vacation."

"We can sure try. We still have two nights left."

Laughing, Zurich shook his head. "So we do, Hailey. Sounds like a challenge to me."

While organizing her things for later packing, Hailey gasped as she spotted the brand-new digital camera she'd purchased specifically for this trip. She suddenly realized she hadn't taken a single picture of anything or anyone during her entire vacation. She felt as if she had nothing to show her parents and friends of this beautiful spot in America's Texas.

The one person she definitely wanted several pictures of was Zurich, so she'd have to make sure to take his picture when they got together later in the evening. Deciding to at least take pictures of the fabulous hot spots and other idyllic areas around the hotel resort, she grabbed the camera and her purse and then headed straight out the door.

The elevator ride down to the lobby was smooth and fast. The first person she spotted, unexpectedly, was the hotel deliveryman, the one she'd forgotten to tip when he delivered the package from Zurich. Hailey quickly reached into her purse and pulled out a five-dollar bill, which she offered to the young man without explanation.

He looked at her with a puzzled expression. "What's this for, ma'am?"

Hailey smiled warmly. "For a delivery you made to my room nearly two weeks back. Sorry for the long delay in getting your tip to you. I also want to say thank-you."

He nodded. "Ma'am that was a long time ago. But I do remember now that you've brought it up. It was the basket with the purple cellophane wrapping, right?"

Hailey beamed. "That's the one!"

He handed Hailey back the money. "The guy paid the delivery tip in advance, at the same time he purchased the gift basket. I've already been well taken care of."

Hailey looked stunned. "Unbelievable!"

"That he'd pay the tip in advance?"

"That, too, but I was referring to your honesty. You deserve the extra tip. I insist on you keeping it. Integrity is always worth a reward."

"Thanks, ma'am. I appreciate it."

"You're welcome," Hailey said in parting, rushing to the outdoors.

Out in the courtyard, adjacent to the pool areas, Hailey dropped down on one of the lounges. Thinking of Zurich's many kindnesses filled her. She guessed it wasn't so unusual to pay the tip in advance, but it wasn't something she would've thought to do. It was an act of kindness no matter how you looked at it.

As she went over their earlier conversation in her mind, she couldn't help smiling. He wanted them to stay connected. That he wanted them to remain friends no matter what gave her a good feeling. Zurich was a man of many surprises, a man of great integrity.

Familiar laughter had her looking in the direction it had come from. It surprised her to see Zurich in the Jacuzzi, but it positively stunned her to see who else was in there with him: the woman who'd thrown herself at him on the evening of their first date. She suddenly felt like a spy of some sort, but she also felt as if she was rooted to the spot. Without thinking of the implications of what she was doing, Hailey began taking pictures of Zurich and the very attractive sister. All sorts of things went through her head as the shutter clicked away. She couldn't see Zurich's expressions that clearly, but the flirtatious smile on the woman's creamy brown face left little to interpretation.

"Playpen" came to mind. His having called the resort his playpen instantly came to mind. Could he have been seeing this woman all along? Had the woman only backed away from him because she thought Hailey really was his wife?

As Zurich's laughter rang out loud and clear, Hailey shuddered inwardly.

His laughter hurt her like a hard slap across her face. Abuse came in many forms: physical, mental, and emotional. Right about now she felt emotionally abused. But why she felt that way was inexplainable. Here she was judging something that she wasn't even sure about, just as Zurich had regarding Mr. Cobb. Eyes could be as deceiving as the tongue.

Well, she thought, there was only one way to find out. Approaching them wasn't even an option, but if she acted like she hadn't seen them no one would be any the wiser. With her trusty camera in hand, Hailey began taking pictures of everything in sight. As she edged closer and closer to Zurich and the woman, she hoped she wouldn't have to cut him down after he managed to get himself hung from the tallest tree branch.

Hailey was so intent on taking the pictures and nervous about getting too close that she failed to closely watch her step. When she turned around, backing up to get a wider shot, she lost her footing. As she landed in the Jacuzzi, practically right in Zurich's lap, she wanted to die on the spot. Zurich and the woman's mocking laughter only made her feel worse.

Hailey had made an utter fool of herself and had no one but herself to blame. Indulging in spying as a twenty-seven-year-old woman was bad enough; getting caught at it was mortifying. Thank goodness Zurich had saved her camera.

Hailey tried to climb out of the water, but Zurich pulled her back and settled her onto his lap. "Hold on, Mrs. Kingdom, what's your rush? You're all wet now."

As he turned her around to face him, Hailey's eyes spit bullets at Zurich. "And so are you, Mr. Kingdom. You just have no idea how wet you really are!"

The fact that Zurich had referred to her as "Mrs. Kingdom" let Hailey know that she had been dead wrong in fearing that Zurich had something going on with the other woman, and was playing them both. Deep down inside Hailey had known better from the start—and her utter embarrassment was a small price to pay for daring to doubt him.

Zurich brought Hailey into his arms. As his lips tenderly came into contact with hers, all she could do was gasp wantonly. His firm hold on her grew tighter as his tongue gently worked itself between her clenched teeth. With no strength or desire to resist him, Hailey succumbed to his insistent passion.

Hailey and Zurich were so lost in each other they didn't even see the other woman leave.

* * *

The passion between them had been hot and heavy all the way from the pool, into the elevator, and on the ride up to her floor. Once the door in her suite closed behind them, Zurich had stripped Hailey out of her wet clothes in a matter of minutes.

Slowly backing her down the hallway, Zurich practically two-stepped her into the bedroom. While dancing down the corridor in the buff was almost laughable, what was happening between them was no laughing matter, despite Hailey's euphoric state of mind.

With his forefinger, he lifted her chin and looked into her amber eyes. "You want to undress me so we can be look-alikes?"

A smile spread across Hailey's face as she pushed Zurich back on the bed. Falling on her knees before him, she started by removing the rubber flip-flops he had on his feet. Swimming trunks and a T-shirt were the only other articles of clothing that he wore, unless she counted the towel around his neck. Hailey figured that the wet trunks might be tough to take off, but since they had the rest of the night she wasn't the least bit concerned about time.

Hailey hoped he had a condom this time so she wouldn't have to go through the embarrassment of producing the ones she had purchased. His attire was an indication that he was more than likely condom-less. There wasn't a single visible pocket on his swimwear.

She briefly thought about the promised *karaoke* night in the hotel club. Instead of hearing her voice, Zurich would just have to listen to her body singing sweetly for him. The little voice inside her head told her there would be no turning back. Hailey was sure she wasn't misinterpreting what she was hearing his body saying to hers, or what they both were feeling.

As her body shivered from the cold gust of wind blasting from the air conditioner, he took her into his arms and kissed her until she moaned against his lips. His hand sought out her breast, kneading it tenderly, kissing her breathless all the while. Her legs nearly gave out when his hand came to rest between her legs. As his fingers gently manipulated her moist flesh, Hailey trembled within.

The tip of Zurich's tongue in her ear had her squirming about in his arms. As his hands reached around to stroke and squeeze her firm buttocks, Hailey lost herself in the waves of ecstasy coursing through her. The size of his erection drove her to wild and crazy thoughts of him inside of her, taking her over and over again.

Zurich held her slightly away from him for a couple of seconds, only to bend his head and take an erect nipple into his mouth. While suckling her breast, his fingers gently probed her inner treasure, causing the moisture within her flower to increase. His teeth gently nipped at each of her ears. Then his head lowered and his lips traced the base of her throat with butterfly kisses.

She impatiently waited with bated breath for him to put the condom on. Zurich was finally going to make love to her, and Hailey couldn't be happier about it.

The gentle thrusts of Zurich's body inside of hers brought Hailey untold pleasures. The man was being super-tender, treating her body like it was his own sacred temple; to her it *was* consecrated. It was as if her satisfaction was his main objective. His passionate murmurs and whispered sweet words in her ear only intensified her desire, her need to have all of him. He was an excellent lover, patient and extremely considerate of her emotions.

Hailey thought of a few spine-tingling positions she'd love to try out, but she was content to let him lead. He made her feel extra-special, cherished and loved. As his thrusts went deeper and deeper, Hailey felt as if he was nearly ready to burst forth inside her, and she wanted to be along with him for the ride into sweet oblivion.

Hailey also wanted to sail Zurich right into heaven on a white fluffy cloud. To heighten his need to reach his climax, which would also spur on her own release, Hailey stroked his buttocks and tantalized his spine with the tip of her fingernails. Her tongue sought out his ear as her free hand rubbed the back of his muscular thigh. To Zurich it felt as if her hands were all over his body—and everywhere at once.

As she undulated wildly beneath him, his moans of ecstasy sailed on the air. In the next couple of seconds the pent up pressure inside of them sent their bodies into an uncontrollable frenzy of tremors. Hailey's body danced without restraint to the enchanting tune of Zurich's rocking rhythms as she trembled like crazy beneath him.

The explosive end left them heaving and panting heavily yet happy and utterly content.

Eight

Sunlight streamed in through the open drapery as Hailey lay in her bed, wide-awake. With her head propped up on one elbow, she watched Zurich's chest rise and fall methodically with the peace he appeared to have found in sleep.

Memories of their previous night had her on cloud nine. They hadn't made it out to the club, but they'd had the pleasure of hearing plenty of sweet music. To accompany the harmonious tunes that their bodies had strummed, Zurich had gotten up between lovemaking sessions and put on an Earth, Wind & Fire CD. He'd even ordered a variety of appetizers from room service, which they'd eaten in bed and had taken pleasure in feeding each other.

The night had been perfect—glorious and fulfilling.

Zurich reached up and pulled her head down into the well of his arm. After turning up on his side, he kissed her deeply. "Morning. Did you sleep well?"

She kissed his chin. "I barely slept at all."

He looked concerned. "Are you sick?"

Hailey raised her head slightly and looked down at him. "This girl is as healthy as can be. I lay awake thinking of every detail of our deepest expressions of physical love. I may have dozed off for a minute or two here and there. But then I'd wake up to make sure you were still here and that I hadn't dreamed of our blissful moments together."

"No, baby, you weren't dreaming. Last night is one memory that I'll carry with me forever. Our first time making love was unforgettable for me. I hope you won't forget it either, Hailey."

"Noway, nohow could I ever forget last night, Zurich Kingdom."

He stroked her hair as she rested her head against his chest. "Are you up to going out for breakfast, Miss Hailey?"

She smiled up at him. "Breakfast in bed?"

"I like your idea better. But can we wait an hour or so before calling room service?"

"No problem. You want to sleep a little longer?"

He brought her head to him and kissed her full on the mouth. "More sleep is not on my agenda. You are. Got another condom handy?"

Hailey blushed as she reached over to the nightstand and picked up a foil packet. "I put out a couple of extras just in case we were feeling extra-frisky."

Zurich threw back his head and laughed. "How many of these babies did you buy?"

"A dozen."

He cracked up. "Eight more to use by tomorrow. Girl, we'd better get busy. We have our work cut out for us."

"Work?"

"Bad choice of words, Hailey. If making love to you is work, I'm willing to do double overtime. Am I forgiven?"

Her tongue gently flicked at his lower lip. "I'll let you know after you make love to me."

"You drive a hard bargain, lady."

She wrapped her hand around his stiff manhood. *"Hard* is a word that I like. Now, we'll have to wait to see how deep you're willing to go with your bargaining power."

"Hailey, you have no idea how deep I can go!"

Turning over until she lay flat on her back, she gave him a taunting look. "Show me."

Freshly showered, but dressed only in terry-cloth robes, Hailey and Zurich were having their breakfast in bed—

scrambled eggs, sausage links, cold cereal, fresh fruit, and cinnamon rolls. Both had ordered orange juice, but Zurich was also having coffee. The daily newspaper was on the bed, spread out between them.

"Do you want anything else, Hailey?"

"I'd like to read the daily horoscopes if you're finished with that section."

He handed her the portion of the paper she'd requested. "You really believe in that kind of stuff?"

"Not really. But I do believe that God sends us little messages in all sorts of ways. I've read things in my horoscope that have actually helped me resolve some issues in one way or another. God speaks to us through so many ways. I always keep my ears and eyes open for any visible or audible signs from Him. With that said, what sign are you?"

"Dollar!"

Hailey cracked up at the crafty grin on Zurich's face. "That's funny. I've never heard that one before. I'll have to use it the next time someone asks me my sign. At any rate, I'm an Aquarius. And I do love the water."

He grinned. "Me, too, on both counts. January twenty-sixth."

"February second. Only seven days apart."

"Yeah, but you forgot to tack on the years. How *do* you feel about being involved with a man seven years your senior?"

"Let's just say I like my men mature and sure, without being bores. But I draw the line at anything over a ten-year age difference."

"Why's that?"

Hailey took a sip of her orange juice and set it back down on the nightstand. "I think there's a lot more to consider when there's too much of a difference in age. When I'm sixty, he'll be seventy-one or older if I go over the ten-year limit. I realize age and health aren't synonymous, but health can be a major concern as we grow older. Women also outlive men, according to statistics."

"So if I'm fifty-seven and you're only fifty, you don't see that as a problem?"

She shook her head. "I really don't. I didn't make a big issue out of or even explore it in depth when I decided that ten years was the cutoff, for whatever reason. Maybe I should've put more thought into it, but I didn't."

Zurich stuck his finger into the icing on his cinnamon roll and held it up to Hailey's mouth. Without hesitation, she sucked it from his finger. Their eyes connected in a knowing way as her tongue circled the tip.

"I wanted to taste you in that way last night, but I wasn't sure how you'd respond. Do you think you would've enjoyed it?"

The color in Hailey's cheeks deepened. "I'm all for finding out."

"Do you have any objection to tasting me?"

Hailey lifted an eyebrow. "Maybe we shouldn't discuss it. Spontaneity in foreplay is what works best for me."

Making direct eye contact, he threw up his hands. "I catch your drift. But I'm a man who likes to know his woman's every like and dislike, in and out of the bedroom. Is there something wrong with that?"

Hailey gave a nonchalant shrug. "That's fine. It just seems to me that you're trying to find out if I've ever indulged in oral sex before. That's neither here nor there. What's important in this instance is that each new adventure we share will be our first with each other."

The expression in his eyes showed his fascination with her. "For a female, you're very rational. You seem to operate more on logic than emotion, which is usually a guy thing. I like everything about you, Miss Hailey. And I do mean everything!"

"I like you, too. Whether you know it or not, you've just paid me a very high compliment. Being logical is a good thing. Thank you."

"You're welcome. Is it okay if we get back to the subject of what you like in bed?"

Hailey quickly cleared off the bed. She then stretched out alongside Zurich and gave him her sexiest smile. "Now that I've made the bed a safer haven, I can answer your question." She licked her tongue out, curling up the tip until it touched her upper lip. Slowly, eyeing him intently, she sucked it back in. "Zurich, are you ready for us to indulge in that first taste-test?"

He tugged at her lower lip with his teeth. "Baby, I love to have you threaten me with a good time! Let the testing begin while the sweet flavors are flowing."

Hailey had already laid her clothes out for the evening. She'd had both elegance and comfort in mind when she'd chosen a long black skirt with a discreet split up the side. The delicate top was sprinkled with tiny black pearls that shimmered. She and Zurich had planned to dine in the room by candlelight. They were more desirous to spend time alone than to sit in a restaurant or be inside a club with a lot of people hanging around. Time was precious, and not much of it was left for them.

After grabbing hold of her purse, Hailey made her way to the door. She had a couple of errands to run before getting herself prepared for the evening. A delicious hot soak in a mountain of bubbles would come as soon as she got back to the room. But the first thing on her agenda was to check out the hotel's specialty shops and boutiques where she could purchase a nice gift for Zurich. She wanted him to have something to remember her by. Not that he could ever forget her, she mused, smiling with smug satisfaction. Nor could she ever forget him.

Their morning rendezvous had had enough dangerously hot ingredients to classify it as top secret, a top-secret rendezvous. She remembered telling Zurich that she couldn't wait for them to have their very first top-secret rendezvous. Mission accomplished.

A handsome, charcoal-gray cashmere sweater had been beautifully wrapped for Hailey in a decorative foil paper with a sports theme. As she made her way back to the elevators, the lingerie store, Lacy's Sweet Boutique, suddenly caught her eye. Thinking a sexy gown and robe done in black lace might be even more appropriate for evening wear than the outfit she'd already picked out, Hailey stopped to take a quick glance in the window before going inside.

Hailey's head immediately jerked forward, her eyes bulging, as she spotted Zurich with the same woman from before; the lady was loose on her man again. Twice may've been a coincidence for them to have been seen together, but a third time was ridiculous, especially for two people who claimed not to know each other. What was Zurich playing at? This situation was downright unreal. Jealousy burned in her eyes as she looked on.

As the woman handed Zurich a hot-looking number done in red satin, Hailey's stomach brewed with an acid-churning sickness. It was obvious that he didn't like the chosen lingerie when he frowned. Shaking his head in the negative, he gave it back to her. A few seconds later she handed him a stunning black lace gown and matching robe, something Hailey definitely would've purchased for herself. It was only drop-dead gorgeous, as was Zurich.

As Zurich took the proffered lingerie set and marched toward the counter with it, Hailey died a little inside. Frozen in the spot where she stood, she watched Zurich take out his trusty American Express card and hand it to the clerk. She looked back at the woman, still busy looking through the rack at other choices in flimsy bedtime or after-dark playtime attire. Hailey's issues weren't with the woman. Zurich was the one she'd take issue with.

Even as Hailey hastily made her way to the elevator, her mind was busy forming an appropriate counterattack. The last thing she wanted to do was cancel their evening, but she hoped Zurich didn't think for one second that he was getting one over on her. It came to her mind for a brief second that he might be the one to do the canceling, but she quickly decided not to worry about that unless it happened. On their last night in what he often referred to as paradise, she thought she might have to rename the island. "Hell on Paradise Isle" worked nicely for her. There was no doubt in her mind that she'd tell him she'd seen him with the *other* woman, and in no uncertain terms. But the revelation would have to come later, much, much later.

It was unlike her to play games with anyone, but Zurich had chosen this one; she was simply going to best him at it. She had believed in her heart that she and Zurich had laid all the cards out on the table. But he was no longer playing with the hand that had already been dealt.

Hailey let herself into the room. Soon after storing her purchases in the bedroom closet, she went back out. Putting her plan into action would take very little mental and physical effort. Putting her heart into it was going to take all the strength and willpower that she had.

Although up to her neck in muscle-relaxing hot water and jasmine-scented bubbles, with the bathroom glowing in soft candlelight and soft music dancing on the air, Hailey was still having a hard time giving herself up to the tranquility of her surroundings.

Seeing Zurich with the woman for a third time in such a short period had her plagued with doubt. His helping her choose sexy lingerie was the most irritating of all the incidents. Was she reading too much into what she'd seen? Was there really something clandestine going on between them? It sure seemed that way to her. If she believed Zurich was cheating on her right under her nose, she would have to completely nix the idea of them having a long-distance relationship. It just wouldn't work. Hailey Hamilton was not the type of woman to become any man's number one of two or one of many.

Hailey Hamilton had to be the one and only woman in her man's life, period.

Realizing she wasn't getting the benefit she'd hoped from indulging in a good soak in the tub, Hailey stood up and turned on the shower to rinse the bubbles from her body. She thought of taking a short nap, but there really wasn't time for that. Besides, how would she manage to sleep if she couldn't even relax in the tub? It just wasn't happening as she'd planned.

As she towel-dried her body, she couldn't keep her thoughts from returning to the memories of their first shower together. It had been better than good, superior to fantastic. Zurich knew how to find and arouse every sensitive spot on a woman's body, at least on hers. The crisp shower spray pinging against her breasts was nipple arousing enough, but Zurich's tender mouth suckling on one while the water electrified the other had been one incredible experience. There wasn't a single spot on her body that Zurich hadn't stimulated in one way or another.

The unforgettable grand finale had taken her to a place somewhere in paradise, far beyond rapture, a place she couldn't wait to return to with him. Their shattering climax had come while he'd held her tightly in his arms, her back against the shower wall and her legs wrapped high up around his waist. Had she been standing, Hailey was positive her legs would've given out on her. She was still trembling even after he'd stood her on her feet a few minutes later.

As she massaged lotion into her body, she recalled the way he had oiled down her skin after he'd dried her off. He had this delightful fetish of loving to kiss and caress each and every inch of her anatomy before he dotted it with the lotion, even her toes. She blushed as she thought of the unmentionable tender places he loved to pay very special attention to. His way of handling her was slow, gentle, and deliberate as he delivered extreme care to her flesh.

An almost quiet knock came on the door. For a reason Hailey didn't understand, it felt as if the hairs on her neck were standing at attention. Sure that it wasn't Zurich, Hailey put her bathrobe on and tied the belt tight. At the door, she put her ear to it and listened for any outside noises. None came. "Who's there?"

"Delivery service."

Remembering Zurich's perfume gift basket, Hailey smiled, wondering what thrilling surprise he'd sent her now. Without another concern, she flung the door back. Adrenaline began to pump wildly through her veins as she saw what appeared to be a human bulldozer coming straight at her.

Before she could act, the door slammed shut and her escape route was blocked by the drunken, abusive man who'd caused her nothing but problems since she first laid eyes on him in the hotel club: "J. Smooth." At the moment, his real name eluded her.

His eyes were red and swollen. He was so close to her she could smell the stench of stale liquor mingled with tobacco on his breath. Getting him to back away was her first task. He obviously hadn't had enough of her yet. Her eyes quickly darted around the room for something to defend herself with if her hands and feet weren't able to render him helpless. She spotted on the coffee table the cigarette lighter she used to light candles.

"Who's gonna' help you now, Ms. Bruce Lee?" he slurred. "No woman makes a fool out of me and lives to tell about it. I've been watching and waiting for you to be alone. Your man ain't here to save you now. I'm gonna' show you what a man does to a disrespectful woman."

You must've forgotten that my man didn't save me before. She didn't think it was a good idea to get into a conversation with him at this point. It would be better to let him do all the talking. That way, he wouldn't know what she was thinking or doing. For her to remind him that she'd already taken him out once would only agitate him more. She already had enough to contend with, and she didn't want to add any more fuel to the fire.

"Cat got your tongue?"

Hailey looked around for her cell phone. Then she remembered it was in the bedroom.

He came closer and Hailey immediately backed away. Each step she took backward, he took one forward. The only thing on Hailey's mind was to get to the cigarette lighter. He was drunk and she felt sure she could take him, but with the lighter in her hands her defense would be strengthened. Hailey had to make a slight turn in order to get over to the coffee table.

Just as she made the barely noticeable turn, he lunged at her. She sidestepped him, and his forward momentum caused him to stumble halfway across the room. Quicker than greased lightning, Hailey had the lighter in her hand.

The look in his eyes frightened her only because of what extent she might have to go to in order to take him down. Hailey knew she would kill before allowing herself to be killed. But she couldn't let him see any signs of fear in her. She took several unnoticeable deep breaths to keep the panic at bay. People like him could smell fear in a woman, which probably made him successful as an intimidator. He had been drunk when he'd accosted her before—he was drunk now. She figured he hadn't been able to determine that she wasn't the type to be intimidated.

Hailey stood stock-still as he came at her again. She allowed him to get right up on her before she ignited the lighter and shoved it in his face. His hair caught fire first, and then she held it up to his shirtsleeve. While he was screaming and jumping around trying to put the flames out, Hailey took him down hard. Her foot then connected several times with his private area for good measure. His screams rocked the air before he passed out. Sure that she'd put him totally out of commission, Hailey ran and got several bottles of water out of the refrigerator. After opening one container, she poured it on his shirt, which was only smoldering slightly. Whatever he had in his hair had really fueled the fire, and she poured a full bottle of water on his head to make sure all the flames were out. She then called hotel security.

Once security took a report from Hailey, they wished her well and left her alone to deal with the aftermath. Corbin Whitehall, "J. Smooth," had long since been carted off on a stretcher by the local EMT team. They'd offered to transport her to the hospital or call a doctor for her, but she'd declined. Hailey felt just fine.

The only ordeal she'd really suffered was the shock of seeing him rushing into her space. As far as she was concerned, he hadn't ever posed a real threat to her. He hadn't showed her a weapon; that alone had allowed her to feel that she could maintain control. "J. Smooth" was a drunk and an abuser, but he'd twice proved to be no match for her.

As Hailey pondered the incredible events of the last hour, she decided that it was best not to tell Zurich what had happened during their last evening together. She would tell him on the way to the airport in the morning, since he'd offered to drive her. They already had enough unfinished business to deal with. The J. Smooth story could wait since no real harm had come to her.

With his feet propped up on the coffee table in his suite, Zurich was talking on the phone with one of his best friends from Buckley Academy, Haughton Storm. Haughton was slightly older, and had graduated a few years before Zurich. Because Zurich was mature beyond his years back then, the older guys had accepted him into their small, intimate group of star athletes.

Haughton laughed into the phone. "How did that happen,

and so quickly, my man? I just left your side not too long ago. You certainly work fast."

"I don't know. One minute I was offering to buy her a drink and the next minute I was dreading the end of our vacation. We laid down a lot of ground rules in the beginning, but neither of us has been able to stick to them. The girl is beautiful and smart. I'm in big trouble, brother."

"Why do you say that?"

"Man, you're on active duty in the military, so you should know all the problems that come with trying to have a meaningful relationship. You also know that I don't think the military and marriage can mix well for me. One bride at a time has always been my motto. I have yet to tell Hailey what I do for a living. She hasn't revealed her career field either—and she's as secretive about her job as I am. The question I want to ask you is if I should tell her the truth and let the chips fall wherever."

"Kingdom, I can't make that decision for you. Can you trust her with the truth of what profession you're in?"

"Hailey is very trustworthy, Storm. I'm just afraid that my career may turn her off. You know how unpredictable this man's military is. All she knows is my home of record and just a little about how quickly things can change for me. She's going to a new job location, but she hasn't even told me where, and I sense some reluctance on her part to do so. The only addresses we've exchanged are to our parents' places, a sure way to make contact no matter where we end up. Wherever it is, we're going to have to try and maintain a long-distance relationship. Is that even possible in today's crazy world, man?"

"Do you love her?"

Zurich grunted. "I wish you hadn't gone there, Storm."

"Why not?"

"Because I'm not so sure I'm *in* love, but I do love her. Hailey's a special woman. The only thing I'm sure about is that I don't want us to lose contact." Zurich sighed hard. "Who the hell am I fooling? I'm so in love with her I don't dare think about a life without her. But, Storm, there's another not-so-little problem. I hope your ears can stay tuned in just a wee bit longer."

Feeling both excited and apprehensive, but completely over her earlier ordeal, Hailey dressed with special care for her last evening with Zurich, paying very close attention to her hair and make-up. As part of her last-minute preparations, Hailey sprayed her pulse points with Tresor.

Her bets were still on Zurich when his integrity came into question. If there was a plausible explanation for what she'd witnessed, repeatedly—him with the woman, she felt certain that he'd come clean if she were to pointblank ask him to. Although she still intended to put her clever plan into action, she hoped it would be all for naught. However, his reaction would tell the story.

All an earthworm knew how to do was squirm—but she hoped that Zurich wouldn't make the slightest wiggle.

Zurich's familiar knock came on the door just as Hailey reached the front of the suite. Showtime or showdown? She prayed it wasn't the latter. Without pretense, Hailey greeted him with a smile and a passionate kiss. As usual, his attire was nothing short of simple elegance. The man sure knew which clothes best accentuated his muscular physique. He seemed to love darker colors, which was evident in the navy blue pants and shirt he wore. His linen sports coat was done in shades of navy, burgundy, and camel.

Zurich kissed the tip of her nose. "You look like someone I'd love to be seen with on a regular basis. Your outfit is gorgeous. You're sure-enough working that side split. You look hot enough to keep me steaming, Miss Hailey."

Hailey laughed. "Thanks, I think." She made a gesture toward the sofa. "Let's have a seat. Room service isn't scheduled to deliver our meal for another ten minutes or so. Are you as hungry as I am?"

"I haven't eaten since our little breakfast-in-bed tryst. I'm ready to chow down." His expression grew sentimental. "I've missed you, Hailey."

"Even though we've only been apart a few hours, I missed you, too."

He hugged her tight. "Go ahead and sit down, Hailey. I'm going to light the candles for us. I see you have a couple of new ones. Been shopping, huh?"

Hailey perched herself on the arm of one of the chairs in the living room. *I'm not the only one who's been shopping.* "I purchased them in the gift shop earlier today. Once the votives have burned down, I'll clean the frosted glass holders and put them away. They're small enough to pack in between the softer items inside my suitcase so that they don't break."

Zurich didn't have a chance to seat himself before the food arrived. Hailey had excused herself for a moment, which meant that he had to get the door. After all the dinner items were set on the table, Zurich had a brief chat with the waiter. He then gave the middle-aged man a hefty tip to show his gratitude for such great service. The second Hailey returned, Zurich pulled out a chair for her. He then seated himself. This time, Hailey offered the blessing.

Tender breasts of chicken simmered in golden mushroom sauce with wild rice and fresh snow peas served as the main entree. A clear glass bowl held iceberg lettuce and red cabbage garnished with cherry tomatoes and thin slices of sweet red onion. A loaf of freshly baked sourdough bread and whipped butter accompanied the meal.

After Zurich placed his napkin across his lap, he poured two glasses of chardonnay. "Everything sure smells good. Since it's something we haven't discussed, I'd like to know if you've got any skills in the kitchen," Zurich said.

"Serious ones, if I may say so myself. I don't get many opportunities to show off my culinary skills, but I can definitely put a smile on a person's face. What about you? I bet you sure know how to throw down in the kitchen."

"Bernice Kingdom taught her boys to cook at an early age. No shame in my game! Like you, I don't get to rustle up the grub often enough. But I can make you hurt yourself on my soul food. What's your best dish?"

"I guess I could say buttermilk fried chicken. It's my dad's recipe, but I've perfected it. My pot roast is easy enough to fix; I simply throw the vegetables and beef in a cooking bag and slow-roast them. But the delicious gravy I whip up makes it heavenly; cream of mushroom soup simmering in the natural juices of the meat helps to tenderize it."

He looked pensive. "I'm hoping that in the very near future we'll get to have dinner at one of our places. But from all indications, it may be a while. Hopefully our schedules will click before too long." He lifted his wineglass to propose a toast. "Here's to that upcoming dinner. It doesn't matter which one of us prepares it. I just want it to happen."

She clinked her glass with his. "Me too."

Hailey realized she'd missed out on another opportunity to tell Zurich where she'd be living; fear had once again caused her to pass on it. She still planned to tell him in her first letter. Hoping he'd understand her reasons for not telling him sooner, she made a silent promise to pen the letter before leaving the States.

Hailey and Zurich had danced to several romantic, slow songs before she'd slipped away to change into something comfortable. Anxiously, Zurich kept a watchful eye on the bedroom door while waiting for her to reappear. Every single second counted. Nervously tapping his feet, he looked at his watch. Her early morning flight to Florida was less than thirteen hours away. He didn't know where all the time had gone; he just knew that it was rapidly disappearing.

Hailey's hands trembled as she practically tore herself out of her clothing, but she managed to make quick work of things. After another light dabbing of Tresor to her pulse points, she was off to where he waited for her.

The stunned look on his face caused her heartbeat to slightly falter. The deep scowl told her all that she needed to know. Her spirit sank as she saw the look of deep disappointment in his eyes. That she wore the same exact robe and gown that he'd purchased for the woman had affected him greatly. His entire demeanor was a dead giveaway.

She sat down on the sofa, but at the opposite end from him. "What's wrong, Zurich? Don't you like what I'm wearing? I picked it out with you in mind." Relieved that she'd kept the sarcasm out of her remark, she sighed with discontent.

Zurich quickly recuperated from his initial shock. "As a matter of fact, I love it. I couldn't have made a better choice for you myself. Scoot over here so I can enjoy it up close." He was puzzled by why she'd seated herself so far away from him, but he didn't pass comment.

As Hailey drew closer to him, he lifted her up and placed her onto his lap. His nose nuzzled her neck and ears. "You smell as good as you look. I'm glad you like the perfume I gave you. I'm flattered that you choose to wear it when we're together. Let's get dessert out of the way so I can begin to feast on you."

Hailey smiled, but she felt totally empty inside. Zurich had played everything off like it was no big deal, like he wasn't bothered by what she had on. There was no mistake about his immediate recognition of the lingerie she wore, no doubt that he'd been stunned by it. If only she could get inside his head and know what he was really thinking.

Zurich lifted Hailey and placed her on the sofa. He then went over to the table, retrieved the silver-domed dessert tray, and carried it back to where she sat. "Here's your dessert. I had it whipped up especially for you. I hope you like it. But I have a feeling you're going to love it."

Hailey's fingers shook as she lifted the top from the tray. Instead of the delicious-looking dessert she had expected to find, she found the exact replica of the black lace gown and robe she had on. Zurich had brought the lingerie set for her, not for the other woman. Hailey felt downright foolish for the way she had set herself up. Doubting Zurich was inexcusable. The only way to redeem herself was to tell him the reason why she had on the same articles of lingerie he'd obviously purchased as a gift for her.

He unfolded the lace set and held it up. "I see that I'm not the only one who thought this outfit was perfect for you. You're not going to believe this, but I ran into Jillian Carter while I was in the lingerie shop. She sort of helped me pick this out for you. Jillian is the same woman I first met in the gift shop, the one from the strange encounter in the area near the club. I asked for her advice because I've never before purchased intimate apparel for a woman. Some of the things she recommended were distasteful to me, but this one had your name written all over it. I guess I don't have to ask if you like it. I'll take this sexy one back and pick out something else for you. But I'll have to send it to you since you'll already be in the sky when the shop opens. Unless you'd rather have the money to reimburse yourself for the one you have on."

Hailey kissed Zurich on the mouth as she lightly fingered the lace sleepwear. "Thanks for such a lovely gift, Zurich. Sorry I put a damper on your surprise package. Hiding it under a serving dish was an excellent way to present it. You're very creative. I like your style. I think I'll keep it for a future rendezvous. A girl can't ever have too many sexy nightgowns."

Looking downcast, Hailey thought of the right words to tell him what she'd suspected him of. Then she remembered the gift she'd gotten for him. Happy for the temporary stay, she immediately jumped to her feet. "I'll be right back."

In a matter of seconds Hailey came back into the room

carrying her wrapped gift. Smiling sweetly, she handed the package to him. "I hope you like it, Zurich."

His eyes connected with hers. "I'll love it just because you bought it for me."

Zurich did love the sweater, but not only because she'd given it to him. It was beautiful and he was sure he hadn't seen another one like it anywhere else. He held it up to his chest. "Looks like a perfect fit. Thank you, Hailey. I'm going to think about you every time I wear it." He leaned over and kissed her cheek. "Now that we've exchanged gifts, you can tell me what's wrong. You're uncomfortable about something. Besides the troubling storm brewing in your eyes, you've darn near twisted your thumb off. Was the gown too intimate of a gift from me?"

She shook her head. "It's nothing like that. I have a confession to make." She swallowed the lump forming in her throat. "I doubted you in the worst way, Zurich. I saw you today in the lingerie shop with . . . uh . . . what's-her-name? I thought you were buying the gown for her since I'd seen you two together twice before. I began to believe you might be a cheater and a liar, thought you two were somehow intimately involved. I was wrong and I'm terribly sorry for mistrusting you, Zurich. But I'm glad I was badly mistaken, not that it's any comfort to you."

"Might be, Hailey? This is something I wouldn't have guessed at from you." He looked hurt. "I have spent practically every waking moment with you for the last two weeks, so when did I have time to cheat on you and lie to you? How did you ever manage to come to such a unsavory conclusion?" He held up his hands. "Maybe you shouldn't answer that 'cause I don't think I want to know. In fact, I'm sure of it. It can only deepen the hurt I feel."

Her eyes burned like crazy from her need to shed the tears she'd been holding back for the longest time. In hurting him, she had also hurt herself. He hadn't deserved her mistrust; that had been proven beyond a shadow of a doubt. She reached for his hand, only to have him rebuff her attempt to touch him. He had instantly withdrawn his hand from her grasp.

Looking troubled, Zurich got to his feet. Without so much as a glance at Hailey, he walked across the room and stood in front of the window. His breath caught at the magnificent sight of the orange sun as it began to bow in preparation for its final descent. This was an awesome moment, one that he should be sharing with Hailey instead of standing at the window alone sulking over something he couldn't ever change.

As he thought back on the few times Hailey had seen him with Jillian, his heart began to soften: in the lobby outside the bar, the Jacuzzi, the lingerie shop. He could now see how she'd think they might be involved, but that didn't stop him from wishing Hailey's belief in him was much stronger than what she'd displayed. Perhaps he hadn't done his job in convincing her otherwise.

After turning to face her, he stretched out his hand. "We have an awesome sunset about to take place over here. Please come join me, Hailey. I want us to share this moment wrapped up in each other's arms. This is our last sunset on the island. We don't want to miss out on it."

Although she had a hard time believing her own ears, Hailey wasn't going to waste any time second-guessing her hearing, especially not when Zurich's outstretched hand indicated that she'd heard him right. He wanted her to watch the sunset with him, and by his side was exactly where she longed to be.

The moment Hailey reached him, he took her in his arms. Forgiveness for her serious misjudgment of his character was ablaze in his eyes. After kissing her gently on the mouth, he turned so that they both faced the window. As he stood directly behind her, resting his chin atop her head, his hands spanned her tiny waist.

Basking in the strength and the security of his embrace, Hailey tilted her head back until it made contact with his chest. She then covered his hands with her own and laced their fingers together. Glad that he'd forgiven her, she gave a quiet prayer of thanks.

In the romantic candlelit setting of her hotel suite, happy to be in one another's arms, they watched the sun slowly go down. Zurich's hands tightened against her abdomen when he heard her deep sigh of contentment.

With her back planted firmly against the front of his body, Zurich gently nibbled on her ears and neck as his hands caressed the flat of her abdomen. Hailey began to melt under his heated touch. As his hands gradually inched her gown up around her thighs, she trembled within from the eager anticipation of what was likely to happen. His hands remained tender while massaging her, but the rub-down grew in intensity. His hardened maleness could be felt as his body slightly gyrated against her firm buttocks. As his lips sprinkled juicy kisses along her collarbone and shoulders, his hands kneading her breasts all the while, Hailey's legs began to weaken. By the time his fiery hands found their way to the soft flesh between her inner thighs, the muscles all over her body had jellied. As he drew her lace panties down over her legs, Hailey felt as if she had to suck in several deep breaths just to stay conscious.

Reaching around behind her was awkward, and Hailey's hands fumbled a bit until they found the buckle on his belt, which she instantly unbuckled. Through a few clever maneuvers on her part, his zipper came down next. Although it was a difficult operation for her to execute with her back to him, she reached inside his zipper and freed his manhood through the opening in his slacks. For several moments, tenderly, she stroked the sides of his erection. Then her delicate hand wrapped completely around his hardened flesh while her roving thumb vigorously stimulated his manhood.

While their positions were somewhat awkward, the mounting pleasures derived from the exhilarating foreplay left them unable to quell their raging desire to come together as one. Zurich carefully dropped down to the floor. With one rapid-fire motion, he removed his pants and briefs. His shirt came off next, followed by his socks and shoes. He made quick work of removing one of Hailey's remaining condoms from his wallet.

He then drew Hailey down onto his lap, where he continued to probe her sweetness with his fingers and mouth. After raising himself into a sitting position, Zurich lifted Hailey up and then positioned his latex-protected manhood at the opening of her moist flower. Slowly, he drew her down onto his throbbing organ. In completing the delicate act of penetration, he gently thrust himself forward until he was deep inside of her.

With Zurich's burgeoning sex locked deeply into her treasure cove, Hailey lifted her arms high up over her head for him to remove her gown. She couldn't even remember the moment when he'd removed her robe, but it had somehow disappeared.

As his burning desire for her went berserk at the sight of her nakedness, his mouth hungrily sought out her nipples, suckling and laving them until each stood erect beneath his tongue. Using the pads of his forefinger and thumb, he massaged her soft flesh. She moaned and writhed from the exotic delights of his pleasure-evoking mouth and hands. More than ready for whatever he had in mind for them, Hailey wrapped her arms around Zurich's neck.

At three A.M. Zurich awoke Hailey with gentle kisses to her bare back. "I'm going to miss you, sweet Hailey. What am I to do without you, lady?"

At the delicious sound of his deep voice, she quickly rolled over and went straight into his arms. Smiling, she looked into his eyes. "What are we going to do without each other? I'll miss you, too, Zurich. I've grown very attached to you."

"That's good, since I'm feeling the same way about you.

Over the past few days, I've made several attempts to define my feelings for you. It hasn't been an easy assessment. That's why I discussed our relationship with one of my friends. After listening to me go on and on about us, he eventually asked me if I was in love with you." Zurich told Hailey the first answer he'd given to Haughton Storm. "Then I confessed the truth to him, Hailey. Told him that I was so much in love with you that I didn't dare think of life without you. I do love you, Hailey."

Hailey gulped hard. "Love! What a meaningful word, though often abused, misused, understated, overstated, and overrated. I've been around love all my life; my parents' love for each other is one wonderful example. But I've also been around hate masquerading as love, seen it firsthand. Kelly and Will's relationship was a perfect example of that."

Hailey fought hard to hold back the surging sorrow she felt over Kelly's death. Kelly had loved and lost, but it didn't have to turn out that way for her. Thanks in part to the loving and kind ways of Zurich, Hailey was pretty sure that she'd never allow herself to become a victim of domestic violence, unwittingly or otherwise. Zurich had taught her to trust in romantic love. But could he help her get over the guilt of feeling responsible for the significant part she played in her friend's death? On some level of her psyche, Hailey didn't think she deserved to be happy when Kelly would never experience joy again.

Yet she owed it to both herself and Zurich to give their love a serious try.

Her amber eyes held love and tenderness as she looked at Zurich. "I've finally decided that I can't let others' experiences with love, good or bad, continue to jade my way of thinking. I admit to lots of uncertainty, and to having entertained numerous negative thoughts about romantic liaisons. Because of that negativity, I also misjudged you and then dared to unjustifiably question your character. You've altered my opinions of being in love, and you've also changed me on the inside, Zurich Kingdom. I know we have a few obstacles ahead of us, but we're both strong individuals, with even stronger wills. We can work all of this out if it's truly what we both want. As confessions go, here is mine. I love you, too, Zurich, very much."

He gazed into her eyes and caressed her cheek with the back of his hand. "I'm not going to try and explain to you how happy I am that you're in love with me. I want us to spend the rest of our time showing each other just how deep our feelings run." He took a momentary glance at the clock. "For me to get you there in time for your flight, we need to leave for the airport around six o'clock. Until then, we're going to indulge ourselves in a lot of showing and telling."

Nine

Seated at the passenger terminal at Rhein Main Air Force Base in Germany, Hailey waited for her unit sponsor to arrive. Even though several days had come and gone Hailey, felt sicker than a rabid dog as she, only for the hundredth time, thought back on what she'd seen in the lobby of the ticketing and baggage check-in counter at the airport in Harlingen, Texas. All through her brief, four-day stay in Florida with her parents she hadn't been able to think of anything but the emotional devastation she'd experienced during her final moments with Zurich Kingdom.

She knew that there was no future for her and Zurich because of what he did for a living. When he'd accidentally dropped his wallet on the floor, his easily recognizable U.S. Air Force identification card had come into plain view.

It wasn't just the ID card; the gold leaf cluster pinned on the inside of his wallet was the real culprit. The gold leaf cluster represented the rank of major, O-4. From all indications it appeared that Zurich Kingdom was a military officer in the United States Air Force.

If he had realized she'd seen the ID card, perhaps they could've talked about the serious ramifications before she passed through the security checkpoint, an area which he hadn't been allowed to enter because of all the recent airport security measures. Unfortunately, he hadn't noticed the ID card or the look of shock she was sure her face must've revealed. There was no way that she and Zurich could be involved in any sort of relationship, romantic or otherwise.

Air Force Policy Directive 36-29 addressed fraternization between an officer and a noncommissioned officer. Zurich was an officer, and she was enlisted. While there were a variety of issues covered in the Air Force Policy Directive, the gist of the directive was very clear to her. Air Force Instructions 36-704 addressed the disciplinary measures for violation, which ran the gamut from a simple verbal warning to, in severe cases, court martial. Fraternization was a serious infraction of the military code of justice.

Their love affair was forbidden, plain and simple. When they'd first met, they hadn't been aware of each other's military service or status, but that wouldn't matter if they continued to see each other now that one of the members was aware of it. Her possession of the knowledge pertaining to their ranks dictated what action she and Zurich must take from here on in. Otherwise, they'd be in violation of said directive, which was subject to punishment.

Tears came to her eyes every time she realized she had to give up the man she loved.

The nature of the letter she had written to reveal to Zurich where she'd be living had already been changed to a farewell note: "nice while it lasted," a *Dear John* so to speak.

Hailey wiped the tears from her eyes. It would be terribly embarrassing for her sponsor to catch her crying. As a proud seven-year veteran of the United States Air Force, the last thing she wanted to portray were any signs of weakness, especially in front of a colleague. This was a new duty assignment for her and she wasn't about to put anything but her best foot forward, the same as she'd always done throughout her military career. Her service record was extraordinary.

A very attractive young woman wearing an Air Force uniform suddenly plopped down on the seat that was back-to-back to the one Hailey occupied. She then turned and tapped Hailey on the shoulder. "I'm here to pick up Staff Sergeant Hailey Hamilton. Would you happen to be her?"

The familiar voice caused Hailey to turn with a start. Seeing her dear friend, the stunning Alicia Richards, seated directly behind her came as a big shock. "Staff Sergeant Richards, what the heck are you doing here at the terminal?" Hailey screeched, reaching across the seat to hug her friend.

Alicia laughed heartily. "Picking you up! Are you ready to go?"

Hailey was delighted to see her close friend. Alicia possessed a warm brown complexion and stood around five-seven. She kept her nutmeg-brown hair extremely short and wavy, but she wore it so well. She had a friendly smile and a great figure. Alicia also had a refreshing sense of humor, one that wouldn't quit. She was the same age as Hailey, twenty-seven. The two women had become instant friends during basic training at Lackland Air Force Base in San Antonio, Texas, where Alicia was actually born and raised. Alicia was a bona fide Texan.

Like Hailey's, Alicia's father was also a retired military officer, but both men had begun military service as enlisted members. Following in the footsteps of their dads, both women had enlisted in the Air Force after completing only two years of college. Each had recently earned their college degrees while on active duty. Alicia was assigned to the base hospital as a pharmacy technician and was close to realizing her goal of becoming a pharmacist. All the things that the two women had in common were very instrumental in the instant bond of friendship that they'd easily formed.

Once Hailey walked the aisle and came around to face Alicia, the women embraced again. "I didn't expect you for a couple of weeks. How you'd manage to pull this one off?"

"The girl's got skills! But since I talked your sponsor

into letting me pick you up, you're stuck with me. I wanted to keep my date of arrival as a surprise. I wasn't sure if your sponsor would go for me picking you up in place of her, but she did."

"So you knew you were reporting to the base earlier when we were in San Antonio?"

Alicia nodded. "I did, but I haven't been here that long. Keeping it as a surprise was hard, but I managed. Knowing the unit you were assigned to made it easy for me to find out your sponsor. Technical Sergeant Lila Briggs was really nice about the whole thing. Let's get going, Hailey. We can chat in the car. I want to hear all about your time on the island. You have a certain glow about you, one that I haven't seen on you before. There has to be a man involved in this new look."

Hailey moaned inwardly. Her stay on the island had been the most exciting time she'd ever had in her entire life. Meeting Zurich Kingdom, the man who simply had it all, and then falling in love with him, was one of the best things that had ever happened to her. Their last night on the island was breathtaking, practically unbelievable. Zurich had shown her the time of her life. The man had made love to her in so many delicious ways, ways she'd never dreamed of.

But she wasn't eager to talk about how it had to end. The unfathomable pain was fresh and raw. Having Alicia to confide in was a mixed blessing. Transitions were always difficult to adjust to, but actually knowing someone at a new duty assignment normally helped to make the move a bit easier. Arriving at a new place with a severely broken heart only served to further complicate matters for Hailey.

Nonetheless, Hailey still had to report for duty, and she had to be both mentally and physically prepared to execute her duties, which, for now, had to remain her top priority in life.

* * *

During the drive to the other side of the base, where the Air Force Inn and other airmen living quarters were located, Hailey went into great detail about her two-week stay on beautiful South Padre Island. As she told Alicia about the new man in her life, Hailey positively glowed. Her feelings for Zurich were apparent in her every breath.

"Zurich is a wonderful man. He's the only man who's ever been able to make me reassess my views on love and romantic relationships. He makes me feel so good about life in general. I feel really blessed to have met him." Hailey went on to tell Alicia about all the magnificent and romantic adventures she and Zurich had experienced while on the island.

"Ugh, living in a base hotel room for a minute doesn't appeal to me. I just recently left a luxury one." Hailey dropped down on the double bed. "But I have to admit that this one is really nice. I can't believe they won't have a dorm room for me for a couple of weeks. But I should know by now to always expect the unexpected when in transition."

Alicia seated herself in the wing chair. "Welcome to our great way of life!" Both Hailey and Alicia laughed. "I'm just joking. The Air Force *is* and has definitely been a great way of life for me, and I wouldn't give it up for anything in the world. As for the dilemma with quarters, I might have a solution for you, but you'll still have to be in the hotel for a short while. You can move in with Staff Sergeant Kila Billings and me. We work at the base hospital together. We've put a deposit down on this great three-bedroom apartment off base. Our quarters allowance and cost of living allowance are more than enough to pay for it. But if we split the rent three ways, we can all have more shopping and travel money. What do you think about the idea?"

"It's a great one for someone who can live with other

people. I'm afraid I'm not good at sharing space, but you already know that. You also know that I'm not as neat as I should be, clean as a whistle, but definitely not neat. Besides, I need to be alone for a while to sort things out. My broken heart will more than likely make me horrible company for months to come. That wouldn't be fair to anyone, especially not you and your future roommate."

"I'm sorry for what happened to you just before you left the island. It's a hurting thing to have come about after you two had such a glorious time with each other. Zurich sounds like a truly wonderful guy. But I wouldn't give up on the relationship just yet. There are still lots of options out there for you guys. Also, you're still waiting on the special letter that could easily solve all of your problems."

Hailey frowned. "That's certainly a long shot. But you're right. I have to weigh all my options. Since Zurich and I are living so far apart, it might not be as big a problem as I'm imagining. But I know I have to come clean with him as soon as possible. I deeply regret not saying something at the airport. It didn't seem appropriate when we were already suffering because we had to tell each other good-bye."

"I got the visual. I know it must've been hard on both of you. But you can always get out when your enlistment is up if your dream goal doesn't come through. Of course, you have to at least meet your three-year commitment, since you accepted an overseas assignment. I have one more suggestion regarding your living arrangements. Why don't you apply for an apartment in the same building I'm moving into? There's also a two-bedroom that'll be available at the same time the three-bedroom is ready. It's right across the hall from mine. There are only four apartments to begin with, two on each level, and the owners live in one of the ones on the ground floor. Will that work better for you, Hailey?"

"Sounds like you've been busy. It's a super plan. When can you take me to see it?"

"You need to get some rest after such a long flight, but first thing tomorrow morning is good for me. I'll call the landlord and ask him to please hold it until you see it. Herr and Frau Schuller are really nice people. You'll like them. When are you scheduled for base orientation?"

"Not until Tuesday. I have the entire weekend and Monday to acclimate. I already did the international driver's license application through Triple A, so I don't have to go through that portion of it. Since tomorrow is Saturday, I certainly don't want to infringe on your time if you have the day off. We can go see the place on Monday."

"Don't give it another thought, Hailey. I have it off, but nothing important is scheduled. Besides, we need to act on the apartment as soon as possible. This is a super-hot property. Off-base housing is extremely difficult to come by these days. I'm just hoping the owners haven't already rented it out. So, taking all that into consideration, are we on for tomorrow morning?"

"You bet! Thanks for going to all the trouble of arranging to pick me up, Alicia. I can't tell you how glad I am that we were able to get assignments on the same base for the next three years. I'm thrilled! At this difficult time, knowing that you're here is one huge comfort."

"Glad to hear that, sweetie. Don't hesitate to call on me for anything. I'm going to run now so you can shower and rest. You'll find me right downstairs in the lobby at 0900. See you then, Hailey." Alicia warmly embraced Hailey as her final farewell.

Throughout the rest of the previous day and evening, no matter what Hailey had tried to do to take her mind off Zurich—reading, watching television, writing in her journal, even meditating—nothing had worked thus far. She had even taken a brisk walk around the hotel and the outside grounds before retiring for the night. Nothing had helped to ease the agony of missing him so much.

Every minute detail of their brief love affair was still so vivid in her mind. It was as if she could feel his every touch and taste their every kiss. Mentally blocking out the lovemaking sessions had proved impossible. Locking him out of her heart was just not going to happen, not ever. The memory of those glorious two weeks was imprinted on her brain.

Their reluctance to talk about their professions and other important aspects of their private lives all made sense to her now. They had merely been practicing extreme caution, which was just a part of the drastic changes that had occurred because of September eleventh. Why she hadn't immediately guessed that Zurich was in the military eluded her. She didn't have to think back on it to recall how he'd carried himself with military dignity and pride. Zurich was an officer and a gentleman. As she took a minute to think about how he'd reacted so strangely when she'd called him "commander," the reason for his reaction suddenly became crystal clear to her.

Hailey had been right all along. While she hadn't experienced this kind of love firsthand, she'd been around enough romantic relationships to know that being in love did hurt, a lot, under both good and bad circumstances. She couldn't help thinking of the hurt Kelly had suffered in the name of love. The pain of Zurich being torn from her arms by an Air Force policy directive, one that she didn't fully understand, yet must respect, was deeper than she could adequately express.

Fraternization between a military officer and a noncommissioned officer was a definite no-no.

Deciding to eat a light breakfast in the cafeteria, Hailey grabbed her purse and headed for the door. Alicia wasn't due to arrive for another hour and a half, which meant she had plenty of time, especially since the cafeteria was located only a few yards from the hotel entrance. Before exiting the room, she ran back and quickly checked her appearance in the full-length mirror. Jeans, a crisp white shirt, and sneakers were all appropriate apparel for apartment hunting.

Hailey had just set her breakfast tray down when, very much to her surprise, she found herself being kissed hard on the mouth. Unable to keep from succumbing to the familiar taste of passion racing through her, Hailey lost all thought to where she was and what could possibly happen as a result of whom she was kissing. Her heart entered into a relay race with her brain in trying to reach a state of calm. Hailey had lost herself inside a world of wonderful dreams, a fantasy world that she had no desire to awaken from.

Grinning broadly, Zurich held Hailey slightly away from him. "Oh, my God, Hailey, what are you doing here? What an unbelievable but pleasant surprise! I was so worried about the distance. You really are an undercover agent of some sort, aren't you? I don't know if you're FBI or what, I just know I'm happy you're here! I couldn't believe my eyes when I saw you coming toward me. I wish we could've told each other we'd be living in Germany. This is perfect!" Thrilled to see her, he pulled her to him again for another passionate kiss.

Hailey was still in a state of shock as she trembled in his strong arms. The last person she expected to see halfway around the world was Zurich Kingdom. She opened and closed her eyes several times to make sure she wasn't actually dreaming up this wild and crazy scenario. Zurich was as real as real came. His mouth on hers was a definite, and sweet reality.

As his kiss deepened and nearly took her breath away, a deeper reality set in. They couldn't be together as a couple, not as long as they were in the military. Fearful of what she knew could happen to their careers, Hailey had to use every ounce of strength she had to push him away. "Zurich, we can't do this. Not here. We're out in public."

Thinking she was embarrassed by his wanton display of affection, he laughed. "Can't do what? Show how much we love each other? Don't answer that yet. Let me grab a cup of coffee so we can sit down together and do some serious catching up. This is nothing but a miracle."

Zurich suddenly realized his behavior was unprofessional, but seeing Hailey like this again made him all but forget who he was and what prestigious organization he belonged to. He was just a man crazy in love when he was with Hailey Hamilton.

While Hailey assessed his passionate response to seeing her, she noted that Zurich was also out of uniform, which made his ardent behavior toward her just a little more understandable. She couldn't imagine him kissing her so passionately while on duty. In fact, she didn't think he would've kissed her at all if he'd been dressed in his official military uniform.

After several moments of pondering how to break the bad news, Hailey just dug into her purse and came up with her active duty military ID card. Hating what she was forced to do, she quickly handed the laminated plastic card to Zurich. Her heart grieved as she watched his eyes cloud with pain. She then saw his facial expression turn from bewilderment to one of anger.

He practically threw the ID card back at her. "You knew about this in Texas, didn't you? How long you've known about this is what I'm really interested in hearing from you. Save that answer, too. I'll be right back with you. You and I need to sit down and talk this over."

The accusatory ring in his voice surprised her. As she watched him storm toward the cafeteria line, the urge to run away without looking back had grown stronger. Hailey looked at her food, and pushed the tray away. Her appetite no longer existed.

When Hailey heard loud giggling, she turned around for a brief second and saw two black women seated behind the table that she occupied. Their heads were drawn closely together as they whispered, loud enough for Hailey to hear. These two women were oblivious to everyone and everything but the sound of their own gossiping voices.

"She must be a fairly new officer here," one woman remarked. "He's only the most sought-out eligible bachelor on the base. Looks as if his status is about to change. She should consider herself blessed. That was some kiss he put on girlfriend. Their affair is going to be the talk of the entire base. Congratulations to her for landing the righteous Major Kingdom come!"

"Brand new," Hailey said. She didn't know what to think about their gossipy remarks, but she knew that trouble was definitely brewing. An officer, she wasn't. But they'd find that out soon enough—and so would everyone else. That was exactly the kind of trouble she was afraid of.

From the sisters' remarks it seemed to Hailey that Zurich may have been stationed in Germany for a while. And here she'd been worried that he'd be upset because she hadn't told him she'd be residing on another continent. Their situation was unbelievably complicated.

Boy, talk about what can happen when secrets kept in the dark came out into the light!

Never once had it dawned on Hailey that Zurich was in the armed forces. She had been certain that he belonged to a covert organization of some type, but she hadn't placed him in a military environment. A Secret Service agent was closer to what she'd had in mind.

Her statement about him "commanding an entire army" suddenly rang in her ears again.

Zurich sat down across from her. For several unnerving seconds he just stared at her.

Just to have something to do with her hands, Hailey pulled back her shirt cuff and looked at her watch. "I've only got a few minutes, Zurich. I have an appointment this morning."

He eyed her with suspicion. "To do what? Most business squadrons are closed down on the weekends."

"To check out an apartment. Why do you ask?"

"Just curious. When did you first learn that I was in the military?"

She swallowed hard. The harshness in his tone was beginning to arouse her anger. It made her think of how Will used to speak to Kelly. In an instant, she decided she wasn't going to take any amount of disrespect from him. It wasn't like she had set out to dupe him. "You know something, I don't like the tone of your voice. If you want me to answer your questions, you'd better show me more respect." Thinking of Kelly had turned up the heat under her rising anger. Kelly's battered face had a way of appearing in her mind without any warning. Will's fist smashing into Kelly's beautiful face and body was a recurring nightmare for Hailey.

"Talking about respect, that cuts both ways, Hailey. Did you think you were showing me respect by not telling me you knew all along that I was in the military?"

"You know, you're good at jumping to conclusions, Kingdom. You're doing me the same way you did your mother about Mr. Cobb. Why do you have to assume the worst about people?"

He raised both eyebrows. "I can't believe you said that! Aren't you the same person who assumed I was having an affair with another woman, though I was spending all my time with you? What about the serious altercation you had with J. Smooth? The one you didn't mention until we were on our way to the airport. Or am I confusing you with someone else, *Hamilton?*"

Sighing, Hailey looked regretful. "This conversation isn't going very well. To answer your question, I didn't know about your career choice until we were at the airport in Harlingen. When you dropped your wallet, I saw your active duty military ID card. But it wasn't until I spotted the gold oak-leaf cluster pinned to the leather flap that I realized you were an officer."

Only one of his eyebrows went up this time. "You saw me go into my wallet numerous times while we were together. Are you saying you didn't see either the card or the emblem on any of those occasions?"

"Are you suggesting that I'm lying, Zurich? If so, what would I have to gain by it? Furthermore, from what you just stated, I could easily come to the conclusion that you intended for me to see your officer's emblem each time you opened your wallet. What about that?"

He shoved his hand through his hair. "You're right, this isn't going well. Things are complicated enough without me making matters worse. I'm sorry. To answer your last question, I didn't even think about my ID when I opened my wallet. But enough of that. What squadron are you assigned to, Hailey, that is, assuming you're assigned to this base?"

"I'm assigned to a detachment of the 25th Weather Squadron." His loud groan momentarily startled her. "What was that all about, Zurich?"

"Even though I knew your dad was a meteorologist, I still felt that you were way too knowledgeable about weather phenomena just to have learned a few things from him. Then, when you didn't say anything to the contrary, I just chalked everything up to all the years you lived at home with a weatherman for a dad. It looks as though I was right about what I thought. I saw the rank of E-5 on your ID card when you just showed it to me. Forecaster?"

"Right. As for my rank, I was promoted last time around. I have a line number for E-6. I have a few months yet to go before I can sew on my Technical Sergeant stripes."

Hailey had purposely left out the fact that she'd recently earned her B.S. degree in applied sciences, which made her a full-fledged meteorologist, education-wise. Her experience as a military-trained forecaster would also carry plenty of weight, especially when it later came to applying for a job in the civilian sector. But Hailey's goals and dreams went far beyond that.

"What's your area of expertise, Zurich?"

"I thought you would've guessed by now. I'm also a meteorologist. I'm assigned to Headquarters, 25th Weather Squadron, which is where my office is located." Zurich shook his head. "This is an impossible situation to be in. I can't believe this is happening to us. You're going to find this next revelation utterly amazing. I'm TDY to your detachment beginning on Monday. As the squadron's operations officer, I'll be conducting a staff assistance visit, SAV. I'll be hanging around your unit for several days."

Looking downright frazzled, Hailey moaned. "This situation keeps getting more complicated." She shook her head in disbelief. "At least it's only temporary duty."

Hailey really didn't know what else to say. What could she say? Her heart was in shambles and, from the look of things, so was his. Hailey glanced at her watch again. She then got to her feet. "I hate to run, but someone is waiting for me. I truly don't know what to say about any of this, Zurich. I wish I had all the answers." She shrugged. "I just know that we can't resume our personal relationship, not without serious consequences."

"Who's waiting for you, and where, Hailey?"

"My girlfriend is coming to the hotel, the one I told you about, Alicia Richards. My short stay here has already been full of surprises. Alicia reported earlier than I expected. She kept it a secret. Seems like plenty of secrets have been kept. It looks like you might just get to meet her."

"Wow! I see what you mean about the surprises and the secrets. At any rate, I need to see you again. We have to resolve this sticky situation we've unwittingly gotten ourselves into. We can't let things end here. Not like this. I just have to see you, Hailey."

"I'm not sure that's such a good idea, Zurich. We both have a lot at stake here."

He sighed hard. "Tell me about it! Still, we have to talk this through. I'll come over to the hotel later on. What's the room number?"

She frowned. "I don't know about that, Zurich. It's a pretty risky idea."

"Let me worry about the risk involved." The expression in his eyes softened. "I'm always going to protect you, Hailey. You can count on that. Okay?"

She managed to hold back her tears. "Room 204. I'm really sorry about all of this."

"Me, too. But I've got a feeling we're going to be a lot sorrier if we don't find a way to work this out. The military rules are clear to us, but what the hell do we tell our breaking hearts?" He smiled weakly. "Forbidden or not, I love you so much, Staff Sergeant, soon to be Technical Sergeant Hailey Hamilton."

Hailey lowered her lashes to half-mast. "Major Kingdom, I love you, too," she whispered. Feeling terribly dejected, Hailey turned to walk away, her head hung low. The sadness she felt had already overwhelmed her. She didn't know if she'd ever be able to smile again. Losing Zurich would leave her with nothing to smile about.

"Hailey," he softly called out to her before she'd taken another step. "Wait a minute."

Forcing a smile to her lips, she turned to face the man she was absolutely crazy for. "I know what you're feeling, Hailey." He got up and came over to her. "Try to keep your chin up, baby. I just refuse to believe that God brought us together only to have us torn apart. I *won't* believe it. Hold on to our love, okay? I need you to do that for both of us. I promise not to let you down. I'm not going to run out on my responsibilities to you, to us. You are not in this alone. I know of many instances where the woman has had to make all the sacrifices in situations like this. You don't have to worry about that happening in this case.

Accepting the four introductory books for FREE (plus $1.99 to offset the cost of shipping & handling) places you under no obligation to buy anything. You may keep the books and return the shipping statement marked "cancelled". If you do not cancel, about a month later we will send 4 additional Arabesque novels, and you will be billed the preferred subscriber's price of just $4.00 per title. That's $16.00* for all 4 books for a savings of almost 40% off the cover price (Plus $1.99 for shipping and handling). You may cancel at any time, but if you choose to continue, every month we'll send you 4 more books, which you may either purchase at the preferred discount price. . . or return to us and cancel your subscription.

* PRICES SUBJECT TO CHANGE

THE ARABESQUE ROMANCE CLUB: HERE'S HOW IT WORKS

PLACE
STAMP
HERE

THE ARABESQUE ROMANCE BOOK CLUB
P.O. BOX 5214
CLIFTON NJ 07015-5214

Please believe and trust in me, Hailey Hamilton. Our love is strong enough to withstand this."

All she wanted to do was run to him and throw herself into his arms. Every part of her wanted and needed him badly. She needed to be in his arms for solace, but she also wanted and needed him to make love to her to ease the tension and the brutal pain attacking her heart. But that couldn't happen, might never happen again. Just the thought of it made her ill.

Out of the corner of her eye she saw that they had a rapt audience. She couldn't bring them into full view, not without turning to look at them. But she could imagine the two sisters sitting on the edge of their seats, their knuckles white from gripping the chairs too hard.

It was at that very moment that she realized how much Zurich was putting on the line for her. If word of their personal relationship got out, his reputation could be damaged. He didn't seem to fully understand that his career could be hurt by their love affair. But she did. She understood all too well—and her unconditional love for him would never allow his profession to be jeopardized in this manner, not if she could help it. Zurich meant way too much to her for her to let that come to pass.

Hailey suddenly realized that she wasn't as nearly concerned about her reputation as she was worried over his. She found that odd since her Air Force career meant absolutely everything in the world to her. That this situation could damage her chances for moving on to bigger and better career choices should've been her main concern. But it wasn't.

For Hailey, this was all about the most important human emotion: love.

"We'll do whatever it is that we have to do, Zurich. And I do trust you, with all my heart. I made the mistake of mistrusting you once. I don't plan on giving a repeat performance. I really have to go now. We'll talk. I'm hoping that it's not a punishable offense for us to just talk."

"Rest assured that it's not. Before coming up to your room, I'll call you from down in the lobby. Keep yourself cool and calm. I know we can pull this off without either of us having to suffer any dire consequences. We'll be just fine, baby. Just remember that we're in love."

In parting, Hailey mouthed the words *I love you, too*.

Though it was his heart's desire, he didn't try to touch Hailey again, because he too saw how intently the two black female airmen were watching their every move. He could only imagine that for them it was like watching the daytime soaps, but he wasn't going to give away any more of the plot for them to spread around as gossip about Hailey or him. In his opinion, they'd probably already seen and heard too much. Watching Hailey walk away from him was as hard as it had been when he had to watch her leave him behind at the Harlingen Airport in Texas.

Hailey had her head hung so low that she practically ran right into Alicia as she was rushing toward the hotel. Alicia immediately noticed the troubled look on her friend's face when Hailey lifted her head. She slipped her arm around Hailey's shoulder as they fell into step with each other. "Rough morning, sister? You don't look so hot."

"You may not want to know how rough." Hailey managed to force out a believable smile. "Good morning, my dear friend Alicia. I'm happy and relieved to see you. You can't possibly know how relieved I am that you and I are stationed here in Germany together. We are so far away from home. Thanks for being here for me, Alicia. I'm glad I don't have to do this alone."

"Anytime, Hailey. Do you have to go up to your room? Or are you ready to leave now?"

"I have everything I need. Let's go. I'm really eager to see the apartment. I'm also dying to tell you everything that happened in the cafeteria. There was drama up in that place like you wouldn't believe. I still don't believe it myself. Then again, you probably will since military installations are often referred to as the "Peyton Place"s of the world. By the way, I never got to eat the breakfast I paid for. My appetite was completely blown away by what happened in there."

Eager to hear all the juicy gossip, Alicia opened the passenger door of the late-model Porsche she'd borrowed from a close male friend before sliding into the driver's seat. Her own automobile, a bright red Mazda Miata, was being shipped overseas, as was Hailey's Chrysler Sebring, but neither one had yet arrived in the German seaport of Bremerhaven.

Hailey made sure her seat belt was buckled. Alicia had a heavy foot, and Hailey knew there was no speed limit on the autobahn from previous visits to Germany while on vacation leave. This was Hailey's first duty assignment to Germany, but she had been stationed in England several years back. During that time she'd traveled to numerous European cities, including many German ones.

"So, let's hear what happened in the cafeteria. It sure has you riled up, whatever it was."

Hailey told Alicia all that went on with her and Zurich, and about the two airmen who had been privy to practically everything that had gone down.

Alicia had a strange look on her face. "That *is* an amazing story! What a hell of a coincidence that you two ended up at the same base. Your secret is definitely safe with me. Earlier I thought there was something familiar about your story, but I couldn't think why until now. Kila's best friend found himself in a similar situation with a young female lieutenant. But they both knew their ranks from the start. Not only that, the lieutenant was married to a captain. Kila's friend didn't know that the lieutenant had a husband. Are you sure Zurich isn't married, Hailey?"

Hailey pressed her lips together. "That's certainly interesting information, but it's nothing that we haven't heard before. In fact, numerous times. Zurich isn't married. I'm sure of it."

Alicia frowned. "Hailey, you may have to watch your back, in more ways than one. If he's as fine as you say he is, there may be a few jealous women who might want to cause you major trouble if they hear about your affair. You need to be extremely cautious."

Hailey laughed. "Major trouble!"

Alicia laughed, too. "No pun intended."

"At any rate," Hailey continued, "other women are the least of my worries. Zurich and I are too dedicated to our careers and to the Air Force to handle this situation in a reckless manner. Yet I can't say that I'm sorry we got involved. I hope we'll never have to face any sort of disciplinary action because of it. If we'd known about our jobs and ranks from the beginning, we wouldn't have gotten involved. I'm positive about that."

Alicia carefully backed the Porsche out of the parking space. "Oh, Hailey, I'm sure a lot of people believe that. But it's the hearts that get involved. People are attracted to each other for all sorts of reason, but if the heart's not in it, they aren't going to get very far in building a relationship. It sounds like you and Zurich fell in love almost instantly, even before you knew a lot about each other. Nowadays people just aren't telling all their business when they first meet. With most everyone in the armed services so extremely sensitive about terrorism, we're not readily sharing with outsiders our personal and professional information. You don't know who or what the heck you're dealing with these days. We can't be too careful."

"For real. That's the reason Zurich and I remained very tightlipped about our jobs."

"Not to change the subject, but Allen is coming to see me next week. He's going to catch a hop. He's stationed in Italy. Besides you being here, you know that having Allen nearby is another reason I wanted to be stationed somewhere in Europe. You know how much we love each other."

"Yeah, I do know. Allen and Alicia Richards, the adorable twin sister and brother who love each other like crazy. It'll be nice to see him again."

"Most definitely. I haven't seen him in three months. I wonder if he still has a mean crush on you. He used to try and talk to me to death about you."

"Don't start that again. You're talking about something he joked about way back when we were in basic training. He only said that if he weren't dating someone, he could really get into me. You took that meaningless statement and ran with it. Allen has never looked at me as anything but a friend. I've been around your brother many times since then, Alicia, and he hasn't shown any romantic interest in me whatsoever."

"I know. But you two are my favorite people. I love you both."

Hailey smiled. "We love you, too, Alicia."

Alicia exited the autobahn and turned left at the light. She drove two more blocks and made a sharp right turn. She parked the Porsche in front of a fairly new structure and cut the engine. "This is it." She pointed at the first corner building. "You ready to meet the Schullers?"

"Ready or not, here we are," Hailey joked. "Let's get out of the car. I'm really eager to see the place now. This looks like a great neighborhood to live in. I'm impressed." She looked over at Alicia with deep curiosity in her eyes. "By the way, who in the Sam Hill does this red-hot Porsche belong to, anyway? I've been dying to ask." Hailey closed the car door.

"A close friend."

"How close? Male or female?"

Alicia's smile was delightful, but kind of smug. "Now, you know no sister is going to lend me her expensive Porsche. Anyway, it's the same guy I was wildly attracted to while I was TDY in Spain last year. He's a civilian, has a wonderful job, and he's single. We've kept in touch, but I hooked up with him again by mail right after I got my orders. I mentioned him when I saw you in San Antonio, but I didn't go into great detail. Does the name Phillip Lankster ring a bell?"

"You've talked about him off and on, but I never really got the impression that you were involved with him in any romantic way. I guess I was wrong. Is he just visiting you here?"

"He's working on this base now. He's in the AAFES organization, upper management."

Hailey nodded, a light of understanding shining in her eyes. "I get it! It looks to me like you weren't trying to get stationed in Germany because of me after all. Is it possible that Phillip was your main reason for wanting this assignment?"

Alicia laughed heartily, throwing up both her hands. "I'm busted! What can I say? There are also some issues with civilian and military fraternization, but not so much in our particular instance. However, we've decided to keep our relationship on the down-low. It's not that serious between us anyway. Don't get me wrong here; we're more than just a tad interested in each other, but we're content to wait to see how things develop."

"How do you figure you're keeping your relationship quiet? You're driving his fire-engine red Porsche all over the base for goodness sake."

"I know. But good friends loan each other their cars. We've done it enough times. We want to develop a solid friendship first. Phillip and I are in no hurry to go off the deep end."

"That's a smart way to look at it, Alicia. I look forward to meeting Phillip. I only wish that Zurich and I had had more time. We laid out all the ground rules for our two-week stay on the island, but we couldn't keep our hearts under control. Our hearts ended up controlling us."

Hailey stopped before entering the apartment building. "I wish for the best outcome for both of us. We deserve nothing but the very best and the utmost respect out of any kind of relationship—it is imperative that we demand nothing less than that. One thing that Kelly's death seriously reinforced for me was to constantly keep those boundaries in place. If you don't set up any perimeters for yourself, someone is going to jump your fence."

"In a heartbeat. Your gut-wrenching rendition of Kelly's violent death still haunts me, too, Hailey. I can remember how hard a time I had getting to sleep after we talked about it."

"I'm really glad you've been there to help me get through it, Alicia. How about a hug?"

The two women embraced warmly before proceeding into the apartment building.

Ten

Just when Hailey was about to give up on Zurich showing up as he'd promised, a light knock came on the door. He had told her he'd call first, but it couldn't be anyone but him on the other side of the door. It was well after ten P.M., much too late for Alicia or Hailey's squadron unit sponsor to be dropping by. Other than Zurich, they were the only other people who knew her hotel room number. Butterflies flew about in Hailey's stomach as she made her way across the room.

"Who's there?" she called out through the door, smoothing her hair with the palms of her hands. Hailey sighed a breath of relief that she hadn't already changed into her nightclothes.

"Zurich, Hailey. It's okay to let me in."

As she opened the door, she saw that Zurich carried a large white box. She smelled the delicious aroma coming from the pizza carton at the same moment he entered the room.

Although his hands were full, he still stopped and kissed her on the cheek. "I thought you might be hungry. I brought you a pizza, loaded with the works just the way you like it."

All of the hotel rooms were fully equipped with a mini-refrigerator, microwave, and a variety of small appliances, as well as dinnerware, flatware, and glasses. A bed, dresser, nightstand, desk, and a small dining table and four chairs completed the modest furnishings. Zurich placed the pizza box and the two liter-bottles of Coke on top of the microwave oven.

Turning back to face Hailey, he took both of her hands. "I know you're nervous about me being here. But I can assure you that it's okay. I won't do anything to cause us to compromise ourselves. As hard as it's going to be for me not to take you in my arms and make love to you until we're both too weak to do anything but fall asleep, I promise to keep my cool."

"Zurich, please don't say things like that. The images of us together like that are way too powerful for me to combat without serious difficulty. If thinking about us making love is a punishable offense, I'm going to have to do hard time."

The anguish on her face caused his heart to ache. He placed his hands on her shoulders. "Listen to me, Hailey. We haven't done anything improper since we've both become aware that a possible fraternization situation might exist. Neither of us knew the real situation while we were on the island, and I didn't know you were an NCO when I kissed you in the cafeteria. We haven't violated any rules since the discovery."

"A *possible* fraternization situation *might* exist! Come on now. I knew, Zurich."

"Yes, but you didn't know I was here in Germany—and you sure in hell didn't know I was going to be in the cafeteria, let alone that I was going to kiss you. Let me reiterate our position on this matter, Hailey. We've done nothing wrong. Okay? Am I coming in clear?"

"Clear enough."

"Good, now let's sit down and eat. Once we're through with the pizza, we can try and figure this whole thing out. No matter what else occurs, I want the responsibility for this situation to lie solely with me. You are not to admit to any type of culpability under any circumstance should our relationship become an issue. I'm the go-to man."

Keeping his eyes fastened on her, he picked up the pizza

box and Cokes and brought the items over to the table, where he set them down. Zurich then retrieved plates from the cabinet and filled two glasses with ice. He summoned Hailey over to the table and pulled out her chair before seating himself. He wasted no time in saying the blessing.

Hailey couldn't take her eyes off him even as she bit into the freshly baked dough. Zurich was a take-charge kind of guy, a leader—and a commander. Her beginning assessment of him hadn't at all been a crock of bull. Her intuition had allowed her to see him as he actually was, although her reference to him commanding an army of men and women had only been in jest. Still, she had failed to recognize him as a member of the armed forces. Looking back, she couldn't figure out how she'd missed it, especially given the dignified way in which he'd always carried himself. Whether or not it was because she now knew the truth about him, Zurich definitely had *commander* written all over him.

"You still look mighty worried, Hailey. Are you going to be okay?"

She gave him a bright smile. "Yeah, I'm just fine, and so are you, Major Kingdom. Since looking at you might be all I'll ever be able to do, I'm sitting here getting me an eyeful of your beautiful self. It's hard for me not to reach over there and touch you, Zurich. Real hard."

"I know the feeling, baby. But all we can do right now is talk. We don't want to lend any credence to this situation. How much longer do you have on your current enlistment?"

"I only have seven years in, and my goal is to stay active all the way up to retirement. I love the Air Force, Zurich. I'm passionate about my job and fiercely dedicated to the overall mission of the agency. To answer your question, I recently re-enlisted for three years. From what you said before, I already know that you're a lifer. With seventeen in, you only have three years left, unless you're going for the maximum of thirty."

"Thirty years active is my goal. At least, it was before I met you. Hailey, I did a lot of thinking about us after I ran into you this morning. I'm willing to get out at twenty, but only if and when we're sure that we are in this forever."

She gasped with disbelief. "I can't ask you to do that! That wouldn't be the least bit fair to you. The military has been your whole life."

"You *didn't* ask me. It's a decision I made on my own. You're right. The military has been my entire life, but if I'm to have a meaningful one in the future it has to include you. Let me just say this. We may be jumping the gun here. Nothing may even come up about us, but I admit there's cause for concern." He shrugged. "I don't know. But if it does come up, I want us to have a game plan. Do you feel as if I'm someone you could spend the rest of your life with? In other words, do you love me enough to marry me?"

Her hands flew up to her face. "Are you asking me to do that?"

"Hypothetically speaking. I just want things to be clear."

She felt a twinge of disappointment. "In theory, yes, to both questions."

He shook his head. "I sure botched that one! Hailey, I know we haven't even come close to discussing marriage, but I wanted to be damn sure of our feelings so I know where we stand should someone question our involvement. Do you understand?"

"I do. I also understand that I love you. Now let's move on. Neither of us is comfortable with the subject. Is talking about sex a compromising activity?" *What a silly question.*

He grinned. "We're going to have to figure that all out. This isn't going to be easy on either of us. My desire to make love to you has never been stronger than it is right now. Oh, Hailey, I don't know how we're going to get through this madness, day in and day out being so close but unable to make love. But I do see a lot of cold showers in my future."

"What a chilling statement, yet it did nothing to cool me off. Moving right along, on to easier-to-deal-with topics. Do you live on base?"

"Off base in a quaint little picturesque town surrounded by a beautiful forest. A babbling brook runs through the middle of the property. My three-bedroom apartment is nice and comfortable, and I love living there. The place has a great balcony with a splendid view. You'll love it, too, if you ever get the chance to see it. How did your morning house-hunting go?"

Hailey rubbed her hands together. "Very well, thank you. Alicia actually turned me on to this place. It's about five to seven miles from the base. She and another girl had already rented a three-bedroom apartment in the same building. Alicia wanted me to move in with them, but I declined because I'm no good at living with others. Since there was another, two-bedroom, apartment for rent right across the hall from theirs, she offered to take me to see it."

"How are you ever going to get married if you can't live with someone?"

"Married to someone is a totally different situation than living with two female roommates. Besides, there're way more fringe benefits for a woman living and sleeping with her husband every night." Hailey batted her eyes in a flirtatious manner, making Zurich laugh.

"I'm feeling you. What's the status on the place you looked at?"

"According to the owner, a guy had filled out an application for the place, but he never came back with the required deposit in the time frame he was allotted. The landlord was eager to rent it and I had the money to put down the deposit. It's pretty much a done deal. I can move in next week, so I hope my hold baggage is here by then. Since I opted not to ship my furniture, I'll have to use base issues. Did you have your own furniture brought over?"

"I didn't have any furniture until recently. I started accumulating pieces here and there over the past year or so. I like a lot of open space, uncluttered. All I have in my bedroom is a bed, one nightstand, and a comfortable chair. I just recently purchased a schrank for the living room, but I plan to give it to my mother when I leave here. Do you know what that is?"

"Of course I do, an entire wall unit constructed out of fine hardwoods. I plan to buy one shortly before I DEROS. Speaking of uncluttered space, I'm not such a neat freak. I tend to be a little messy, clean but terribly unorganized."

"A unorganized person in the military! I'm surprised that you survived basic."

"Oh, I did what I needed to do to pass muster. You only have to see one time what happens to the others when one person doesn't take her duties seriously. I wasn't going to make the mistake of having everyone pay for what I failed to do. I pretty much sailed through basic. I always kept the right attitude. I knew why I'd come to the military, was never in any doubt."

"Why?"

"I wanted to make something of myself. I wanted to be a part of a huge world mission. The benefits are extraordinary, which helps make up for the shortage in pay. Where else can a young person, especially those straight out of high school, get a job where they start out with medical, dental, optical, room and board, thirty days paid leave, travel privileges, and training in a worthwhile career—and get paid for it. The commissary and BX are two other great benefits. Education and veteran's benefits alone are invaluable. I think I forgot to mention three square meals a day. I've been around the military all my life, so it was a way of life that I was familiar with. I knew what I was getting into before I enlisted. I knew exactly what was expected of me. I often feel as if I'm receiving way more than I'm giving. Satisfied with my answers?"

"Tremendously."

"Why did you join the military, Zurich?"

He gave her question a minute's thought even though he already knew the answer. "Joining the military probably kept me out of a lot of trouble. I was angry at my circumstances, extremely angry with my parents. I hated what Dad did to Mom, but I was more upset with her than him. I didn't understand why she stayed. More than that, I believed that she failed to protect her children, which should come naturally to a mother. I came into the military because I had no alternative. I needed to leave home for obvious reasons." Zurich took a swig of his Coke.

"With that said, I came in with the goal of becoming nothing short of a success. I worked hard at whatever job I was given. At the same time, I continued with my education during off-duty time. A career in weather was chosen for me; it wouldn't have been my choice, but I accepted the challenge and was determined to be the best at it. I have not had a moment of regret. I later earned my degree and applied for officer's training school. The rest is history."

"So, Zurich, it seems we're both clear on why we joined the service. I wish we had been able to talk about all of this when we first met, but in a way I'm glad that we didn't."

"Why's that, Hailey?"

"Because the issue of fraternization would've kept us from taking our relationship to the level that we did. Do you agree?"

To warm his hands after handling the ice-cold glass, Zurich rubbed them together. "I'm not so sure about that. If I had in my mind that we'd probably never be stationed on the same base, I probably wouldn't have practiced the same degree of caution. Now, with us in the same career field, I might've given things a bit more thought. But I still can't say I would've backed away from you altogether. However, I would've known that that's what I should do. We did take our relationship to an intimate level, and now we have to deal with the consequences. I still feel confident that we'll work it out."

"Do you think there are a lot of military people facing the same dilemma we are?"

"Absolutely, all the time. What I'm not so sure about is if they would be facing it in the same manner we are. Most people would go ahead and do it regardless, figuring they'll never get caught at it, especially those who aren't taking the relationship seriously. How we're trying to handle this is probably the exception rather than the rule. If we weren't so self-conscious about who we are and what we do, we'd probably just throw caution to the wind. This is an extremely hard situation to be in, especially when we weren't aware of all the issues until after becoming intimate with each other. Our hearts are also very much involved in this. For two people who decided on no hassles, hang-ups, or heartaches we're certainly experiencing them all."

Hailey smiled. "I know what you mean. What we're going through is a definite hassle. Our feelings about what's happening can be looked at as our personal hang-ups, and we're both brokenhearted over all of it."

"I second that sentiment. Listen, when did you say you were moving into your place?"

"Next week. I'm going to check on my hold baggage on Monday. I have a lot of business to take care of before I officially report for duty. Orientation is on Tuesday."

"I'll help you get settled in."

"You don't see that as a problem?"

He shrugged. "Just helping out a friend. Besides, your military neighbors will help keep us honest. Don't worry. I know how to control myself."

Hailey look worried. "You might not like this, but I told Alicia about our situation. However, she promised not to ever breathe a word to anyone."

He frowned. "That's all well and good, but what's she going to do if you two ever have a serious disagreement about something? I'd be real careful from now on what I reveal and to whom. You never know when a spark of interest may develop out of something someone says unintentionally. We just have to be cautious."

"Alicia is not like that, but I understand your concerns. The only other person who knows about this is my mother. I can assure you she's not going to blow the whistle on her only child."

"What about your dad? Are you saying he doesn't know?"

Hailey shook her head in the negative. "He loves me dearly, but he's not always able to be objective about my involvement in personal relationships. I didn't mention it to him because I didn't want to hear a lecture on doing the right thing."

Zurich raised an eyebrow. "Won't your mother tell him?"

"I told her not to."

"Really! So, it sounds like you play your parents against each other. Is that right?"

Hailey gave Zurich a strange look. "No way! How did you reach that conclusion?"

"I don't know. It just sounded that way. But that's not important."

"The hell it isn't! You make a bold statement like that and then you tell me it's not important. You've got to be kidding."

Zurich was surprised at her sudden outburst of anger. Without thinking about the consequences, he found himself kneeling in front of her chair and bringing her into his arms. "I'm sorry, Hailey. I didn't mean to upset you."

She pushed him away. "But you did. It sounds to me as if you're trying to find out if I'm a spoiled brat or not. I'm not. I didn't tell my dad because it might upset him to think that I could be brought up on charges for having an affair with an officer. He already worries too much about me when I'm on overseas assignments—and I didn't want to add another burden. Dad was enlisted, too, before he became an officer. He talked about how tough it was on him because he had so many NCOs as friends, and how those relationships seemed to have changed because he was an officer. It was even harder once he realized that changes had to be made. No matter what base he went to, he always knew someone there. That was all there was to me confiding in my Mom. On top of all we're going through, your doubting me doesn't make me feel very good."

He risked taking her into his arms again. "Will you accept my apology? I meant it."

Hailey couldn't help remembering how forgiving he was to her when'd she'd doubted him on more than one occasion. He'd forgiven her. "I accept. Under normal circumstances I'd seal it with a kiss. But these aren't normal circumstances."

"A light peck won't hurt." He put his cheek against her lips.

As Hailey pressed her lips deep into his cheek, her thoughts ran wild. His lips were only a short distance away from his cheek and there were no probing eyes to witness her indiscretion. The desire to forget the rules they'd agreed to play by was stronger than her will. Hailey eyes closed as she instantly conjured up his mouth beneath hers, their tongues entwining, their passion exploding. Just imagining their passionate kiss gave her thrilling goose bumps.

Zurich didn't dare flinch. His thoughts ran pretty much the same as Hailey's, wild and crazy. He also had a bigger problem than she did in hiding his desire. The crotch of his pants was protruding with his excitement. A mere touch from her was erotic. The nude image of her looming in front of his eyes was just as tempting to him as seeing the real thing.

Hailey finally managed to drag herself away from her fantasy. It hurt to leave a fantasy place she'd become accustomed to, had grown quite comfortable in, a place she wanted to stay in forever.

His fingertips slow-danced across her lips. "We have to think of creative ways to get our needs met without indulging in the ultimate act." He wanted so badly to guide her hand to his erection, but he knew it wouldn't or couldn't end there. They would end up in her bed if her hand came anywhere near his pulsating desire. Of that fact, he was sure. It was time to split.

He got to his feet. "Good night, baby. Wait for me to make contact with you. I don't want you jeopardized in any way. I promise that your wait will be a short one. Good night, my love."

"Good night, Zurich. I'll be waiting."

Hailey rushed off the base shuttle and hurried into the chapel. She had woken in the wee hours of the morning with a strong desire to go to church and pray inside the Potter's house, though she knew He always resided within her heart. She also needed spiritual guidance in the worst way. Every time she talked things out with God, He never failed to direct her onto the right path. She needed to kneel before the altar today. She needed to welcome His presence into her situation. God had not failed her yet. Her only wish was that she'd consulted him before she went against His wishes in the first place.

Shocked to see Zurich sitting on the front pew, Hailey decided it was best to take a seat in the back of the sanctuary. Although his back was turned to her, she could easily pick him out of a room full of brothers. She would go to the front during altar call. If he knelt too, he might not see her. But if he did spot her, she knew he'd practice discretion and would expect the same from her. For them not to outwardly acknowledge each other would hurt, she knew it was necessary. The path to their future was dangerous and rocky.

The moment she made herself comfortable on the bench seat, she pulled out the precious greeting card she'd found under her door just before she'd left the room. It was from Zurich. Finding it then had told her that he'd either placed it there early that morning or after he'd left her the previous night. It was a sweet and loving gesture, either way.

The words on the "Missing You" card were sweet, sentimental, and encouraging. The faint trace of his cologne on the card had caused her senses to desert her. Up until now, she thought only women dabbed their favorite scent onto correspondence to a loved one. She didn't know if he'd intentionally done it, or if it had occurred from just him handling the card; the whiff of his scent was all that mattered to her.

Hailey put the card away and tuned into the comforting voice of the base chaplain, Captain Carlton McGuire. While Hailey had grown up on the fire-and-brimstone preaching, she preferred the calmer way in which the chaplain was delivery this morning's message. She had yet to experience any of the fiery preaching since joining the military. Except when stationed overseas, her parents had always attended church off base while her father was on active duty.

Hailey remained seated after the call to the altar was made. She had waited to see what Zurich would do. Once he was settled on his knees, she didn't go up front until there were several rows of people in place, which would keep them separated. If he was as in tune to her as she was to him, he just might catch her scent if she were right behind him.

The moment the chaplain began praying, Hailey closed her eyes. She had a few prayers of her own to send up and she quietly voiced them inside her heart. While she didn't think asking the Master to work things out for her and Zurich was wrong, she felt guilty about bringing forth this particular supplication when so many other world issues needed prayer.

* * *

All sorts of things went through Hailey's mind as she stood at the base shuttle/share-a-ride stand waiting to be picked up. It bothered her that she'd had to slip out of the service just before it was over so as not to put Zurich in an awkward position. She had also saved herself the pain of seeing him and knowing she couldn't be with him the way she wanted to. But it hurt, anyway, like the dickens.

Hailey's attention was quickly drawn to the brand-spanking-new shiny black Corvette that had just pulled up in front of the stand. When the passenger window rolled down, she got a full view of the handsome driver, Major Kingdom. "Need a lift, Staff Sergeant?"

Hailey tried to hide her shock, but failed. She couldn't believe he was doing this. She stepped over to the car, looking all around as if someone were spying on her her. "This is not at all cool. And you know it. We can't do this," she whispered, though no one was within earshot.

"There are no rules against offering a ride to anyone needing one. Rank is not at issue in this case. Giving someone a lift is the whole purpose of the share-a-ride stand. Get in, Hailey. All I'm doing is giving you a ride." His tone was gentle and undemanding. Her hesitancy was obvious to him. He stretched across the seat and opened the passenger door. "You don't want me to get out and put you in the car, now do you? That might draw way more attention to us than if you were to just get in of your own free will."

Hailey knew she was in big trouble the moment she moved forward to obey his last comment, which had been more of a command, or even a softly veiled threat. It suddenly became apparent to her that her carefree heart had decided it would follow this man and his big heart wherever they led. She just hoped their hearts wouldn't lead them straight down the path to destruction. But she wasn't going to explore that for now. At the moment, her man was in control since she knew he'd make good on his threat.

The powerful car was off and running the same instant

Hailey finished buckling herself in. While he was obeying the speed laws for driving on base, Hailey could easily imagine him letting the car completely loose on the open road. Autobahn driving was for fast cars like his.

Zurich's broad smile caused her heart to careen. "You look beautiful."

"Thank you. You're not looking too shabby over there yourself. Love the double-breasted jacket." She gave him a slight frown. "Are you sure you know what the heck you're doing?"

Laughing, he shrugged. "No, not really, but I'm having fun at it. It's almost like tasting the forbidden fruit. You know you shouldn't give in to the temptation to taste the sweetness you're almost sure you'll find within, but you just can't seem to help yourself. That's how I feel whenever I catch the slightest glimpse of you, Miss Hailey."

She rolled her eyes at him. "Every time you have that particular thought, you should also think about what happened to Adam and Eve, Zurich. I'm tough enough all right, but I don't want to be tossed out of the Garden of Eden, which is the Air Force for me. You feeling me?"

Zurich laughed heartily. "It's all good. Just sit back in your seat and relax, baby. Like I said before, I'm just supplying a ride to someone in need."

Hailey laughed, too. "You can psych yourself up all you want, but don't try to make me buy into your insanity, Major. Okay?"

"Girl, you just need to go ahead and admit the facts to yourself. We're both insane, insanely in love with each other. If need be, we can use that as our defense. Maybe we can call on Navy Commander Harmon Rabb and Marine Lieutenant Colonel Sarah MacKenzie to defend us if we catch a case. Even if they won't admit it, they're intensely in love with each other. Their compassion and empathy for us will make them work even harder at winning."

Hailey sucked her teeth to show her intolerance of his

bull. "I'm sure I don't have to tell you that what's happening with us isn't just a television episode of *JAG*. Think about it. For now I'm not going to say another word on the subject!"

He grinned devilishly. "Promise?"

Hailey's amber eyes softened as she looked into the eyes of the man she adored. "I promise, despite your smart-behind retorts."

Zurich turned on the CD player. "Let me help you get mellow. I can't stand seeing you so uptight. I purchased this disk knowing how much you love it." He went straight to the number of the song she loved so much.

Hailey's eyes lit up when she heard LeAnn Rimes's voice singing "How Do I Live." The title of that song had become her reality; it was a question she asked herself a hundred times a day. How was she to live without him? "You do pay attention to a girl's likes and dislikes, don't you? I love that about you. But you'd better be glad we have certain set rules to play by."

"Oh, yeah! Why's that?"

"If no rules existed, I'd have you pull this car off into one of these dense forests, into a secluded place where I could spread out a blanket and then strip your body bare. I'd have my way with you in every position one can imagine. We could even make love sitting up in the deep curve of a tree if we so desired. Might be hard for your naked butt to handle the rough bark, but I think your firm backside is tough enough to hang with it." Though it was difficult for her, Hailey held her laughter within. It was even harder for her to keep her physical desire for him at bay.

His eyes danced with the mystery of black magic. "Oh, so you want to go there, huh? I'm not the only one who'd need to worry about the bark. I know for a fact that your sweet, soft behind couldn't handle the roughness of it. What do you have to say to that?"

"My sweet buns wouldn't have to deal with it, period. Because you'd be inside of me while I'm sitting on your lap. Just imagine our legs dangling from the high limb of a tree as we made sweet, passionate love. How do you like that for an inflammable image? Whew! I can already feel the moisture."

"Uh-oh, it done got mighty hot up in here! I'm too scared of you, Staff Sergeant Hailey Hamilton. What other juicy tidbits you got for me, girl? I like the way you make me burn for you."

While envisioning the unusual, white-hot scenario Hailey had just painted for them, they both cracked up. Zurich had to curb his desire to reach over and place his hand on her thigh. If he was honest with himself, his desire was more than just to touch her. Completely ravaging her lovely body was more what he had in mind. Hailey had his manhood stiffer than stiff.

"I can't believe I went there. Didn't we just get out of church? I am too sinful," Hailey confessed. "Oh, but what delicious sins!"

Zurich cracked up. "See, even you were tempted into going for the forbidden fruit."

Hailey slammed her eyes shut the minute she spotted the obvious bulge in his pants. What lay in wait for her inside his silk boxers was definitely not a balled-up pair of socks. She had firsthand knowledge of that. Being in the intimate confines of his car was almost too much for her to handle, especially when all she had to do was reach over and unzip his slacks to caress his rising need. She couldn't even allow herself to think about what she'd love to do for him to relieve the pain of his need. That is, not without acting upon it.

"Zurich, uh, do you happen to have the phone number for Commander Rabb and Colonel MacKenzie? If we keep this up, we just might need to hire them after all."

"We? Baby, you're the only one who might need a lawyer. I've been trying my best to be good over here—and you just went off on a wild tangent and pulled out all the stops. All I'm guilty of is offering you a ride home."

Realizing they should've been at the hotel a long time ago, Hailey looked out the window. They were already off the base. She had been so into sexually taunting him that she hadn't even seen them pass the guard shack. "Where are we going? Since we're no longer on the base, this route is surely not on my way home."

"I don't recall saying whose home I was giving you a ride to. Do you?"

Another shock to her system had come without warning. "I don't think I even want to try to answer that one. I'm just along for the ride. The less I know, the better." Hailey closed her eyes and rested her head back against the headrest. "However, this is kidnapping, you know."

"Yeah, baby, but it's just my word against yours. And I don't think either one of us is silly enough to bring charges against ourselves. Since you're just along for the ride, please open your pretty eyes. You don't want to miss the beauty of the scenic route we're about to take."

As if she had no other desire in life but to please him, she immediately popped up her lids. The endearing smile she gave him warmed his heart.

Ten minutes later Hailey understood perfectly why Zurich had told her to keep her eyes open. On her prior visits to Germany she'd only had enough time to visit the bigger cities. Exploring the rural areas and the quaint little towns and hamlets this time around was already on the top of her agenda of things to do and see. She could clearly see that her fascinating journey was about to begin. The breathtaking landscape before her held promises of a glorious afternoon in the presence of God's creations and in the engaging company of her handsome tour guide. Nature in its entire magnificent splendor surrounded her.

His place was warm and spacious. She liked it. His signature was written upon the strong character of the apartment, limited in furnishings yet comfortable. Hailey had once again shown hesitancy when he'd parked the car out in front of his building, but Zurich had managed to convince her it would be okay for her to come in for a few minutes.

He came to stand behind her as she looked out at his view of the forest. "You like it?"

"I love it. You have a serious view, so serene. It's a very nice place."

"Want to see the bedroom?"

She turned around and looked up at him. "Are you taunting me?"

"No more than you were baiting me earlier." He took her hand and led her down the hallway. Once they got to his room, he pushed the door back and turned on the light. "Go on in. I'll wait for you up front."

With a look of uncertainty on her face, Hailey stepped inside his private space. The European-style bed didn't look too comfortable, but sleeping in it with Zurich would make up for any discomfort. She figured he had a wardrobe chest in another bedroom, since most German housing didn't have closets. He didn't have a single picture on the off-white walls, which she thought was odd since he had such a big family.

As she looked out on the balcony, she smiled warmly. His all-white goose-down feather bedding and pillows were hung over the railing, a German custom. Every morning the family bedding was put outside for airing out. The hardwood floors gleamed with a fresh coat of wax and the white hand-woven throw rugs were spotless. The room was just as he'd described it, spacious and uncluttered. Hailey took another couple of minutes to look around his space before returning to the front, where she found him in the kitchen.

Hailey leaned against the doorjamb. "What are you doing?"

"Fixing you something to eat. I imagine you must be hungry by now."

Hailey couldn't believe how incredible this man was. "What are you cooking?"

"Nothing fancy; just an easy stir-fry concoction of fresh veggies and garlic shrimp. I get my vegetables at the local market just around the corner. It's already after noon so I thought we'd do lunch as opposed to breakfast. Did you have something planned for today?"

"Yeah, I did. I was going to stay in bed all day and dream about you and me making love. But don't you think you should've asked me that question before you kidnapped me? What if I'd had something important to do?"

"Had that been the case, you would've told me in no uncertain terms. When you saw that we were already off base, you had a second opportunity to say something but didn't. So bring your lovely behind on in here and have a seat. I'll have everything ready in a minute or two."

"Is that an order, Commander?"

"If that's how you want to take it. How'd you know I've had my own command?"

Hailey sat down. "I didn't. It's just written all over you. I knew you were a leader; I just didn't know who you were leading. Some people are born to lead, and others are born to be led."

"Which one are you, Hailey?"

"Both. I'm a leader in my professional life, and I love to be led in my very personal one, but only within reason. I give up control to no one but God. However, I let you take control today. If I were you, I wouldn't count on it happening too often."

He laughed. "I heard that! By the way, do you have any hang-ups about commissioned officers, more so when it comes down to taking orders on the job?"

"Don't even try it. I have many issues with officers, but I also have them with NCOs. I take issue with anyone who doesn't carry his or her weight on the job. Don't give me something to do that you can darn well do yourself, especially when it's your duty assignment in the first place. I don't like to be unfairly pushed around simply because someone outranks me."

He grinned broadly. "Ouch! I seem to have touched a nerve. Are you one of those NCOs who feel that noncommissioned officers are the backbone of the military?"

"Let me put it like this. When a doctor writes an order for his patient, who carries it out? You were an NCO before you became an officer. I'm sure you can answer your own question. I just hope you're not one of those ex-NCOs who likes to throw his weight around after receiving a commission. I'm sure you've been around the type I'm talking about, the ones who start smelling themselves, yet don't ever seem to realize they stink."

"I've been around too many of them. I can assure you that I'm not that type. What have your APRs been like?"

"I'm not sure I like the reason why you might be asking, but I'll answer, anyway. My airman performance reports have all been straight nines thus far."

"Okay now! The best rating one can get. What do you think my reason was for asking?"

"It sounds like you were trying to find out if I'm insubordinate. I'm not. I know how to go through the chain of command—and only when it's absolutely necessary to do so."

"Sounds like you know exactly what you're about. I like that. Now let's eat so I can get you back to base before your friend puts out a missing person bulletin on you. I'm sure she's concerned if she's been to the hotel and you weren't there."

"Alicia and I are strong, independent military women. We don't consult each other on our every move. If I'm not there, she'll just try back later. Knowing that you're stationed here, too, she probably has already put two and two together if she did stop by."

"In that case, I just might keep you here with me a little longer."

She smiled. "I'm still willing to let you lead, for today."

"Smart girl. How's your food?"

She pulled a face. "I've had better, but I've also had much worse."

"I think that was an honest answer. I'm glad you felt bold enough to come clean. Now I'm going to have to punish you for insulting the heck out of me in my own kitchen."

"What kind of punishment do you have in mind?"

"Well, it's not serious enough to justify a court martial, but I might consider giving you life if you don't watch yourself!" He winked at her. "A lifetime with me."

Hailey's smile glowed brightly. "That was sweet. I love you, Major."

His eyes glowed every bit as much as her smile. "I love you, too, Staff Sergeant."

Eleven

As usual, Hailey saw that she was the only African-American, but not the only person of color, in her unit, as her sponsor, Technical Sergeant Lila Briggs, took her around to meet everyone assigned to the 25th Weather Detachment. Two Hispanics, male and female, a Philippine-American female, a male from St. Thomas, Virgin Islands, and numerous Caucasians made up the work force. Feeling a genuinely warm welcome from each member, Hailey sighed in relief.

The diversity of a unit always made for interesting conversation, and she positively loved the animated exchanges of cultural ideas. When unit potluck luncheons or dinners were held, she always looked forward to the swapping of recipes on the different styles of foods and how they were prepared. She liked the fellowship and eating parts best. She felt as if she would fit in well with this group of smiling Air Force personnel. Everyone seemed pretty nice.

Once the tour was finished, Hailey settled down at her workstation and began to organize her desk tools and store her personal items. The previous day's orientation session had been a long one, as usual, but was very necessary. A lot of vital information was exchanged during the course of the day. Understanding the host nation's laws, driving and otherwise, was an absolute must. When venturing off base, the laws of the land also governed U.S. military members. Knowing and obeying the laws of the host nation was an absolute requirement.

Hailey was only working half-days for the rest of this

week, but come next week she would be on full duty as an integral member of the weather support team. Hailey loved her job as much as her father had loved his. Providing weather support to the base's flying squadrons was a major function of the unit. She loved meeting all the visiting pilots who came up to the counter for weather briefings before taking off into the wild blue yonder. Hailey had a deep fascination with the fighter pilots, but only because she was in awe of what they did. They didn't look too bad in their flight gear, either.

As her thoughts turned to the conversation she and Zurich had had about their prospective jobs, a lazy smile came to her lips. Major Kingdom was extremely knowledgeable in meteorology. The brother had it going on in the applied science department. She'd felt as if she was having a conversation with a heavy-duty physical science textbook.

How they'd managed to get through an entire evening without so much as a kiss, yet go away utterly fulfilled, still amazed her. Zurich had dropped her off in front of the hotel, only squeezing her hand with gentle affection as he bade her a farewell and pleasant dreams. His eyes had expressed his deepest feelings, his unconditional love for her. She'd lain awake a long time after going to bed just thinking about all the things they'd discussed.

Knowing they had more than just a physical thing going for them actually excited her to no end. It only heightened her desire to be an important part of his life. Their conversations often left her fascinated and enlightened. Hailey was so in love with Major Zurich Kingdom that she didn't want to even try to imagine her life without him.

They certainly had a lot in common. Their highly technical jobs were only one among many common interests. Two meteorologists in one household was a riveting thought. If they were blessed enough to marry one day, there would be three atmospheric science nuts in one family. That would really drive her mother insane. Her inward laughter bubbled.

They both loved sports, romantic movies, traveling, and watching the Weather Channel, the Discovery Channel, and nature shows like Wild Kingdom. Hailey also loved to watch the true-to-life stories on the Lifetime Channel, which she was going to miss sorely since television programming was limited overseas. Zurich preferred Star Trek and other science fiction series. He was particularly fond of the Star Wars movies, and owned the complete set of videocassettes. He also loved war movies. *Tora! Tora! Tora!: the Attack on Pearl Harbor* was his favorite. *Midway* and *In Harms Way* came in second and third. He wasn't terribly fond of the films on Vietnam.

Hailey didn't have to look up to know that Zurich stood there. What she wasn't prepared for was how devastatingly handsome he looked in his uniform. The brother was fine, and he looked impeccable in his Air Force blues. From his head down to his spit-shined shoes he was a magnificent work of art. Hailey's heart continued to swoon like crazy while she tried to figure out why the women's military uniforms didn't do the same thing for them as the men's did.

While the unit commander introduced Zurich to her as the weather squadron's operations officer, she did her best to hide any flicker of recognition. He, on the other hand, had an undeniable twinkle of devilment in his eyes. Zurich did very little to ease her discomfort with his taunting, flirtatious smile. She was going to have to talk to that boy, she told herself.

Hailey hoped he'd check himself before she had to read him or before someone else began to easily read them both. The knowing looks they often shared had to be curbed. She and Zurich had developed a natural way of looking at each other, as if they were about to or had just finished making heart-stopping love. Their eyes always communicated soulfully.

As Zurich moved on with Lt. Colonel Raymond Paul in

the lead, he made a slight turn of his head and looked back at her. When he winked, Hailey did everything in her power to keep herself from blushing like a fool. The fact that she failed at that mission didn't surprise her one bit. Her face wasn't the only part of her anatomy feeling the heat.

Hailey couldn't deny the warm feelings Zurich always left her with. The man did it for her on every level. She still couldn't get over the fact that they were stationed on the same base in a foreign country—and that he was actually her man. She wasn't sure how long she could claim him as such, but forever was a very nice thought to entertain, habitually so.

Freshly showered and dressed in a bathrobe, Hailey hung up her uniform and then fully stretched herself out on the bed. She hadn't expended a lot of energy at work, but she felt tired. The time difference was partly responsible for her fatigue. Having watched Zurich strutting here and there around the office had also tired her out, because she'd had to work so hard to keep her mind off of him, not to mention the nights they'd been so free to make passionate love to each other. She had to wonder if they'd have that sort of freedom ever again. For now she'd have to rely on her memories and her creative imagination to get her through the lonely days and nights.

Well, she had to admit that she hadn't had time to be lonely; Zurich was seeing to that.

Zurich used his cell phone to put a call in to the hotel. He asked for Hailey's room the moment the operator came on the line. He grinned broadly when he heard her sweet voice come over the line. "Hey, Staff Sergeant, what's happening with you?"

"You! Where are you?"

He laughed. "In my car, riding around this base trying to figure out how I can manage to see you before I go home. I came up with a good idea. Put your jogging clothes on and meet me at the share-a-ride stand. Not the one in front of the hotel. Walk across the street to the one near the BX. How much time do you need?"

"Zurich!"

"Hailey, no lectures please, not right now. Just agree to do it or say you won't, okay?"

"*At your service*, Commander!"

Dressed in a navy blue Nike jogging outfit and white Nikes, Hailey slipped into the passenger seat of the black Corvette. The bright smile Zurich gave her kept her from acting unpleasant. She loved being with him, but she still feared them getting caught up in something they couldn't handle. She was also worried about them spending so much time with each other, since it only served to fuel their sexual appetites. They physically turned each other on. Hailey wanted to make love to him every time she laid eyes on him, and the I-want-you looks he always gave her revealed his answering desire.

"Mad at me?"

She cut her eyes at him, noticing that he'd already changed out of his uniform and into athletic gear. "I guess not. I'm just starting to get a little fearful."

"No need to be. Everything is under control. Trust me, Hailey."

"Under whose control?"

"Hailey, relax. Arguing about this isn't going to help. Our time together is short. Let's enjoy the little time we do have. Please."

Surrendering to his plea, she relaxed against the seat back. She could either be willing to deal with any and all consequences in order to be with him, or she had to stop giving in to his demands. This was her life, not his, and she had to make her decisions according to what was right for her. Not wanting to deal with any unpleasantness, Hailey closed her eyes and conjured up a place where no stress existed, a place where she could completely free her spirit.

The thirty-minute ride was accomplished without them uttering a word. Only the music from the radio had prevented a deafening silence, yet the aura felt tension-free. He parked near the entry of a beautiful park surrounded by a dense forest. Looking out the window at all the splendor of God's creation, Hailey waited until Zurich opened her car door before getting out.

Leaning on the car, he pointed in one direction and then in the other. "I'll take this path and you take that one. Stay on the straight-away. Don't make any turns and it will bring you into the center of the forest. The path I'm taking will meet up with yours. I'm anxious to see who gets there first. Do we have a race?"

"You're on!" Hailey took off running, wanting badly to win.

Just so she could show him that she could outdo him at something, she kicked her butt into high gear. Zurich needed to come down a tad off his role as a commander, she thought, laughing as she tore up the solidly packed dirt path. She was no stranger to jogging or other strenuous exercise. She hadn't kept her body in such good shape by ignoring it. Besides, the Air Force required their members to take physical-fitness endurance and aerobic tests on a regular basis. Hailey groaned when she realized she'd left her water and towel bag in the car. To turn around now would mean a sound defeat for her and a sure win for him. *No way.*

Hailey couldn't believe that Zurich beat her to the clearing. But what she really couldn't fathom was that he'd had time to spread a blanket under a tree and put out food and drink. Then she spotted something shiny hidden behind a high bush. A closer look allowed her to see exactly what was gleaming. It looked as if the man had ridden a bicycle to the rendezvous point while she had run her buns off. She hadn't noticed a bicycle rack on the back of his car the first time she'd seen it, but it must have one unless the bike had appeared out of thin air.

While waiting for him to 'fess up, Hailey sat down on the blanket. The sight of various types of German sausage, bratwurst and rindwurst being her favorites, made her mouth water. The aluminum container of red-potato salad looked smooth and creamy. A couple of plastic containers of fruit juice caught her eye. She immediately reached for one. She then spotted the bottled water and opted to put the juice back. Water best suited her thirst after such a hard run.

"Nice spread you got here, Kingdom. How'd you manage to carry all this food and drink while jogging through the forest?"

"You know me." He shrugged. "I got skills and I'm very innovative."

She raised an eyebrow. "I would've never guessed." She bit into the sausage, chewed it up very slowly, and then swallowed it. "Why you trying to play me, Kingdom?"

"What are you talking about, Hailey?"

"Like you don't know. I'd better eat so I can keep my big mouth shut. But I owe you one! And I am going to deliver on that promise."

Hailey suddenly spotted movement in the bushes and her on-guard antenna went up instantly. When a teenage boy emerged from the dense greenery, pushing a shiny bike equipped with a good-size metal basket, she became really curious as to what was going on. She now knew that the bike didn't belong to Zurich.

Zurich said something to the boy in German. Then he pointed at Hailey, smiling broadly. The boy vigorously nodded his head in agreement that she was beautiful as he took the wad of Euros from Zurich's extended hand.

The young man thanked Zurich in his native tongue and took off. It puzzled Hailey that he didn't take the bike, but then she thought that he had to be coming back.

"Let me guess. You paid him to bring all this stuff into the park."

"You got it right on the first try, Hailey. He's my landlord's son. Heinrich runs a lot of little errands for me. He's a really good kid, and he agrees with me on your beauty. Wants to be a fighter pilot. Not long after I moved out here, I learned how crazy he was about flying, so I arranged for him to meet some of my friends who are also fly-boys. In case you didn't notice on the way in, this is the park right behind my apartment, the one you can see from my bedroom."

Shaking her head, she blushed at the reference to her looks. "Okay, this rendezvous point makes sense now. That was generous of you to introduce the kid to your pilot buddies. I'm sure he was ecstatic. Now back to you. How'd you plan this nice little picnic in the park so quickly?"

"I told you I have skills, girl, major ones. I just called Heinrich from the base and told him what I needed him to do. The family owns a small market. As you can see, he accomplished the mission for me. Are you impressed with my little surprise for you?"

"Genuinely! But I'm afraid I have another confession to make. I thought you rode the bike in here while I jogged my tail off. I really do have to stop doubting you."

He cracked up. "I *did* ride my bike in here while you worked up a sweat and a good appetite. Heinrich was waiting for me in the parking lot with my bicycle, just as planned. I keep it on the balcony, and he already knows where I keep the spare key to the lock. We came into the forest together to put the blanket and food out. The rest is no mystery."

She was visibly stunned. "You blow me away. If that's your bike, where's his?"

"He chained it up a little ways back. There are several racks throughout the park."

She shrugged. "Okay, mister. Now, tell me this, are you planning to ride back to the car while I walk or jog?"

He grinned. "You don't expect me to leave my hot wheels out here, do you? Of course I'm going to ride back—and so are you. Either on the handlebars or behind me; you get to choose all by yourself."

Her eyes cut him down to size. "Aren't we generous in allowing Hailey to make her own choices. But I have a better idea. I'll ride the bike back to the car while you jog back, which is how it should've been in the first place. We were supposed to be racing. You catching my drift?"

He laughed heartily. "I'm quite a bit bigger than you, Hailey. That gives me the edge."

While rubbing her hands together, she gave him a cynical look. "J. Smooth was a lot bigger than me, too. I hope you haven't forgotten what happened to him, twice, within a two-week period. I'm as well trained as you are, if not more so. Just so you'll know up front, I recently took a specialized training class in hand-to-hand combat. I passed with flying colors."

The mention of her personal nemesis made him cringe. While he'd understood Hailey's reasons for not telling him about that last incident sooner than she had, he wished she hadn't waited until they were on the way to the airport. On the other hand, she'd done what she'd thought was best. Hailey had known that he would've tried to track the guy down before he left town, even it meant going down to the jail, which could've landed Zurich's butt behind bars, too. Knowing that she had been right about him had allowed him to get past her not confiding in him.

"I'm sorry. I can see that I've walked into a dicey topic. Are you still upset with me for not telling you right away what happened?"

His eyes connected with hers. "No, baby, I'm not upset with you. It just bothers me to know that I wasn't there for you at the time. I didn't do anything when my father repeatedly beat my mother, and I've failed to come to your rescue on two occasions now. I ran off to the military rather than stand up and confront my father like a real man would've done. I was more concerned about what could happen to me if I took him down rather than being concerned about what was happening to Mom. I also left my little brother there in the midst of all that abuse and turmoil. It's not something I can ever be proud of." His shame was there in his eyes.

He threw up his hands. "I bear the heavy burden of my guilt every single day, Hailey. No matter where I go or how far away from home I get, I carry the scars with me. I have yet to learn how to turn those scars into stars."

Nothing could've stopped her from scooting across the blanket and taking hold of his hand. The Judge General Advocate could've been looking on and it wouldn't have mattered in the least to her. Zurich needed to be comforted. She understood him perfectly because she carried similar feelings of profound guilt regarding Kelly. Her own burden was something she had held within for a very long time. She felt every bit as guilty as Zurich did.

"You've already turned your scars into shining stars, Zurich. You've made something of yourself. You left home to keep out of jail. For you to abuse your father physically would have been far more damaging than any other course of action. You did the right thing. You see, we have choices in this life. You need to accept the fact that your mother made a conscious decision to stay in the abusive situation. That was not your choice for her. On the other hand, you made the choice, a very wise one I should say, to get away from the violence so that you wouldn't end up suffering dire consequences. Are you hearing what I'm saying to you?"

He squeezed her hand. "Every word of it. Thanks for always trying to shed some light on the dark path I sometimes find myself on. I'm sure that your experiences with your girlfriend help you to understand what I'm feeling. We both loved people who we couldn't save. That's just one of the things we have in common, but I'm not sure that's such a good one to boast on."

"It's a great thing for us to share, Zurich. It's one of the things that has led to the compassion and understanding between us. As much as we wanted to save them and rescue them from their horrific circumstances, we couldn't. We didn't even have the power to save them from themselves. We're blaming ourselves for something we couldn't control. But knowing that for a fact doesn't always relieve the guilt and asking the "what if" questions. Are we back on the same page?"

Leaning into her, he kissed her on the cheek. "Same book, same page. Did you get enough to eat?"

"I'm going to eat a little more if you don't mind. Since you're riding the bike out of here, I need to store up some extra energy for pounding my way back to the car. I'm a leader, so the back of the bike won't cut it. That metal basket is daunting, which makes the handlebars a no-go, too."

"The basket is completely removable. It can lock into the back grooves or the front ones. What if I move it to the back?"

She smiled brightly. "In that case, you have a passenger." She looked at her watch. "It's getting late. We both have early-morning duty. Let me take these last few bites so we can wrap everything up and be on our way. Sound like a plan?"

He squeezed her hand again in response. "You go ahead and fill yourself up. I hope you can eat and listen at the same time. I've got a few things to run by you." He locked his fingers together. *Here we go.* "I think you and I should get away for a weekend, away from prying eyes and inquisitive minds. I'd like us to fly to Mykonos . . ."

"As in the Greek Isles?" she interjected.

"The one and only. Hailey, I'm not suggesting we do

this so we can be all over each other because we'll be out of the public eye."

Her head jerked up. "Oh, that's too bad. I rather like the idea of us being all over each other, as well as being totally into us. Like it was on the island."

He smiled gently. "I know, but we're not on the island now. This is a tough situation we're in and we're both uptight about it. I don't show it as much as you do, but I do have deep concerns. I'm studying all the issues in depth. While I'm interested in the Air Force directives, I'm paying closer attention to the instructions, which deal with the penalty phases. I never really paid much attention to the rules because I just accepted them as cut-and-dried. I never thought I'd be in that type of situation, so I really didn't see any reason to research the matter of fraternization. The strongest thing that we have going for us is that neither of us knew."

"But there's still the matter of us knowing it now. Why do you insist on us getting any deeper into trouble than we might already be? Being here like this can be considered unprofessional, irresponsible behavior. And now we're talking about going away together. Maybe we should've just gotten married in Texas."

"Delicious thought, Hailey, yet it's only hindsight. The fact that we're in love with each other won't amount to a hill of beans if we're not sure where this relationship is headed. We owe it to ourselves to get away from the base environment and really talk things through. Think you can warm to the idea?"

Her eyes were soft with liquid as she looked at him. "You once spoke about wanting to be the only one to take the responsibility for whatever might come our way as a result of our love affair. But I have to ask you this: Are you saying that because you feel you have to save me, in the same way you felt you couldn't save your mother?"

"That's a fair question. Unfortunately, I can't give you an honest answer without searching deep within. Can you give me a couple of days to explore the issue? I promise to answer your question soon as I have the answer."

"Take all the time you need, Zurich. But if that turns out to be the case, I want my voice to be clear on this matter. I'm not looking for a rescuer or a savior. I'm capable of saving myself and being my own champion, but only with help from above. The Lord is the only savior I'll ever need. He has already rescued me more times than I can remember. Therefore I don't *need* you as a rescuer, nor do I need your friendship and your love. I simply *want* it, even if that's with something akin to desperation. The difference in want and need is this: I need food and water to survive. The love of a man will not satisfy my need for nourishment. On the other hand, I very much want the love of a good man, one who will enhance my joy, and revel in my peace with self. Are you feeling me on all that?"

"You have my full attention. I like what you have to say. But are you saying that you don't need me for anything? If so, that scares me."

"There are countless things that I might need you for. I can't have a baby without you, but I'd have to *want* you as the father of my children before the need would arise. All I was saying is that I don't want you to feel that I need you to be responsible for me in the areas we just discussed. I know how to hang tough. I need you to kiss me right now, need to have you relieve me of my pent-up sexual frustrations, but I know that can't happen. Cold showers don't work for me, not when I'm hopelessly hooked on the type of lovemaking a certain Major doles out."

"We're both hooked, Hailey. Make no mistake about that. But why can't it happen?"

She sucked her teeth. "There you go again. You already know the answer."

"What I want to know the answer to is this: Why can't I relieve your sexual desires without being inside of you?"

Hailey blushed. "You can, but it would still require

physical contact." The thought of him relieving her in other arousing ways excited her.

"You sure about that?"

She shook her head. "I'm not sure of anything anymore but what I feel for you. If you can take me over the top without touching me, I'd love to go there. But I'm rather partial to having you touch me deep within."

Without uttering a word, he began to gather up their belongings. After packing everything in the basket he'd transferred to the back of the bicycle, he deposited all the trash in the metal cans provided by the park services.

Zurich gripped the handlebars, rubbing the metal base to warm them up. "Ready to park your sweet butt on these hard babies?"

"I can think of another, harder place I'd prefer to park myself on, but I wouldn't want to be accused of taunting you. The heat's already rising."

"If that wasn't a taunt, I don't know what is. The heat you're now experiencing ain't nothing compared to what you'll be feeling before I'm through with you."

"In the words of Major Kingdom, I love it when you threaten me with a good time!"

The handlebars felt very uncomfortable so Hailey dismounted and placed her folded jacket over them. She then got back on, fidgeting about until she made herself comfortable.

Zurich leaned forward and briefly rested his chin on her shoulder. "Are you comfortable now, baby?"

Hailey laughed. "I wouldn't use that exact term, but I'm good to go."

Hailey began to giggle as Zurich set the bicycle in motion. She hadn't ridden on the handlebars of a bike since she was a small child. Zurich had complete control of the two-wheeler, which kept it from zigzagging all over the place. She was grateful for that.

Thoughts of Kelly instantly came to mind, wonderful thoughts of the times they'd played with dolls and shared numerous sleepovers. The memories of them laughing all night long were fresh in her mind. Their lives had been so easy and carefree. Feeling the wind in her hair was exhilarating. This was fun. As they whisked by the tall trees, Hailey's laughter filled the air.

The sound of her joy excited Zurich. He'd never before heard her laugh with such wild abandon. She was being downright silly, but he didn't find her girlish behavior the least bit distasteful. It seemed as if someone was tickling her; perhaps it was the fingers of the wind, he mused, smiling at the thought. In hopes of prolonging the thrilling ride for her, he decided to take the long way around. For the next twenty minutes or so Hailey and Zurich basked in the beauty of nature and reveled in their deep feelings for each other as they rode along in sweet harmony.

Hailey watched from the car as Zurich chained his bike to the rack. He planned to come back and retrieve it after he got her back to the hotel. He jogged through the park every evening, so he would just leave the car at home and jog back. Her adoring eyes followed him from the bike rack and up to where he disappeared behind the car. Seconds later he was seated beside her, right where she hoped he'd always be.

Zurich got back out of the car and walked around to the passenger side and opened the door. Kneeling down, he set about the task of adjusting the seat into a position that would maximize Hailey's comfort.

It seemed to Hailey that his thoughtfulness was without end.

Back inside the car, he buckled his seat belt and turned on the ignition. "Ready for that trip we talked about?"

"To Mykonos?"

His gaze locked into hers with a look that nearly set her soul on fire. "No, silly. The one to paradise without me physically touching you."

Hailey laughed nervously. "Do we really want to go there?"

The look in his eyes was sweetly challenging. "That's entirely up to you, baby."

Laughing, she rechecked her seat belt. "Ready for blast off!"

"Rest your head back and close your eyes. You're going to have to rely on your imagination for the scenes; my voice and the content of the story will provide the rest."

Zurich set up the scenario by telling Hailey about a man and woman who were deeply in love, but the woman was still a virgin and wanted to stay pure until their wedding night. The guy wanted to play by her rules, but was really hot for her. So he decided that he had to be innovative in his way of thinking. He came up with the idea of creating a heated situation that would hopefully leave them both physically fulfilled without actually engaging in the act of lovemaking. He then told Hailey that the story he was telling her was probably like the ones told by the person who'd created phone sex. They both held their laughter so as not to spoil the mood.

Hailey was already on the edge of her seat and Zurich hadn't even begun the story.

"It's late in the evening and the couple have come back to his place after a evening of fine dining and listening to romantic music. He creates a sensual mood by filling up all the slots on the CD player with Luther Vandross recordings. To further relax her, he pours a glass of wine and sets it in front of her on the coffee table. After he has her stretch out on the sofa in a comfortable position, he props up her feet on a couple of bed pillows. That will be the extent of him touching her outwardly. Now he knows he has to do his thing in touching her inwardly, using only his voice and his creative mind."

Zurich turned down the soft music playing on the CD in his car. "Now that his woman looks relaxed and ready to be lulled into another galaxy, he seats himself in the leather recliner and adjusts the chair it to a position that suits his needs. 'Close your eyes,' he tells his woman.

"'I'm going to now speak of the things we're going to indulge in on the first night of our honeymoon. As you stand before me in your flowing white satin gown, I can see that your skin is soft and fresh with the dewdrops of the lotion that I've just massaged into your body. My first thought is to lower the gown down over your shoulders so my lips can gently dust your beautiful neck and shoulders with butterfly kisses.'

"The slight trembling of her untouched body excites him, making him wonder if he can really go through this and come out of it not wanting to make love to her even more. 'As my finger reaches up and lazes across your full bottom lip, I feel you shudder.'

"That caused him to continue caressing her lips with his fingertips. When her mouth parts slightly, he places his finger at the opening. As though she knew exactly what he wants from her, she drew his finger into her mouth and tenderly sucks on it. He closes his eyes since that erotic gesture makes him imagine her mouth elsewhere on his anatomy as he moans with undeniable pleasure."

Zurich paused for a moment, as if he was thinking. He then continued on. "Then he realized that her pleasure had to come first. It was his desire to make her first journey into his sexual fantasyland a memorable one. With that in mind, he lifts her hand and begins to taste each of her fingertips. One by one, he tends to them with loving care. He then draws her forefinger into his mouth and treats it to a thrilling seduction. His hands then go back to her gown and lowers it until her full, ripe breasts come into view. He gasps with desire when he sees that her nipples are hard and erect, as if in eager anticipation of the feel of his tender hands and mouth. He has to swallow hard because his mouth has gone dry."

Zurich took a moment to look over at Hailey. Her eyes were still closed and that made him smile. It told him she was deep into the story, or that she was bored and had fallen off to sleep. He shuddered at the latter thought.

"Unable to control his desire for the taste of her delectable flesh, he dips his fingers in the wine and sprinkles it on her breasts. He then bends forward and sweeps his lips across her heaving mounds. Her sensual moans urge him on. His tongue darts out but he only allows the tip of it to tease her nipples until her breasts are ready for submission. As she begins to squirm, he takes one of her breasts fully into his mouth but his fingertips keeps the thrilling pressure on her other nipple. While gorging himself on her sweetness, his hands move down and rove over her body with the gentleness of a butterfly. Her moans grow louder as his manhood continues to outgrow his briefs. His hands and mouth suddenly develop a mind of their own. He can't seem to control either as they work her beautiful body into a nearly uncontrollable frenzy. His mouth is everywhere while his hands urgently find the soft flesh between her legs. His fingers slowly caress and massage her inner sanctum until she screams out his name. Prolonging the sweetest agony he'd ever known, he lowers his head and allows his tongue to go anywhere it so desires. As her body trembles with her dire need for him to take her to the paradise he's described for her, his tight control instantly breaks free. He then nestles his manhood deep inside of her, thrusting, stroking, and rocking her world until his release entwines with hers and comes like a raging river."

Hailey's pleasurable moans had Zurich pulling the car off the road and into yet another area of dense forest. As promised, he had taken her to paradise—and without the slightest touch of his hand to her lovely body.

While towel-drying her body, cherishing the never-to-be-told secrets she and Zurich had vowed to hold within, Hailey wore a tantalizing smile on her face. She felt as if there were a magical aura surrounding her as she selected from the drawer a white silk gown that reminded her of the flowing one the woman wore in Zurich's erotic tale of love and seduction.

In a way, she felt as if this was *her* honeymoon night, too. Her skin flushed as the memory of their first night of making love flashed in her mind. Zurich had a way of making her feel like a blushing bride every time he looked at her or merely touched his hand to any part of her anatomy. The way he so lovingly caressed her face was the most sensual of all. Zurich's hands were always warm and tender, just like his wonderful caring heart. She loved both.

No one could've ever made her believe that she would enjoy a man spinning erotic tales for her while she relaxed in the seat of his car, let alone completely succumb to the ecstasy of them. Zurich had kept his promise to her, and she couldn't begin to imagine him breaking his word to her. He had won her complete trust and unwavering loyalty. Her heart was in his hands.

Hailey never realized men like Zurich existed in the world. Although her father was a wonderful man, he was just that, her father. Her mother had always carried the glow of love and happiness on her face and in her eyes, but Hailey never even dared to think of her parents in the biblical sense. As far as she was concerned, they were just two people happy and in love.

Hailey believed that her and Zurich's relationship was a masterpiece of rare beauty. They only seemed to fully blossom when in each other's company. If their feelings were painted on canvas for the world to view, she imagined it would be an awesome portrait to behold.

How something that felt so natural and so right could be considered a criminal offense under the military code of justice was way beyond her comprehension. Yet, deep down inside her heart, she knew there had to be just cause for the country's national defense organizations to impose any sort of penalty on the craziest of all the emotions, this wonderful thing called love; the only crazy thing the world needed more of.

Stretched fully out in his bed, laying flat on his stomach, Zurich intently studied the Air Force directives and instructions on fraternization in the thick manual open in front of him. He couldn't believe how much material had been written on the subject, which meant he had tons of reading to do. Reading it was one thing, but he had to fully understand the policies, not as they were written, but as to their actual intent and application.

Before the fat lady could even get the chance to weigh in with her song, Zurich was sure he'd more than likely have to pay a visit to the Area Defense Counsel. The ADC functioned independently of the Judge Advocate General (JAG), which could possibly give him other options to consider. As it stood now, he was beginning to feel the ever-growing conflict between his personal life and his sworn duty to his country—and he darn well needed to know all the options available to him and then some if he was to avoid devastation in both vital areas.

While he fully realized that it was premature to consider a feasible defense, he was determined to find out exactly what he was up against. Every action that he'd taken thus far, as it pertained to their relationship, had let him know how serious he was about Hailey Hamilton. It was crystal clear to him that his feelings for Hailey were nothing akin to a foolish case of misguided lust.

A man who'd risk his lifelong career for a beautiful woman was a man deeply in love.

Twelve

Hailey looked around her new apartment as if she was seeing it for the first time ever. It looked totally different with her hold baggage stacked up all over the place. Glad that she had the entire weekend to put things in some kind of order, she set about the task of opening one of the boxes in the kitchen. The movers had been gracious in putting away the labeled boxes, each one with the designated room clearly marked on it with a black marker.

An unexpected knock came on the door and Hailey was almost happy to put her work on hold despite the fact she hadn't even begun. The only person it could be was Alicia, because she was the only one who knew exactly where Hailey lived. Seeing that she was right as she looked out the peephole, Hailey eagerly opened the door. While she was thrilled to have Alicia pop over, she wasn't prepared for all the brawny males trooping in right behind her dear friend. The very last person she expected to see was Zurich bringing up the rear, yet she wasn't all that surprised. He simply had his own way of doing things. He had already known about her move.

"Hey, girl," Alicia sang out. "I've rounded up all these muscled guys so they can make light work of getting this apartment in shape. Where shall we start?"

Alicia quickly raised her hand in a halting gesture. "Wait a minute here. I'm totally going about this the wrong way. Please forgive me for not first making the introductions. Guys, meet Hailey Hamilton, one of my best friends, my hanging-out partner. We went through basic together. Like me, this girl knows how to have a real good time. Hailey, these are all friends of Phillip's." Alicia took his hand. "This is the Phillip I've been whispering to you about."

Hailey extended her hand to the good-looking brother who had the kind of muscles that most men wished for. "Nice to meet you, Phillip. Thanks for coming to help out."

"You're welcome, Hailey." Phillip then took the liberty of introducing his friendly work crew, consisting of two head-turning brothers, Ron and Justice, and two nice-looking white guys, Tim and Art. Too cute for his own good was a strapping Hispanic guy, Carlos.

"Phillip and his buddies are all civilians assigned to AAFES. And this nice guy here," Alicia dared to say about an officer, "is a dear friend of another very close friend of mine. Zurich offered to help out when he overheard me asking for volunteers to help get you-all settled in. Now that all the introductions have been made, let's get this party going."

Hailey had a difficult time acting like she didn't know Zurich. When he extended his hand to her, she looked almost afraid to take it, knowing she might very well melt from his touch.

"It's nice to meet you, Hailey."

She lowered her eyelashes to veil her feelings for him. "Same here."

"Hey, you two, let's get to work! You guys can explore that love connection thing you got going later on," Phillip joked. He then turned to Alicia. "I got a feeling you've been playing matchmaker. Am I right?"

Alicia gave Phillip a withering look. "Like you said, let's get to work, 'cause you're embarrassing the hell out of all of us with that silly nonsense. Zurich happens to be engaged to one of my dear friends. Hailey, where do you want us to start?" Alicia asked.

Hailey nearly went through the floor at Alicia's outright

lie. Zurich obviously thought her remark was comical since he was laughing to beat the band. In fact, everyone was laughing but her. *Loosen up,* she scolded herself inwardly, *you are way too uptight.*

Hailey noticed that Alicia didn't seem the least bit worried that Phillip had easily observed what was going on with her and Zurich. On the other hand, Hailey was worried sick about it. It was going to be interesting to find out how Zurich really happened to be here; Hailey wasn't buying Alicia's tall tale of him volunteering his services. But then again, she couldn't be sure. Alicia and Zurich both had the same kind of devilishly defiant streak in their personalities.

"I was just getting started in the kitchen, but that might be a good area for a couple of the guys to start in. Do you mind supervising the kitchen duties, Alicia? You'll know just where to put everything since you're so organized. Then you'll have to tell me where to find it all."

Both women laughed.

Once the duties were all decided upon, Hailey went into the bedroom she'd chosen for herself. It didn't surprise her to have Zurich follow her since he'd already made his working preference clear to the others in a joking manner. The guys thought Zurich was following up on Phillip's assessment of him and Hailey just to prove Phillip wrong; they had no clue.

"You are incorrigible! What are you doing here, Zurich?" she whispered through clenched teeth, her back to the door.

He instantly went into his innocent act with a nonchalant shrug. "Helping out a friend of a friend. What does it look like to you?" he whispered back.

"Okay, okay." She found that she couldn't withhold her smile from him. No matter how incorrigible he was, she loved him. What was the use in trying to pretend otherwise, at least when no one was looking?

"I love you, too," he whispered as if he'd read her mind.

He then gave her his customary wink, one of the things he often did when he was practicing pure devilment.

All she could do was smile.

Only a couple of hours had passed, but the entire apartment was practically in complete order. Hailey had just come back into the bedroom after checking on the others up front.

She sat down on the bed. "Everything is almost put away. I can't believe how quickly this is going. All the help extra help sure came in handy."

Zurich held up a pair of lace bikinis and a black lacy matching bra. "Where do you want all these itty-bitty things in this box to go?"

The color rose in Hailey's cheek. "In the top drawer, thank you." Hailey hated giving him the satisfaction of showing him that he knew exactly how to embarrass her to no end.

"Aren't you glad that I'm the one who opted to help you out in here?"

"Why's that? I'm sure all the guys have seen women's underwear."

"Maybe so, but not yours. Are you saying it wouldn't have bothered you if one of the other guys had unpacked your skimpy little bras and panties?"

"First of all, you're the one who chose bedroom duty. Whether you were here or not, no, I wouldn't have let anyone near these boxes. Don't you think I knew exactly what was in them? For your further information, *I* boxed up my personal items, not the packers. I do have my pride."

"Don't get so haughty. I'm just having a jealous moment. Just the thought of your boys in there seeing what only I should see got my blood boiling a bit."

Zurich looked too adorable when he'd admitted to being jealous. He actually seemed embarrassed by indulging in the emotion. He was so sure of himself. Jealousy just wasn't something she'd expected him to show, let alone confess.

He turned his back to the door to make sure no one could overhear him. "I'm not the jealous type, Hailey, if that's what you're looking so worried about. You didn't do anything to cause that little streak of green to unexpectedly rise up in my eyes. I know you're not the type."

"What type?"

"The kind of woman who makes an art form of trying to make her man jealous. You know, the kind who loves to flaunt herself in another man's face while she knows for sure her man is looking on."

Hailey got to her feet. "You're right. I'm nothing like that." She quickly formed a steeple with her hands and held them against her mouth for a brief moment. "I have an idea. We're finished in here, so why don't we join the others? That way, we can steer clear of trouble." Her eyes encompassed the bed and then slowly roved over his delicious anatomy.

He gave her a winning smile. "You may have something there, Staff Sergeant. I can see that you can also be an incorrigible brat. The pot should never call the skillet black."

"Pray tell, Major!"

Hailey looked around at all the areas that had been filled with boxes just a short time ago. Her place would never again look this uncluttered. Alicia had supervised the unpacking in an expeditious and orderly fashion, just the way she organized her entire life. Hailey wasn't an envious person, but she'd certainly love to have a little of Alicia's organizational skills rub off on her. Zurich was another one who had a place for everything and everything in its place. Thinking of how much she lacked in the neatness department often made her wonder if she'd missed out on some important lesson while growing up. She surely hadn't developed her bad habits from her parents. You could eat off the floors in their clean and neat-as-a-pin home.

"Are you going to feed us, kid?" Alicia asked. "That's the least you can do. We've been your workhorses today."

Hailey looked embarrassed. "If you can find anything in my refrigerator, I'll be happy to cook for everyone. Alicia, you know I haven't been grocery shopping. I only received all my things today. But I *can* take you all out to eat."

Alicia walked over and hugged Hailey. "I'm just kidding. Anybody want to go across the hall to my place? I have a huge pot of spaghetti just waiting for a bunch of hungry folks to show up and eat it. My garlic bread is to die for. I even have warm beer, the way our German hosts love to drink it." She pulled a face. "My brother is coming today. He likes his beer warm, too."

All the guys but Zurich nodded their approval. Hailey understood his reluctance.

"Alicia, could I see you in private for a moment. I need to give you something. Will you all please excuse us?" Hailey's question got the same nods of approval.

Zurich just eyed her curiously, wondering why she suddenly appeared to be upset.

Hailey opened her purse and took out several twenty-dollar bills. "Will you pay the guys for me. I know they won't take it if I try to give it to them."

"So you want me to insult them for you, huh? They're not going to take your money. Those guys enjoyed helping out. Everybody's not out for monetary gain. They did a good deed. Say thanks and give them your sweetest smile. That'll be more than enough. After I feed them, they'll be happier than mud-bathing pigs."

"Well, I guess you've told me!" Hailey took Alicia's hand and squeezed it affectionately. "One more thing before we go back. Zurich didn't look too comfortable about coming to your place. We have to be so careful. Do you understand?"

"Of course. Aren't you curious about how he got here in the first place?"

"I've been afraid to ask. Who initiated what? You or him?"

"I ran into him at the BX during lunchtime a while back. I introduced myself first and then I told him a few of my civilian friends, emphasizing civilian, were going to help you get settled in to your new apartment. He said count me in. I gave him the address even though I was sure he already had it. The rest is history. Pretty clever of me, huh?"

"Really? That means he'd already known he was coming here for some time now. You two are the world's worst and its very best. I'm going to come over to your place, but I want a couple of minutes to say good-bye to Zurich. I'm sure he's ready to go by now. Thanks for that big white lie you told. I know you did it to protect us. I appreciate it."

"These guys don't have a clue about anything to do with military codes of justice. They have top paying jobs at AAFES. Phillip is the least likely to want to cause any trouble for someone. Don't work up a sweat over it. By the way, what do you think of Phillip?"

"I definitely noticed those muscles of his. He's very handsome. I think you picked out a winner. I hope it works for you two and that you find in each other whatever you're looking for. I found the pot of gold at the end of the rainbow on South Padre Island. I just wish I wasn't so fearful of losing him to regulations. I hope you and Zurich can get to know each other one day. He's a really great guy."

"He sure is fine enough. And he *was* wearing the hell out of his uniform when I first saw him. The pictures you have of him don't do him a bit of justice. Come on. We'd better get back out there before they send out a search party. I'm sure the guys are hungry."

"Hold up. I need to ask you one question. How in the

heck did you get up the nerve to approach Zurich in the first place? With him being an officer, I would've been afraid that he might chew me up and spit me out with a mere glance."

"The man is flesh and blood. And I'm sure you're familiar with the flesh part. Officers breathe the same air we do. They just happen to wear shiny metal on their shoulders and we wear cloth stripes. Everyone with hang-ups about officers being anything other than flesh-and-blood people needs to get over it, including you, especially you. Our dads are retired officers despite the fact they started out as NCOs."

"I can always count on you to bring it straight to me, Alicia."

Alicia blew Hailey a kiss. "That's what friends are for."

Hailey stood in the doorway until Alicia and her all-male crew disappeared inside her apartment. She had a great friend in Alicia Richards and she was grateful to have her friendship. Zurich came up behind her just as she closed the door. When she turned around, they practically stood toe to toe.

He brushed an errant strand of hair from her face. "Tired?"

Hailey sat down on the floor and Zurich dropped down beside her.

"Not so tired that I can't hang out for a while longer. Alicia is expecting me to come over for a minute or two. I don't want to disappoint her. It appeared to me you weren't thrilled with the idea, but I can understand it. Appearances, appearances."

"Me? You're the one who looked upset. Your face wasn't a happy one. Did I happen to miss something in that look?"

"If you're talking about what I think you are, that look was about how I was going to offer the guys payment for all their hard work. I guess I was concerned they wouldn't take it from me. That's why I tried to give it to Alicia to pass on." Hailey made a face.

"Let me guess. She told you not to insult them by trying to pay them, right?"

"That's close to how she put it. She was a tad more vocal about it." Her eyes gently caressed his. "I'm sorry I don't have a thing here to offer you to eat. You must be hungry. Do you want me to have Alicia make a plate for you to take with you?"

"Am I going somewhere? You work me like a dog and now you're ready to throw me out. It's like that, huh?"

"I see you've still got jokes. At any rate, you should let me go over there and bring you something back. You can eat it here."

"I'll tell you what. I'll go over there and fix my own plate. I'll just tell them that I couldn't stop thinking about the spaghetti. You wait a few minutes and then come on over. Sound like a plan?"

"It sounds like we're getting into the nasty habit of lying. I don't like it, but I'm too hungry to debate the issue."

"If it'll make you feel better, I won't lie. I'll just out-and-out tell them that you and me are sleeping together. Is that honest enough for you?"

"I'm feeling you. Alicia is the one who told the lie about you being engaged, but we can't undo it now. Go on over. I'll be there in a few minutes. Love you, baby."

"Would you like it if she'd been telling the truth?"

"I'd say not. Since she had you engaged to one of her other friends."

Zurich laughed. "I don't think you were listening. The friend she was talking about was definitely you."

She looked doubtful. "You think so?"

"No doubt. Now answer my question. What if I were engaged to the best friend she was referring to? Would you be happy about it?"

Hailey's heartbeat quickened. "Beyond thrilled! Now scoot on over to Alicia's before too much time elapses."

Ecstatic over her answer, he blew her a kiss. "Don't take too long, baby. I'll miss you."

Hailey closed the door behind Zurich and sat down on the standard-issue sofa. The furniture wasn't all that bad considering she didn't have to pay anything for it, she thought, looking around the sparsely furnished room. Besides the sofa, she'd been issued two chairs, a coffee and two end tables, a dining room set, bedroom furnishings, and a desk. The kitchen appliances and the washer and dryer had also been included. She already missed her own things, which had all been fairly new. But they'd be there for her when she got back to the States, that is, if they didn't get badly damaged during the transfer to the storage unit.

The question Zurich had asked her regarding Alicia's lie popped into her head. Her answer had been an honest one. She'd be thrilled to be engaged to him. But there were so many unresolved issues and uncertainties standing in the way of their happiness. Besides, if her lofty dream came through, she'd have a couple of serious choices to make. Choosing between Zurich and her lifelong goal would indeed be hard. On the other hand, it would also remove both of them from the problematical situation they were in, as she'd have to return to the States, Texas of all places. Since none of her choices would have to be made anytime soon, she decided to give herself a break from agonizing over them. Her friends were waiting on her.

As she got up from the sofa, she realized there was at least one decision that had to be made without delay. She hadn't either accepted or rejected Zurich's offer of Mykonos. In giving his suggestion a lot of thought, she'd come to the conclusion that they should get away from the base atmosphere. It might not be the wisest choice to make, but it was necessary if they were to really confront the seriousness of their issues. Though she somehow felt the trip might bring everything to a head, that it might also bring their love affair to an abrupt end, she was willing to take the risk.

They simply had a need to know how far they were each willing to go, and at what cost.

Hailey ran right into Air Force Captain Allen Richards as she came out of her apartment. Immediately recognizing her, Allen took her in his arms and gave her a warm, friendly hug. He and Alicia looked so much alike it was uncanny. But they were twins. He was the strong, silent type with the rugged good looks. Alicia was the much softer replica of him, pretty and willowy, but every bit as strong as her adorable brother.

He looked puzzled. "Did I somehow write down the wrong apartment number?"

"You were headed in the right direction. This is my apartment. Alicia lives across the hall. I was on my way over there for chow. Shall I escort you in?"

"Works for me, Hailey."

Hailey knocked on the door while Allen opted to stand off to the side. He didn't want his sister to see him right away. He loved to see her get overly excited. She was a riot when caught off guard. He was the older by seven minutes; she'd spoiled him rotten while growing up, treating him as if he were the little sibling rather than the big brother. He'd enjoyed letting her do so.

Alicia answered the bell, and Hailey immediately stepped inside. As Alicia was about to close the door, Allen jammed it with his foot. Just as he'd expected, his twin leaped into his arms, screaming like someone who'd won some type of grand prize. Alicia's beyond-effervescent welcome for Allen kept them outside for several minutes.

Hailey was concerned when she didn't see Zurich among

the guys. *Had he decided to leave without telling her? Had something happened to make him uncomfortable?*

Then she spotted him out on the patio. Seconds later she saw that he was talking with someone, a female someone. Kila Billings, Alicia's very sexy roommate. Since he seemed to be thoroughly enjoying himself, judging from the thrilling sound of his laughter, she headed for the kitchen to fix a plate, steaming within. Seeing him with another woman, a very attractive single one, was not at all a good feeling. It didn't so much bother her that he was talking with Kila, it was the fact that they had isolated themselves from the rest of the group that had her so upset. Not only that, she remembered Alicia telling her that Kila was a huge flirt.

Alicia had certainly put out a healthy spread. To go along with the spaghetti she had also prepared a tossed salad, fried chicken wings, and a divine-looking chocolate cake and dozens of chocolate-chip cookies with macadamia nuts. Alicia had it going on. The nice thing about it was that she knew it. Alicia had unwavering confidence in herself. Hailey figured that most of the goodies were prepared in Allen's honor; the twins were chocoholics and cookie monsters.

Once Hailey had her plate fixed, she wrapped it with aluminum foil for take-out. Since Zurich was still outside with Kila she didn't see much of a reason for her to stick around just to be miserable. His parting comment that he'd miss her seemed doubtful at best.

Hailey once again thanked the guys for all their help and then quietly slipped out. Before she could make it to her own door, Alicia called out to her. Hailey walked back and met her friend in the middle of the landing.

Alicia frowned. "What's up with you? Why are you slinking off to your place looking so dejected? You seem really upset."

"Just tired. Don't worry about me. I'm ready to take a hot shower and enjoy my first night in my new apartment.

We'll talk tomorrow." It was obvious to Hailey that Alicia hadn't seen Zurich and Kila together. If she had, she would've had her say, in Kila's favor or otherwise. Alicia had no compunction whatsoever about calling a spade a spade.

Hailey didn't like lying about things, but she didn't want to get into any discussion about Zurich and Kila either. In no way did Hailey want Kila to know that she was upset about her talking to Zurich. Often, when a certain type of woman knew another woman's weakness, she wasn't above using it against her. She didn't know Kila well enough to know what type of woman she was, but she wasn't taking any chances. Besides, Kila didn't know she and Zurich were romantically involved. But he did.

Hailey stood in front of the mirror and brushed her hair. It was getting a little too long for her liking. It was time for a good trim. She glanced at the clock. Over an hour had passed since she'd left Alicia's. No sign of Zurich. Her shower had lasted all of three minutes so she doubted that he'd come and gone that quickly. The thought of him still enjoying himself with Kila made her stomach queasy. Sharing her man with another woman was not the least bit appealing to her despite the growing trend of such carrying on.

Since her phone wouldn't be installed until Monday, two days away, she couldn't call Alicia to find out if Zurich was still there, so she decided to listen to some music and read. Then she thought about picking out her clothes for church the next day. Hailey realized she was just trying to stay busy in hopes of keeping her mind off the man she loved.

Once her clothes were laid out she wasn't sure if she should lie down on the couch or in the bed. Being such a sound sleeper, she might not hear the doorbell from the bedroom since it was so far back. She still had hopes of Zurich dropping by before he went on home.

Within seconds of her last thought, the bell pealed. Her hopes soared.

Hailey's hopes crash-landed when she saw Alicia outside her door. She quickly removed the lock and granted Alicia access.

"I'm on a quick mission. Can only stay a second. Zurich wants to know if it's okay for him to come back? He thinks you left because you were uncomfortable with the situation. He doesn't want to do anything to cause you any anxiety. Let me tell you this first. He and Allen know each other. They've been busy catching up for the last hour. How's that for a coincidence?"

Hailey wanted to laugh and cry at the same time. Instant relief filled her up. Zurich had stayed on because of Allen, and not Kila. Hailey suddenly felt like singing.

Hailey's mood suddenly changed. "Allen doesn't know about us, does he?"

"I promised you that I wouldn't tell a single soul. You should know by now that my word is my bond. Besides, it's nobody's business. If Allen did know, he would definitely understand. He's been where you are. I won't break his confidence by going into any details, but if you ever need someone to talk to about fraternization he's the man."

Hailey looked stunned. "You never mentioned this before."

"I know. That's why you don't need to worry about me telling your secrets. I've got to go. What should I tell Zurich?"

Hailey's smile was wicked. "That I'll leave the door unlocked for him."

"All right, now! Don't do anything that you know I *would* do. I'm the defiant one, not you. Goodnight, Hailey. Get you some rest."

"I'll keep what you've said in mind." Hailey hugged Alicia. "Pleasant dreams, sweetie. And thanks again for everything."

When Hailey opened the door for Alicia, Zurich was

already standing there, looking undecided. Hailey's heart opened wide at the sight of him. All she could do was stare into his eyes. He kept her mesmerized.

Alicia couldn't help but smile. The look in Hailey's eyes was easy enough to read. Her friend was hopelessly in love. Alicia flashed Zurich a warm smile. "Couldn't wait for me to come back with the answer, I see. Now that you're here, Hailey can give you the bad news herself. Sorry. Goodnight, you two," Alicia said, giggling inwardly.

"Bad news! Does that mean I can't come in?"

Hailey stepped aside for him to enter. "Once you get to know Alicia, you'll come to understand her. She loves to mess with folks, especially when she learns that she can. She was coming back to tell you that the door would be unlocked for you. Let's go sit down and make ourselves comfortable."

"That means I owe her one. I love payback."

Hailey laughed. "I'm not surprised by that. You two are a lot alike in the category of one-upmanship and keeping score. I guess I have to include myself in that, too."

Looking relieved and totally at ease, Zurich followed Hailey into the living room, where they both got situated on the couch. Seated on the opposite end from him, Hailey drew her legs up under her and picked up a sofa pillow, which she hugged tightly to her.

Zurich had a moment of wishing she had chosen him as her pillow. She was talkative enough, but he sensed an air of tension about her. Hailey had something troubling on her mind. The fact that there was so much physical space between them was a good indication of that. Regardless of their situation, they always stayed in close proximity to each other when alone.

"You're acting weird, Hailey. Talk to me."

She shook her head. "That's not true. I'm fine."

Zurich eyed her suspiciously. "If it's not true, why did you leave next door without telling me? In fact, I didn't even know you were there."

"I guess not. You were otherwise engaged."

"Kila?"

"It didn't take you very long to figure that one out. That memorable, huh?"

"Now it's you that has the green streak going on. Jealousy becomes you. You look beautiful in envious green."

Hailey busted up laughing. Zurich had eradicated the tension with ease. "Thanks for letting me keep my dignity. It was slowly slipping out of my control."

"That's why we're such a winning combination. We understand what's important in a relationship. Therefore, we're careful not to intentionally tamper with each other's pride. I hope we keep it that way. Did you eat, Hailey?"

"I lost my appetite the moment I saw you out on the balcony with sexy Kila. I guess you think that's really stupid of me."

"Not at all, Hailey. That's just human nature. No one gets pleasure seeing their lover talking to a member of the opposite sex, especially if they don't know the person. I was admiring the balcony view and she just popped up. Kila is kind of like the women we talked about earlier, a definite flirter, but in an innocent sort of way. Just so you'll know, I find her to be a very attractive woman, but certainly not my type. Are we clear on that little misunderstanding?"

"Crystal clear, Zurich. Thanks for being so considerate of my feelings."

"No more than you are of mine. That's why we have so much going for us. Where's the food you brought home from Alicia's, baby?"

"On the kitchen counter. It was still too hot to refrigerate."

He got to his feet. "You should eat. I'll warm it for you. How do you like your food, moderately warm or real hot?"

Hailey laughed, remembering the Tabasco sauce fiasco. "Hot, as in temperature. No hot sauce for me tonight!"

The memory of that comical situation amused him, too.

"Coming right up is your order of hot food; hold the Tabasco."

From where she was seated Hailey could see Zurich moving about the kitchen in a very competent way. It was easy to tell that he was no stranger to getting things done in the easiest and speediest manner possible. On the opposite side of that coin, Hailey was aware that she had a tendency to make everything overly complicated. He'd be a great complement to her in that area.

Zurich's caring nature still amazed her after all this time. In a lot of newly blossoming relationships it often didn't take very long for the sweet taste of the wine to turn bitter. While they had been together but a short time, there were a lot of things about Zurich that told her he was true to his nature, which allowed him to be true to her.

Zurich returned with a paper plate of food, a fork, and a couple of napkins and set the items down on the coffee table. He quickly dashed back into the kitchen and grabbed the glass of ice water he'd poured for her, as she didn't have anything else in the house to drink. He sat down, took Hailey's hand, and then said the blessing. Her smile showed her deep appreciation for his kindheartedness.

He took the fork from Hailey's hand, wrapped a mouthful of spaghetti around it, and held it up to her lips. "Open up, baby, let Daddy take care of his only girl," he joked.

Hailey laughed and her eyelashes batted wildly. "You are the best daddy in the whole wide world," she mocked him in a babylike voice. Having no intention of letting him continue to feed her, she attempted to take the fork. When he resisted, she had to wrestle the fork from his hand. She eventually got it in her possession, but only because he'd decided to let loose of it.

"I guess Daddy's little girl is all grown up now. She can feed herself. Yea for Hailey," he sang out, clapping his hands.

Hailey totally ignored him and his cutesy antics as she

dug into her food with gusto. The first bite was delicious and she couldn't wait to shovel in the second one. Alicia had once again cooked to perfection one of her specialty pasta dishes. The fresh marinara sauce was kicking.

Minutes later, Zurich looked at her empty plate and laughed. "You *were* hungry, weren't you, child? You ate everything but the spaghetti sauce staining the plate. Should I call Alicia on my cell and have her bring you over some more of everything?"

Hailey playfully punched him in the arm. "I am full and satisfied. I don't even have any more room for the cake and cookies I also wrapped up. Now I'm ready to go to sleep."

"Is that the clue that says it's time for me to leave?"

"The thought never crossed my mind, but aren't you tired too? I don't want you falling asleep at the wheel on your way home. It is late, you know."

"In that case, you go ahead and get in bed. I'll stretch out on the sofa for about an hour, then I'll hit the road." He rubbed his eyes. "I am suddenly feeling a little sleepy," he teased.

"If you can behave yourself, you can lay down in the bed with me."

"I can't believe that proposition coming from you as scary as you've been acting. At any rate, I know how to behave myself, but my good-boy resolve might be a little weaker than normal tonight. It might be easier for the bad boy in me to get the upper hand. All evening I've been thinking about all that sexy underwear I had to unpack and put away in the drawers. The alluring visions just won't go away. If I get in that bed with you, I'm going to want to see what type of skimpy lace or satin you're wearing under your nightgown."

"I can solve that tiny problem for you with ease. I don't wear anything under my gowns. And furthermore, there are many nights when I simply sleep in my birthday suit. Since you've rejected the offer of sharing my bed with me,

I'm going to do as you suggested. Good night, Zurich. Just slip the bottom lock in place on your way out."

Hailey had no desire to go to bed and leave Zurich in the room by himself, but she was actually dead tired. She was also glad that he'd decided to take a short nap before leaving. Her concern for his safety was genuine. A person had to be extremely alert, period, when driving, but even more so on the treacherous autobahn. With no speed laws to adhere to, even safe drivers were tempted to accelerate to speeds that could easily get out of their control.

He brought her to him and gave her a warm hug. "What's on your agenda for tomorrow?"

"Church first and then the commissary. I can't wait to stock my kitchen with a bunch of goodies and drink items. I happen to be a late-night television watcher, so I've got to have plenty of snacks on hand when I get the munchies."

"Make sure you pick up a couple of packages of oatmeal-raisin cookies for me. Okay?"

"Sounds like you plan on breaking a few more rules."

"Just walking the tightrope, hoping and praying that I don't fall off, that's all. Sleep tight, angel. Our paths will cross soon. I'm still waiting on your answer about Mykonos."

"I'm still waiting to come up with one. Good night."

His look was thoughtful as he watched her disappear into the bedroom. In the next instant, Zurich plopped back down on the sofa and took his shoes off. He took a quick glance in the direction of Hailey's bedroom as he stretched out on the couch and put a pillow behind his head.

Thirteen

Hailey moaned as a breath of warm air fanned her cheek. As she turned over, she saw Zurich kneeling by her bed, his eyes moist from his feelings for her. She then looked at the clock. Three A.M. He had obviously slept longer than originally intended.

He reached up and brushed her hair back from her face. "Baby, I'm leaving now. I just couldn't seem to get out the door without seeing you again. Sorry for waking you up, but I'm glad I did. Just seeing you lying there looking so sweet and sexy does real crazy things to me."

She scooted over in the bed to give him room to sit down by her side. He did so without hesitation. Hungry for the warmth of each other's bodies, they locked themselves up in a riveting embrace, one that lasted for several minutes. He kissed her gently on the mouth before releasing her. Then Zurich covered Hailey up and started for the door.

"Zurich, before you go, I'd like to tell you a story, if that's okay. It came to me earlier as I lay here thinking about you and me and all that we're going through. Interested in hearing it?"

He came back and sat down on the side of the bed. His hand slipped under the nape of her neck. As he pulled her forward, he kissed her forehead. "Mind if I stretch out beside you?"

She softly stroked his cheek. "I'd be disappointed if you didn't. I want your undivided attention." She gave him one of her three pillows to put under his head. After he made himself comfortable, she looked over at him and smiled. "Ready?"

He winked at her. "Ready, baby."

Hailey propped herself up in bed by putting the remaining two pillows behind her back. Feeling a little nervous, she cleared her throat. "This is a story about a man and a woman who love each other like crazy. It's told from the woman's point of view. This couple can't be together like they want to because of a lot of official rules and regulations. Until they're fully aware of all the ramifications and penalties for having a forbidden love affair, they have to continuously find ways to keep their relationship fresh and exciting. Before knowing what they were up against, they'd made love, wonderful, beautiful love. That caused their love addiction to deepen. Not being able to continue making sweet love to each other is one of their biggest challenges."

Hailey paused as she looked over at Zurich. "Shall I go on with the story?"

His expression was soft. "Please do." It didn't take a genius to figure out that her story was about them. *Leave it to Hailey to create a story built on their realities.* "What happened next, Hailey? You have really aroused my interest."

She laid her head back and closed her eyes. "Well, the lady's man had told her a very erotic story one evening. And she later found herself constantly trying to think up one to tell him. So, now that she has one, here's the story she decided to share. It goes something like this:

"When the handsome man asked his lady to go away for a weekend with him, she wasn't sure what to do. But she later agreed. The couple ran away to his very rugged hunting cabin located in the southern region of Texas. In honor of the weekend, he'd had it furnished with all the creature comforts that he thought she would enjoy. While the furniture was rented, he'd made sure that everything was top quality. Knowing how much she loved candles, he'd purchased all sorts of wax products formed into a variety of shapes and sizes. It was his plan to light every single one of them every night of their stay. The fireplace had been cleaned, and the bin filled with sweetly scented woods. The refrigerator and pantry had been stocked with her favorite food and snack items, and he had designated himself the head chef. He wanted to exquisitely prepare in her honor whatever her palate desired. Assorted wines were also on hand for their drinking pleasure, though they were only light drinkers.

"Each night after eating dinner by candlelight during their brief stay, she'd run a steaming-hot bath for them. Tonight was no exception. She found great pleasure in bathing him with tender care and then towel-drying his body. The part she loved best in the process was oiling him down and having him do the same for her. She liked to make love to him when his anatomy was slick with oil so that their bodies could slip and slide all over each other as they practically burnt friction holes in the sheets. The love-making was always wild and hot and usually reoccurred all through the night. The couple was tireless in physically satisfying each other, and they loved to try out different positions—daring ones. Her favorite place to make love to him was standing up in the shower. He was rather fond of taking her in front of the fireplace."

Hailey knew she was blushing, but she didn't care. In essence, she was telling him exactly what she liked. Seeing the passion and lust in Zurich's eyes turned her on, so much so that she didn't know if they were going to survive this hot story. Their willpower was already on the line.

"After she led her fine, naked man to the bed," Hailey continued, "she turned down the white satin sheets and prompted him to climb in. She loved the feel of satin beneath her nude body. Even though the sheets always got stained with the hot oils mingled with their sweat, she wouldn't think of using any other material for their late-night rendezvous. The slippery feel of the sheets only added another element of sensual pleasure.

"Stretch out on your back, lover, she told him in her most seductive voice. Naked as the day she was born, she straddled him at mid-waist. With her secret treasures only inches from his, she began kissing and fondling his upper anatomy. Her hands were as soft as a feather as they stroked and caressed his tender flesh. Then she leaned forward. Her tongue laved each of his earlobes and tickled his inner ears as the palms of her hands massaged his broad, hairy chest. His nipples loved the attention that her warm, moist mouth and tongue gave to each. She loved to tweak them between two of her fingers; she knew it drove him wild. She was into doing whatever brought a bright smile to her man's handsome face or lusty moans to his sweet lips."

Hailey wiped the sweat from her brow as she began to get into the crux of the story. She was already red-hot for him. She hoped he was just as on fire for her, even if it did spell trouble.

"Slowly, she inched her body back toward the lower half of his while her mouth kissed and her teeth sank gently into the tender places on his anatomy. Lower, lower, she worked her way down his body, until she reached his majestic tool. Upright and rigid, his manhood throbbed with his uncontrollable desire for her. As she took control of his need with her hands and mouth, he groaned from the sheer ecstasy of it all. After several minutes of working him to near completion, she seated herself onto him in one fluid motion. The boy nearly flipped out.

"With his woman in full command of his body, he had no choice but to also surrender his will to her. Looking into his eyes, glazed with lust, she worked her sweet magic on him. As she felt his explosion nearing, she immediately increased the pressure with a flurry of mind-blowing grinds and deep gyrations, sending them both into a spasmodic climax. There, in each other's arms, they shuddered and trembled from their erotic release until emotional control was eventually restored. Her mission to fulfill her man's needs and desires had been accomplished."

Half-crazed for the feel of her against his throbbing manhood, Zurich reached out to Hailey at the very same moment she opened her arms wide to him. Their lips and tongues came together in a hungry kiss, and their bodies feverishly meshed together.

Hating to go, yet knowing that he had to, Zurich slipped out of bed and headed for the door. The sweet smell of her was all over him and he inhaled deeply of her tantalizing scent. His head spun with the fiery memories of one of the most blazing nights of their brief affair. His desire to climb back in bed with her came at him from every direction. The constant stiffening of his lower anatomy at just a mere thought of her seemed uncontrollable.

Tears of joy fell softly from her eyes. "Mykonos is a definite go," she whispered before he got out of earshot.

His heart leaped inside his chest as he turned around and looked back at her. "Just tell me when, baby—and I'll take care of the rest." With that said, he turned on his heels and left.

Zurich looked around when he heard his name floating on the cool night air. Because it was so faint, he couldn't tell if it was Hailey's or not. He looked back at Hailey's apartment door even though he didn't think it had come from that direction; it was still closed. Then he saw her, curvy hips and all, leaning against the car parked right next to his.

Kila Billings, Alicia's roommate. The last person he wanted to encounter.

His pulse rate increased considerably. *Had she seen him come out of Hailey's place?*

Well, he thought, even if she hadn't, there weren't any other apartments he could've come from. He certainly hadn't been asleep in hers and Alicia's. He cursed under his breath at his carelessness. The rules of fraternization quickly came to mind.

Kila wouldn't even have known he was an officer had Allen not called him by his rank. Allen and he had met when Zurich had done a staff-assistance visit at Randolph Air Force Base in Texas, which had been a while back. But then again, he thought, she may've already known his rank. He'd once heard that he was often the subject of female conversations around the base.

Looking back and forth between him and Hailey's front door, Kila eyed him with obvious suspicion. "Where are you coming from so late, Major?"

Though nervous, he smiled with confidence. "I could ask you the same question."

"I'm not coming, I'm going to work. I'm heading into the base a little earlier to pull the last couple of hours of a friend's shift. Then I start my own. Where are you off to?"

"Home. Have a good day, Kila." Zurich hopped into his car before she could ask him anything else. This was one conversation he wasn't interested in having with her. She had interrogated him enough for one night. During their brief conversation, she'd hit him with every personal questionable imaginable; *are you married* was the one she seemed most eager to know the answer to. Hailey had just calmed him down in her own sweet way and now his nerves felt as if they were being stretched to the absolute limit.

She tapped on the window before he could pull away.

Reluctantly, he pressed in the button powering the driver's window. "What's up, Kila?"

"Are you okay, Major Kingdom? You don't seem yourself."

How would she know whether he was himself or not? He certainly hadn't talked to her that long, at least not long enough for her to assume that she knew his every mood. "I'm fine. Just in a hurry."

"I can tell. If you're ever out this way again please feel

free to drop in on me. I'd love to get to know you better. You seem like a very interesting man. You have a good day also, Major."

"Thanks. Be safe, Kila."

No way was he going to commit to any such thing as that. Getting to know Kila was the last thing on his mind. Zurich now realized that he should've gone home right after Hailey was all settled in. Even if he'd stayed with her a little longer, he shouldn't have gone to Alicia's. He wouldn't have met Kila and the offer she'd just made to him wouldn't have been possible.

Kila didn't seem like a troublemaker, but he didn't know what she'd be like if she somehow felt rejected by him. Her *get to know you better* didn't sound as if she'd meant it in terms of just being friends. Kila Billings had a little more than friendship on her mind, despite their military rankings. If he was correct in his assessment—and Kila had actually seen where he'd come from—then she felt comfortable approaching him because she figured that he was already into breaking the rules. Zurich was having none of it. He was already in enough trouble. Even if Hailey wasn't in his life, Kila wouldn't be the one he'd turn to. She wasn't his type.

Hailey was the only delectable dish that had ever completely satisfied his spiritual and physical appetites. If there was such a thing as a soul mate, Hailey Hamilton was his.

He had to smile when his thoughts turned to her last whispered statement; *Mykonos is a go*. He was happy enough about that, but he had a six-week TDY coming up fairly soon. He was waiting for his orders to be cut. If they didn't get away before it was time for him to leave, they would have to wait until his return. That didn't appeal to him. He hoped Hailey could get a weekend off before his assignment.

Happy that he had gotten at least a few hours of sleep, Zurich opened up the Corvette by pressing the pedal to the metal. He still had to shave, shower, and get into his church clothes in order to attend the seven-thirty A.M. service. It was just a coincidence for him to have been at the second Protestant church service last weekend, the same one Hailey had attended.

In a little over twenty-four hours a new workweek would begin. Come Monday morning, he had to be seated at his desk by seventy-thirty A.M. With a job that no longer required him to pull shifts, Zurich had worked Monday through Friday from seventy-thirty A.M. to four-thirty P.M. for several years now.

Hailey's mind was still on the church service as she continued to wheel the blue plastic coated metal grocery cart through the aisles at the commissary. The chaplain had delivered a very compelling message on forgiveness, something she'd needed to hear. While listening intently to the sermon, she realized that if she was ever to be forgiven her sins, she had to find a way to forgive Will Brockman. Up until this point, she had thought that to be an impossible feat.

Alicia and Allen had gone to church with her. After the service, they'd dropped off Allen at one of his friend's, a first lieutenant who lived in base housing. Allen had rented a car, but he preferred Alicia to run him around since she was way more familiar with the base than he was. He'd been to Rhein Main Air Force Base on a temporary duty assignment before, but it had been a long time ago. Allen was now assigned to a bioenvironmental health squadron at Aviano AFB in Italy.

Practically finished with her grocery shopping, Hailey looked at her watch. Alicia had gone on to the BX after dropping her off; they'd agreed to meet out in front of the commissary. They'd allotted each other an hour and a half to complete their missions. Their plans included picking up Allen once they were ready to go back home.

Hailey took out her shopping list to see what items

hadn't been checked off yet. A big smile came to her face. The only item unchecked was the oatmeal-raisin cookies Zurich had requested. This was just another request of his that would definitely be fulfilled.

Vivid images of other delicious dessert snacks filled her head. She could almost taste the sweetness of Zurich Kingdom as she conjured up his beautiful nude image.

While lying across the bed, Hailey checked over her duty roster to see when she was scheduled to have a weekend off. Because she worked rotating shifts, she rarely ended up with more than one full weekend off in a single month. The only reason she'd had this one off was because she was still involved with the business of base in-processing.

Ugh, she thought, thinking that next weekend might be too soon for Zurich. But it was her first shift break that included a Friday, Saturday, and Sunday. All she could do was run it by him and let him figure out the rest. Though she still wasn't sure it was the smartest thing for them to do, she was going for it anyway.

Now that she'd really taken the time to think about it, the Greek island was the last place two people in their situation should venture off to. The magnificent island was a hopeless romantic's fantasy world. Although she'd only seen pictures of the place, she could easily conjure up a perfect postcard image of vividly white stucco houses structured on sloping hillsides, boasting azure domed roofs; the same color blue as the Aegean and Ionian seas. She could imagine the variety of colorful, open-air markets ascended. She could almost taste the distinct flavor and spices of the islands and feel the tantalizing rhythm of bouzouki music.

Zurich just loved taking her to paradise. Hailey leaped off the bed and went into the kitchen, where she fixed a light snack of sandwich and chips and carried it over to the kitchen table. No sooner than she sat down to eat, the bell rang. Hailey pushed her chair back and ran for the door. As she looked out the safety window, she saw Alicia standing outside. It surprised Hailey to see her friend looking rather anxious. She quickly opened the door and gestured for Alicia to enter.

"Hi, Alicia. I didn't expect to see you again today. Is everything okay?"

"Let's sit down. We need to talk."

"Come on in the kitchen. I just fixed a snack. I can prepare something for you if you'd like me to."

Alicia raised her hand. "No, that won't be necessary. I can't stay that long. Allen and I are going to a gasthaus for dinner tonight. I'll just grab a Coke from the fridge. We'd love you to come out with us if you'd like to join us."

"No thanks. I want to rest before duty tomorrow. I go in a little late because the phone is being installed tomorrow. It was nice of Lila to offer to pick me up until my car is delivered from Bremerhaven. It should be here by Tuesday. What about your ride, when are you expecting it? I know we both opted for the earlier shipment dates."

"Mine is already here. I'll be picking it up tomorrow when the trailer unloads. I got notification on Friday. Just forgot to mention it." Alicia pulled out a chair and sat down opposite Hailey. "Listen, you and Zurich might need to cool it for a bit. Kila's thinking he came out of your apartment in the wee hours of the morning. Although she didn't see exactly where he came from, there are no other choices unless he was at the landlord's place; fat chance of that."

Hailey looked horrified. "Oh, no, this can't be happening. As if this situation isn't already intense enough. He shouldn't have come to your place last night. It was a big mistake. No one would believe he slept on the couch because I was concerned about him falling asleep at the wheel of his car. We all know how treacherous the autobahn is."

Hailey wouldn't dare tell the rest; she practically melted within from the detailed memories of their arousing "story hour."

"We were all so tired, Alicia. But you're right; we need to be extremely cautious from here on in. With that as my intent, I'm not going to talk to you about Zurich anymore. I don't want to involve you more than you already are. It's not fair to drag you into our duplicity. I don't want you as an accessory to such an unbelievable mess."

Alicia shook her head. "Hailey, you need someone to talk to, and you should always have someone there for you. I'm here and I'm not concerned about being involved. I'm your best friend since Kelly passed away. I'm not deserting you; you can forget that whole idea."

"Thank you for that, Alicia. Who'd ever believe that Zurich's and my only crime of passion is that we deeply love each other. We love each other so much it hurts. Is pain all we're ever going to get out of our loving relationship? If two people ever belonged together, Zurich and I are the ones. Neither of us expected what was supposed to be an emotion-free two weeks of vacation to turn into the real thing, the love of a lifetime."

Hailey broke down emotionally for the first time since she'd realized their precarious predicament at the airport in Harlingen. She had found love on an island paradise, and now there was a good chance her paradise would be snatched away.

Alicia held Hailey in her arms as she cried like her heart was breaking. Alicia couldn't help but cry with her. Alicia, too, had been unlucky in love once upon a time. That's why she was so cautious in developing her relationship with Phillip. She felt the same as Hailey did; hearts were too precious, too tender, and too loving to be ripped to pieces at the uncaring hands of another human being. Hailey had often expressed her fear of love to Alicia, fear brought on by what Hailey had seen happen to Kelly, what she'd seen unfolding right before her own eyes.

"Hailey, it's going to be okay and it's okay to cry it all out. You and Zurich are tough. You're going to figure out how you can be together without being brought up on charges. You're new to the base, so no one really knows you. He's not in your reporting chain of command at your squadron, so it could be a worse-case situation. As for Kila, I've already handled her without revealing your secret. I told her that Zurich is engaged to one of my friends and that she needs to back off of him and find someone else to dig her claws into. Believe me, she got the message."

Through all her anguish, Hailey had to laugh. Sniffling, she wiped her eyes. "You keep telling everyone that Zurich is engaged to a friend. Why's that?"

"In my estimation, he is; to you, my dear friend. His heart is engaged to yours and vice versa. If you two don't end up at the altar, it will surprise the heck out of me. You were made for each other. I saw the way you guys looked at each other. What's between you is undeniable."

Alicia hugged Hailey again before getting out of her seat. "Allen is probably fit to be tied by now. Five minutes has turned into thirty. Sure you don't want to go out to dinner with us?"

"Thank you, but I need to get myself together. I don't want to turn into a basket case. You two have a wonderful time. Don't eat too much German cooking. Good night, Alicia."

While she'd been waiting for the guy to finish installing the telephone, Hailey had written a letter to her parents. As she affixed her signature to the bottom of the African-print stationery, she recalled the lengthy note she'd penned to Zurich before leaving the States, the Dear John letter. Glad that she hadn't mailed it, Hailey retrieved the letter from the desk drawer and read it over again. It stressed her heart to see how she would've broken his had she sent it as planned.

Hailey was happy that things had turned out altogether differently, even if there still was a chance that hearts could get broken—a very real chance.

Hailey looked over at the phone and smiled. Her first call would be to Zurich if she had his in-country cell number. She didn't dare call the weather unit number, no matter how tempted she was. She would at least get to see glimpses of him throughout the week as he went about executing his duties as operations officer. That he was TDY in her unit was still unbelievable to Hailey.

With Zurich's sexy, uniformed image in her mind, she hurried and dressed for work. Lila was picking her up within the next thirty minutes.

During duty hours, as the administrative specialist for the unit, TSgt Lila Briggs was the drill-sergeant type, gruff and tough in demeanor. But Hailey had already gotten to see another side of her, which was very sweet and kind. She had been a big help in seeing that Hailey got settled in to her new duty assignment. Then came the kind offer of giving her rides to work until her car was delivered. Hailey had really apreciated it. It also meant no share-a-ride stands for her.

The weather unit personnel were in an uproar when Hailey and Lila arrived on the scene. Everyone was gathered around the weather-briefing counter, with each person giving their account as to what may have happened. It didn't take long for Hailey to learn that a cargo plane had taken a lightning strike during its climb out from the airfield. The concern was whether the aircrew had been properly briefed on potential thunderstorm activity prior to takeoff.

SSgt Leon Anderson, the duty forecaster, had received a pilot-to-forecaster radio call while the aircraft was still on the ground. The crew had questioned a weather echo depicted on their radar screen approximately twenty miles southeast of the field. The forecaster had advised the crew of potential thunderstorm activity in varied directions within the twenty-mile range—and to use caution. Not only did SSgt Anderson have a copy of the weather briefing he'd given, but other unit personnel who had been present could attest to the radio call and to Anderson's verbal response.

However, the wing commander was questioning crew awareness, in terms of their having been properly briefed by the weather duty forecaster. He was also very concerned about potential damage to the aircraft. He wanted proof in the form of the recorded radio briefing before he drew his conclusion as to the nature of the incident and where to place liability.

The weather unit was merely one of several base operation units in upheaval over the incident. Crash rescue, audio-visual, and maintenance recovery, among other equally vital units, were now on alert, awaiting the aircraft commander's decision to return to the base or to continue on to the next destination once damages were assessed.

With nothing else to do but wait until weather maintenance had recovered the tape recording for delivery to the wing commander, and then await the commander's assessment, all personnel returned to their duty stations to get on with the business at hand.

Hailey had been well aware of Zurich standing in back of the room observing everything that had gone down. She caught a glimpse of him as he turned and went back into the commander's office, where he'd set up his operation. His job was to review and evaluate the unit's operation readiness.

As far as Hailey was concerned, what had just happened was a perfect incident for Zurich to have observed in determining the unit's readiness and response to emergency situations. She would say that the unit had passed with flying colors. Since she hadn't been there to hear the actual forecast, she'd have to wait on the final outcome. Although from what had already been said, it appeared to her that the duty forecaster had followed the proper procedures right down to the letter.

Although Hailey would have to work with another forecaster for a couple of weeks before taking a solo shift, her capabilities were already apparent to her coworkers in her forecasts and her one-on-one flight-crew briefings. She knew her job and what was expected of her. Hailey was confident in her meticulous briefing technique and believed wholeheartedly in every forecast she delivered. When in doubt, she was adept enough to seek out assistance from her peers.

Having her car delivered from the shipping port was one of the highlights of the beginning of Hailey's week. Getting settled in at work and in to her new apartment had been a breeze, especially with all the help she'd had. While she hadn't expected everything to go so smoothly, she was grateful that it had.

Knowing that she and Zurich would be getting away at the end of the work schedule was what she looked forward to most. As it turned out, scheduling their trip for the upcoming weekend had worked out great for him. He was now in the process of taking care of everything.

Alicia was a little sad that her brother was leaving in a couple of days, but Hailey had been there to comfort her and remind her that all things had to end, but that it wasn't *the* end. Since Allen was also stationed in Europe, he and Alicia could see each other more than if one of them were assigned to a stateside base. It was as if the twins had been joined at the hip at birth. Each of them seemed to feel every single thing that the other one felt. It was amazing to Hailey. To have that kind of soulful and spiritual connection with someone had to be awesome.

It *was* awesome, she mentally corrected herself. Though it took a different form, she and Zurich also had a soulful and spiritual connection.

Hailey looked at her watch. She then did a check on the scheduled briefings that needed to be completed before her shift was over. She'd already done several of them. She had also sent out numerous weather advisories for expected inclement weather.

Five flight crews had already come through during her shift. Everyone seemed to wear their flight gear like it was nobody's business. Well, practically everyone, she corrected. She'd had no interest in checking out the female pilot on one of the crews to see if she had really tight buns. She was always happy to report to her female comrades that all the guys had the kind of derrieres that she loved. Not as attractive as Zurich's, but firm and round nonetheless.

Hailey laughed out loud at her crazy self, drawing the attention of the other forecasters and the administration specialist, Sergeant Briggs. She wished she could tell the entire world about Zurich.

"What have you been all smiles about over there? We've been unreasonably busy, but you haven't cracked a single frown today," Sergeant Briggs told Hailey, laughing.

'Cause I'm going away with my man in a couple of days, away from prying eyes and eavesdropping ears. "Hey, what can I tell you? This girl just loves what she does on this job and she is so happy to be alive. Is it okay for me to feel that way?"

"I guess so. But you're sure acting wacko over there, constantly laughing to yourself and grinning like a Cheshire cat. Are you in love, Hamilton?" Sergeant Briggs asked jokingly. "If not, you're sure acting like it."

"Of course I am. With my job! Didn't I just say that?"

Hailey was so in love she could barely see straight. She did love her job, but her love for Zurich was what had her heart so wide open. No way could she ever close it to him.

"Whatever you say! Have you heard the good news about the incident, Sergeant Hamilton?"

"Yeah, I did. It was unbelievable to learn that the aircraft's radar had been out of alignment by a whopping thirty degrees. From all indications, the situation could've been much worse. I'm sorry about what happened with the lightning strike, but I'm happy the weather section has been exonerated of all liability. Everyone seemed sure that the right forecast had been given out. I'm sure Sergeant Anderson breathed a sigh of relief when he got the word."

"I'll bet. I think Major Kingdom was happy with our section's overall performance. He was certainly watching everything like a hawk. You think we won his approval?"

Hailey wondered why Briggs was asking her that question. *Was she suspicious of them?* She quickly shook her head, chalking her foolishness up to a bad case of paranoia because of the upcoming weekend getaway. "I think we won it with ease. The major seemed very pleased."

Lila looked over at Hailey with a thoughtful expression. "Are you into bowling, Hamilton? If so, we need another man on our team. One of our regulars has a sprained wrist. Interested in joining us?"

Hailey laughed. "Another man? Do I look like a guy to you, ma'am?"

Briggs cracked up. "Just a figure of speech. Think you can fill the slot?"

"Depends on when you need it filled. I do have a life, you know," Hailey joked.

"This coming Saturday is a crucial tournament for us. Are you free?"

Hailey's heart nearly stopped beating. Saturday was absolutely out of the question. She just hoped she wouldn't be questioned as to why she couldn't make it. "You're fresh out of luck. Saturday is booked solid. Sorry."

Hailey excused herself to go to the bathroom to keep from answering any questions about her plans. She certainly didn't want to mention Greece. If she had to take formal leave, she'd have to put her destination on the leave slip. But since it was a scheduled weekend off, she didn't have to report her whereabouts. Not even Alicia knew she was going away. True to her word, she was keeping Alicia out of her and Zurich's complicated mess.

The end of the workweek found Hailey in dire need of rest and recuperation, R&R. She was dead tired yet enthusiastic as she packed her weekender for her and Zurich's mini-getaway. They were to catch an evening flight into Venizelos International Airport, and she could hardly wait.

Three days with Zurich was like drinking milk; it would do a body good.

Fourteen

Mykonos was a magnificent place where golden beaches met the aquamarine sea in a bold statement of beauty. The most expensive and heavily visited of all the Greek islands, the popular resort also had the most chic nightlife. The heat on the island was often tempered by the *meltemi*, the northerly wind.

Nearly blinded by the dazzling sunlight, Hailey and Zurich stood on the blooming-bougainvillea-and-clematis-plant-adorned balcony of their sloping hillside hotel suite. The breathtaking view boasted a magnificent coastline dotted with a variety of boats in all sizes and shapes, as well as gleaming-white, square structures grouped around a colony of waterfront domiciles belonging to the fishermen. Just as Hailey had imagined in her postcard image of the island, bright-blue church domes offset the blinding white buildings.

While there were many island attractions to visit, and colorful markets and trendy boutiques to browse around in, sightseeing and shopping weren't the top priorities on Hailey and Zurich's agenda. This long weekend was really about them and the serious issues surrounding their relationship.

"Now that we're settled in, are you ready to take a walk around the island, Hailey?"

Hailey could barely contain her excitement. "Let me put some comfortable shoes on. I want to be able to handle the hilly terrain with ease. Do you think we could start out at the picturesque fishing village below?"

"Wherever you want to begin."

It only took Hailey a couple of minutes to change her shoes and meet up with Zurich at the front entrance. Instead of going down to the lobby, they let themselves out of the side entrance, which put them right on the narrow stone steps leading down to the coastline. Zurich held her hand as they maneuvered the rocky, uneven pathway.

As they grew closer to the village, Hailey felt the rhythms of the enchantment surrounding her. While looking up into the sun-drenched hills, she could see the brightly painted balconies running rampant with large colorful blooms. The natural beauty nearly took her breath away as she pointed out her discovery to Zurich. Both Hailey and Zurich had traveled extensively throughout Europe, which was simply a cache of rare and unimaginable scenery. This lively Greek island, thus far, was no exception to the magnificence they'd already experienced on other parts of the continent.

The friendly villagers waved to them as they made their way around the island. Although American forces had been asked to leave Greece, there didn't seem to be any hostility toward them from the native islanders. Of course, no one knew for sure that they were active duty military members.

"It looks as if American are welcome here despite the fact we were asked to get out," Hailey said.

"That wasn't something all Greeks wanted. I was here once and felt very welcome."

Zurich could remember all the old-world charm around Athens, where Hellenikon Air Base was once a major operation. The troops had often jokingly referred to the base as "hell in the can." The Apollon Palace, located in a coastal area of Athens, had been one of Zurich's favorite military haunts of long ago. The large military complex, located right on the beach, had at one time housed under one roof all the kinds of recreational facilities, restaurants, clubs and shopping venues that one could imagine.

"Are you hungry, Hailey?"

"I'm too excited to even think about food, but I probably should eat something before we go back to the hotel. What about one of the little cheaper eateries around here? I'm not hungry enough for a full-course meal."

He pointed down the road. "We can eat at the tiny place right there. It has a great view of the water. If the food is as good as the view, we may have found us a winner."

Hailey and Zurich trudged further down the village streets to the cozy eatery nestled near the water's edge. Seats on the balcony were plentiful, and they found one of the tables that gave them an unobstructed view. The weather was very nice, not too hot or too cool.

Hailey ordered souvlaki, skewered grilled meat in pita bread. Greek foods were invariably served lukewarm. Zurich was fond of the country salad, *horiatiki,* the mainstay of the Greek diet, consisting of cucumber, tomatoes, onions, feta cheese, and olives lightly doused with a mixture of virgin olive oil, ground oregano, and a dash of salt and pepper. Their meals were served rather quickly since their orders had been simple ones.

"You mentioned Hellenikon. Were you stationed there, Zurich?"

"Just another TDY. It seems like I've been all over the world on temporary duty. I used to love to travel. I still do, but only for leisure. Duty travel has gotten tedious."

"You mentioned a TDY as soon as we get back. Do you have your orders yet?"

He moaned. "Not yet. I'll be doing staff assistant visits at various bases in the European theater. The majority of them will be here in Germany. There are lots of bases in this country."

"Tell me about it. I'm sure Alicia and I will visit as many of them as we can. By the way, have you talked with your mother since you've been back? Does she know I'm over here?"

He grinned. "My mother knows mostly everything there

is to know about you except your rank. I purposely withheld that information. The less she knows, the better off she is."

"I think I understand." Hailey yawned. "I'm getting sleepy. A nice nap with the sea air blowing into the bedroom is an appealing thought. If you don't mind, as soon as we finish eating I'd like to go back to the hotel and rest."

Zurich nodded in agreement. "I could use a little shut-eye myself."

Hailey looked on at Zurich as his eyes skimmed the beauty of the island from the balcony. He'd been unusually quiet during their walk back to the hotel. She still couldn't figure out what was on his mind, but she knew it was serious and that it probably had everything to do with their relationship. Fear of his answers was what had kept her from asking questions. There was no doubt in her mind that she'd know what was on his soon enough.

"This is an amazing island."

"It is that, Hailey. If you're okay for now, I'm going to go on in and lie down. I'm feeling a little off-color for some reason."

Without making any physical contact with her, Zurich turned away and walked indoors.

Curious as to what was really going on with him, Hailey followed Zurich inside to the bright but modestly furnished two-bedroom suite, and walked into the front room.

She sat down in the low European-style chair. "Is that why you were so quiet on the way back here? You hardly said anything at all."

Zurich sat down in the chair opposite Hailey. Both chairs were situated in front of the large window offering a panoramic view of the island. It was hard for Zurich to get serious when all he wanted to do was explore this exotic island with the woman he loved. It had been his intent for them to have a carefree couple of days and get into the more serious issues on the last evening of their stay. It didn't seem to be turning out that way.

He sighed hard. "Hailey, I wanted us to have a great weekend before we sat down and had a heart-to-heart. I'm finding that hard to do now . . ."

"To do what, Zurich? You're scaring me. What's this all about?"

He scooted his chair closer to hers and took her hand. "You know I've been reading everything I can get my hands on that has to do with fraternization. Hailey, we're in a no-win situation with this one. There's no way out of this . . ."

Her loud gasp matched the look of horror on her face. "What are you saying?" She held her head high. "You brought me all the way to Greece to tell me that it's over between us, didn't you? If that's the deal, I think you're pretty cruel. How could you bring me to a place as beautiful and romantic as this just to kill my spirit and break my heart? How do you dare?"

Before she could utter a protest, he had picked her up and carried her over to the sofa, where he sat down and placed her on his lap. "I know this seems cruel to you, but I didn't know what else to do. If I cancelled the trip, we were still going to suffer through this. I somehow thought if we took the trip anyway that it might be easier on us. I can see that I was wrong."

Her eyes welled with tears, but she quickly dashed them away with her knuckles. "Damn wrong!" She jumped up and ran into the bedroom she'd chosen when he'd given her first dibs on the sleeping accommodations. "You should've taken me to some dark, Godforsaken place to tell me it's over. Why'd you have to bring me to paradise to do it?"

He followed her into the room and instantly took her into his arms. "I'm sorry, Hailey. I really didn't know what would be the right thing to do in this instance. Please sit down and listen to me. There's so much more that needs to be said here."

She pulled away from him and sat on the very end of the bed. "Haven't you said enough? I get the picture, Zurich. I understand what's happening here. But what I don't understand is why you're trying to rub my nose in it. I already know how bad it stinks."

He hated what this was doing to her. If he could just get her to listen to what he had to say, maybe she'd understand that he had no choice in the matter. It wasn't as simple for him as she seemed to think. His heart was no less distressed than hers was, but he understood that her pain was too raw to even try and feel his.

Hailey got up and began to throw her clothes back into the suitcase. She had no idea if there was even another flight off the island since the one they'd taken out of Athens had been the last one from there, but she had to find out. The only way to do that was to take a taxi back to the airport; she'd sit there all night if she had to. She couldn't stay here with him and be humiliated for the rest of the weekend. This whole thing had been such a mistake. She should've sent the *Dear John* letter right after she wrote it to him. The minute she'd learned he was an officer was when she should've found the nerve to take a hike. At least she'd still have her dignity to walk away with. Now she had nothing but a broken heart.

He turned her around and gently pushed her back down on the bed. "Look, you're not going anywhere until you listen to what I have to say. You're acting crazy with me for no reason. You're not even trying to hear what I have to say, yet you're already jumping to all sorts of conclusions. You're good at that, though, aren't you?"

She openly glared at him. "I guess you're going to hit me if I refuse to obey your orders! Is that what happens next, Major Kingdom? You've already broken my heart. Are you now willing to smash in my face in order to put me in my place? Isn't that what you abusive, egotistical men always do to maintain control of your feisty woman when you consider her to be out of line?"

Zurich nearly doubled over from the pain of her hard-hitting remarks. For several seconds he could only stare at her in disbelief. "Is that what you really think about me, Hailey? God, I hope not. If you believe I'd hit you, then you don't know me at all. Go ahead and pack your clothes and leave if it will make you feel better. I won't try to stop you. You can rest assured of that." Disgusted by her downright cruel remarks, he turned away from her and left the room.

He came back immediately. "There are no more flights this evening, so you'll be wasting your time going to the airport. But knowing you as I do, you'll probably go anyway."

"Zurich, wait," she called out to him. "I'm so sorry."

If he'd heard her, he didn't bother to acknowledge her apology. That made her feel horrible, especially for the terribly unfair things she'd said to him in her anger and disappointment. How childish of her to want to hurt him because he'd dealt her a painful blow.

In her frustration, she snatched a few articles of her clothing out of the suitcase and threw them up in the air. Now that a living hell had caught up with paradise, Hailey had no idea how to keep herself from being burned alive.

Doing her best to keep from breaking down completely, Hailey threw herself across the bed and muffled her frustrated screams in the pillow. It was devastating for her to know how much she'd hurt Zurich, the only man she'd ever loved. Of course she didn't think he would've hit her. But that was no comfort to him. The damaging words had come flying out of her mouth, recklessly; there was no way to take them back now. But she still had to ask his forgiveness, beg for it if necessary. He hadn't deserved the verbal attack on his character.

Given Zurich's fear that he could turn out to be just like his dad, her careless remarks probably had him questioning himself all over again. Zurich wasn't an abusive man, yet she'd willfully accused him of being just that.

Her violent reaction to losing him had come unexpectedly and had shocked her senseless. Just the thought of it being over for them was killing her inside. They both had hoped and prayed, and now hope had run out on them and their prayers were left unanswered. Perhaps they'd read more into destiny than God had intended them to.

Fate simply never failed; it wasn't designed to do so.

Hailey looked at the closed door knowing there was yet another one that kept them separated. She had heard his door slam right after he walked out on her. Her desire to go to him and beg for forgiveness was strong; her fear of rejection was even more overpowering.

As she thought back on their time together, she saw that she had doubted him so many times already, without just cause. All he'd asked her to do was hear him out. Yes, he'd pushed her down on the bed, but there hadn't been anything violent in his manner. He'd been as frustrated as her, yet his gentle shove probably hadn't revealed half of how deep his frustration ran. What should've been a beautiful weekend was now a complete washout, and Hailey felt as if she had no one but herself to blame for that.

Her cruel remarks alone had put them where they were right now.

Regretting that he'd dared to put his hands on her, no matter how gently he'd pushed her, Zurich wasn't having an easy time figuring out how to salvage the rest of the weekend. Since he hadn't heard Hailey leave, he assumed that she had decided to stay on at least until the morning. He would've gone after her. There was no way he would've allowed her to travel alone to the airport by taxi, military training or not. Her safety was always his main concern, despite the fact she had proven she could darn well take good care of herself.

There was a lot of terrorist activity all around the different areas of Greece and its surrounding regions. Zurich was not the least bit fooled by the beauty and the serenity of the island. Treacherous folks often lived among the peacekeepers as a way to camouflage their true identities and mask their evil intents. It was the unorthodox skills of those who practiced this kind of dark deception that had allowed the United States to fall prey to the visiting enemies residing within her too-gracious boundaries.

Hailey stood at Zurich's bedroom door, waiting for him to answer her knock. Several seconds passed without a word from him. She knew he was in there since she hadn't heard him go out. She had only been waiting with bated breath for any sounds of movement from him.

Not caring that it was the wrong thing to do, Hailey turned the knob while praying he hadn't locked the door, which didn't seem likely. That was more of a woman's method of operation than it was a man's way of gaining the upper hand. The man normally stalked out, not to return for several hours or even until the next day.

His eyes connected with hers as he looked up from the book he was reading. "What is it that you want to say now, Hailey?"

She kept her hand wrapped around the doorknob. "I think we should talk. I'd like to hear you out if possible."

"Now that you've established me as an abuser, why would you want to hear anything that I have to say, Staff Sergeant?"

Hailey dared to come inside the room and seat herself in the chair near the bed where he was completely stretched out. "We both need to grow up here for a minute or two, don't you think, Zurich?"

"Oh, so now I'm childish as well as an abuser. Got any other character assassinations that you want to stab my guts out with?"

"Oh, please, at your age I thought you were above all of this nonsense. I *am* way above it, so let me start over here.

Zurich, I came in here because I'm so sorry for assassinating your character the way I did. I don't believe you are an abuser. In fact, I know you're not. I was angry and frustrated when I lashed out at you. I deeply regret being so cruel, even though it was intentional at the time. You didn't deserve the things I said. I sincerely apologize. My mouth is now crammed full of undercooked crow. Can I please have your permission to swallow before I gag on it? The feathers are stuck in my throat."

It was hard for him not to laugh, but he managed to refrain. He kept a straight face.

"Sarcasm should never accompany a sincere apology, Staff Sergeant. Nonetheless, I will accept it. Won't you please come in and have a seat?"

Hailey fought the urge to roll her eyes at him for being just as sarcastic as he'd accused her of being, since she was already in the room and seated. Hailey tried hard to figure out what to say next. The right words weren't coming to her now that she'd apologized to him.

"I see that you still haven't completely swallowed all the crow, so I'll do my best to get this conversation started if you're willing to listen this time." He looked to her for a response.

"I'm listening, Major Kingdom."

"It's about time." He rubbed his hands down each side of his face. "Sorry about that. That remark wasn't necessary. But, Hailey, what I was trying to tell you before is this. I've read and reread all the policy directives and instructions as they pertain to fraternization. I even had the intention of seeking out help from the ADC, but I found that my interpretations of the materials were quite adequate. I didn't need anyone to tell me what I already knew."

He threw up his hands in frustration. "Hailey, fraternization is terribly complicated in its dozens and dozens of meanings. I'm so much clearer now on its intent and application than before I began my research. It wasn't mandated to punish different-ranking service members who love each other, nor was it designed to initiate penalties just because one member wears metal and the other wears stripes. It has more to do with the impact on good order, discipline, respect for authority, maintenance of unit cohesion, and mission accomplishment, which are the very things cited in the military standards. It goes so much deeper than what appears on the surface, so much more than I ever could've imagined without studying it closely. You suddenly look so perplexed. Tell me what's on your mind."

She blew out a stream of air. "I've always known in my heart that there had to be good reasons for these policies to exist, but I admit to having a different interpretation. People tend to think that commissioned officers look down on NCOs and that they think they're better than us. I know that not to be true. Still, our job is just as important and our dedication to the mission is no less than theirs. As far as it coming down to personal relationships, we both know that if our relationship comes into the light nothing serious would happen to you. The consequences would be all mine to bear. You've already said as much yourself. Male officers break the rules all the time, but the female members, both NCO and officers, are the ones who ultimately pay the price. Male NCOs are subject to the same unfair application of the rules as the women. That's just the way it is. The same way it has always been."

"For sure, that's the way it used to be. Things have changed considerably. But you're right, nothing serious would probably happen to me beyond a verbal cease-and-desist order."

"I'm glad you've never backed away from the truth of the way things are and from acknowledging the differences in treatment of females versus males. I understand the concept that you can't always command or order someone to do something when you're hanging out with your workers as buddies. The same rules apply in the civilian world. If you're out drinking and partying with the people you supervise, you're setting yourself up for the possibility of them balking when you give them something to do that they don't want to. The situation can end up with them not taking you seriously as a leader, just as it can in the military. Business and pleasure don't mix."

Hailey wrung her hands together. "If I love you, will I be able to order you into combat? Or will I send someone else into a war zone in your place just to spare you? Will I promote you over someone who deserves the promotion more, because I'm sleeping with you? I clearly get the implications. But what I need to know now is what's the bottom line for us? What conclusions have you drawn about us in all of this? Where do we go from here?"

He anxiously rubbed his hands together. "Hailey, we both joined the military, voluntarily, even if we did it for different reasons. We both love what we do, we take it seriously, and we have literally dedicated our entire lives to our country. There is no such thing as separation of personal life and military life in our case. We are what we are, what we consciously chose to be. We are on duty twenty-four seven, three hundred and sixty-five days a year."

He got off the bed and knelt down in front of her chair. "I believe that we can still have a life together, but not until after we've separated from the service. I don't want us to put our careers at risk because we can't control ourselves. Yet, if I were willing to put my career at risk for anything, it would be for us, which I think I've already proven time and time again. It's just that we've both come too far and have invested way too much in this country just to walk away empty-handed or to find ourselves saddled with a dishonorable discharge. Don't you agree?"

She leaned forward and rested her forehead against his. "Yes, with everything you've said thus far. I'm just sorry that it has to end this way, even though in my heart I always knew it would end exactly like this—so much for our enthusiastically anticipated top secret rendezvous. Even if I was willing to walk away from my career to save our relationship, I still have a three-year commitment, just as you do. So the line in the sand has been clearly delineated. This is where dedication to country takes precedence over our love and devotion to one another. When duty calls, our response can only be this one: *At your service.*"

Hating to see her looking so forlorn, he kissed her forehead. Unable to keep his hands off her for another second, he lifted her up, sat down in the chair, and put her on his lap. This rough, tough, and ready woman, trained in hand-to-hand combat, with her I-don't-take-any-mess-off-anyone (especially men) attitude, looked so vulnerable that it nearly made him weep. Was it possible for him to love her any more than he did at this moment? He imagined so, only because he found himself falling more and more in love with her every single minute of the day.

Gazing into her eyes, he gently stroked her cheek with his forefinger. "I'm willing to retire at twenty as opposed to thirty. That's how much I want to be with you. Not only do I want to be with you, I want us to get married one day and be together for the rest of our lives."

His words of eternity had utterly shocked her. Tears threatened to break her emotionally.

"Are you saying you want to marry me, Zurich Kingdom? Is that what you're saying?"

He kissed her softly on the mouth. "Yes, Hailey Hamilton. That's exactly what I'm saying. I know three years is a long time to wait; that's why I won't ask you to do that. I don't want you to commit to something you might come to regret. It would be unfair. Just know that I love you and that I'm all yours. Once my three years are up, I'm yours in every sense of the word, for all eternity. That is, if and when you decide you want to marry me."

Her tears finally spilled over as she kissed him passionately. "Of course I want to marry you, Zurich! You're my every dream. I've never been surer about anything in my life. I love you, too. Like you said, three years is a long time. But I'm not the only one who has to wait it out. If any unfairness exists in this instance, we're on equal footing. We're both in the same boat. I don't want to see it sink. I want our ship to sail into the sunset with both of us aboard."

He kissed her tears away. "I don't think I can put it any better than you just did. Three years is going to seem like forever to me, but I know I can withstand the wait if it means I end up with you as my wife. Losing you is what I can't endure."

She looked deeply into his eyes. "We have to believe that we won't lose each other. Then we have to make sure that we don't allow it to happen. I'm willing to make that promise."

He reached up and fingered a strand of her hair. "So am I. I promise to never take my love away from you." He suddenly looked pensive. "You know, Hailey, you've said a few things today and in the past that have me a little worried. I know you apologized for all the nasty things you said a while ago, but I have to be sure you didn't mean them. How can I be sure?"

She pressed her lips into his forehead. "I was dead wrong. I meant those cruel, cruel words at the time but never for a second did I believe in what I was saying to you or about you. How could I believe that, knowing you? Whether you know it or not, you're my hero, Zurich. You've shown me the difference between controlling love and freeing love, the difference between obsession and passion. You've allowed me to be myself through it all. You're so capable of both giving and receiving love freely. That's the kind of man I fell in love with. You're the only man I've ever really fallen in love with. You can be sure that you're everything I desire in my man."

His heart was fully satisfied with her response, yet he had one more important question. "Do you remember telling me you had a secret that you would only tell to your husband if you ever married?"

She nodded.

"Now that you're considering taking me on as your husband, do you feel good enough about me to let me share in your secret? Since I believe it's a spirit-damaging one, I think you'll feel completely whole once you've let it out."

She couldn't believe he remembered that she had a secret. Zurich obviously had listened intently to everything she'd told him. He also had a way of looking into her heart and seeing the good and the not-so-good. Did she trust him enough to share her destructive secret with him?

She smiled, despite her anguish. "Since I trust you with my life, I'd have to say yes."

His sigh of relief was huge.

Ashamed of what she was about to say, Hailey nervously fiddled with her hair. "My father was the one to tell Kelly's parents about the physical and emotional abuse she was suffering at the hands of Will. He told them immediately after I asked him to. It turned out to be of no avail, since Kelly moved out of her parents' house and in with Will right after her parents confronted her with what they now knew. Then she married him rather quickly. I still feel responsible for all that occurred after Kelly's well-kept secret was out. You see, her death followed shortly after that chain of events; death at the very hands of the man she loved."

Hailey had to take a deep breath to maintain control of her emotions.

"If I hadn't asked Dad to talk to Kelly's parents in hopes of getting the abuse stopped, Kelly might not have moved in with Will or married him—and she might not have died the way she did. This was the one covert burden that I thought I'd always carry, even to my own grave. This was no secret that I'd been the one to tell about the abuse, but no one knew about the guilt I carried around inside. The guilt of feeling responsible for her death has been my darkest secret."

He ran his fingers through her hair. "You may not feel

instant liberation, but it will come. I'm willing to bet on it. It's now outside of you, where you can now begin to deal with it."

"I believe you're right. Thanks for prompting me to share. I love you. Kelly's death has haunted me day and night since it happened. A man she would do anything for did nothing but torture her and make her life miserable. I don't know if she stayed with him out of fear or not, but she had every right to be fearful of him. But Kelly really did think she could help him. She thought that if she helped him get through whatever was going on with him that he'd go back to being the man she fell in love with, the man who, in the beginning, treated her like she was his black queen. I'll probably never understand her way of thinking, or why she put up with all that she did, but I tried hard not to judge her. I just knew that I couldn't desert her, that I had to be there for her. There were many times when I didn't offer any input, times when I sensed that she just needed to talk and have someone listen. She wasn't looking to me to resolve her issues with Will. She just needed her best friend to be there for her to lean on."

Knowing that she needed to get all of her feelings out in the open about Kelly's violent death, Zurich just sat there and listened, wiping her tears away as they continued to fall.

"For some reason or other, Kelly must've felt that she deserved to be treated that way. Through it all, up until the end, I hung right in there with her. Yet we lost her anyway. Everyone who loved Kelly had lost her to someone who hadn't put any value whatsoever on her precious life. In the middle of the night, as she lay sleeping, he strangled her to death."

"As we both know, issues of domestic violence are complicated, rarely making any sort of sense to anyone except to the person it's happening to. When I confronted my mother about Cobb, she told me some things that finally made sense. From her account, my father had threatened to kill her if she left him. But that obviously didn't matter to her since she ended up leaving him later with the same threat hanging over her head. It was the threat he'd made to kill her precious babies, and the strong belief that he was capable of doing it that kept her shackled to him. Once her babies were grown and gone, she did what she had to do for herself. She only dared to make that move after her children were in a safe environment. So, you see, you'll never know the real reason why Kelly stayed with Will; her voice has been silenced forever. It may have been a very good reason, one similar to the threat my father made against his own flesh and blood. My mother might have gone to her grave with her darkest secret had I not confronted her. She only told me then because I let her know how badly it was affecting my life. Once again, you'll never know Kelly's reasons. It's time to give up the ghosts of the past."

Zurich was right; it was time to let go of the past. They had cleared their issues regarding the people they loved yet couldn't save. It was time to move on.

Hailey quickly decided that she wasn't about to let a dark mood invade her spirit any further. In the wake of her and Zurich's voiced desires to eventually marry, she wanted to celebrate their love, not mourn Kelly's death. Kelly would have been deliriously happy for them.

Hailey repositioned herself on Zurich's lap. "With all that's been said, done, and finally settled, we're still both flesh-and-blood humans. If I have to walk away from you, I desire something of you to take with me. We've skated and flitted around the rules long enough; I'm now ready to completely break them for the next couple of days. At this very moment, as far as I'm concerned, we're just two ordinary people who came away for a romantic weekend. I don't know your rank and you don't know mine. We're those same two people on South Padre Island, the ones who didn't want to know anything about what the other did for a living. All we have is right now, this very moment.

We may never make it back to where our love affair began, because tomorrow doesn't come with a guarantee. Please take us back there now, Zurich. Please!"

He was amazed at the passion in her eyes. "Hailey, do you know what you're saying?"

Ignoring his question, she pointed out the window at the panoramic view, her tears flowing hotly. "As you can see, heaven has also found us here in the Greek Isles. If only for a while, in every way possible, I want to passionately share this romantic spot with the man I love. For the rest of our stay here, I want you to make nonstop love to me. I want you so deep inside of me, buried so deep within that we'll always feel as if we're a part of each other's soul. Do we dare ignore what we may never have again, Zurich? Do we dare forsake paradise?"

His eyes darkened with matching passion as he looked deep into her tearful amber gaze.

"Do you know what Adam said to Eve when she asked a similar question, Hailey?"

"I can only imagine, Zurich."

"Are you aware of the possible consequences? And are you prepared to accept them?"

"Yes!"

"Lead me into the Garden of Eden and over to the tree bearing only the forbidden fruit."

Hailey got up from his lap and pulled him forward, urging him out of the chair. She led him over to the bed and gently nudged him down to the mattress. She then stepped away and took a minute to put on some dance music by Marc Anthony. The CD she'd chosen to slide into the portable player also had lots of romantic ballads sung by the same golden-voiced artist.

The very same moment the Latin music took to the air, Hailey began to show off her artistic dance skills with a sultry salsa rendition. As she danced in perfect harmony with the funky rhythms of "I Need to Know," she moved about the room as if she had wings on her feet.

As the music slowed down, so did Hailey. Keeping her passionate gaze locked onto Zurich's, she began to gently sway her hips back and forth to the tantalizing tempo. The take-me-to-heaven look in his eyes spurred her on. Hailey's fingers trembled with excitement as she slowly worked loose on her white shirt the first button of many. Her exhilaration grew as she reached the bottom of her blouse. In one seductive motion, she opened her shirt and slowly slid it back over her shoulders as she continued to sway to the tempestuous music.

As though she were privately painting a masterpiece as a personal gift for Zurich, using her body as the paintbrush, she slowly moved into a wildly beguiling striptease routine. While licking her pouting lips in a most provocative way, she made an absolute art form out of dramatically removing her jeans, black lace bra, and lacy bikini briefs.

Hailey had suddenly transformed herself into an alluring vision of erotic pleasure.

Zurich immediately recognized the set of lacy unmentionables as the same ones he'd twirled around on his finger when he'd helped her put her things away. While his heart rate had already gone bananas, his manhood was also fervently responding to every single movement she made. As she continued to lather him up, he saw no use in trying to hide his erection or his eager anticipation of eventually being inside of her. If he didn't get out of his jeans within the next few minutes, he knew things were going to get mighty uncomfortable for him inside of there. He could barely breathe as it was.

To further provoke him, Hailey sucked on her finger in a very demonstrative way. Hailey then crooked the same wet finger at Zurich, summoning him with a sexy, come-hither gaze. Moving in slow motion, thunderstruck by her burning sensuality, Zurich got off the bed. Dying to have her take him out of his misery, he came and stood before this exotic woman he barely recognized as the sweet innocent he'd fallen so desperately in love with. He had to admit that he wasn't sure which personality he liked the best, but he was more than thrilled to death by both.

As Hailey danced around him, she began to touch him softly, intimately. Slithering up to his back, she reached around his waist and moved her hands upward until they reached the top button on his shirt. Once every closure was popped free and his upper body was completely revealed, her capable hands massaged the hairy expanse of his chest. Within a matter of minutes, she'd removed his shirt altogether. Her busy little nimble digits then went to work on his belt.

While continuing to gyrate against him from behind, her mouth and tongue hotly seduced his nude back as her scorching hands tenderly kneaded his strong abs. Seconds later, Hailey's hands melted into the waistband of his jeans and continued the march right on down into his black silk boxers. As her soothing hands wrapped around his manhood, she felt him shudder.

Zurich had never before found himself in a situation such as this, especially one that he didn't have full control of. Hailey had seduced him into a very vulnerable position. She was the one calling all the shots. He felt helpless against her allure and he didn't feel one bit ashamed of it. The flesh was weak, and his body was getting weaker and weaker by the second. Hailey had just about worn him all the way down. He didn't think he could take much more.

His undoing nearly came when Hailey inched his jeans and boxers down over his hips until they fell down around his ankles; yet another defenseless position he'd never before been in. He was the one who normally took pleasure in unwrapping the physical gifts. Hailey had unwrapped him and now she was busy unraveling him. It didn't look to him as if she was going to stop until she had him completely dismantled. While it was a very unfamiliar road for him to find himself on, he didn't find the fiery path she was taking him on the least bit undesirable.

Hailey urged him to turn around and face her. Her

mouth engaged his in a lingering kiss. She then looked into his eyes. "The forbidden fruits of this tree are all yours for the taking."

Zurich didn't need any further prompting. All the foreplay had already hotly achieved its goal. Swift action on his part was now required. He backed her up until the straight chair at the desk came into view. Reaching around her, he pulled the chair completely out and away from the heavy piece of furniture. He then seated himself, but left her standing.

As she stood before him, his hands and mouth worked feverishly to bring her to where he already was, white-hot and just barely in control. Hailey's sweet moans of ecstasy coursed through him as his hands unhurriedly fondled her breasts. The tip of his tongue torched the inner part of her navel as she squirmed with her need for him. The same instant he inserted his long, slender fingers into the core of her essence, Hailey's knees all but buckled on her.

Zurich reveled in her weakened condition, which told him she was almost there.

As the flowing moisture of her core revealed to him its reckless craving to receive him, he tenderly drew her down onto his throbbing erection. Zurich's manhood completely filled her up as they wildly rode the crest of their uncontrollable passions toward an exotic fulfillment.

Awakening just before the sun came up, though they'd only been asleep for a couple of hours, Zurich cuddled up to Hailey and pulled her fully against him. The intimate celebration of their last night on the island had kept them up until the wee hours of the morning.

His mouth greeted hers with a passionate kiss. Hailey moaned as she made herself comfortable in his arms. He looked into her eyes. "The forbidden fruit was divine, Eve. We've been really bad for the past three days, and now we have to deal with the consequences. In punishing ourselves for breaking all the rules, I hope we don't severely overdo it. Just remember that we're human and that our rendezvous wasn't merely a defiant act on our part because we lack respect for self and our country. We didn't purposely set out to defy anything or anyone. We are in love. We fell for each other long before our prospective duties to our nation were discovered. I don't know how we're going to manage to live separate lives for three years; I just know that we'll make it through this. Are we still on the same page with our three-year plan, Hailey? Think you can keep from judging yourself too harshly?"

She brushed her fingers across his lips. "There'll be no judging, period. We've decided to take the honorable approach because we do respect our country and ourselves. We could continue this duplicity and possibly never get caught. But we're no longer willing to take that risk, because we've come to understand what's really at stake here. We're handling this just as we should. I love you, Major Zurich Kingdom."

He kissed the tip of her nose. "By taking responsibility for our actions, and complying with the cease-and-desist order before it's ever demanded by our superiors, we're taking full control of our own destiny. No one else will have to decide our future for us. The three-year plan will work because we're both committed to making it work, just as we've been committed to our military careers. I can't wait until the time has been served out. It's also a good decision that we're going to wait until then to decide who actually gets out. Staff Sergeant Hailey Hamilton, I love you, too."

Zurich reached under his pillow and brought out a royal-blue velvet jewel case. He flipped open the box. "I want to give this diamond promise ring to you to seal the oaths we've made to each other. This is merely a small token of the unfathomable love I feel for you. It's nothing like the one I plan to give you when we officially get engaged, but it's nonetheless special. I love you. Will you accept this ring and my promise of forever, Miss Hailey?"

With tears flowing down her cheeks, she kissed him passionately. "I do, Zurich. I will cherish this ring every bit as much as I cherish you. I'll be looking forward to our next rendezvous. After three years of abstinence, that long-awaited rendezvous will be off the hook."

"And no longer classified as top secret," Zurich chimed in.

Epilogue

The content of the letter was still blowing Hailey's mind as she held it in her hand while perusing it for the umpteenth time in the past several weeks. Her dream had finally come true. Her big promotion was coming through. She couldn't believe it the day it happened, and she still couldn't fathom it even though she was already back in the States attending classes. She hadn't called her parents and shared the good news with them until she'd reached Lackland Air Force Base in Texas, where she'd do her extensive training. Both her mother and father had been ecstatic for their beautiful, high-spirited daughter.

Even in all of Hailey's euphoria, it hadn't taken long for reality to set in.

To prepare for her promotional duties, Hailey had had to leave Germany, leave behind all the people she'd just gotten to know and had come to feel extremely comfortable with. There was a slim possibility that, after her initial six weeks of intense training, she might not go back to Rhein Main Air Force Base at all. Details were still being worked out, as notification of class opening had been extremely short.

Not only had she had to leave the country, she'd had to leave rather quickly.

According to what Hailey had learned, she'd initially been selected for a later class, which would've given her way more time to prepare for the move. But a class slot had come open unexpectedly due to another candidate's sudden illness. Rather than lose the spot altogether, the European Weather Wing had decided to select Hailey to fill the earlier space as opposed to the later one. Time and need was of the greater essence.

Alicia had kindly offered to see to it that Hailey's belongings, including her car, would be shipped back to the States if she somehow ended up having to make a permanent change in duty stations. In turn, Hailey had gone to legal services and signed a power of attorney giving Alicia the right to handle certain affairs on her behalf. Hailey was praying no changes would occur.

Missing Zurich like she did also had Hailey more than a little crazy. He had been gone two weeks by the time she'd left Germany. True to their word, they hadn't seen each other as lovers beyond Greece. With the exception of him slipping by her place to tell her good-bye before he'd gone TDY, Hailey and Zurich had only run into each other on the base a couple of times.

The only things they'd exchanged between them on that cool evening were a few warm hugs and numerous tender glances of longing. It had been more difficult for them to see each other than for them not to. All their self-enforced restrictions had made the visit more intense than it would've been otherwise. Sitting in the same room with someone you love and had repeatedly made heart-stopping love to, without being able to go to that idyllic spot with them again and again, was the worst kind of punishment she'd ever had to deal with, the type that no one should ever have to endure.

Hailey had no spare time for reading books and magazines, or watching television for recreation. Her studies took up her all time. Hailey at times was bored stiff after completing her assignments. Even if there had been tons of fun things for her to do, she had just lost interest in the kinds of hobbies that used to bring her so much joy. The only warmth she had in her life came from the numerous sweet memories that she and Zurich had made together within a very short period of time. Although treating Zurich as unfairly as she had in Greece was the worst of their memories, she was keeping that one super-bad memory around as a constant reminder of how she should never dare to treat him again.

Hailey looked around the dorm room and felt like screaming. Her life was a lonely place to begin with when she had to be alone, but it was even lonelier without Zurich there to brighten up her days and make her laugh. And she'd had the nerve to tell him that she didn't need him to make her happy. Well, she thought, she didn't need him in order for her to be happy, but he certainly had enhanced her joy tenfold.

The only real unhappiness Hailey had carried around with her was the part she'd always believed she played in Kelly's death. She now knew much better than that, thanks in part to Zurich. Hailey admitted to herself that she wasn't unhappy now. Her present state of mind had more to do with loneliness and missing Zurich more and more each day.

Three years, equaling one thousand and ninety-five days, was a long time indeed to be separated from someone you loved as much as she did Zurich. She'd even figured up the hours.

The color of blushing heat flooded Hailey's cheeks as she thought about the last days of their mini-vacation on Mykonos. She had been a downright sex maniac, but she didn't regret any of what she'd done. Her behavior had been so out of the ordinary, but she'd only acted out the extraordinary things she'd felt. Zurich had a way of bringing out the naughty girl in her.

Remembering that she hadn't read her mail, Hailey looked through the letters she'd received early in the afternoon. The letter from her mother surprised her, as she'd just talked with her. Marie hadn't mentioned writing to her. As she tore it open, she saw that another envelope, also addressed to her, was inside the larger mailer. Euphoria rushed to her heart.

It was from Zurich. The postmark read Ramstein AFB, Germany.

Hailey ripped open the envelope as she stretched out on the bed to peruse her letter. Just as before, when he'd left the greeting card under her hotel-room door, she caught a whiff of his engaging cologne, which she now figured was intentional on his part.

The opening greeting immediately caught her attention, causing her heart to laugh.

Hi, Adam's Eve,

I hope this note finds you in good spirits. All is well with me. I know we promised not to do much in the way of communicating unless we just happened to pass by each other on the base, but that's not likely to happen anytime soon since we're now in different locations. I'm writing to you for the same reasons I couldn't leave the country without at least saying good-bye to you; it would've killed me not to do so. Although I'm mainly writing to say hello, I have so much more than that to say to you, but I know the rules we agreed to. I sent this letter to your parents' address so as not to leave any sort of paper trail, though I doubt anyone is paying us one iota of attention. This is hard for me, and I'm sure it's not any easier on you. Three years of us being apart will be like doing three years of hard labor as a prison inmate in a third-world country. I'm a strong black man, but there are some things that strength just can't make up for. Missing you so much.

I love you,
Eve's Adam

P.S. Thinking of just getting a mere glimpse of you once this assignment was up has kept me going. Now I understand I may be going elsewhere before returning to home base.):

Tears sprang to her eyes. She loved the fitting code names he'd chosen for them. Their sinful three-night rendezvous in the Garden of Eden partaking of the forbidden fruit had certainly earned them the interesting monikers. The word *sinful* was an understatement when used in describing their every morning, noon, and night physical trysts. She couldn't even remember them looking at a clock for the first two days. Not a word had been mentioned about time since they both were aware that it was quickly running out on them.

The fact that he didn't sign his name didn't surprise her. She was aware that he'd just been playing it safe. That he still even dared to play at all astounded her. He'd been so adamant about them seeing their careers through to the end without the slightest blemish on their military records. Love had a way of making you do crazy things and taking unnecessary risks. She certainly could attest to that; her insane actions were proof enough.

It seemed so odd to her that two people in love didn't even positively know each other's whereabouts. He thought she was still in Germany, and he was constantly moving from base to base. She could only imagine his expression when he got home and learned she was gone. The other really strange occurrence was that she'd never mentioned the nature of her lifelong goal to Zurich in case it didn't come through. And now it was coming true; that is, if she didn't wash out. She wasn't even sure the promotion would make a difference in their dilemma, but she was sure hoping. With so many rules and regulations governing fraternization, she just didn't know what to think or to expect.

While stretched out on his bed, Zurich still couldn't digest what he'd just learned about Hailey a few days ago. He'd come back from TDY with high hopes of spotting her somewhere on base. To learn that she was back in the States in school had come as a real big shock to him. He'd found out his first day back at work by casually asking someone in his unit about how the new weather observer was doing in her new assignment. Much to his surprise, though she was classified as a weather observer, she had just recently earned her degree in meteorology.

After receiving the shocking news, he'd immediately tracked down Alicia Richards and found out everything else he needed to know about Hailey being in Texas, of all places. As Zurich thought about what this could possibly mean for them, he couldn't help smiling, yet he didn't dare get his hopes up too high.

Hailey had applied for OTS, officer's training school, and had actually been accepted. If she completed her training, she would become a full-fledged officer and wear the rank of 2LT. This was incredible news, despite the concerns that still remained.

That Hailey had kept all of this a secret was the most unbelievable part, yet he understood why she would do so. If her appointment hadn't come through, she wouldn't have had to suffer the embarrassment of others outside of the command staff knowing she didn't make it. That was probably where her head was. He knew what that was all about. No one other than the powers that be had known he'd applied for OTS, either. He and Hailey had one more thing in common.

It seemed that a couple of extraordinary events were about to go down in Texas. His mother was having an engagement party.

Hailey was nervous as a cat on a hot tin roof as she sat stiffly on the podium with her graduating class. Her parents had flown to Texas as a surprise and to lend her their support, but Hailey still felt as if she needed to be hit right between the eyes with a tranquilizer dart. She hadn't slept very well over the past week, and she'd be glad when this was all over so she could get her sleeping routine back on schedule. She was completely wired.

Hailey expected the ceremony to possibly be rather long and drawn out, but the program was moving right along. No matter how long it took, Hailey couldn't think of anyplace she'd rather be. As she looked slightly to her left, she nearly fell out of her chair. Her heart practically stopped at the sight of him as he slipped into the only empty seat. The reason for him being there totally baffled her.

It wasn't just that he was in attendance at the ceremony; Zurich was seated among the prestigious presenters. What was he going to present and to whom? She wouldn't even allow herself to think that he might be there for her.

As the names of her peers were called out, Hailey watched intently as they walked up to the podium to receive their graduating certificates and have the official military insignias pinned on their uniforms. When her name was called out, her heart stopped and restarted several times before she even got out of her seat. Zurich's mission was now crystal clear to her since he was now at the podium.

He was there to represent Headquarters, 25th Weather Squadron.

Major Zurich Kingdom was going to present her with the gold bar representing the rank of 2LT. How he'd pulled this major feat off was something she couldn't wait to hear him explain. She was in no doubt that he'd pulled a few strings to be here.

Hailey's parents had just left the Hilton Hotel on San Antonio's famed Riverwalk after having had a wonderful dinner with their daughter and her love interest. Major Zurich Kingdom had been an instant hit with Martin and Marie Hamilton. Zurich had asked Hailey and her parents to join him for dinner shortly after the ceremony had come to an official close. Martin had been left totally in the dark about the love affair until Hailey and Zurich had brought it up after dinner. Martin was simply glad that he hadn't known.

Zurich had booked a suite in the Hilton rather than stay at the Lackland AFB VOQ; visiting officers' quarters. Now that they'd had their very private, passionate reunion, Hailey and Zurich were seated on the sofa in the living room. He had just finished explaining to Hailey how he'd come to be at her ceremony.

She smiled. "That's all there is to it, huh?"

"Yeah, for sure. I just went in and had the commander approve my leave to make it here for my mother's engagement party. The rest is history. Of course, I pulled a few strings in order to present at the ceremony, but you don't need to know all the details. Just consider it classified."

Laughing, Hailey laid her head on his shoulder. "I think I'll take your suggestion." She lifted her head and looked into his eyes. "I know we're not home free yet since there still may be other issues for us to deal with. I'm now a 2LT, but you definitely outrank me. Since you're the one who studied the rules in depth, where do we stand?"

"Together. I don't know how much of an issue it might be, but I'm not in your reporting chain of command. You're assigned to the detachment, and I'm at headquarters. But for now, we're not going to worry about any of that, nor are we taking any chances of being separated. If I get my way, we're going back to Germany as husband and wife. I'm willing to let the chips fall where they may. But what I'm not willing to do is live another day without you. We've suffered enough being apart. Are we on the same page?"

Hailey kissed him passionately. "Same page, same chapter, same book. I love you, Eve's Adam."

He brought her into his arms and kissed her thoroughly. "I love you, too! Will you marry me right away, Adam's Eve?"

Crying and laughing at the same time, Hailey threw her arms around his neck. "In a Texas minute."

For a sneak peek at
the next book in
the At Your Service series

Courage Under Fire
by Candice Poarch

Coming in July 2003
from BET Books/Arabesque

Just turn the page . . .

Prologue

Ronald Taft wore dress blues. Although his wife couldn't see the shoes, she knew they were spit-shined black.

The officer's dress blues were his favorite Army uniform. He wore them with a sense of pride and honor for his country and for the fact that he—a black man who came from little—had progressed so far. He loved the Army and even more, he loved his status as an officer.

Arlene Taft remembered when Ronald had taken her to her first formal military function. Since it was his ball, she'd elected to wear a blue gown instead of her dress uniform.

Just a smattering of African-Americans had been in attendance.

"We'll go far in the military," he'd said to Arlene. They were both stationed in the Washington, D.C. area. Although it was unusual to get assigned to the same location for years, he'd lucked out with his posting at the Pentagon. Since she was a nurse, staying in one location wasn't unusual for her. She'd been at Walter Reed Army Medical Center for years.

As the years passed, Ronald's postings required more and more travel—so much, in fact, that it was easy for him to take a vacation with a mistress without his wife's knowledge.

Arlene sat through her husband's funeral with strained emotions. What was she to feel except betrayal, disillusionment, and a deep burning anger that she couldn't appease?

Her mother-in-law sniffled and moaned her grief beside her. She held on to the woman's hand, perhaps too tightly at times, but Nancy Taft didn't complain. She was swallowed up in her own grief and she didn't even notice. The nurse had already revived her once with smelling salts. Ronald had been Mrs. Taft's only child—a truly beloved son. And somewhat spoiled. But she didn't blame Mrs. Taft for being a loving and giving woman. She'd accepted Arlene into the fold as if she were her own child. Nancy was a rarity. She seldom spoke a disparaging word against anyone.

Arlene's father was present with his new wife, a woman who was merely a few months older than Arlene. She was so unlike Arlene's mother that Arlene wondered what he saw in her except for the obvious appeal of a younger woman. Arlene's mother had died three years ago, and Arlene supposed this was his way of moving on. He certainly dressed younger. His wife stood out in her lavish black attire. The skirt was higher and tighter than Arlene thought appropriate, but who was she to judge? She only wished she could see more of her father. Their relationship hadn't been the same since her mother's death.

The preacher's words droned on. They could have been disjointed ramblings, because Arlene didn't hear any of it. She didn't know why she was grieving.

Her husband died on a boating trip with his lover—a lover Arlene must have subconsciously known had been out there. Did she have blinders on? The reality that he spent so little time with her should have been one clear indication. Randy army officers rarely went without physical pleasures. She'd only deluded herself into thinking that her man was made of sterner stuff.

Arlene shook with his betrayal. She wondered if his army buddies who laughed and joked in front of her knew of his exploits behind her back. Had their wives, who called themselves her friends, also been privy to the information? The military community was small. People knew each other's business, and they told. Yet no one had seen the necessity of informing her.

Somehow Arlene got through the funeral. She barely startled at the gun salute, and made polite conversation at the reception held after the gravesite service. Her father and his wife left.

Arlene stayed on for a few days to console her mother-in-law. Then she flew back to Washington, D.C., telling Mrs. Taft that she would stay in touch and that she would send her mementos of her son.

It was Friday night when she unpacked her suitcase in the row house she'd lived in for years. The message machine was beeping. Ignoring it, she stood under the shower a long time, then went to the closet to pull on a robe, even though the outside August temperature hovered in the nineties.

Ronald's suits and clothes hung in the closet beside hers. What happened next seemed to be outside of her control.

She came back to her senses when she heard the doorbell ring. Shelly Bailey, her girlfriend since kindergarten, stood on the cement steps, a suitcase beside her.

Arlene glanced around the room. It was a disaster. Every piece of Ronald's clothing was flung about the room. A stack of black garbage bags was hidden under more clothes on the cocktail table.

Shelly glanced at Arlene's ravished features. Then she glanced around the living room, a worried expression on her face.

She tugged Arlene into her arms and held her tightly. "Girlfriend, I'm here. We're going to work this through together."

One

Some days were better than others. Arlene wanted to pull the covers up to her neck and spend the next few hours in her warm bed.

At nine she made an effort to rise, but never made it up. She dozed again, off and on for two hours. A siren blared from afar, but that wasn't so unusual in the city.

The clock closed in on eleven when she finally considered actually getting up. She didn't feel too guilty. After all, she'd worked the eleven-to-seven shift at the hospital the evening before.

Arlene contemplated calling in sick—perhaps to spend the rest of what was left of the day in bed. Half of it was gone anyway. This was totally out of line for her. She'd never called in sick when she wasn't. But many things had changed in the last month and she didn't feel quite herself.

Suddenly the phone rang, a loud and unwanted sound in the quiet of her bedroom. Lazily she reached out a hand, plucked up the receiver, and barked out a groggy "Hello."

"Lieutenant Colonel Taft, we need you here stat!" the hospital scheduler told her.

Now! Was that woman crazy? Arlene wanted to avoid the day altogether, but she wouldn't dare say so out loud. A soldier was on call twenty-four-seven. If they needed her, she'd have to go.

"Due to the disaster, we need more nurses, especially specialists," the woman said.

"What disaster?" Arlene asked.

"Haven't you seen the news?"

"No. What happened?" Sitting up in bed, she reached for the remote. It was too far away. Now that she thought about it, she had heard more sirens than usual, but it hadn't pierced the fog that had settled on her.

"The Pentagon has been bombed. And both towers of the World Trade Center are gone. And that's just the beginning."

"Gone? *Impossible.*"

"Just turn on the TV. Every station is broadcasting. We need you here. Now."

"I'll be there as soon as I dress." Arlene fumbled the receiver back onto the hook and scrambled for the TV remote to press the power button. Every channel focused on the tragedy. It didn't take long for her to get the gist of the earth-shattering disaster. A deep sense of dread and sorrow flowed through her for the suffering these people were experiencing and that someone would dare do this in America. She saw it in the news when it happened in Europe and Israel. *But here?* The U.S. seemed isolated from all that, but global involvement had brought the entire world closer—for the good as well as the bad.

With a quick prayer, she rushed out of bed so fast her head swam. Tugging off her nightgown and thrusting it aside, she headed to the shower. After taking the fastest shower in history, she listened to the news as she quickly donned her uniform. Her new hairdo of short red curls only took a moment to rake a comb through. Turning off the TV, she paused only long enough to grab a bagel and cream cheese to eat in the car as she drove the short distance to the hospital. Depending on the number of injured, finding time for a break once she arrived could be next to impossible.

At the hospital, she was quickly directed to the trauma section. It was a beehive of activity.

"Lieutenant Colonel Neal Allen is one of your patients," she was told. "He has multiple fractures, scorched lungs and throat, and internal injuries. Right now we're trying to keep him breathing on his own to clear his lungs and increase his chances of survival."

Arlene recorded his vital signs on his chart. He was still heavily sedated from surgery.

Neal Allen. That name was indelibly etched in her mind. Could this be the Neal Allen who lived next door to her in middle school? Arlene shook her head at the foolish thought. It couldn't be. Of all the people for her to run into.

The Neal Allen she'd known back in Texas had been the bane of her existence. She would never forget the time he'd taken her red-and-white panties off the clothesline, attached them to a piece of cardboard, scribbled her name in huge bold letters across the front, and hung them on his father's flagpole. Her panties had flown for hours where the man had so proudly flown his American flag. All because she wouldn't walk to the movies with him. She'd already accepted a date with someone else, but even if she hadn't, she wouldn't have gone out with Neal. *What was that boy's name?* she wondered. Perhaps she hadn't been the most diplomatic with her refusal, but she didn't deserve that.

As Arlene looked at him, she realized he *was* that Neal Allen. Determined to find something to dislike about him, she noted his physical appearance had changed a lot in the last twenty-one years from the gangly youth she'd known.

It was immediately evident that he worked out regularly. His relaxed state failed to mask his underlying strength. His chest and shoulder muscles were amazing. She felt the steel beneath soft skin when she attached the blood-pressure cuff. His dark lashes covering his closed eyes were much too attractive. His hair was cut short, yet still managed to look striking. As Arlene gazed down on him, she wondered if his character had changed as much as his appearance.

She shook the memories away and got back to the business of keeping Lieutenant Colonel Neal Allen alive.

* * *

The next day, when Arlene reported to duty, the patient was looking better. She wondered if he remembered her.

"How are we feeling today, Lieutenant Colonel Allen?" Arlene asked him as she slipped the pressure cuff on his arm.

"Good to be alive," he whispered in a raspy voice she could barely hear. It was tinged with the smoke and heat damage from the fire.

"Oh, you'll be feeling better in no time." After making a notation of his blood pressure, she slid the thermometer into his ear, then recorded his temperature. It was only slightly elevated.

"How did the others—"

"You saved quite a few people. They've been calling about you."

"But—"

"Don't try to talk. Save your throat." She smiled. Whatever their past, he was her patient and she was determined to give him the best care. "You're a hero."

"No . . . So much destruction. So many people injured—" he whispered.

"And many generous people who are out there offering help. You did your part; now let us help you."

"It wasn't enough."

Arlene patted his hand, wanting to ease his distress. "You gave all you could. No one could ask for more."

He closed his eyes.

Arlene didn't know if her words had had any effect. She only hoped they eased his pain.

She kept peeking at him as she attended to his injuries. His concern for the others touched her more than she wanted. Could he have changed so drastically from that obnoxious kid she knew so long ago?

* * *

"Well, Little Miss Leave-Me-Alone."

Arlene stopped in her tracks, her hackles rising. She forced herself to present a calm front. "We must be feeling better."

"Thought I'd forgotten you, didn't you?"

Arlene had hoped so.

"Were you trying to hide your identity?" His voice rose barely above a whisper. She strained to hear him, but she heard nevertheless. His cute brown eyes were dancing with merriment for the first time. Even though it was at her expense, she was glad for it.

She'd hoped he'd forgotten about her past, darn it. After all, she couldn't look the same, and her last name had changed. Back then, he'd loved to tease her. "I don't have anything to hide. My life is an open book. I see you haven't changed from that obnoxious kid who lived next door to me."

"In some ways—in many, many ways—I hope I have. Changed, that is."

"Hummm." He had changed, all right. Even with his numerous injuries, she hadn't missed the striking proportions of his body. As his nurse, she'd seen all of him, and to her chagrin, she liked what she saw.

"We'll just work on getting you healed right now, okay?"

His smile faded. "How are the others who were brought in?"

"I don't know. I'm sorry. They were taken to hospitals all around the area." She pulled the sheet up to his chest. "I want you to rest your voice. Your throat is still raw. It must be painful for you to talk."

He clasped her hand in his, imprisoning it with a grip that belied his condition. "I need to know."

"I know you do. Believe me, we're all doing our best for all the injured. Trust me."

"Can I trust you?" The seriousness of his tone surprised Arlene.

"Why wouldn't you?"

His stare was intense, as if his eyes spoke words he wouldn't say aloud. Then suddenly he glanced away from her to the picture beside his bed.

She regarded the photo, which a nurse had found in his pocket. A pretty young girl with two thick pigtails. Arlene had brought a frame for it and put it on his bedside table, hoping the photo would give him pleasure. From her conversations with his mother, who called often, she'd garnered that the child was his niece, a cutie named April.

"Your mother and your niece have called several times. They're very concerned about you."

"What did you tell them?"

"That you're better, and that we're taking excellent care of you. As soon as your voice heals, we'll let you talk with them. But right now, I want you to rest your vocal cords."

He glanced at the clock. "It's time for you to leave?"

"Yes," Arlene said. "My shift is over."

"Can't you stay a little while?"

"Why?"

"I don't know. To talk about home. To read to me. Something—anything. I can't sleep."

She stopped the urge to stroke his forehead. "They'll give you something to help you sleep," Arlene said softly. "You need your rest."

"I don't want any more medication."

Arlene knew very well that she had nothing to rush home to. Her husband was dead—had seldom been around when he was alive. Since his death, things hadn't changed that much, actually. Except for the expectation of his arrival. When she looked back on her marriage, she saw that it hadn't been that great. She'd been complacent. And that was sad.

Arlene had nothing to go home to.

"All right. I'll read to you. What kinds of books do you like?"

"Anything will do." Neal just wanted to listen to her

voice. Her soothing voice intrigued him, not the story. He was disgusted with himself for wanting her near. Most of his waking hours were spent watching the disaster on TV. His unit would be one of the groups dispatched to Afghanistan. He was disappointed that he wouldn't be among them.

Now he was punishing himself by listening to Arlene's voice, even though he knew she'd been responsible for his sister's, and thereby April's, unhappiness and pain.

But Ronald Taft *had* been Arlene's husband. He'd already been married, and Bridget had no right to him.

Arlene smiled—a smile he remembered so well from when she was up to mischief. "Would one of my romance novels work?"

He smiled, and the image was amazing.

"How about a mystery?" Arlene amended, knowing the skewed notion men had of romance novels. "I'll find one that will keep your heart pumping for hours. Or I might get you something soothing enough to help you sleep. What's your preference?" She found herself stroking his hand even though she'd cautioned herself not to.

"Excitement, please."

There was that smile again—the one he'd used just after he'd teased her in middle school. Back then, Arlene had hated that smile, but now she found it sexy. She chuckled. "I'll be back soon," she said, and went to meet with the nurse who would replace her.

"Arlene, we're transferring a call. This kid insists on speaking to you and only you."

For a change, Neal was sleeping peacefully. Arlene's hand hovered over the phone so that she could catch it before the ring woke him.

"Nurse Taft?" a young voice asked in a firm tone.

"This is Lieutenant Colonel Taft," Arlene responded.

"Good. I'm calling about Uncle Neal. I'm worried

about him. When can he come home? I miss him. I *need* him." The little girl sounded as if she were near tears.

"Are you April?"

Silence greeted Arlene. Then a hesitant, trembling voice said, "Yes."

"Your uncle is much better, April. He's responding well to the medication. But he needs time for his body to heal. It might take a little while."

Arlene heard sniffles on the end of the line, and her heart cracked.

"Is your grandmother there, or your mother?"

"My mommy's dead. Uncle Neal is supposed to take care of me now."

"I'm so sorry, honey." Arlene's heart went out to the motherless little girl. She remembered Bridget well, and was saddened to hear the young woman was dead. Neal seemed to be the child's security blanket.

"Grandma's worried about Uncle Neal. She wants to come there but Grandpa's too sick. Grandpa wants to come, too. But he can't."

"It won't be easy catching a plane right now, anyway. Maybe it's best they stay home. Anytime you're worried about him, just call me, all right?"

"Will you tell me the truth?"

Arlene closed her eyes, moved by the hope in the child's voice. "Always."

"Uncle Neal's really doing better?" she asked with a skepticism too old for one so young.

"Yes, he's much better. I promise." That much wasn't a lie. Arlene wouldn't lie to her.

"He's really not going to die? Grandma said he wouldn't, but I thought she was just trying to make me feel better."

"No, he's definitely not going to die. I wouldn't lie about that."

"Thank you."

"You're very welcome, dear. Did you get your grandparents' permission to call?"

"Uncle Neal gave me lots of phone cards so I can call him anytime I want to."

"And you know how to use them?"

"Sure," she said with a confidence that belied her age. "He showed me how to use them. And I've been reading for years. I can read directions."

Arlene smiled. "You're a big girl, aren't you?"

"Yeah. I can do lots of things."

When Arlene hung up the phone, she caught Neal's steady gaze as he watched her. He was always watching her in that strange way. Why? What was he looking for? "I didn't know you were awake," Arlene said finally. "I'm sorry I woke you."

"It's okay," he whispered. But a deep sadness seemed to steal over him. She understood some of what he felt, only her grief was different. Her sorrow was tinged with adultery, mistrust, and hurt. The loss of a beloved sister was so much worse.

"I'm so sorry about your sister," Arlene told him.

He nodded and turned away from her. Nothing could be said to ease the sorrow of a loved one's death. She wouldn't even try to ease what she couldn't anyway.

She thought of Bridget again. She'd been five years younger than Arlene. They'd known each other, but their ages were too far apart for them to run in the same circles. But Bridget had looked up to Arlene. And Arlene sometimes baby-sat for Mrs. Allen. Bridget had been as full of energy as her precocious brother, but not quite as mischievous. Their mother was practically useless when it came to handling two such active kids. Sometimes it seemed she didn't even try.

Arlene glanced at the photo on Neal's bedside table. "April is very pretty. She resembles you."

"You think so?"

"Yes. Although she also reminds me of Bridget at that age. She definitely has your nose and your smile."

His smile was not filled with humor.

"Are you comfortable?" Arlene asked, straightening his covers.

He nodded.

With nothing more to offer, Arlene touched his hand and left the room.

Considering the meticulous care she gave him and the gentle comfort she offered his family, it was difficult to believe that Arlene was the vindictive woman who wouldn't give her husband a divorce, even after she'd already agreed to do so, simply because she discovered another woman was pregnant with his child. According to Ronald, his relationship with his wife had been over years ago. He'd finally decided to end it, and she'd agreed. Then, when she discovered Bridget was pregnant with his child, she refused to give him the divorce, threatening to ruin his career if he tried to get one.

Ronald and Neal were both Army career men. The threat of adultery could damage a black man's career in a heartbeat. White officers could sometimes get away with unsavory behavior. Even with the barrage of publicity, only a few cases actually amounted to anything. The press usually died down after a short while. Besides, officers protected each other. Today as much as in the past, black men lived by a different, more cautious code.

Another worry nagged relentlessly at Neal. He was responsible for raising his niece. Would he heal well enough to return to his post so he could properly care for her? He wasn't ready to retire. But if his body betrayed him, he would have no other recourse. He wanted to expose her to the world. There was so much for her to learn—so much to see.

April had lost a mother and father only a month ago. And now her guardian was in the hospital. His parents were too infirm to care for a rambunctious eight-year-old. And April had always been full of energy. Every week since his sister's death, his mother had called to tell him about some mischief April had gotten into. He'd lecture the child, but her deeds weren't that serious, and Neal didn't put that much energy into the lecture. She'd lived through enough traumas. He wouldn't make her life any more unbearable than it already was. He needed to be with her.

Neal had paid for a live-in nanny to care for her until he could take the responsibility for her.

She was on her third nanny so far. The second one had been frightened away when April put her hamster in the woman's bed. The woman had woken in the middle of the night to find the hamster crawling up her leg.

Neal had hoped to get April in a few weeks. Now, there was no telling when he would be able to return to the real world and care for her.

He could imagine the frightening thoughts running through her head, especially with his accident so close on the heels of her parents' deaths.

It was Saturday. Neal had been in the hospital for two weeks now. It was Arlene's day off, and she debated going in to visit him. He expected to see her every day. They had fallen into a routine of sorts, although sometimes his mind seemed to wander. Some deep, dark secret from the past, perhaps. Arlene got the feeling he didn't like her for some reason. But she certainly couldn't be part of whatever troubled him.

When she arrived, the phone in his room rang. By now it was second nature for her to reach for it.

"It's time to send Uncle Neal home," April said, when Arlene answered it.

"He's healing very nicely," Arlene told her. "But he isn't quite ready to return home."

"But I need him *now.*" Every situation was urgent as far as April was concerned.

"He misses you, too, sweetheart."

"My nanny is a witch." A long, labored breath followed that pronouncement.

Arlene smothered a laugh.

"How so?" Arlene couldn't help but ask.

"She doesn't understand me."

"Maybe if you explained your problem to her—"

"She doesn't understand, though. She's too old. I need help!"

"Honey—"

"Can you believe she got mad because my guinea pig got out of the cage and went to her room?"

"It just happened to get out?"

Silence greeted her. Arlene surmised the rodent had had plenty of help.

"I may have *accidentally* left the door open when I took her out to play with me. Maybe I didn't latch the door good enough. But it was an *accident.* Everybody makes mistakes. Why can't I make them?"

"I see," Arlene said. Evidently Nanny didn't like little animals scurrying around the house.

"And my hamster won't stay in the cage. Nanny keeps calling it a mouse and threatening to kill it. Can you believe she'd kill my hamster? I told Grandpa on her too. He told her not to kill my animals. She's a mean old lady."

"Let me get this straight. The hamster gets out of the cage on its own. You didn't give it any help?"

"No. Never."

I just bet it did, Arlene thought.

"Is it my fault he keeps getting out? I do everything I can to get him to stay in, but every morning when I wake up he's gone. And he stays away until he gets hungry. Then he comes back looking scrawny and starved."

"So after the hamster got out of the room on its own, it found its way to your nanny's room, too?"

"What can I do about *that?"* April asked, affronted. "He got out on his own. It's the hamster's fault. Why doesn't she blame him?"

"She can't exactly talk to the hamster."

"I talk to him all the time. But does he listen when I tell him to stay in a cage? Nanny's mean. He's got to be careful around her, and I told him that, too. But Grandma says that's a man for you. They never listen."

Arlene couldn't contain her laugh.

"And then there's my dog."

Did the child have a zoo in that house? Arlene wondered. "A dog?"

"Nothing worth getting mad about. It just chewed on her raggedy old house shoe. And then it peed on the carpet in her room. But that was her fault. She shouldn't have scared him. If I was a baby, I would have peed too if that old hag had frightened me. It's just a puppy."

Arlene peeked at Neal to make sure he was still sleeping. "I take it she doesn't frighten you."

"Not really. I hate her!"

"Have you spoken to your grandparents about this?"

"They don't understand because the mean witch always gets to them first before I even get a chance to tell them *my* side." A long, defeated sigh came over the phone. "Now I'm stuck in my room until I learn to behave. I'm going to spend the rest of my life cooped up in this room. Can I come to Uncle Neal? Please? Please? I'll take care of him. I won't bother him. I promise to be good."

Arlene's heart clenched. April desperately needed her uncle. "Sweetheart, you *are* good." She was just an eight-year-old acting her age.

Early Monday afternoon, General Ashborn presented Neal with the papers and eagle for his promotion to Colonel. He also received a special commendation for his rescue efforts.

Arlene borrowed a disposable camera from one of the nurses and snapped pictures.

"Congratulations, Colonel," Arlene told him once the general had left.

"Thank you," he said.

"This is absolutely wonderful."

He studied the commendation as if it held the secrets to the universe. "So many people were hurt far worse than I was. So many lives lost. I don't feel I deserve this."

"That doesn't mean we can't recognize our heroes. You deserve your commendation, Neal. You have something to be proud of."

Neal's phone rang, and Arlene picked it up as if it were her own.

"My hamster's dead!" April wailed over the phone.

"What happened?" Arlene asked, ready to go to battle with the mean old nanny who had the nerve to kill a child's animal.

"My dog bit it."

"Your dog?" Arlene pressed a hand against her chest to still her quickened heartbeat.

"It got out of the cage again. It wouldn't listen to me. And Pickles ate it. He was bloody and dead on my carpet this morning. I didn't even hear him last night."

"Oh, I'm so sorry, honey."

"I want Uncle Neal. Please can I come?"

"Honey, your uncle is improving daily, but it will take some time before he's ready to come home. You can't stay in a hospital."

"I'll be good, and I'll be quiet, too. I promise."

Arlene's heart ached for the little girl. "Who will keep your animals if you leave?"

"I'm mad at Pickles. She ate my hamster."

"It's not quite Pickles's fault, honey. His natural survival instinct encourages him to eat animals. Dogs are made that way."

"It's mean."

"It seems like it. But those instincts keep them alive

when they don't have someone special like you to take care of them."

"I feed her. I even give her food from my plate sometimes, even when Nanny gets mad."

"I'm sure you take very good care of her. And you must continue to do so until Uncle Neal is well. Okay?"

A few sniffles came over the wire before a weak, "Okay."

"Good."

"I buried him in a shoe box in the back yard. Grandpa said a prayer over his grave."

"That's good."

"I made a cross out of some sticks, and planted a flower by his grave. My mama's flowers were prettier. You think he'll like the flowers?"

"I'm sure he loved them."

"I miss my hamster and I miss my mom."

"I know you do, sweetheart." Arlene struggled to hold back tears.

A couple of sniffles preceded, "My friend Keanna has a boyfriend. I'm never going to date a boy."

Arlene smiled and swiped the wetness away from her eyes. "You might feel differently when you enter high school."

"They're so hardheaded. Grandma said that's why my hamster's dead. Because boys are hardheaded. They're the devil's spawn, she said. They always do what you tell them not to. I don't want any hardheaded boys. It hurts too much. I'm not getting any more boy animals."

"Oh, sweetheart. They aren't all bad." Thinking back on Neal when he was a boy, Arlene thought April wasn't too far off the mark.

"Grandma says they are. Nanny agreed, but I don't believe anything she says. She wanted to dump my hamster in the trash. Can you believe that? She wanted to treat him like he was trash."

This woman was toast if Arlene had anything to say about it.

"Grandpa wouldn't let her. He made her keep him so we could bury him."

Arlene closed her eyes briefly. So much grief for one so young. First she buried her mom. Now her pet. Arlene's own pain seemed minuscule in comparison.

"What's the devil's spawn? Nanny called me that, and I'm not a boy."

"You're not the devil's spawn. Put your nanny on the phone."

"She'll be mad at me."

"Right now."

A few seconds passed before an older woman answered the phone. "Hello?"

"Mrs. Carter, I'm Colonel Allen's nurse. He has asked me to speak to you about April."

"She's a handful, I'll tell you that."

"All little eight-year-olds are handfuls," Arlene said.

"Mine weren't."

Did the woman think she'd raised angels? They were probably just good around her. "You do understand that she's just lost her mother, and her uncle who is now her guardian is gravely injured. He would appreciate it if you can keep things calm for her and give her a little consideration."

"He wants me to spoil the child?"

"Consideration means not calling her bad names that might label her for life. Children are very sensitive about that. She also loves her animals. If you could be a little generous toward them, he would be grateful." Arlene chose her words carefully. After all, Neal couldn't search out a new nanny in his condition. Still, the nanny should show some kindness toward the child. No child should be labeled the devil's spawn. Of all the nerve!

When Arlene hung up, she wondered if she'd overstepped her authority. She glanced at Neal. He was watching her, his emotions unreadable. Even regarding his illness, she couldn't always read him. He hated taking pain medication. He was so good at hiding emotions that she couldn't always tell when he was in pain. What else was he covering up?

"I hope you don't mind," she said.

He shook his head.

Neal seemed always to be thinking, always considering some matter. Arlene wondered what was going through his mind. Sometimes she felt he was measuring her, and wondered why. She wondered if she came up lacking.

Near the end of Arlene's shift, as she recorded Neal's vital signs on a chart, a gorgeous, honey-brown–hued woman wearing an Army uniform entered Neal's room.

"Hello, Neal. I was told you were improving," the woman said as she walked to the bed.

He nodded.

"Just ring the bell if you need anything," Arlene said to Neal, and prepared to leave.

"Hello, I'm Natasha, Neal's wife."

Wife. A ring hadn't been among his possessions, and he'd never mentioned a wife.

"Nice to meet you," Arlene said, and left the room.

Neal's wife *would* be what men considered a knockout. Why hadn't Natasha visited him before? Or called him? Perhaps she was stationed elsewhere and had trouble getting to D.C. April called every day. Surely the wife could have called him once.

For some indescribable reason, a shaft of disappointment swirled through Arlene. *You weren't falling for your patient, Arlene. So what's going on?* She took a deep breath and continued the last of her duties of the day. Neal was thirty-six—certainly old enough to have married at least once.

* * *

Neal watched Arlene leave the room, surely thinking he'd lied to her.

"Why are you here, Natasha?"

Natasha approached his bed. "I know this is bad timing, but the sooner we get this divorce moving, the better. If you sign the papers now, the divorce will come through in six months. I got the papers a couple of weeks ago, but I wanted to give you some time."

"How generous," he whispered. His voice was a little stronger than it had been, but not much.

"Give me the papers."

Natasha took a manila envelope out of her huge purse and retrieved the papers.

"The lawyer tagged the areas where you should sign," she said.

Neal activated the remote for the bed so he could sit up.

"I'll help you with that."

"I have it," he shot back. If he could handle a divorce, he could damn well handle a remote. He scanned the papers, making sure he wasn't signing away everything he'd ever saved. A five-year marriage that only halfway worked for the first three years wasn't worth everything he'd ever worked for.

Now Neal was grateful Natasha had insisted on a prenuptial agreement, fearing that if things didn't work out, he'd end up with the little her father had left her. He knew very well his assets amounted to more than hers. He wanted to keep it that way.

Neal signed the papers and handed them to her.

"How is April?" she asked, as if she really cared.

"She's fine."

"Good." Natasha checked the clock. "Well, I have an appointment. I hope everything turns out well for you."

"You, too," Neal told her, knowing very well that she was rushing off to be with her new boyfriend.

Now uncomfortable with him, she quickly left. A part of Neal's life was nearing a close. He shouldn't feel anything, should be grateful to see the last of her. Still they had been married for five years, and parting wasn't easy.

He glanced at the clock and wonndered if Arlene would stop by once again before she left. He was falling for her, just as he had as a lovesick thirteen-year-old. Every time she came in the room, his system went into overdrive. He had to work at keeping his emotions contained. She was forever leaning over him or touching him in her warm manner. And her touches set his heart thumping. He watched the clock, waiting for her to return.

She didn't, and he was even more disappointed than he'd been with the ending of his marriage.

Arlene had the next two days off, and for the first time since Neal had arrived, she didn't go by the hospital to visit him. They were the longest two days of Neal's life.

She returned on Thursday. When she came into his room, she was very businesslike. She did the chores she usually did, and was about to leave the room when he grabbed her arm.

"What's going on?" he whispered.

"Nothing. Did you have a good weekend?"

"I expected to see you."

"Wasn't your wife with you?"

Neal sighed. He needed to clear the air. "We're separated. She brought the separation papers by for me to sign."

With an unbelieving glint, Arlene's eyes widened. "She brought you papers while you're in the hospital?"

Neal shrugged. "They needed to be signed. My marriage has been over for years. We're just getting it done legally."

"I'm sorry, Neal."

"I'm not."

"Are you okay?"

Neal nodded.

Arlene squeezed his hand and went about her rounds,

wondering at the cruelty of people, or was it just that they didn't care anymore as long as their needs were taken care of. She hoped she would never be that uncaring.

April had called practically every day since Arlene's conversation with the nanny. Somehow, the energetic child brought Arlene out of her own grief.

"Are your bags all packed?" Neal asked.

"They are. Most of my things have been shipped to Korea," Arlene said. Korea was her next tour of duty. She was scheduled for a short stay there.

"Aren't you going to miss this place?"

Arlene nodded. "I'm definitely going to miss the D.C. area. The beautiful old homes. The rhythm of the city. The museums and activities on the Mall. The theaters. Cherry blossoms in the spring. The restaurants. But it's time for me to see other parts of the world." The things she'd mentioned were only a few of the activities Arlene would miss, but the day after she returned to work after burying Ronald, she'd asked for a change in location. She realized she'd grown stagnant. She was pleased the change had come through quickly.

Neal was leaving the hospital today. He was taking a flight to Dallas to finish his recuperation near his family. April needed to see that he was still alive and recovering. Arlene had halfway fallen in love with the child over the last few weeks. She would miss their lively conversations. If she'd had a child, she would have wished for one like April.

She would also miss Neal. Darn it. Tears clogged her throat. How had she fallen for him so quickly? She hadn't fallen in love with him or anything stupid like that. It was just . . . in their month and half together, they had formed a bond of sorts.

Neal, too, had mixed feelings about Arlene. He'd grown to respect her skills, and had even fallen in love with her a little over the last several weeks. It was difficult to reconcile the vindictive woman Ronald had described to Bridget, with this tender, caring woman who dealt so well with April, his parents, and his concerned friends.

Perhaps Ronald had been wrong. It was possible that Arlene had refused to give him a divorce because she was in love with him. After all, he had been her husband. She had first dibs on him. Bridget, the baby sister whom Neal had loved so much, had found her happiness on the dregs of another woman's lost dreams.

It hurt to think about his sister. The two of them had always been protective of one another. It seemed his connection to family stability had been broken with her death. Family was special to him. Sometimes he thought the only thing keeping his life in perspective was April, simply because she needed him.

For the last month she'd called almost daily, wanting him home with her. The doctors wanted him to stay in D.C. another week or so before he went to Texas, but he couldn't. He was going home.

Arlene drove him to Dulles International Airport. The trip on 66 West was almost bumper-to-bumper traffic. Normally he would have flown from Washington National, but their full flight schedule hadn't resumed yet. From Dulles, he wouldn't have to change planes.

From the passenger seat he assessed her. He was accustomed to seeing Arlene in her nurse's uniform. She was beautiful today in dark blue slacks and a matching V-neck top and gold necklace. She looked elegant and fetching.

"Thank you, Arlene, for all you've done for me and my family."

"You're very welcome," she said.

Words couldn't express his gratitude. He'd received many letters of good wishes from the families whose loved ones he'd saved, and his friends from Buckley Academy had called him often—even sent flowers and cards. But

Arlene had been his steady champion. And he couldn't think of the words to express how indebted he felt.

When they arrived at the airport Arlene let him off at the terminal and requested a wheelchair. He went through check-in while she parked the car. The lines were long due to increased security. Although he could stand for short periods, he was glad she'd insisted on the wheelchair, as much as he hated it.

An athletic man his entire life, an Airborne Ranger, even, he found it humbling to be pushed through the airport to his gate while Arlene walked beside him carrying his cane. He shouldn't complain. After all that had occurred, he was grateful to be alive, and well enough to even take the flight.

"Can I get you anything?" Arlene asked him. "A sandwich, maybe?"

"Nothing. Thanks. Just sit and relax."

She sat in a chair by his wheelchair. He took in the beautiful elegance and warmth of her face, the tenderness in her eyes, and wondered if he would ever see her again. He hoped that another twenty-one years wouldn't pass before their paths crossed again.

He started to ask for her phone number—ask if he could visit her once he healed, but decided against it. April was his responsibility now. And he couldn't ask Arlene to be a part of her husband's baby's life, to have her pain thrown in her face on a daily basis.

The fact that he had gotten custody of April had been the final breaking point of his marriage. Natasha had made it clear that she didn't want a kid of her own, much less to take care of somebody else's. He certainly couldn't expect Arlene to care for her husband's child.

This would be their final good-bye.

Preflight boarding for his flight was announced, and Arlene started to stand. Neal caught her hands, leaned toward her, and, with a gentle tug, pulled her toward him until their lips touched.

He expected her to jerk away from him. When she didn't, he swiped his tongue over her lips. Her sweet essence mingled with a touch of perfume and the sweetness of the kiss was almost painful.

She opened her mouth to him, and for the first time in his life, he kissed the lips that had tempted him as a horny fourteen-year-old, standing on the cusp of tomorrow without a clue about how to deal with the girl who'd snubbed him. Even now she enticed the full-grown man. The emotional distance between them seemed as palpable as it had years before.

With a pressing need to touch her, he captured her warm face in his hands, tasted her, felt her soft skin—knowing this was all they would ever share. The realization was heartrending. A knot rose in his throat.

"Thank you," he whispered, while gazing into her eyes. There, he saw the same need that held him in its grip. Slowly, he slid his hands down her arms. Holding both her hands in his, he carried them to his mouth and gently kissed her knuckles, closing his eyes against the strength of his need.

They had come so close once again, only to have the future snatched away. When she opened one hand to caress his cheek, his gaze jerked to hers. All that he felt was reflected in her pretty brown eyes. There was so much he wanted to say, yet he felt compelled to remain silent. With hundreds of words left unspoken between them, the attendant wheeled him away.

He'd been given a commendation for courage, but he felt far from courageous when he caught one last glimpse of Arlene looking after him. The attendant whirled the wheelchair toward the gate. He didn't dare glance back with longing for what he could never have. Dear Lord, fate would have it that he could only move forward—toward April.

[illegible]

[illegible] gives a commendation for courage [illegible]

[illegible]

For a sneak peek at
the next book in
the At Your Service series

The Glory of Love
by Kim Louise

Coming in August 2003
from BET Books/Arabesque

Just turn the page . . .

Prologue

Franklin "Amadeus" Jones had gone completely mad.

Carl Baer stared at his lifelong friend with a rancid mixture of pity and revulsion.

"What do you think, Carly?"

Carly! He hated being called that. But he'd put up with it for the twenty-five years that they'd been friends. Carl swallowed, forcing a bitter rise of bile back into his stomach. Yes, he admitted; he'd put up with a lot.

Carl's nerves flickered with unease. "I think it's time to get him back before the toxident wears off."

Amadeus cackled, then strutted around like a peacock, as though the world were in his hip pocket, as though they all weren't living on borrowed time.

There were three other men in the motel room. Amadeus's muscle looming quietly in the shadows. They had helped to incapacitate and carry the soldier. After they got him on the bed, they bound him so that Carl could *do his thing*. The injection had taken only seconds to administer, and the man on the bed started talking soon after.

Amadeus had hurled a barrage of questions at the soldier. Pulling out his innermost feelings had been like extracting a tooth, and Amadeus played the masochistic dentist role to the hilt—drilling, picking.

Needling.

He acquired more information from the soldier than he could ever use.

"Look at him, Carly. A warrior. A killing machine. They

don't come any better than Chief Storm, here. He'll be perfect. Don't you think?"

Amadeus hadn't lost *all* of his faculties. He was right about that, at least. A Nubian king. The hard detachment of a warrior. Bulky. The guy tied down on the bed looked as though he could rip a man in two with his bare hands and had probably done so on several occasions.

"He will be formidable," Carl admitted. It was one of those times that he couldn't stop staring at his friend. Pillsbury Dough Boy complexion and bright yellow hair. He was the only individual with albinism Carl had ever known personally.

Drool glistened at the corners of Amadeus's mouth. "What about the sample?"

Carl pulled a long, thin syringe from a case. The surgical steel glinted angrily in the harsh overhead lighting. As a scientist, what he was about to do had thrilled him once. And God help him, aspects of it still did. But the implications of his actions felt like hands choking him sometimes, made him physically ill.

Amadeus turned to him before he had time to mask his wave of repugnance. The pale man drew closer. Just a soft whisper above skeletal, his body gave new meaning to the word gaunt. He always dressed more like Beethoven than his namesake, and Carl could smell the scent of mental decay rising like rotting flesh from Amadeus's pores.

He closed in. That thin mouth and those tiny teeth grinning. Desperation sparked inside Carl and he slapped Amadeus quickly across the face. Knowing his own strength, he was sure the blow sounded much worse than it felt.

To no avail. The grin was still there. Still moving toward him. Carl closed his eyes for his punishment, but what he received was a cold kiss on the cheek from lips that weren't quite there.

He shuddered.

He'd always been afraid of Amadeus, especially the light

flickering just behind his eyes that made him look like a wolf on the verge of being rabid. He hadn't wanted this friendship. But they were *both* freaks. They'd been outcasts since birth, and had found each other.

Like the man lying on the bed, their fate was sealed.

One

He would need surgery soon. Commander Haughton Storm lay low in the dry night air, obscured by brambles and thin, lifeless bushes. Just when he thought he'd be going home, his squad had gotten an order for recon in Gabon.

The pain slicing across his lower back stemmed from an old football injury. In the past, if he'd ignored it, the pain would give up and go away. This time he'd had it for a week and it only gotten worse. Soon he might be forced use a hot pack or buy, God help him, Icy Hot.

He squinted his eyes against the darkness. The heat of the tropics began to cool. Storm's search-and-rescue unit had been stalking for hours. The inch-by-inch crawl toward their target would have sent ordinary military forces packing for home, but his team of highly trained Navy SEALs was the best at what they did. As SEAL operators, they consumed a regular diet of search and rescue, demolition, and recon. The kind of dirty work he lived for.

He listened, and slid forward another inch. His recent-issue fatigues could barely be seen beneath the leaves and twigs he'd covered himself with. Any potential sweat or shine from his face was obscured by the black hue of burnt paper he'd covered his face with.

Another inch and they would be in range.

A twinge of pain vied for his attention. It had been years since he'd had any serious lumbar problems. Years. The slow, dull pain felt more like a warning, a premonition of bad things to come. On mission after mission, he'd learned to trust what his body told him. By the pounding, his body was preparing him for something out of the ordinary. He summoned his training and turned his mind from the ache. Just like a switch, he shut the pain off.

En route to the target, four of Storm's seven men swept the perimeter in preparation for their seizure of the building. They would ensure there were no outside threats.

Almost there now. He and his men inched closer and reached for their assault rifles, which they'd kept tucked beneath them. War in slow motion, he thought as each man drew up his weapon and took aim.

First, they would take out all personnel they could see, both inside and outside the building. Then, in a swift rush forward, they would advance.

Storm gave a barely perceptible nod. A thunderstorm of shots bombarded the still night air. Guards fell like targets on a shooting track. And those who didn't, ran into the hills after seeing the bodies of their comrades shatter and explode in the barrage.

A short whistle, a sweeping hand, and they attacked. Scouts, patrolling the perimeter, covered them as Storm and three of his squad took snake formation and entered the building single file.

Storm moved in first. Their mission was to search and secure the building where an American scientist was being held, and bring him home.

Checking corridors. Checking rooms. Searching. Looking. Hands on weapon. Mind on mission. Haughton Storm had never lost a man during a mission and had had very few wounded. His gut told him to make this quick or that fact might change.

His operators called out from above and below. "First floor, secure!" "Third floor, secure!" Check hallways. Check doors. Gunfire! He was being shot at. Storm got off a round, ducked behind a door, and slapped in another magazine. One operator was on his left. He signaled him to go around to the other side of the hallway and into the holding room.

The picture they reviewed in the mission briefing had not done justice to the man they'd been sent to rescue. The photo was bad, but this guy looked worse. Storm could tell he was African-American. The problem was he looked as though a vampire had come along and drained all the blood from his body.

His second in command took out the last guard in the room.

Storm ran toward the pale man. "Are you injured?" he shouted.

The man shook his head and his eyes widened and seemed to dance a bit. Storm registered that the man had one gray eye and one ice-green eye.

"Then down on the ground! Now!" As per his training, he treated all rescued personnel as hostile.

The man did as he was told.

"Put your hands behind your back!" Storm had drawn his nine-millimeter handgun and had it pointed toward the man's head. He patted the man down on all sides. "Are you armed, or concealing anything that can be used as a weapon?"

"No," the man said, with what sounded like a smile in his voice. Storm was immediately distrustful. While one of his operators trained his weapon on the man's head, Storm put him in handcuffs and yanked him up.

"Let's move!"

Again, his men maneuvered into snake formation. This time, the hostage was in the middle. With eyes like eagles, each one of his men checked side to side, above, and below. Their movements were precise like the internal workings of the finest watch. The enemy could be anywhere.

When they reached the lower level, three men from his squad fanned out to sweep the area for their departure. They took the hostage with them.

There was a rhythm to mission deployment, something a few soldiers tuned into like a sixth sense. Sensing like a hawk or panther exactly when to move, when to strike, when to retaliate. Many of his men said he had it—the rhythm. He wasn't sure what he had, but he knew it was like a pulse in the earth pounding in his brain. A tremor only he could feel sometimes. It told him when to strike, when to stay put, when to lie low, and when to take risks. And that tremor was telling him now that his squad was in danger. Maybe something in the orders they'd received was off, but the game had changed within the space of the last few minutes. And suddenly the whole thing smelled like rotten flesh.

Storm made a series of gestures with his hand. Closed fist. Open. Open. Point north. Three fingers, two circles. Closed fist.

They had to get out of there now.

The message traveled quickly, and the men of Cobra One fanned out one by one and pulled back from the edge of the enemy camp.

Storm's skin prickled. Closed fist.

Footfalls in the jungle. They were in trouble.

Shots fired. They hit the deck, each man rolling and scampering behind the shelter of the dilapidated building. The familiar surge of adrenaline charged through Storm's body as he barked orders through his headset. As customary, his team was in perfect sync. They followed his commands as if they had read his mind before he could think his thoughts.

Back out.

T-formation.

If he could get the men back to the perimeter, they could return to the extraction point and be lifted out by helicopter.

"Alpha Six this is Cobra One!"

"Alpha Six, over."

"Need extraction! ETA ten minutes!"

"Copy that."

Over a dozen enemy soldiers scrambled from the shadows, guns drawn.

Storm tagged a guard, who buckled with the impact and went down.

Gunfire filled the jungle night. Explosions lit up the sky like an erratic strobe. As his men fought for their lives and their country, Storm defended himself and swore that whoever was responsible for setting this trap would pay.

"I'm hit!" a voice said, slicing through the thunder of gunfire.

"Sharky!" Storm shouted, recognizing the call of his second-in-command.

A sniper pinned Storm down in a thicket. If Storm didn't take him out soon, he'd never get out of there to help Sharky.

Storm jerked himself against a tree for cover. His pulse pounded loud and hard. Jungle shadows provided some cover for him. His eyes swept the perimeter quickly. Bullets whizzed by on both sides of him. The enemy was behind them, stationary, not following—yet. He had to get to Sharky before that was no longer the case.

The footfalls and suppressing fire from his unit told him they were regrouping, but not fast enough. Without his men to cover him, he would have to run unprotected to where Sharky lay, at the foot of a thick bush, unmoving.

He could see one leg. The rest of his comrade's body was motionless. A bolt of pain struck Storm in the middle of the chest, and he sprinted toward the man's location.

For years he'd trained against letting the sight of injuries, wounds, or blood affect him. Every SEAL had. But for a millisecond, he lost his training as a sliver of remorse slid though him. Then it was gone and he knew that the man, shot in the side but still reaching for his gun, needed and deserved every bit of military training Storm could summon to get them out of the ambush.

"Just get me on my feet and put my gun in my hand,"

Sharky said, stark determination making him seem much older than his thirty-two years.

"You got it, soldier," Storm replied.

More shouts and bootfalls as the SEAL Team Cobra One aborted their reconnaissance mission. Storm hefted Sharky up and handed him his weapon. With a nod from the injured man, they scrambled toward the extraction point, arm in arm, rifles drawn and blazing.

"SEALs, we are *lea-ving!*" Storm shouted when his unit had regrouped.

The enemy was following close now.

"Alpha Six this is Cobra One, over."

"Alpha Six, go ahead."

"Zone is hot. Repeat, zone is hot, over."

"Roger that, Cobra One. What's your ETA?"

Storm tightened his hold on Sharky.

"Two minutes, and we got injuries, over!"

"Two minutes, Chief. We'll prep for medical, over."

"Copy that. Cobra Out."

"Alpha Six, out."

Storm's breathing matched the pace of his run with Sharky through the heat and brush. He sensed the anxiety of his team. "Cobra team sound off."

"Sandman, on your six, Sir!"

"Hardgrove, side by side, Sir!"

"Mills, on the move, Commander!"

"Fox, still in the pocket, Chief!"

"Tuxedo, kickin' up dust, Sir!"

"Faison, bringing up the rear!"

Good. His team was intact. He'd be damned if he'd lose any men to an ambush, which is what this was.

As the sound of gunfire grew behind him, he realized that what they'd experienced was a brush-off. If the guards had wanted a confrontation, he and his men would have had to do a lot more fighting than simply retreat.

Why did this feel like a test?

When they arrived at the extraction point, the chopper flew in, cannons blazing. All seven of his men were by his side, and ready to lift out.

"Go! Go! Go! Go!" Seconds into the helo, and Storm issued the command to leave.

The helicopter lifted up and away sharply, guns still blazing.

"What happened back there?" one of the pilots shouted.

"Ambush. Somebody set us up." After making sure the hostage was secure, Storm knelt beside his teammate. He and Sharky went all the way back to Hell Week in BUDs training. They had endured every horrendous test thrown at them. He was the closest thing Storm had to a brother.

Sharky was getting worked on pretty good by Raymond "Doc" Collins, the best med tech Storm had ever worked with. If he couldn't save Sharky, no one could.

Doc looked up. "Punctured lung. I'm going to intubate and patch to keep his lung from collapsing. He's bleeding like a stuck pig, but I'll get it stopped and he should be okay."

Relief slowed Storm's raging pulse.

Sharky trembled on the floor of the helicopter. His eyes widened. It was the first time Storm had ever seen anything close to fear in his eyes in all the years they'd served together.

"Suck it up, soldier!" he barked. "That's an order!"

He touched Sharky on the shoulder. "You're gonna make it," he said.

"I gotta . . . gotta make it," Sharky replied, heaving with each word. "Or else there'll be no one who can keep . . . keep your . . . sorry carcass in line."

Storm grinned and nodded. Sharky was going to be fine.

Relieved, he sat back, reflecting. At the beginning of each

mission, Storm would take a mental snapshot of his platoon. Every time, he etched their faces into his memory.

Failure is not an option to a Navy SEAL. Each mission is carefully planned and rehearsed to be successful without casualties or injuries. If either occurs, the commander has made an unacceptable mistake.

His head rocked back and forth against the cold metal of the chopper. Vibration from the propellers strummed inside the vehicle like the heartbeat of a giant bird.

He shifted, as his back sent out another twinge for good measure. The hostage hadn't said a word. Not "thank-you." Not "much obliged." Not "kiss my behind." He only sat in silence with a strange grin that gave Storm a jolt of unease.

He knew his men. Their body language was clear. Seven men, twitching and snorting like nervous bulls. The inside of the helicopter was uncharacteristically quiet, and their gazes moved to and away from the man. Something about the man they'd rescued put them all on edge.

Storm closed his eyes and wondered why his green-faced warriors, a platoon of the most highly skilled soldiers in the U.S. military forces, were spooked by a tiny little man.

For a sneak peek at
the next book in
the At Your Service series

Flying High
by Gwynne Forster

Coming in September 2003
from BET Books/Arabesque

Just turn the page . . .

One

Nelson Wainwright, Colonel, United States Marine Corps, glanced at the overcast sky, dropped his briefcase, and switched on the television. He hated getting wet when he was fully dressed; in fact, he disliked untidiness and considered a wrinkled uniform the its epitome. He turned on the television to check the weather, and read the news beneath the picture: Sixty-eight and cloudy. Rain likely. Cooler than usual for May.

"What will a man endure to achieve his aims?" the motivational speaker said, as Nelson reached to switch off the television. The question mocked him, enticed him to linger and listen. "How much will he sacrifice? What will he give? What will he gain? And what can he lose?"

Ordinarily, Nelson did not allow media gurus or other self-styled motivators to impress him, but those words hounded him as he drove from Alexandria, Virginia to his office in the Pentagon. He had spent eighteen of his forty-one years in the Marine Corps, and as recompense for working so hard and shaking hands with death more times than he wanted to remember, he intended to retire with four silver stars on his collar. He'd love to retire with five stars, but nothing less than four-star general would satisfy him.

Nelson knew two reasons why, even with good fortune, hard work, and shrewdness, he had a less-than-even chance of retiring as a full general. His superiors did not know that an injury to his neck pained him sufficiently to make him unfit for duty, nor did they know of his failure to report a corporal whom he'd discovered sleeping while on guard duty in Afghanistan. He didn't doubt that if his superiors knew of the unremitting pain he suffered, they would force his immediate retirement. And if he managed to camouflage that, he could be dismissed, or at least disciplined, for not having reported that marine's misconduct. Either meant he would finish military life as a colonel.

He parked in the space reserved for officers of his rank, and as light rain drops spattered his shoulders, he dashed inside the Pentagon. But as he entered his office, an eerie feeling settled over him, and very pores of his skin jumped to alert as if he were back in Afghanistan anticipating a missile. He rushed to answer the telephone even as dread washed through his system.

"'Morning. Wainwright speaking."

"Good morning, Sir," a female said. "This is Lieutenant McCafferty in the Commandant's Office, and I'm sorry I have to give you this sad news."

Nelson leaned forward, mentally bracing himself, and listened as she told him that his brother had perished in an automobile accident that morning.

"You're listed as next of kin, Sir, and as guardian for Commander Wainwright's child, Richard Wainwright. Let us know what we can do for you. This office will send you an order for two weeks leave beginning now."

He sat there for an hour dealing with his emotions and collecting his thoughts. Joel, his younger brother and only known relative other than little Ricky, had been looking forward to a great future in the Navy, and now . . . Well, what was done was done. The navy would take care of Joel; he had to look after four-year-old Ricky.

As the days passed, Ricky didn't respond favorably to the succession of foster mothers with whom he placed the boy, and he couldn't help noticing negative changes in the child's behavior, from bright and cheerful to sullen and quiet.

"That does it," he said to himself when, on one of his daily visits, Ricky clung to his leg in a fit of tears and wouldn't let go. He picked the child up, paid the foster mother for the remainder of the month and took Ricky home with him.

He wasn't a religious man, but he gave sincere thanks when Lena Alexander, whom his secretary recommended, walked into his house. She greeted him, looked down at Ricky, who loitered behind, dragging a beach towel, and her face lit up with a smile as she bent to the child and opened her arms. "My name is Lena, and I love little boys. What's your name?"

When Ricky smiled at her and told her his name was Ricky Wainwright, Nelson relaxed. Seconds later, Lena was giving Ricky a hug, and the child was telling her about his imaginary friends. The next morning, he moved her personal belongings to his home and settled her in a guest room.

It had been years since he had shared his living quarters, not since the four months during which he lived with Carole James, the woman who had brought another man—his closest friend—to the bed they shared, and had cared so little for him that she let him catch her cheating. The woman who would have been his wife within six weeks. In the more than five years that followed, he had enjoyed the quiet, though not the loneliness, and hearing Ricky's joyful noises and Lena's humming as she worked and her laughter with Ricky buoyed his spirits. Home was suddenly a pleasant place, especially at dinner when he had company for the delightful meals Lena prepared.

"What's the matter with your neck, Colonel?" Lena asked him at breakfast several days after joining his household. "Looks to me like you always favoring your neck. Better get it looked after. Trouble don't stand still in this world; either gets better or worse. You know what I'm saying?"

He did, indeed. Didn't the pain in his neck get worse daily? "I'm dealing with it, Lena. Don't let it bother you."

"Ain't bothering me none, Colonel. You the one that's uncomfortable. I declare, I wish somebody'd tell me why men so scared of a doctor. In the almost thirty years that I worked as an LPN—you know, licensed practical nurse—I never yet saw a male patient who didn't wait till he was half dead before he went to the doctor. You better do something before you get a problem with your spine."

He didn't have to answer her because she left the breakfast room humming what he suspected was her favorite hymn. "What's the name of that tune, Lena?" he asked when she came back with a carafe of hot coffee.

"If you don't know that song, you in trouble. Even the devil knows 'Amazing Grace.'"

He held his breath, watching while she filled his cup to the brim. When it didn't spill over, he bent over and sipped enough so that he could raise the cup to his lips without spilling the coffee.

"That surprises me, Lena. I would have thought the devil was more creative than to . . ."

He stopped. Her expression amounted to wonderment at his low level of intelligence. "Colonel Wainwright, I never said he sang the song; I said he knew it."

She walked with him to the door, holding Ricky who enjoyed telling him good-bye and getting a hug "You go see a doctor today, Colonel."

"See a doctor, Colonel," Ricky parroted.

"Ricky, you have to call him Uncle Nelson," she heard Lena say as he headed for his car.

"You sit down here and build your castle or read your book while I tend to a little business," Lena said to Ricky one morning about a month later as soon as Nelson left home. Ricky talked to the pictures in his books and pretended to read.

She dialed the hospital. "Let me speak to Dr. Powers, please."

"Dr. Powers speaking. How may I help you?"

"Audrey, honey, this is Aunt Lena. I love my boss. He's a wonderful man, so good with his little nephew. I wish—"

"Aunt Lena, I am not interested in your matchmaking. I'm glad the guy is a good father, and I'm glad you like your job. Now—"

"Hear me out, Audrey. Something is wrong with this man's neck. If he's not holding it and rubbing it, he's got something wrapped around it, and I can't get him to see a doctor. It's free for officers at Walter Reed Hospital, but I can't get him to go. Last night, he stopped eating his dinner, got up and put something around it. I hate to see him suffer like this. Come over one night, or maybe this Sunday when you're off, and have a look at it. He's such a good man."

"If it bothers him enough, Aunt Lena, he'll do something about it. I'd rather not meddle in that."

"Well . . . I, I just don't know what to do. It's not like he was hiding from the law." Lena hung up. She would find a way to get him to a doctor, he could bet on that.

"You didn't commit no crime, did you, Colonel?" she asked Nelson one night at dinner. When he stopped eating and stared at her, she pretending not to notice. "I mean, you not hiding out or something. You know what I mean, don't you."

He half-laughed and pointed his fork at her. "No, Lena, I don't know what you mean, and stop needling me." Then he laughed outright. "It just occurred to me that you're a blessing to my ego. I get so damned much deference in the Pentagon that I've started to believe I deserve it, but I can count on you to bring me down front and keep my feet to the fire, so to speak."

She turned her back in order to get the piece of celery that had lodged in the gap between her front teeth, then turned back to him. "I didn't mean to get familiar, but—"

He laughed. "I don't believe you said that."

"Well, truth is I care about what happens to you, and I've had plenty experience with people who've been injured, so I know that neck of yours is a serious problem."

"That's right. Sometime I forget you're a nurse. Lena, I'm not entirely foolish. A missile hit the helicopter that I was piloting in Afghanistan, and when the copter crashed, I got some injuries, and this whiplash was one of them. My other injuries healed; this one is taking a little longer. That's all."

"Hmmm. You had that before I came here, and I've been working for you over three months. That's more than long enough for a whiplash to heal. Why don't you go over to Walter Reed and let them take care of it?"

"I can't do that, Lena. If my superiors find out that my neck is still giving me trouble, they may force me to retire. It's bad enough that I'm still on desk duty."

"Oh, dear. I see what the problem is. And if you go to a private doctor, it'll be reported. Well, I'll pray for you. I sure will."

He seemed relieved to get that subject out of the way, but he didn't know that she wasn't used to accepting defeat. She put Ricky to bed, and while Nelson read the child's favorite story to him, she figured it was a good time to call her niece.

"Audrey, could you do me a favor?" she asked, after they greeted each other. "I want to go on my church's outing Saturday, day after tomorrow. They're going to Crystal Caverns down in Strasburg, Virginia, and I always wanted to go. Year before last when they went, I couldn't get away from work. Could you look after Ricky"—she didn't dare mention Nelson—"for me Saturday? Just give him lunch and read him some stories. He's no trouble, and sweet as he can be."

She listened to the silence until she thought she would scream. Finally Audrey said, "What time do you think you'll get back there?"

"Around seven."

"All right. I'll do it this once, but you know I don't cook."

"Sandwiches will do just fine." She hadn't planned to take the excursion, but she phoned the organizer and got her seat. Maybe she could kill two birds with one stone. Nelson Wainwright was a catch for any woman.

Audrey Powers did not relish the thought of babysitting, not even for half an hour. But her aunt had been so supportive during her struggles first to get through college and then to complete her medical training that she could hardly think of anything she wouldn't do for Lena. She stuffed half a dozen Chupa Chyps into her handbag, and stepped out of her house at barely sunup. Owing to the sparse traffic, the drive from her house in Bethesda to Alexandria, circling Washington on the Beltway, took her only twenty minutes early that Saturday morning. She parked in front of the beige-colored brick town house at 76 Acorn Drive. Lena greeted her at the door. "You're just in time. My taxi will be here in fifteen minutes." She turned around and pointed to the little boy. "This is Ricky. Ricky, Audrey is going to stay with you today."

Audrey looked down at the child who stared at her with an almost plaintive expression, and her heart seemed to constrict as she knelt beside him. "Hello, Ricky."

"Do you like little boys? Miss Lena loves little boys." His expression had changed to one of challenge.

"I love boys, especially little ones, and since I don't have a little boy, I can love you, can't I?"

He nodded, but kept looking at her. Suddenly, he smiled. "You can play with my bear and my blanket."

Realizing that that meant acceptance, she hugged and thanked him.

"Nelson will be down for breakfast around eight-thirty," Lena said as the horn blast signaled the arrival of her taxi.

"He'll be . . . Well if he's here, why am I . . ."

Lena closed the door.

Audrey took Ricky's hand and followed him to the refrigerator. When she opened it, he pointed to the milk. "Chocolate milk, please."

She poured the milk, thinking that she couldn't wait to give her aunt a piece of her mind. "I've been had," she said, when she didn't see any cooked food in the refrigerator. "I'm thirty years old, and I let my aunt hoodwink me."

He held the glass up to her. "Sugar, pease."

"I don't believe anybody puts sugar in your milk, but since nobody gave me any instructions, have a field day."

She put a teaspoon of sugar in the milk, stirred it and watched his eyes sparkle with delight. Now what? Her search for cereal or anything else a child would eat for breakfast proved futile.

"What do you eat for breakfast, Ricky?"

"Cake."

"Don't even think it. Try to bamboozle me, will you." She found some bread, toasted it, and, aware that he had a passion for things sweet, slathered the toast with butter and raspberry jam, poured a glass of orange juice, and sat Ricky down for breakfast.

"How old are you, Ricky?"

He held up four fingers. "Five."

She wondered if that was another of his games aimed at addling her, and it occurred to her that she might have to spend ten or twelve hours dealing with Ricky's little shenanigans. While he ate, she looked around for a coffee pot and the makings of a good cup of coffee. She didn't remember having gone so long after awakening without her caffeine fix. As soon as the smell of coffee permeated the kitchen, Ricky held out his glass.

"Can I please have some coffee, Audie?"

She would look back one day and know that that was the moment when he'd sneaked into her heart. "You little devil," she said as laughter spilled out of her. A lightheartedness, a joy, seemed to envelop her, and she lifted him from his chair and hugged him.

"No, you can't have any coffee, and you know it."

His lips grazed her cheek in a quick, almost tentative, kiss, delighting and surprising her. "Now be a good boy and finish your milk."

"Okay. I'm four."

She was about to thank him for telling the truth when the sound of heavy steps loping down the stairs reminded her that they were not alone, and her belly tightened in anticipation.

Nelson stepped out of the shower, and as he dried his body it occurred to him that a man of his height had to spend twice as much time on ablutions as a did a shorter man of slight build. But he wasn't complaining; he liked his six-feet-five-inch frame. He slipped on a red, short-sleeved T-shirt and a pair of fatigues and followed the aroma of coffee, his spirits high as he anticipated getting in a solid day's work at home.

He was used to Ricky now, and thought nothing unusual as he strode down the hallway enjoying the sound of boy's chatter. He stepped into the kitchen.

"'Morning, you two. What's for break . . . What the? Who are you, and where's Lena?"

"Unca Nelson, Audie gave me toast. I love toast, Unca Nelson."

She looked up at him, her lips parted in what was surely surprise, and immediately her lashes covered her remarkable dark and luminous eyes. *Who was she?* Jolts of electricity whistled through his veins, firing him the way gasoline dumped on a fire triggers powerful flames. He thought he would explode.

"I said . . . who are you?" Her grudging smile sent darts zinging all over his body. Poleaxing him. He groped for the chair beside Ricky where Lena usually sat, and slowly lowered himself into it.

"What are you doing here? If I may ask."

"I'm Audrey Powers," she said. "My aunt Lena had to go on a church outing today, and asked me to fill in for her. I can't believe she didn't get your approval."

Dignified. Well-spoken. Yes, and lovely. "Lena get my approval for something she wants to do? She tries, and if she doesn't succeed, she deals with matters in her own way. Thanks for helping out. I have a lot of things to do around here today, and it's good that you're here to look after Ricky. Any chance I could get some breakfast?"

Her reticence didn't escape him. "Cooking isn't something I'm good at, Colonel. I noticed some grits in the pantry. If you can handle grits, scrambled eggs, and toast . . ."

She let it hang, and he knew it was that or nothing, so he didn't mention the sausage or bacon that had to be somewhere in that refrigerator.

"I'd appreciate it, and if you wouldn't mind sharing your coffee . . ."

As if seeing him for the first time, or maybe questioning his temerity, her eyes narrowed in a squint, and suddenly he could feel the tension crackling between them. *Good Lord, I don't need this. I don't know a thing about this woman.*

She got up from the table, exposing her five-feet-eight inches of svelte feminine beauty, rounded hips and full bosom emphasized by a neat waist. He gulped air as she glided toward the kitchen counter, got a mug of coffee, and handed it to him.

"If you want a second cup, the carafe is over there beside the sink."

Her message didn't escape him; she wasn't there to pamper him, but to take care of Ricky. "Thanks. I'm not much good before I get my coffee."

"Somehow I find that hard to believe, Colonel. I'd bet you do what you have to do, no matter the circumstances."

His left eyebrow shot up. "I try to do that, but how did you know?" He gripped his neck with his left hand as the familiar pain shot through him, took a deep breath, and forced himself to relax. Thank God Lena wasn't there to start her lecture. "When it comes to duty, a man ought to set personal consideration aside. And call me Nelson. Do you mind if I call you Audrey?"

"No, I don't."

"I like Audie, Unca Nelson."

"After conning me into putting sugar into your chocolate milk, I guess you do." She looked at Nelson. "He told me he eats cake for breakfast."

He couldn't help laughing. "Ricky is skilled in getting what he wants. He doesn't get sugar in his milk, and I hope you didn't give him any cake."

"He got the sugar, but I knew better than to give him cake."

"I like cake, Audie. Miss Lena makes cake, and it's good, too."

Her gaze lingered on Ricky, and it was clear to him that Ricky had won her affection. "I'm sorry, Ricky, but I have never made a cake in my life. Excuse me, Nelson, while I get your breakfast."

"It's okay. Miss Lena will make the cake," Ricky called after him.

If only his neck would stop paining him. He had to finish installing the bookcases in his den and get some work done on the paneling in his basement.

He finished his breakfast, started upstairs to his den, and glanced around to see Ricky following him with his "blanket," the navy-blue beach towel trailing behind him.

"Rick, old boy, you're going to have to give up that blanket. Wainwright men do not romance blankets." He looked up to find Audrey's gaze on him. "They romance women." Now, why the devil had he said that? He whirled around and dashed up the stairs feeling as if he'd lost control of his life. And he always made it a point to control himself, and, to the extent possible, his life and everything that affected him personally.

"She's not going to detour me," he told himself, "I wouldn't care if she was the Venus de Milo incarnate. And I'm going to give Lena a good talking-to when she gets back here."

Damn! He jerked back his thumb, dropped the hammer and went to the bathroom to run cold water on the injury. If he had been paying attention, if the picture of Audrey Powers sitting at his kitchen table smiling at Ricky hadn't blotted all else out of his mind . . .

I don't care who she is or what she looks like, I'm not getting involved with her. He laughed. Getting involved was a two-sided thing, and she hadn't given any indication that she was interested. He corrected that. She'd reacted to him as man, that was sure, but the woman displayed her dignity the way the sun displays its rays. And she kept her feelings to herself. He'd give a lot to know who she was, but he was not going to let her know that. She was here for one day, and he'd make sure that was all.

Audrey cleaned the kitchen, something she seldom had to do at home, and tried to figure out what to do with Ricky. Finally she asked him, "Where's your room, Ricky?" Perhaps she could read to him or he could play with his toys.

The child beamed with glee, grabbed her hand, and

started with her to the stairs. "Up the stairs, Audie. I have a big room."

She started up with him, and stopped. She did not want to encounter Nelson Wainwright right then, for she hadn't reclaimed the contentment that she'd worked so hard and so long to achieve, the feeling that she belonged to herself, that her soul was her own. One look at Nelson Wainwright, big, strong, and all man with his dreamy eyes trained on her, and she had nearly sprung out of her chair. Like a clap of thunder, he jarred her from her head to her toes, an eviscerating blow to her belly. She thanked God she'd been sitting down.

"Can you play my flute?" Ricky asked her as they walked into his room, a child's dream world.

Her gaze fell on a full-size harp, and her heart kicked over. She had studied the harp and once played it well, but hadn't touched it since her father died. He'd loved to hear her play it and would sit and listen for as long as she played.

"I'm sorry, Ricky, but I've never played the flute."

"Unca Nelson can play it. Can you read me Winnie-the-Pooh?"

She told him she could and he handed her the book, surprising her when he climbed into her lap and rested his head on her breast while she read to him. The prospect of motherhood didn't occupy much of her thought, because her one experience with love and loving had erupted in her face. And since she wanted nothing more to do with men, certainly not to expose herself to an intimate relationship, she blocked thoughts of motherhood and children. But she couldn't deny that Ricky stirred in her heart a longing for the joy of a child at her breast.

When the story ended, Ricky scampered off her lap, ran across the room, and put a compact disk on his player. Then he ran back and looked up at her, waiting for her response as Ella Fitzgerald's "A Tiskit A Tasket" filled the room. To let him know that she appreciated his gesture, she sang it along with Ella, while he clapped his hands and jumped up and down laughing and trying to sing along with her.

"Hey, what's going on in here?"

She settled her gaze on the door and the man who stood there wearing a quizzical smile and a soft, surgical collar around his neck.

Ricky ran to his uncle and tugged at his hand. "Audie read my book for me and I'm playing my CD for her."

He picked the boy up and hugged him. "Don't wear her out, now."

"How old is Ricky?" Audrey asked Nelson.

"He'll be five next week." His left hand went to the back of his neck. "He's made tremendous progress since Lena's been with him. I had him in foster care for a couple of months after my brother died, and that experience set him back considerably. I brought him here to live with me, and I could see an improvement within a week."

She watched as he held his neck without seeming to give the act conscious thought. It was not a good sign. "I'm sure he feels the difference. Some foster parents give a child love and understanding as well as care; others don't, often through no fault of their own. Tell me, do you play the harp?" She pointed to the instrument there in Ricky's room.

He lowered his head. "Wish I could. That one belonged to my brother, Ricky's father. He played it very well indeed. I put it here in case Ricky takes an interest in it."

Speaking of his brother obviously saddened him, and she found that she wanted to know more, but she didn't dare invade his privacy with a personal question.

"I'm hungry, Audie. Can I have some ice cream?"

"May I have some ice cream?" Nelson said, correcting the child. "No, you may not. You get ice cream after you've eaten all of your lunch. You know that."

With innocence spread over his face, he turned to her. "Don't give me much lunch."

She stifled a laugh and got up, surprised by the realization that she had spent half a day enjoying the company of a four-year-old. Still holding Ricky in his arms, Nelson didn't move from the doorway as she attempted to leave the room. Her nerves skittered as she neared him, and when she couldn't help glancing up at him, he looked down directly into her eyes and caught his breath. She managed to pass him, but only the Lord knew how she did it.

Something in him, something hard, and strong, blood-sizzlingly masculine clutched at her. An aura like nothing she'd experienced before jumped out at her and claimed her. And all he'd done was stand there. How she got downstairs she would never know; he blurred her vision and sabotaged her thoughts. Worse, her heart threatened to bolt from her chest. She leaned against the kitchen counter. Nelson Wainwright was just another man, and she had no intention of making a fool of herself over him. A long sigh escaped her. One piece of her father's wisdom claimed that the road to hell was paved with good intentions.

"Girl, you need to get out more," she chided herself. "Stuck in that hospital all the time, you forget what it's like out here."

Within a few minutes, she called up to him. "Lunch is ready, Nelson, such as it is."

He took a long time getting downstairs, and she couldn't help wondering why. "Thank you for taking care of this, Audrey," he said. "I get the feeling this is aeons away from what you normally do."

He stared at the food before him. "I take it you don't cook much. These look good, though," he said of the tunafish salad and cheese sandwiches.

"I cook not at all."

Ricky clapped his hands and laughed. "No potatoes and no veggies, Unca Nelson. I like this. I want Audie to stay with us all the time."

Nelson seemed to wince as his hand went once more to

his neck, and this time there was no mistaking his pain. Without considering her action, she rose from the table, stepped behind him and examined his neck.

"What the . . . what are you doing?" he demanded as her fingers began the gentle massage that she knew would bring him relief. "I said . . . Look here. You're out of line."

"No, I'm not," she said without pausing in her ministrations. "I'm a physician, Nelson, and physical therapy and sports medicine are my specialties. This will make you feel better."

"You're a *what?*"

"A physician. I can't help noticing your problem, and it's clear to me that the pain is killing you."

"Look here! You can't—"

"Don't you feel better already? Fifteen minutes of this and you'll feel like a different man. Just relax and give yourself over to me."

"What kind of—"

"Shhh. Just relax."

"Does it hurt, Uncle Nelson?" Ricky's voice rose with anxiety, and she hastened to assure him that she was helping, not hurting his uncle.

"I'm making him feel better, Ricky. Go on and eat your sandwich. Isn't the pain easing already, Nelson?"

Her fingers, gentle yet firm, kneaded his flesh. "Relax," she'd said, but how could he, tense as he was with the pain that was his constant companion. He thought of pushing back his chair and leaving the table, but if he did that, he could hurt her. How could Lena betray him so blatantly?

"Relax. Drop your shoulders," she whispered.

No one dictated his life, as Lena was trying to do, and he wouldn't have it. He attempted to move, but with deft fingers Audrey soothed him, easing the pain, giving him the first relief he'd had in nearly a year, reducing the throbbing to a dull ache. Her hands massaged him with soft circular movements, squeezing and caressing. He lowered his head and luxuriated in the relief that her gentle strokes gave him. Then, with his eyes closed, he saw her fingers skimming his entire naked body, caressing and adoring him, preparing him for the assault of her luscious mouth.

Good Lord! His eyelids flew open, and he gasped in astonishment. He'd been within seconds of a full erection. Better put an end to that bit of heaven, and fast. He put both hands to the back of his neck and gripped her fingers.

"Thanks. You're right, I feel better, but can I finish my . . . my sandwich now?"

She went back to her chair, but she didn't sit down. "You're not angry, are you? I know it made you feel better. The problem is that the relief is very temporary. Massage is not a cure."

He didn't pretend, nor did he attempt to depreciate the comfort she gave him; Audrey Powers obviously knew her business, and anyway, he didn't want to seem ungrateful. "How could I be angry? I feel better right now than in a year."

She sat down, her eyes wide and a look of incredulity on her face. "You've been suffering like this for a year? How could you stand it?

He let the shrug of his shoulders communicate his feelings. "You do what you have to do. Simple as that."

She leaned toward him. "But it isn't necessary for you to suffer like this."

"It is, Audrey, believe me. The Marine Corps is a unit of men in perfect physical and mental condition. We are the crown of the Service, the cream of the crop. If you can't hack it, you get a letter of thanks, and that's it. I can handle it, and I will."

"But can't you go to Walter Reed, or the Navy Medical Center?"

"Sure, if I want an honorable discharge. I'm not ready for that."

"But . . . You mean your superiors don't know about this?"

He stared at her, and if he seemed threatening, he didn't care. "No, and nobody's going to tell them."

Not many men stood up to him, but he could see from her demeanor that if he pushed her, she would shove right back. Apparently having thought better of an alternative response, she nodded and said, "I see. What a pity."

Even at the tender age of four, Ricky appeared to sense Audrey's concern, for he attempted to pacify her.

"I'm eating all of my sandwich, Audrey."

She smiled and stroked Ricky's cheek, though he could see that her thoughts hadn't shifted from him to the child.

"Am I going to get my ice cream, Audie?"

It amazed him that Ricky had so quickly handed over his care to Audrey. Maybe he just liked women; if so, he wouldn't blame him, and he certainly understood Ricky's preference for this one. She'd gotten to him the minute his gaze landed on her. Not that it would make a difference in his life. He meant to give Lena a stiff lecture about her underhanded little trick, and he didn't expect to see Audrey Powers again.

"If your uncle Nelson says you may have ice cream, I'll get you a nice big scoop," he heard her say to Ricky.

With a smile obviously aimed to captivate Audrey, Ricky said, "Miss Lena always gives me two nice big scoops."

Laughter rumbled in his chest, and he felt good. He couldn't remember when he'd had such a light . . . He pushed the word back, but it returned, and he admitted to himself that he felt happy. He looked from Ricky to Audrey, and tremors shot through him at her unguarded expression. It was there only for a second, but he didn't mistake it; she wanted him. It had been there when they met. He'd had enough experience to know that an attraction as strong as what he felt for her couldn't be one-sided.

Questions about her zinged through his mind. Why

would a medical doctor baby-sit even for one day? Where was her office? She wasn't wearing a ring, not even a diamond, so why was a woman with her phenomenal looks single? He voiced none of them. He didn't like revealing himself, and therefore he didn't request it of others. He pushed back his chair.

"Thanks for my lunch, and especially for that great massage. I'd better get back to work while I'm still pain-free."

He looked at Ricky and marveled that the child didn't jump from the chair and trail after him as he usually did. Ricky ignored him.

"After you give me my ice cream, Audie, you can play with my robot."

He went upstairs, almost reluctant to leave them. As he worked, their chatter and laughter buoyed him, but after a time a quiet prevailed. He walked over to Ricky's room to find them both asleep, Ricky in her lap with his head on her breast and she with both arms around him. The longer he stared at them, the lonelier he felt. Disgusted with himself, he put on a leather Eisenhower jacket, went out in his back garden, and busied himself building a fire in the brick oven. He couldn't say exactly why he did that, but he was certain of his need to change the scene and recover the part of himself that, within a split second, Audrey Powers had stolen. He sat there in the cool and rising wind until after dark warming himself by the fire and reminding himself of Carole James, the one woman, the betrayer, he'd allowed himself to love. Thoughts of her brought the taste of bile to his mouth.

"I'll die a bachelor," he said aloud, shoveled some dirt on the coals, and went inside.

Audrey prowled around Ricky's room, fighting the vexation at her aunt that was rapidly escalating into anger. It was time Ricky had dinner, she didn't know what to give him, and his hot-shot uncle was no where to be found.

"I wanna eat, Audie. I'm hungry."

She looked at her watch for the nth time. Seven-fifteen. Of course he was hungry; so was she. She heard the back door close, grabbed Ricky's robot, and rushed to the top of the stairs.

"Who's there?"

"Sorry, Audrey. It didn't occur to me that I might frighten you. Lena isn't back?"

"No, she isn't, and Ricky's hungry. Maybe you'd better phone a restaurant and have something delivered."

He reached the top of the stairs where she stood holding Ricky's hand, or maybe Ricky was holding her hand. The cloud covering her face and the set of her mouth told him to tread carefully. He didn't enjoy tangling with women in the best of circumstances, and this one was angry. Moreover, she had a right to be.

His hands went up, palms out. "I'm sorry about this. I was out back, thinking Lena—"

"She isn't here, and—"

He wasn't accustomed to being interrupted, but he thought it best not to tell her that. "As I was about to say, if you'll tell me what you'd like to eat, I'll order dinner. I know a great seafood restaurant that will deliver full-course meals within forty minutes.

"I'll take shrimp and whatever goes with it."

A deep breath escaped him. Thank God for a woman who didn't feel she had to wash his face with his errors. "Great, so will Ricky. Be back shortly." He went into his room and ordered dinners for the four of them. He had a few things to tell Lena, but that didn't mean she should be deprived of a good meal.

His hunch told him the less Audrey was required to do, the better her mood would be, so he set the table in the breakfast room and opened a bottle of chilled chardonnay.

"Would you like a glass of wine while we wait for dinner?" he asked Audrey.

Suddenly, she laughed. "I may be furious with my aunt, Nelson, but I won't bite off your head."

"Thanks for the assurance. You had such a dark look on your face that I wasn't sure I should say a word to you. This wine is usually pretty good."

"Thanks, I'll have half a glass. I don't drink when I have to drive. Say, that's the doorbell, isn't it? Mind if I answer it?"

"Uh, no. If it's Lena, give her a chance to explain before you blow her away."

She rushed to the door with Ricky and his "blanket" trailing behind her. "Oh. It's the food," she called to Nelson, looked up and saw that he was beside her. He paid the deliveryman and took the food.

"Come on, you two, let's eat."

They sat down, and the doorbell rang again. She moved as if to get up, but he raised his hand. "I'll get it. You should have cooled off by now."

"I never cool off till I get my due," he heard her say as he headed for the door.

"How you doing, Colonel? I know Audrey's mad by now, but I got back quick as I could."

"Audrey? What about me? I'm the one you've got to reckon with."

"Now, now, Colonel. Give me a chance to get in. I bet your neck feels better."

The audacity of the woman! "Dinner's on the table. I'll speak with you later."

"Miss Lena, guess what? I had toast this morning, and I didn't have to eat any veggies for lunch. Audie gave me san . . . sandwiches"

"I bet she did. Audrey, honey, I'm so sorry."

"No problem," Nelson said. "Audrey's mad at you, but you two can deal with that later. Right now she's going to smile if it kills her. We're going to enjoy our food."

They listened to Lena's tales of the famous Crystal

Caverns and her picturesque account of the scenery during the drive. He knew she meant to placate both him and Audrey, but he didn't think she achieved either.

"I'd better be going," Audrey said when they finished eating. "Be sure and take care of your neck, Nelson. My judgment is that if you don't, you will have serious trouble down the road."

It struck him as silly; he didn't want her to leave. "Uh, thanks. I . . . It was good to met you, Audrey."

"I want Audie to stay," Ricky said. "I don't want her to leave, Unca Nelson. Please don't let her leave."

Audrey knelt beside the child and placed an arm around him. "I have to go, Ricky. I hate to leave you, but I have to go home."

"No!" Ricky ran and stood with his back against the door. "No, you can't go."

He looked down at his nephew and wondered whether Audrey had sprinkled some kind of dust over him and the boy. Then, he reached to lift Ricky into his arms, but the child evaded him.

"I don't want Audie to leave." Ricky sat down on the floor and began to cry. "Unca Nelson, don't let her leave. I don't want her to go."

Lena bent to take the child into her arms. "Ricky, darling," she said. "It's time for bed. Kiss Audrey good-bye and off we go to bed."

He twisted away from her. "No. I want Audie to stay."

"I'll come back to see you, Ricky. I promise."

He stared at her. "Don't tell him that, because you don't mean it."

She squinted at him, and a frown clouded her face. "I wouldn't dare lie to a child. If you don't want me to come see him, say so."

"I'm sorry." He picked up the recalcitrant boy, hugging and comforting him. "It's all right, Ricky. She said she will come to see you, and she will. Now give her a big kiss and let her go home. She's tired."

Ricky reached out to kiss Audrey. "I'm sorry you have to go, Audie. Bye."

Ricky didn't usually hold on to him so tightly, and it struck him with considerable force that the effect of so many losses in the child's young life lay close to the surface of Ricky's emotions. He wondered if Audrey reminded Ricky of his mother. She didn't bring to his own mind any other woman he'd ever met, and he doubted he would forget her soon, if ever. He remembered her promise to visit Ricky, turned, and, still holding the child, loped with him up the stairs to his room. Who was this woman who had changed both their lives? He put the boy to bed and stood looking down at him as he dozed off to sleep. *You will forget her long before I will.* For the first time in seven hours, pain streaked through his neck.

Dear Readers,

I sincerely hope that you enjoyed reading *Top-Secret Rendezvous* from cover to cover. I'm very interested in hearing your comments and thoughts on the story of these two lovers, Staff Sergeant Hailey Hamilton and Major Zurich Kingdom, who found themselves shackled by complicated but necessary military policies. I love hearing from my readers, and I do appreciate the time you take out of your busy schedules to write.

Please enclose a self-addressed, stamped envelope with all your correspondence, and mail to: Linda Hudson-Smith, 2026C North Riverside Avenue, Box 109, Rialto, CA 92377. Or you can e-mail your comments to *LHS4romance@yahoo.com*. Please also visit my website and sign my guest book at *www.lindahudsonsmith.com*.

ABOUT THE AUTHOR

Born in Canonsburgh, Pennsylvania and raised in Washington, Linda Hudson-Smith has traveled the world as an enthusiastic witness to other cultures and lifestyles. Her husband's military career gave her the opportunity to live in Japan, Germany, and many cities across the United States. Linda's extensive travels help her to craft stories set in a variety of beautiful and romantic locations. She turned to writing as a form of therapy after illness forced her to leave a marketing and public relations career.

Romance in Color chose her as Rising Star for the month of January, 2000. *Ice Under Fire,* her debut Arabesque novel, received rave reviews. In 2002, the Black Writers Alliance presented Linda with the prestigious Gold Pen Award in the category of Best New Author. She has also won two Shades of Romance Magazine awards in the categories of Multicultural New Romance Author of the Year and Multicultural New Fiction Author of the Year 2001. Linda was also nominated as the Best New Romance Author at the 2001 Romance Slam Jam Conference. Her novel covers have been featured in such major publications as Publishers Weekly, USA Today, and Essence magazine. Linda's debut inspirational, Ladies in Waiting, has appeared on several bestseller lists since its release in August 2002.

Linda is a member of Romance Writers of America and the Black Writers Alliance. Though novel writing remains her first love, she is currently cultivating her screenwriting skills. She has also been contracted to pen several other novels for BET Books.

Dedicated to inspiring readers to overcome adversity against all odds, for the past two years Linda has served as the national spokesperson for the Lupus Foundation of America. In making Lupus awareness one of her top priorities, she travels around the country delivering inspirational messages of hope. She is also a strong supporter of the NAACP and the American Cancer Society. She enjoys poetry, entertaining, traveling, and attending sporting events. The mother of two sons, Linda shares residences in both California and Texas with her husband.